*New York Times* and *USA TODAY* bestselling author **Barbara Dunlop** has written more than forty novels for Mills & Boon, including the acclaimed Chicago Sons series for Mills & Boon Desire. Her sexy, lighthearted stories regularly hit bestseller lists. Barbara is a three-time finalist for the Romance Writers of America's RITA® Award.

*USA TODAY* bestselling author **Catherine Mann** has won numerous awards for her novels, including both a prestigious RITA® Award and an *RT Book Reviews* Reviewers' Choice Award. After years of moving around the country bringing up four children, Catherine has settled in her home state of South Carolina, where she's active in animal rescue. For more information, visit her website, www.catherinemann.com.

D1512978

Visit millsandboon.co.uk
for more information

# HIS TEMPTATION, HER SECRET

## BARBARA DUNLOP

# THE BABY CLAIM

## CATHERINE MANN

MILLS & BOON

First Published in Great Britain 2018
by Mills & Boon, an imprint of HarperCollinsPublishers,
1 London Bridge Street, London, SE1 9GF

*His Temptation, Her Secret* © 2018 Barbara Dunlop
*The Baby Claim* © 2018 Catherine Mann

ISBN: 978-0-263-93591-2

51-0218

MIX
Paper from
responsible sources
FSC™ C007454

This book is produced from independently certified FSC™ paper to ensure responsible forest management.

For more information visit: www.harpercollins.co.uk/green

Printed and bound in Spain
by CPI, Barcelona

# HIS TEMPTATION, HER SECRET

BARBARA DUNLOP

For CJ Carmichael

# One

$A$s the bride and groom whirled into the first dance at the sumptuously decorated Beacon Hill Crystal Club, TJ Bauer struggled to block memories of his own wedding. It had been more than two years since Lauren had died, and there were days when he was at relative peace with her loss. But there were also days like this when the ache was so acute that his chest balled into a painful knot of loneliness.

"Doing okay?" Caleb Watford approached, handing TJ a glass of single malt, one ice cube, just the way TJ liked it.

"I'm fine."

"Liar."

TJ had no intention of getting into it, so he nodded to the dance floor instead. "Matt's one lucky man."

Caleb watched TJ's expression closely, as if he was debating whether or not to let the topic drop. "I'll agree to that."

"It was touch and go there for a while." TJ forced his mind away from the memory of Lauren, reliving his good friend Matt Emerson's frantic, ring-less marriage proposal to Tasha, her packed suitcases at her feet. "I thought she was going to say no."

Caleb cracked a grin. "It all turned out in the end."

TJ found his own smile for Matt's good fortune. He was genuinely happy that his friend had found love. Tasha was smart, beautiful and completely down-to-earth. She was exactly what Matt needed in his life.

Caleb clapped a hand on TJ's shoulder. "You'll be next."

"Not." The cloud moved back over TJ's emotions.

"You need to keep an open mind."

"Would you replace Jules?"

The question brought silence.

TJ took a swallow of his drink. "That's what I thought."

"It's easy to say never when she's right here in front of me."

Both men shifted their gazes to Caleb's wife, Jules. She was radiant following the birth of her twin girls three months ago. Right now, she laughed at something her brother-in-law Noah said.

"It's hard to get past the never part," TJ said, struggling to put his feelings into words. He liked facts, not emotions. Emotions always tripped him up. "It's not that I'm not trying. I am. But it always cycles back to Lauren."

"I get it," Caleb said. "At least I think I get it. I know I can't possibly understand."

"If I could flip a switch…" TJ let the sentence drop.

Intellectually, he knew Lauren wasn't coming back. He even knew she'd want him to move on. But she was his true love, his one and only. He couldn't imagine anyone taking her place.

"Give it some more time," Caleb said.

"It's not like I have a choice," TJ responded, hearing the irony in his own tone. Time would march along no matter what he did or didn't do.

The strains of the song wound down to an end, and Matt and Tasha moved toward them, all smiles. Her graceful tulle skirt floated over the polished floor. TJ never thought he'd see the tomboyish marine mechanic in full bridal attire. When she wore a dress instead of coveralls, she was quite stunningly beautiful.

"Come and dance with the bride," she said to him, a tinkling laugh in her tone as she linked her arm with his.

"It would be an honor." As the best man, he put a smile on his face and set down his drink, determined to keep his melancholy thoughts to himself.

"Is everything okay?" she asked as they swung onto the dance floor.

Other couples joined them, and the dance floor filled as the music swelled.

"Everything is great," he said.

"I saw your expression when you were talking to Caleb."

"Where did you learn to dance like this?" TJ appreciated her concern, but this was *her* day. She didn't need to be worrying about him.

"What's going on, TJ?"

"Nothing. Well, one thing. I'm a little jealous of Matt."

"Now, that's a big fat lie."

He drew back slightly. "Look at yourself, Tasha. Every guy here is jealous of Matt."

She shook her head and laughed.

"Except for Caleb," TJ felt honor-bound to add. "And the other married guys… Well, some of them, anyway."

Now she looked amused. "That was a very carefully constructed compliment."

"It really went off the rails there, didn't it?"

"You just kept getting deeper and deeper."

"What I mean," he said, "is that you make a radiant bride."

"It's a very time-limited thing," she said.

It was his turn to laugh.

She put on a frown. "I can barely breathe in the corset, never mind walk in these heels. If there's an emergency, somebody's going to have to carry me out of here."

"I'm sure Matt will be happy to carry you anywhere you need to go."

She cast a glance at her new husband, and her expression turned to adoration. TJ felt a surge of envy at their obvious devotion to each other.

"Your mother seems delighted by the posh event," he said, switching his focus.

"I'm doing my duty as a daughter. But I've warned Matt, this may be the last time he sees me in a dress."

"You're going out on a high note."

TJ's phone vibrated in his tux pocket. He had it on silent, but Tasha obviously heard the low buzz.

"You can get that," she said.

"There's nobody I need to talk to right now."

"What if it's one of your investors?"

"It's Saturday night."

"It's Sunday morning in Australia." Tasha was aware of TJ's investment company's global reach.

"So, it's not a workday there either." He had no intention of interrupting the wedding reception with business.

The buzzing stopped.

"See?" he told her. "It went away."

"It always goes away when you don't pick up."

The phone buzzed again.

She stopped dancing. "You need to get that, TJ."

"No, I don't." He gently urged her to move.

"At least see who it is."

"It's nobody more important than you and Matt."

"It could be an emergency."

"Fine." He wasn't about to stand in the middle of the dance floor and argue with the bride.

He discreetly withdrew his phone and started dancing again.

Apparently appeased, she matched his movements.

Glancing down, he was surprised to see the call was from Seattle's St. Bea's Hospital. His company was a longtime contributor to Highside Hospital near his home in Whiskey Bay. But there was no affiliation with St. Bea's. He supposed someone could be soliciting a donation.

"Who is it?" Tasha asked.

He realized he'd stopped dancing again.

"St. Bea's Hospital."

A look of concern came over her face. "Someone could be hurt."

"I don't know why they'd take them to St. Bea's."

He was acquainted with a few people in Seattle, but most

of his friends were in Whiskey Bay or Washington's capital city, Olympia, which was the closest major city. Even in Olympia, there was nobody who'd have him listed as an emergency contact.

The ringing stopped again.

"You better call them back," Tasha said. She linked her arm with his, steering him off the dance floor.

"Tasha," he protested.

"Humor me, or I'll worry."

"If that's what it takes." He hated being the cause of a disruption.

"That's what it takes."

At the edge of the floor, she moved away, giving him privacy.

TJ kept walking to the foyer, where the sound of the band was blocked, so it was quieter. He hit the callback button.

"St. Bea's Hospital, Oncology," a crisp female voice answered.

Oncology? Someone had cancer? "This is Travis Bauer. I'm returning a call from this number."

"Yes, Mr. Bauer. Let me put you through to Dr. Stannis."

"What is this—" TJ stopped talking when the line clicked and went silent.

He waited a few moments, not sure whether to be anxious or simply curious.

"Mr. Bauer?"

"Yes?"

"This is Dr. Shelley Stannis. I'm with the oncology transplant department here at St. Bea's."

A light came on for TJ. "Is this about a bone marrow donation?"

"Yes, it is. Thank you for calling back so quickly. Obviously, I got your information from the registry. We have a young leukemia patient here who is a potential match with you. If you're available, I'd like to set up a consultation and possibly final testing."

"How old?" It was the first question that came to TJ's mind.

"He's nine years old," she said.

TJ didn't hesitate. "When do you need me?"

"Are you saying you're willing to donate?"

"Absolutely."

"Do you have any questions?"

"I'm sure I will, although not right now. I'm in Boston. But I can come back."

There was a pause on the line. "If it's possible, Mr. Bauer, we'd like to do the tests tomorrow. As you can imagine, we have a very anxious mother hoping you'll turn out to be a close enough match."

"I'll be there. And please, call me TJ."

"Thank you very much, TJ."

"Of course. I'll see you tomorrow." He ended the call.

"Everything okay?" Matt had appeared beside him.

"Fine. Hopefully very fine. I may be a bone marrow match for a nine-year-old boy in Seattle."

It seemed to take Matt a moment to process the statement.

"I really hate to cut out on you," TJ said.

"Go!" Matt said, making a shooing motion with his hands. "Go, save a life."

TJ could feel his adrenaline come up with purpose. His next call was to a jet charter company he'd used in the past.

He didn't want to fight for a seat on a red-eye when a young boy and his mother were waiting. And he could afford to fly privately. There were moments in life when it came in handy to be a ridiculously wealthy man.

As she followed the wide corridor at St. Bea's Hospital, Sage Costas's heels echoed against the polished linoleum. Her stomach churned as it had for the past nine days while her son, Eli, had undergone a battery of tests and been diagnosed with an aggressive form of leukemia. The closer she came to the family lounge, the harder her heart pounded. She found herself wondering how much stress the human body could endure before it simply shut down.

She'd barely slept all week, hadn't slept at all last night. She'd forced herself to shower this morning and put on a little makeup. She didn't know why she thought makeup might help. But she wanted to make a good impression. She was terrified the donor would back out.

She could see him now. Through the lounge windows, she could see a tall, dark-haired, smartly dressed man talking to Dr. Stannis. He had to be the donor.

Her steps slowed, and she swallowed. Then she stopped at the closed door. It was more than she could do to push the handle. She'd prayed desperately for this moment. So much was at stake. She wasn't sure she could face it if the process fell apart.

She forced herself to open the door and step inside the lounge.

Dr. Stannis immediately spotted her. "Hello, Sage."

The man turned. His expression was instant bewilderment. "Sage?"

Her world tipped on its axis.

"Is that you?" he asked, stepping forward.

A roar came up in her ears. Her vision switched to black and white, then tunneled down to a pinhole.

"Sage?" Dr. Stannis moved quickly, taking her by the arm.

Sage's brain pulsed a million miles an hour. The room swayed for a moment, until her vision cleared.

He was still standing there.

"I'm fine," she managed to say around the lingering noise inside her head.

"Have you met TJ Bauer?" Dr. Stannis asked with obvious curiosity.

"We went to the same high school." Her voice was little more than a squeak.

How could this be happening?

"It's your son who's sick?" TJ's expression was filled with concern. "I'm so sorry, Sage."

Then his forehead creased, and she could all but see the calculations going on inside his head.

He turned to the doctor. "You said he was nine?"

"Yes."

TJ twisted slowly back to Sage, his words carefully enunciated. "And I'm a likely bone marrow match for him?"

Sage tried to swallow again, but her throat had gone paper dry.

TJ's eyes shifted from blue to gray thunder. "Is he my son?"

The doctor went still. The entire world went still. The ventilation system clicked against the booming silence.

All Sage could manage was a nod.

Dr. Stannis's grip firmed up on Sage's arm. "Perhaps we should sit down."

"I have a son?" TJ asked, his voice hoarse. "You got *pregnant*?"

Sage tried to speak. She managed to move her lips, but no sounds came out.

TJ wasn't having the same problem. "And you didn't *tell* me?"

Dr. Stannis jumped in. "I think it would be best if we all—"

Bitterness suddenly broke through Sage's fear. She found her voice, all but shouting. "You didn't deserve to know."

"Sage." Dr. Stannis's tone was shocked and sharp.

Sage immediately realized her mistake.

They were dependent on TJ. Eli's life depended on this man's good graces, this man who had deceived her, lied to her and taken shameless advantage of her teenage naïveté as a prank to amuse his friends.

She hated him. But he was the one person who could save her son's life.

"I'm sorry," she said, trying desperately to put some sincerity into her tone.

Judging by his expression, she hadn't pulled it off.

"Please don't…" Her stomach cramped up. "Please don't take it out on Eli."

He looked completely dumbfounded. Then he swore under his breath. "You actually think I'd harm a little boy… my own son—" He seemed to gather himself. "You think I'd let my anger with you impact my decision to donate? What kind of a man do you think I am?"

She didn't know what kind of a man he was. She knew what kind of a teenager he'd been back then—unscrupulous and self-centered. She had no reason to assume he'd changed.

"I don't know." She forced the words out.

"Well, *know*," he said. He looked to Dr. Stannis again. "How soon will we be sure I'm a close enough match?"

"A few days," she said. "But given the genetic connection, I'm even more optimistic."

"It's a stroke of luck," TJ said flatly.

Sage couldn't begin to guess at the emotion behind those words.

Dr. Stannis moved to look her directly in the eyes. "Are you sure you're all right?"

"I'm fine." For the moment, she was fine.

TJ was going to help them. They'd figure out the rest later. For now, the bone marrow transplant was all that mattered.

The doctor stepped back. "I'll give the two of you some time to talk."

With a final assessment of Sage's expression, she left the lounge.

Sage had no idea what to say next, and the seconds ticked past.

When TJ finally spoke, there was contained fury in his

tone. "I'm not going to ask you how you could have done something so horrible."

"Me?" Sage could barely believe he'd said it. "You were there. You know *exactly* what happened between us."

He waved a dismissive hand. "That was a stupid stunt by an ignorant kid. We've grown up since then. You've known about this for a *decade*."

"You were a shallow, self-centered jerk."

He squared his shoulders and set his square jaw. "I don't want to fight with you, Sage. This conversation can wait. Right now, I want to meet my son."

Sage staggered and reached to an armchair for support. "No."

"What do you mean no? No is no longer an option for you."

She struggled for the right words. "You can't tell him, TJ. Not now. Not while he's so sick." She stretched her arm expansively toward the door to the rest of the hospital. "There's no way we can expect him to absorb news like that in the middle of all this."

TJ seemed to consider her words. His expression lost its hard edge. "I need to meet him, Sage. We don't have to tell him I'm his father, at least not right away. But I'm going to meet him, and I'm not waiting another minute."

Sage decided she could live with that. "Okay."

"His name is Eli?"

"Yes. Eli Thomas Costas."

TJ didn't react to the name. He walked over to the lounge door and pulled it open, holding it for her. "Take me to my son."

"Whoa, whoa, back up, back up," Matt said to TJ. "You say he's *nine* years old?"

"It was in high school," TJ responded.

There was an open beer on the wide arm of his wooden

deck chair on Matt's Whiskey Bay Marina sundeck, but TJ had no interest in drinking it.

"So, before you met Lauren," Caleb said.

The three men were sitting around the gas fire pit, but it was early on a June evening, so they hadn't bothered lighting it.

"I didn't cheat on Lauren." TJ's tone was hard.

"I'm just getting the time line straight."

"It was a one-night thing. At prom. We danced."

TJ didn't want to own up to participating in the foolish prank that had led him to ask nerdy brainiac Sage Costas to dance with him that night. At least not until he had to. And he hoped that was never.

"And she never told you about the baby?" Matt asked.

"I assume that's rhetorical," TJ replied.

If Sage had told him about Eli, TJ would have moved heaven and earth to have a relationship with his son. TJ's own father had walked out before TJ was born, and there was no way he'd do that to a child of his own.

"What's he like?" Caleb asked, his tone dropping.

TJ's mind went back to the sleepy boy in the stark hospital bed. "He's a great-looking kid."

Eli had been too tired to do much but say hello.

"Like his dad?" Matt joked.

TJ would be lying if he said he hadn't seen some of himself in Eli. He didn't think he was imagining it.

"If he's got his mother's brains, the world better watch out." As he said the words, TJ realized they were entirely true. From a genetic perspective, Eli had a fantastic mother. Back in high school, Sage was voted most likely to save the world or become president.

"When are you going to tell him?" Matt asked.

TJ decided it was time for a shot of alcohol, no matter how weak. He raised his beer and took a drink before answering. "I don't know. When he's feeling better, I guess."

"And the tests?"

"They said the results will take a couple of days. I've got three major private placement deals on the table. I have to close them. Then I'm clearing my desk to go back to Seattle. Whatever happens, if I'm a match or not, he's still my kid, and he's getting the best medical care money can buy."

Matt and Caleb exchanged a look.

"What?" TJ asked.

"That's a good place for your money," Matt said.

"You bet it's a good place for my money."

But money wasn't the only thing his son needed. TJ didn't know what he'd do if he wasn't a bone marrow match. He had to be a match. Nothing else was acceptable.

"You talked to him?" Caleb asked.

"Only a little. He was pretty groggy from all the medication. Sage says he plays baseball, a catcher."

"Have you talked to a lawyer?" Matt asked.

"I've talked to three lawyers." TJ's company Tide Rush Investments had a financial lawyer on retainer and his firm had a family law division.

"What do they say?"

"That I've got a case."

"What are you looking to get?" Matt asked.

"What has she offered?" Caleb's brow shot up.

TJ took another pull on his beer. It was such an incredibly ordinary thing to do—sitting up here with his two friends like he had hundreds of times over the years. But his life had been turned upside down. It would never be the same again.

He'd been considering his position for the past thirty-six hours. "She had custody for the first nine years. I'll take the next nine."

Caleb frowned.

"You can't take that hard a line," Matt said.

"A teenage boy needs his dad. I'd have given anything to have my old man show up in my life when I was Eli's age," TJ said. He had a lot of time to make up for, and he had no intention of letting Sage or anyone else stop him.

"They need their mom too," Caleb said.

TJ knew that. But he didn't want to admit it right now. He wanted to hold on to his anger at Sage for a while.

"She can have visitation," he said. "That's more than she gave me."

"Could you move to Seattle?" Matt asked.

"The Whiskey Bay school is top-notch," TJ countered. "So is the area hospital. And the lifestyle can't be beat." He couldn't imagine a more perfect place to raise a child.

"The neighbors are pretty good," Caleb said with a half smile.

"It's not like I don't have the room."

His wife, Lauren, had wanted several children. She'd designed a six-bedroom house with a massive recreation area in the basement for rainy days and a nanny suite over the garage. She'd been trying to get pregnant when she was diagnosed with breast cancer.

"I can't see it being that straightforward." There was a cautionary note to Matt's voice.

"Nothing's that straightforward," TJ said. "But I'm a determined and resourceful man."

"She's the mother of your child."

"And I'm the father of hers—a fact she seems to have conveniently ignored."

"Do you know why?" Caleb asked. "Why she kept it from you? I mean, she could easily have come after you for child support."

"She wouldn't have had to *come after* me. I'd have stepped up without a fight."

"I know. I know. But you'd think she'd have wanted your help."

TJ knew the whole truth would eventually come out. His friends were too astute, and they cared too much about him to let him get away with a vague explanation. It was both a blessing and a curse.

TJ took the plunge. "She said I didn't deserve to know about Eli."

"Why?" Caleb's question was perfectly predictable.

"Because it was a prank."

Both of his friends looked at him blankly.

"Prom night." TJ gritted his teeth at the memory. "A group of us, the seniors on the football team, we each picked a girl's name out of a hat. I picked Sage."

"I'm guessing they weren't the girls on the cheerleading squad," Matt said. His disappointment in TJ was obvious.

TJ knew he deserved that. "Not the cheerleading squad. They were the nerds, the brains. It was supposed to be a kiss, only a dance and a kiss. That was it. But Sage..."

He remembered the overpowering rush of adolescent hormones. He couldn't say what it was about her. She had been thin and freckled, with this wild red hair. But when he'd kissed her, she'd kissed him back, and they'd both been left breathless. His car had been far too close to the side door of the gym, and they'd ended up in the back seat.

"We can fill in the rest," Caleb said.

"I tracked her down the next day to apologize. But she'd already heard about the prank. She was enraged, punched me square in the chest." TJ's hand went reflexively to the spot where her small fist had connected. "She told me she never wanted to speak to me again."

"You can't blame her," Matt said.

"It was stupid and cruel, I know. But I only planned to kiss her. The rest of it was on both of us. It was more than just consensual. And she's kept my son from me for nine years. The two things don't even compare."

# Two

A week later, mere hours after the transplant procedure, Sage expected to find TJ lounging in his hospital bed. But he was up and halfway dressed, reaching his arms into a crisp white dress shirt.

"Should you be out of bed?" she asked, stepping past the curtain.

"The nurse took the IV out a few minutes ago."

"But you just had surgery."

"I'm aware of that." He adjusted his collar and shifted the lapels across what she'd noted was a magnificently muscular chest.

"You must be sore." She couldn't believe he'd bounce back this fast.

"Only my hip. Dr. Stannis says it'll disappear in a few days. Hanging around here isn't going to help any."

"Can you drive?" Sage asked.

She didn't know where he was staying, but she wanted to be sure he got safely back to his hotel. It was the least she could do—the very least she could do for the man who may have saved her son's life.

"They didn't serve liquor in the operating room."

"You know what I mean. You must be woozy."

"It's not too bad." He finished doing up his buttons. "I'm not crazy about anesthetic. I like my brain cells too much."

"I'm sorry you had to go through that." She struggled to keep her emotions at bay. "Thank you, TJ."

He sent her a sharp gaze, trapping hers for a long second. "You don't have to thank me. He's my son. You don't ever have to thank me for helping my son."

It would be a struggle for her to get used to that. She'd had Eli to herself for such a long time, she couldn't imagine letting anyone else into their circle.

"I need you to understand that, Sage."

"You're going to have to give me some time."

"I've already wasted nine years." TJ took a pewter-gray blazer from a hanger on the wall and put it on over his designer outfit.

She was terrified to ask him what he had in mind. She didn't want to have that conversation. "They're watching Eli for signs of rejection," she said instead.

"Anything yet?" TJ asked.

"It's too soon to tell. Are you staying in Seattle overnight?"

Again, he pasted her with the sharp look. "I'm staying here as long as it takes."

"Takes to what?"

He turned his back to her, punching a code into a small safe on the wall and retrieving his wallet and keys. Then he faced her and deposited the wallet into his inside jacket pocket. He kept the keys in his hand.

"I've been thinking," he said.

She worriedly searched his expression for a clue. "About…"

"I'd like to move Eli to Highside Hospital."

The words blindsided her. "What? Where?"

"It's near Whiskey Bay. It's state-of-the-art—"

"No."

"Hear me out."

Protective instincts rose inside her, along with a healthy dose of fear. "You're not taking Eli out of Seattle."

"It's the best place for him. I've donated to Highside for years, and they have the best doctors, the best technology, he'd be—"

"St. Bea's is a fantastic hospital."

"It's a public hospital."

Her tone went up in defense. "So what?"

"So, they're busy, overworked, stretched for resources."

"They've given Eli everything he needs. They diagnosed him. They found *you*." She stopped, realizing TJ's unique role in Eli's recovery might not be her strongest argument.

"I was in the registry. Any hospital would have found me."

"I don't want him moved." She needed to be close to her son while he recovered.

Whiskey Bay was three hours away. She'd missed so much time at work these past weeks, she couldn't take much more off. She'd planned to work as many hours as she could while Eli was recovering.

"It'll free up a bed for someone who desperately needs it," TJ said.

"What part of no don't you understand?"

"What part of *father* don't *you* understand?"

"He can't be moved yet." She realized her best argument was the medical one.

"I'm not talking about today, or even tomorrow. But as soon as he's strong enough, we can hire a medical helicopter. It'll take thirty minutes, tops."

"Just like that?" She resisted an urge to snap her fingers.

"Just like what?"

"You'll hire a helicopter."

"It's fast. It'll be comfortable. The onboard medics are equipped for anything."

"It'll cost a *fortune*."

His expression was a study in incomprehension. "It's my son's health we're talking about."

She was back in high school again. "You're still the big man, aren't you?"

His nostrils flared, but he didn't answer.

"The star athlete, the guy who got anything he wanted, grants, scholarships, the best parties, all the girls."

TJ opened his mouth, but she didn't let him interrupt.

"The wide receiver with the magic hands, who was going all-state, who could write his own ticket."

"I'm not going to apologize for getting a college degree."

Sage felt like a knife had been shoved into her heart. She'd given up countless scholarship offers to raise Eli.

"I earned my money," TJ continued. "I'm spending it on my son."

She stepped forward. "Your son doesn't need it."

"You want to fight me on this?"

Sage was about to say yes, when the curtain was whisked open.

Dr. Stannis appeared. She looked TJ up and down and smiled. "Nice bounce-back."

"I've been through worse," he said. "How's Eli?"

"He's still in recovery. We're going to keep him there for a few more hours. Do you feel ready for discharge?"

"Absolutely. When can we see him?"

"Later tonight." Dr. Stannis glanced at her watch. "Nine-ish? But he'll still be pretty groggy until morning."

"We'll come back at nine."

Sage was about to protest that she wasn't leaving.

"Make sure you get plenty of fluids," Dr. Stannis said to TJ.

"Is there a good restaurant nearby?"

It took Sage a second to realize the question was for her. "I'm, uh, not sure."

He looked puzzled.

She wasn't about to explain to Mr. Moneybags Helicopter Charter that she normally brought snacks from home to save money over eating in the hospital cafeteria. Forget restaurants. They weren't even on her radar.

"The Red Grill is just down the road," Dr. Stannis said. "It gets good reviews from families of our patients."

"Done," TJ said. He motioned for Sage to go first.

She didn't understand.

"I'm buying," he told her. "We have to eat."

"Fluids," Dr. Stannis said. "For both of you." She gave Sage a pointed look.

They'd had a few conversations about the fact that Sage had lost some weight these past weeks.

"Does Cabernet Sauvignon count?" TJ asked with a teasing smile.

"Only in moderation." Dr. Stannis waved her pen. "Water's better. Tea would be perfect."

"Yes, ma'am."

"And make sure Sage eats."

TJ looked down at Sage with a curious expression. "Anything in particular?"

"Calories."

"Lasagna it is," he said.

"I don't like lasagna." Sage did like lasagna, but she was still thrown off balance by TJ's determination to move Eli to a different hospital. And she resented the way he was organizing her dinner.

"Then order something else," he said easily. "They'll have a menu."

"I'm aware of how restaurants work."

"Good. Then you won't mind taking advantage of one. You are a little thin."

"I'm not thin." She was conveniently ignoring the fact that her favorite jeans were sagging at her waist.

"I didn't mean it as an insult."

"Your opinion means nothing to me."

Dr. Stannis broke in. "And I will see you two later."

"Thank you, Doctor." TJ gave her hand a warm shake with both of his.

Sage wished she could hug the doctor, but she settled for shaking as well. "Thank you *so* much."

"You're most welcome." Dr. Stannis's sincerity was unquestionable. "Go take care of yourself for a couple of hours. Eli is in excellent hands."

"I know," Sage said.

She had complete confidence in the staff at St. Bea's. There wasn't a reason in the world for TJ to move Eli anywhere else.

The Red Grill turned out to have a Southwest flair, with bright colors and lively music in the dining room. The hostess seated them on the patio, which was quieter. She quickly brought them glasses of iced tea and tortilla chips with guacamole.

The pain in TJ's hip was getting worse, but he didn't want to muddle his thinking with any more painkillers. He pushed the tortilla chips toward Sage, but she shook her head.

"Doctor's orders," he said.

She gave him a glare but took a chip and bit down on it.

TJ had so many things to ask her, he barely knew where to start. "Do you have any pictures of Eli?"

She set the chip on her side plate. "I do." She dug into her small bag and retrieved her phone, opening the photo app.

When she handed it over, TJ got the first look at his infant son. The pain in his hip faded as he took in the smiling, cherubic baby.

"How old is he here?" TJ asked.

"Six months in that first one."

He stared at the picture for a long time.

"Are you ready to order?" the waitress interrupted.

"We'll need a few minutes," Sage answered for them.

TJ flipped to the next picture. Toddler Eli was standing in a yard, petting a black Lab that was taller than him.

"You have a dog?" TJ asked.

"No. They're not allowed in our basement suite. Beaumont belonged to a friend. Eli loves animals. He talked me into a gerbil once."

"What happened?"

"He played with it every day, but it was kind of sad. It just wasn't the same as having a dog to walk and play fetch

with. Eventually, the gerbil died and, well, we weren't really supposed to have it in the first place. And I didn't want
to get evicted, so we never got another."

"A boy deserves a dog." TJ could remember how badly
he'd wanted a dog when he was a boy.

"A boy deserves a roof over his head," Sage retorted.

TJ looked up from the screen to see her annoyed expression. "I didn't mean that as a criticism."

"I tried, TJ."

"I know you did. I'm sure you did. I don't understand
why you didn't contact me."

"Well, I'm not going to explain it all over again."

The waitress arrived once more.

"I'll take a beef burrito," TJ said, not wanting to bother
reading the menu and not caring what he ate.

"The same," Sage said, and the waitress departed.

"You didn't look at the menu," he noted.

"Just so long as it's not lasagna."

He couldn't tell if she was joking or not. He flipped to
the next picture.

Eli was in front of a birthday cake covered in blue icing
and decorated with mini balloons. There were three candles
on the cake, and he was grinning ear to ear.

"His birthday?" TJ asked, although it was pretty obvious.

Sage nodded.

Eli had dark, slightly wavy hair, just like TJ's. There was
a familiarity in his eyes and in his slightly crooked smile.
TJ's chest was tight. His heart was expanding to fill every
crack and crevice behind his rib cage.

He had a son—his own son. He'd missed so much of
Eli's life.

He moved to the next picture, but it blurred in front of
his eyes. "I deserve a chance to catch up."

She looked like she wanted to argue. But then she looked
like she didn't have it in her.

"I know," she said. "You can see him as much as you want. I won't try to stop you."

"I want him at Highside Hospital."

This time, she shook her head, and he could see the steel determination in her eyes. "That's not possible. He needs me. He needs me there every day."

"You can stay in Whiskey Bay." The problem was hardly insurmountable.

"I have a job, TJ. I can appreciate this is a huge adjustment for you, but—"

"Adjustment? You call what I'm going through an *adjustment*?" He shifted in his chair, and pain shot through his hip. He struggled to keep his expression neutral.

"You're in pain," she said. "Should we go back to the hospital?"

"No!" He lowered his voice. "We should eat. Starving yourself isn't going to help Eli."

Her jaw clenched tight. "Are you going to give me parenting advice?"

"I'm not." He leaned forward to make his point. "Because I have no idea what it's *like* to be a parent, thanks to you."

"I just apologized."

"You think that cuts it?" He realized his tone was growing louder, and he forced himself to take a beat. They were both raw and tired, and sniping at each other wasn't going to help anything.

Their burritos arrived, along with condiments and utensils.

He slid her phone back across the table. "Thank you for showing me the pictures."

She looked like she wanted to say something more, but she stayed silent.

"You should eat," he told her.

She gave a jerky nod.

He flagged down the waitress. "Can I get a shot of tequila?"

"Painkillers would work better," Sage said.

"It's not for the pain."

They ate in silence for a while.

Despite everything, TJ couldn't help but think it was good she was eating something. He might not agree with her decision to keep him in the dark, but she'd obviously been through a lot taking care of a sick child all on her own.

Then it occurred to him that she might not be on her own. She didn't wear a wedding ring, and her last name remained the same, but that didn't mean she wasn't in a relationship, or even married for that matter.

"Are you single?" he asked bluntly.

Her eyes widened in obvious surprise.

"Is there a man, somebody in your and Eli's lives?" he elaborated. It would certainly give her a good reason for keeping TJ out of the picture.

"No. There's nobody. It's just me and Eli." There was an echo of loneliness in the statement.

"Your family?"

He didn't know if she had siblings. He didn't recall any from high school. But it was a pretty big place, and he certainly hadn't known the entire student body.

"My parents died a few years ago. Not that they were in the picture anyway."

"Did they live out of state?"

"No. They cut me out of their lives. They didn't want me to keep Eli."

TJ's horror was instant.

"They wanted me to give him up for adoption."

"Why?"

"They weren't willing to help me with him and they didn't think I could do it on my own. But they were wrong." Her gaze was firm on him. "I walked out of the house at six months pregnant and never saw them again."

She should have contacted him. Why on earth hadn't she contacted him?

"It was the right choice," she continued. "For all our struggles, I'd do it again in a heartbeat."

He couldn't seem to stop himself. "I wish you'd done some things different."

Her knuckles appeared white as she gripped her knife and fork. "I can't go back in time, TJ."

"I know." He'd lost his appetite, but he forced himself to keep eating.

They could only go forward. And for that, he needed to be at his strongest. If there was anything on earth he could do to help Eli, he was going to do it.

Sage fought the urge to take TJ's hand. It was an irrational urge, since their relationship for the past twenty-four hours could best be described as an armed truce. But her nerves were strung tight as they waited for Dr. Stannis to bring them Eli's test results.

The guest chairs in Dr. Stannis's office were jade-green leather. They were cushioned and comfortable. The room was decorated in muted earth tones, a painting here, some pottery there. It didn't look sterile, not like a waiting room. She couldn't help but imagine it was designed to keep people calm, people like her who were waiting for life-and-death results, or who were hearing the worst kind of news.

"Hey." TJ's tone was soft, and he was the one who took her hand.

She turned to look at him.

"Don't do that to yourself," he said.

He gave her hand a squeeze, which inexplicably made her feel better.

"It's going to be all good," he said.

"You don't know that." Her voice was dry, high-pitched. She tried to swallow, but she couldn't.

He came out of the chair, on one knee in front of her, taking both her hands in his. "Positive thoughts," he said, his voice as gentle as she'd ever heard.

She managed a nod, but she was terrified to be optimistic, as if karma would reach out and smack her if she dared to hope.

The door opened, and Dr. Stannis entered the room. "I won't keep you in suspense," she said briskly, breezing toward her desk. "The results are what we were hoping for. There are no signs of rejection or infection at this point."

Sage thought she might faint with relief.

Before she could move, TJ's arms were around her. He drew her to her feet and hugged her tight.

"Yes," his deep voice hissed next to her ear. "Yes."

His body was strong and solid against hers, warm and welcoming. She was suddenly transported back ten years, to their dance, their kiss, the acute and unexplainable feeling she'd had of coming home, like she belonged in TJ's arms, like she'd been waiting her whole life to be held by him.

She hadn't been able to let go then, and she didn't want to let go now. It was a frightening feeling, and she tried to pull back.

TJ didn't seem to want to let her go either. He held on tight for long seconds before breaking his grip.

"He did it," he said.

"You did it," Sage said.

At the moment, she didn't care who TJ was, what he'd done in the past or what he might do in the future. He'd saved her son, and she owed him everything.

"He needs to get his strength back," Dr. Stannis said.

Sage felt a dampness on her cheek and swiped at it with the back of her hand. She hadn't even realized she was crying.

"And we'll have to carefully monitor his T cells. Infection is still a very serious concern." Dr. Stannis dropped into her high-backed chair. "But at this point, all signs are positive."

TJ eased Sage back into her chair and then took his own.

"How long until he can come home?" she asked. She couldn't wait to have Eli back in his own bed.

"Normally, we'd wait a week," Dr. Stannis said. "But in Eli's case, I'm recommending two."

Sage's euphoria disappeared. "Something is wrong?"

"The chemo was very hard on him. And we've already fought one infection. He's young, and his body has been through a lot."

"Are you sure that's all?"

"I would tell you if there was anything else."

"What about another hospital?" TJ asked.

Sage wanted to shout *no*.

Dr. Stannis switched her attention to TJ. "What do you mean?"

"Highside Hospital, on the coast."

"They're top-notch. There's no doubt about that," Dr. Stannis said.

"I'm affiliated with them," TJ said. "They're world renowned. I want to do everything possible to support his recovery."

Dr. Stannis looked at Sage. "Medically speaking, yes, he could be moved there."

"He'd have a private room," TJ said to Sage. "It would be quieter for him while he recovered. Their equipment is state-of-the-art. If Eli came down with an infection or any other complication, he'd be in the best possible facility."

Sage's hands began to shake. "He wouldn't have his mother."

"You'd come with him. They have a residential facility for parents. You can stay there the whole time free of charge."

"I have a job," Sage protested. There was no way she could take another two weeks off. "After he's out, once he's better, the two of you can—"

"This isn't about me seeing him." TJ's tone was firm. "This is about Eli getting the best care. The nurse-to-patient ratio in Highside is the lowest in the country. They have a pediatric ICU, an extensive on-site laboratory system, and they're an oncology teaching facility."

Dr. Stannis rose to her feet. "I'll leave the two of you to talk."

"One more question," TJ said to Dr. Stannis.

"Of course."

"If Eli was your son, would you choose St. Bea's or High-side?"

Dr. Stannis's hesitation and her guilty look in Sage's direction answered the question.

"I have to be honest," Dr. Stannis said. "Highside is unrivaled for patient care and outcomes."

"Thank you," TJ said.

Dr. Stannis left the office.

"I have to work while he's recovering," Sage said to TJ. "I can't do that from Whiskey Bay." Surely a mother's love counted for something.

"Take some time off. Don't worry about money, I can—"

"It's not just the money." She was embarrassed that her voice cracked. "I've missed so much time lately. They're trying to be patient with me, but they're going to have to replace me if I don't get back there soon."

"Where do you work?"

She found herself raising her chin. "The Eastway Community Center. I'm their event planner."

She wasn't embarrassed by her job. She did meaningful work that helped people in need. But she knew it was nothing compared to what TJ had accomplished since high school.

"Maybe I can talk to them."

"Oh, no, you don't." The idea was offensive. She was an adult. She didn't need some tall, male financial mogul in an expensive suit to advocate on her behalf. "Eli's home is here. His mother is here. My *life* is here."

"And *my* life is—" TJ suddenly stopped talking. He

rocked back in his chair, looking annoyed with himself. "Fine. I'll let it drop."

"Thank you." She was grateful he'd seen the light.

"Right now, we should check on Eli."

She was all for that. "Yes." She nodded rapidly. "Yes."

TJ came to his feet. "We can talk about it some more later."

"Wait. What?" She didn't want to revisit an argument she'd just won.

"I haven't changed my mind. But I'm not unreasonable."

"Not changing your mind *is* being unreasonable." She stood.

"Not if I change yours."

"You won't change mine." Of that, she was positive. If that was what he was waiting for, she was home free. She headed for the door.

It was a ten-minute walk from Dr. Stannis's office to the pediatrics wing. It was almost dinner, and Sage was hoping to coax Eli to eat something, maybe a little Jell-O. He liked red the best.

She couldn't wait for the day when his appetite returned, then his strength and his energy. She couldn't wait for the day when he was an ordinary little boy all over again.

# Three

Once again, TJ was struck by how small and pale Eli looked in the stark white hospital bed. But at least this time he was sitting up. He had a comic book in his lap, and he was slowly turning the pages.

He heard them come in, and he looked up.

"Hi, Mom," he said in a quiet voice.

"Hello, sweetheart." Sage approached his bed and gave him a kiss on the forehead.

There were three other beds in the room. Two were occupied. One with a young girl whose leg was in traction due to a car accident, another by a boy who TJ had learned had his appendix taken out and was in the process of being discharged.

The hospital was spick-and-span. But it was also showing its age, with noisy heaters, worn linoleum and lights that flickered and buzzed overhead. The privacy curtains were a faded yellow, and the table trays squeaked when they were wheeled to a new position.

"Hi, Eli," TJ said.

Eli looked past Sage to meet TJ's eyes. He was clearly puzzled by TJ's continued presence at his bedside. TJ didn't blame the kid. It likely didn't make much sense to Eli for a stranger to show up and keep hanging around while he recovered.

Sage had introduced TJ as an old friend from high school. TJ was dying to tell Eli the truth. But he respected Sage's request to wait until Eli was stronger.

"Hi," Eli answered shortly, looking annoyed.

"How are you feeling?" Sage asked, straightening.

Eli shrugged.

"Are you hungry?" Sage asked.

"Not really." Eli looked back down at the comic book.

"You need to build up your strength." She smoothed his slightly ragged hair.

"I'll try," he said.

"Are you frustrated by the slow progress?" TJ asked.

Sage didn't take the single seat beside the bed, and he wasn't about to sit down and let her stand, so the black vinyl chair was just in the way. TJ maneuvered around it.

Eli shifted to watch his progress. "Are you dating my mom?"

"What?" Sage gasped. "What makes you ask that?"

"No," TJ answered. "I'm not dating your mom. We're old friends."

Sage sat down in the chair and put her hand on Eli's shoulder. "There's something you should know, honey."

TJ stopped breathing.

Eli looked at Sage. "What?"

"TJ donated the bone marrow for your transplant."

TJ let out his breath. He was disappointed, of course. But it had seemed like an abrupt way to tell Eli TJ was his father. It was better that they wait. This was enough.

Eli's eyes opened a little wider. "Are you serious?"

"Yes." Sage took his hand and gave it a kiss. "TJ was your donor."

Eli looked embarrassed. His gaze focused tentatively on TJ's.

"I was more than happy to help," TJ assured him.

Eli's slim shoulders squared, and he seemed to sit up a little straighter. "Thank you, sir."

TJ's heart swelled with pride. "I'm just glad you're getting better."

Eli's expression faltered. "Am I?"

"Of course you are," Sage said, concern clear in her tone.

"I don't feel better."

"You're sitting up."

Eli glanced around the bed, as if the significance of sitting up hadn't occurred to him.

"You couldn't sit up yesterday," Sage said.

"I couldn't, could I?"

"You *are* getting better," she told him firmly.

"It's only a matter of time," TJ said.

Eli gave a ghost of a smile. "I thought they were lying."

"Who?" Sage asked.

"Dr. Stannis. The nurses. They keep saying these things take time, and I should relax and let my body heal."

"They're right."

"That's what they said to Joey." Eli's eyes went glassy with unshed tears. "They told him that right up to when he died."

TJ felt like he'd been sucker punched.

A stricken expression on her face, Sage rose and drew Eli into her arms. "Oh, sweetheart."

"It would be okay," Eli said. "I mean, I'd deal with it if it happened."

"The transplant was a success," Sage said with firm conviction.

"You don't have to deal with it," TJ said. Then he rethought his words.

Eli had plenty to deal with for the next few months.

"It's going to be tough," TJ told his son. "You'll need to be strong. But you are most definitely getting better."

"I can read again," Eli said. "At least a little bit without my head feeling like a baseball hit it."

"I hear you play baseball," TJ said, perching on the corner of the bed.

"I used to," Eli said.

"That's something to look forward to."

"Over the long-term," Sage said.

TJ couldn't tell if it was a rebuke or if she was just carrying on with the conversation.

"For now," she continued, "maybe we can look forward to some Jell-O?"

Eli thought about it for a moment. "I can try."

"Good for you."

TJ found himself smiling at the simple accomplishment. "Is there anything you feel like?" he asked Eli. "Anything at all?"

Eli looked to his mom as if seeking permission. "Could I have a chocolate milkshake?"

"I can run out and pick one up," TJ offered.

"Yes." Sage surreptitiously swiped her hand across her cheeks. "Yes, darling. You can have as many chocolate milkshakes as you want."

"Finally," Eli said with a small smile. "Something good in the hospital."

TJ couldn't believe his son was making a joke. In a hospital bed, weak and frightened, and fighting for his life, he was making a joke. His kid had mettle. Again, pride rose in his chest.

He left the room and took the elevator to the main lobby. There was a fast-food restaurant down the block that served milkshakes. But Eli deserved better than any old milkshake. TJ wanted his first gift to his son to be at least a little bit special.

So he drove to a gourmet ice-cream shop ten minutes away and waited while they made a custom order.

When TJ got back, Eli was semi-reclined in his bed. His eyes were closed, and he was listening to Sage read a story. She was sitting between Eli's bed and the bed of the little girl with the broken leg.

The girl looked to have other injuries too, TJ realized. One of her arms was bandaged, and she had a brace on her other leg.

She looked shyly at the milkshake, and TJ felt like the biggest heel in the world.

Sage stopped reading.

TJ set the milkshake on Eli's table.

"Is there something you'd like?" he asked the girl, moving closer.

"Heidi, this is my friend TJ," Sage said to the girl.

"Hi, Heidi." He offered her a smile. "I should have asked you before. What would you like to eat? As long as it's okay with the nurses, I can bring you anything."

She hesitated.

"Go ahead," Sage told her. "He's rich. He can afford something great."

TJ was taken aback by Sage's description of him. It was true, but it was an odd thing to tell a child.

"Pizza?" she asked shyly.

"Absolutely," TJ answered. "What kind do you like?"

"Hawaiian," she said. "And…" She bit her bottom lip.

"What else?" he asked. "Do you want a soda?"

"Can I have extra cheese?"

"Extra cheese it is." Out of the corner of his eye, TJ saw Eli lift the milkshake to his lips.

Heidi's blue eyes lit up with simple joy.

"This is really good," Eli said.

"Fantastic," TJ said to Eli. He hadn't felt this good about a gift in years.

"I can get you a milkshake, too," he said to Heidi.

Instead of answering, she looked to Sage with amazement.

"Chocolate or vanilla?" Sage asked her. "Or maybe strawberry or caramel?"

"Caramel," Heidi said, sounding breathless.

"What about you?" TJ asked Sage, not about to mess this up a second time. "Pizza and milkshakes all around?"

Sage gave him a grin, and he swore he could feel her joy seep into his very pores.

"You bet," she said. "Surprise me."

"I'm on it." He gave them all a mock salute and walked out of the hospital room feeling ridiculously like a super-hero.

After the pizza and milkshakes, Sage read aloud until both Eli and Heidi were sleeping. Then she said good-night to the nurse before she and TJ walked to the lobby. She was tired, but she was also relieved. Eli was showing definite signs of improvement. He'd finished his entire milkshake and even had a couple bites of pizza.

"I'll be back tomorrow morning," TJ said as they approached the bank of glass doors.

"I know you will."

They were going to have to work this out somehow. But for now, the best she could do was one day at a time.

"Where's your car?" he asked, stopping as she turned left on the sidewalk.

The parking lot was to the right.

"I'm taking the bus."

He closed the gap between them. "Why would you do that?"

She didn't want to tell him. But she didn't want to make a big deal about it either.

She kept her tone blasé, matter-of-fact. "I don't have a car."

He blinked. "Who doesn't have a car?"

"Me."

"Why?"

"Because I don't."

"How do you get to work?"

She could hear the diesel engine and the air brakes of a bus coming up the hill. She pointed to it.

"That's crazy," he said.

She didn't like it much, but she'd sold her car a month ago when they'd started doing tests on Eli. Their meager insurance policy didn't begin to cover all the costs.

"You need a car," he said with authority.

"I had a car."

"Did you crash it?"

"*No*, I didn't crash it. I sold it."

"Why would you—" He stopped, and his brows rose. "The medical bills."

"Yes, the medical bills."

There was no point in pretending. She was a single mother with a low-paying job and a sick child. Of all the things she had going for her in life, money wasn't one of them.

"As of this second," TJ said, "there are no medical bills. You have no medical bills."

"You can't—"

"I can, and I am. How much have you paid so far?"

"None of your business."

"You want me to guess?"

"No, I don't want you to guess." It was her pride arguing with him. There was no practical purpose for insisting on footing the bill herself. From everything she knew, he had money to burn.

"I'll drive you home."

"I have a bus pass."

"It's nearly eleven. You're not getting on the bus."

She folded her arms over her chest. "I'm a functioning adult, TJ. I don't need you or anyone else to take care of me. I've been on this bus dozens of times at night. And I don't need your permission to do it again."

"I'm offering you a simple favor."

"You're…" She paused. She was exhausted, and it was twenty minutes until the Number Seven bus arrived. She had to transfer at the downtown station, which would mean an additional fifteen-minute wait before she boarded the final bus. She was being a fool to turn him down.

She closed her eyes for a second. "Okay. Thank you. That will be quicker."

"Are you always this stubborn?"

She gave him a glare.

"I mean good. My car is this way." He pointed to the south lot.

"I'm used to being self-reliant," she said, although she didn't owe him an explanation.

"Your life has changed," he said.

"So has yours."

He used his remote to unlock the doors to a low-slung red sports car.

"Drastically," she added, contrasting it to the fifteen-year-old minivan she'd recently sold.

He opened the passenger door and stood waiting for her to get in. "We're in this together, Sage."

She didn't like his phrasing. "We have a common interest."

"We have a child together."

She didn't have another response, so she got into the car.

The seats were smooth leather, cool and comfortable, cradling her body, filling the car with a subtle earthy scent. The navigation screen and dashboard made her think of a space shuttle. The seat belt came out smoothly, clipping effortlessly together.

TJ swung into the driver's seat.

"Where to?" he asked, pressing the start button.

"North on Fairton Road."

"You live downtown?"

"It's close to work."

Her rented basement suite was in an older part of the city. Gentrification was taking place near the water, but it hadn't yet made it to Fir Street. That kept rent low, for which she was grateful. But the nearby development was also push-ing trouble closer and closer to her block.

TJ paid the parking charges and exited the lot.

It was a short drive to the highway, and there their speed increased.

The ride was smooth, and the sports car hugged the road. It was like floating on a cushion of air. It was so much bet-ter than the bus. She leaned her head back against the soft headrest and watched the strobe of streetlights above.

Too soon, they came to her exit.

She directed him to her neighborhood and pointed out the right house.

He pulled to the curb, setting the brake and shutting off the engine. He stared through the windshield. "Who are those guys?"

As she unbuckled her seat belt, Sage took in a group of teens and young adults in front of the corner market. There were six of them, scruffy-looking, all male. A couple of them were smoking, another couple were showing an in-terest in TJ's car.

"They look worse than they are." Sage had never been bothered by anyone.

"Are there a lot of drugs around here?"

"How would I know?"

He gave her a frown.

"No more and no less than in other parts of the city. I don't pay that much attention."

She was used to the neighborhood. She saw it every day. Sure, sometimes litter collected in the gutters. And the lawns weren't exactly fine-trimmed. Some of them were barely lawns. But the MacAfees next door were a lovely re-tired couple, and Sage's landlord, Hank Taylor, owned the bakery two blocks down. He was a hardworking, fiftysome-thing man who looked out for her and Eli.

TJ opened his door and got out, staring levelly at the group of boys.

Sage followed and got out her side.

"Ignore them," she told TJ.

"They're trying to decide if they can intimidate me."

"If you don't bother them, they won't bother you."

"I don't want them to bother my car."

"Don't be paranoid." She started across the sidewalk for the worn stepping stones that led to the basement entrance.

"How long have you lived here?" he asked, falling into step.

"Since Eli was two."

"Has it always been like this?" His tone was clearly critical.

"You mean low-rent?"

"This is a little more than low-rent."

She inserted her key into the doorknob and turned it open.

"No dead bolt?" he asked.

"It's not exactly a high crime district."

"Could have fooled me."

Insulted and annoyed, she stepped into the doorway and turned. "Thanks for the ride, TJ."

He looked confused. "You don't want to talk?"

"About?"

"About our situation." His gaze took in the room behind her.

It was clean. Maybe a little cluttered, since she'd spent so much time at the hospital the past two weeks. There were dishes in the drainer and a basket of clean laundry on the sofa. She'd been to the Laundromat but hadn't had time to put everything away.

She realized he had to be used to far more opulent surroundings, but she wasn't going to apologize. She had a limited budget. Eli had a safe, clean place to live. His school was basic, but the teachers were dedicated. And the park down the street was part of a city beautification project and was a perfectly nice place for him to play.

"I'm tired," she said to TJ. "Can we talk tomorrow?"

He glanced at his watch. "I really don't want to leave you here alone."

"It's my home. You're being both ridiculous and insulting."

She'd been aware of the neighborhood slipping in recent years. But it was still a perfectly fine place to live.

"There are thugs on the front sidewalk."

"Those are kids."

"Those *kids* have been shaving for more than a few years. They could be armed."

She'd had enough. "Good night, TJ. Go back to your five-star hotel. Eat some twenty-dollar almonds from the minibar or something."

"Come with me," he said.

In exasperation, she dropped her purse on the bookshelf. "I'm sleeping in my own bed tonight. Just like I did last night and just like I'll be doing tomorrow night."

He opened his mouth.

"Stop," she ordered. She pointed out the door. "Go. I'll meet you at the hospital tomorrow."

"I'll pick you up."

"No, you won't. I already regret letting you drive me home."

"No, you don't."

He was right. She didn't. If he hadn't driven her home, she'd still be standing at the downtown station.

"Why are you fighting me on this?" he asked.

It was a fair question. She wasn't exactly sure. "I think mostly because you're overbearing."

"I'm logical and reasonable."

His answer surprised a laugh out of her. "Is that how you see yourself?"

"I'm staying at the Bayside Hotel."

"Are you bragging?"

He gave an exaggerated sigh. "I'm pointing out my geographic location. It's downtown. It's not even out of my way to pick you up tomorrow." Before she could respond, he continued. "Logic and reason."

"And a little bit overbearing."

"Only a little bit. Eight?"

She didn't want to give in. It felt too much like giving up. "TJ…"

"Eight it is." He gave her shoulder an unexpected squeeze. "Lock the door behind me."

And then he was gone. And her shoulder tingled from his touch. And she wanted to be annoyed with him. But her heart wasn't in it.

Eli seemed to rally in the morning but then faded in the afternoon. The nurses assured them it was normal. TJ made himself scarce for a while to give Sage time alone with Eli, returning to his hotel to touch base with his executive assistant.

While he followed up with the most pressing phone calls, he couldn't get Sage and Eli's apartment off his mind. He understood that it was hard being a single mother. His own mother had struggled to raise him and his two brothers. There was no shame in financial hardship, especially when a woman was juggling both work and parenting.

But Sage didn't need to struggle anymore. She didn't need to worry about money anymore.

He wanted them out of that neighborhood. What was more, he wanted Eli in Whiskey Bay. He might not be feeling quite as hard-nosed about it after the past few days with Sage. But he was still determined to be part of Eli's day-to-day life from here on in.

He didn't know how he'd pull it off, but he knew it would go a lot smoother if he could convince Sage instead of fighting her. As quickly as the thought formed, it also crystallized. If he wanted to win over Sage, he had to show her the possibilities. To show her the possibilities, he had to show her Whiskey Bay.

Back in the hospital, Eli was still feeling low. He barely touched his dinner. And by six he was sound asleep.

"Tomorrow will be better," TJ said to Sage as she kissed Eli's forehead.

"He feels warm." She drew back and cupped her hand on his head.

"The nurse just took his temperature."

"We should ask her to recheck it."

TJ put a hand on Sage's slim shoulder. "They will. They'll monitor it all night."

"What if he gets a fever?"

"You're borrowing trouble." TJ hated to see her stressing herself out. It wasn't going to change the outcome. "We should get something to eat."

"I'd rather stay here."

"There's nothing you can do while he sleeps."

Sage took Eli's hand. "I know."

"There are absolutely no warning signs." TJ wanted to take Sage's hand. "It's simply going to be a long road to recovery."

"I'm telling myself the same thing."

He moved so he was looking at her. "The best thing, the very best thing you can do for Eli is stay strong and healthy yourself."

She gave a ghost of a smile. "Stop being right."

"I can't help it."

Her smile went wider.

He was encouraged. "Let's go get a nice dinner. You've got the nurses' station on speed dial."

She arched a brow. "Are you mocking me?"

"No, I'm trying to cheer you up. He's doing great. You can afford to think positively."

She lifted Eli's hand and gave it a light kiss. "I don't want to jinx it."

"You can't jinx it. There is no jinx it. Your IQ is in the stratosphere. You know worrying yourself sick will have absolutely no beneficial effect on Eli's health."

She looked like she wanted to argue.

"You got straight As in science."

She'd gotten straight As in everything.

"It's true that I'm not superstitious," she said. Her shoulders relaxed.

"I have a very nice restaurant in mind." He had no intention of telling her the details, at least not until he had to.

"Okay. You're right. Dinner would be nice."

"Can you say that again?" he teased.

"Dinner would be nice." She smirked at him.

"I do like being right."

"You have an ego, TJ." She rose from the edge of the bed and gathered her purse.

It was clear she was mocking him, but she could be right.

He definitely liked to accomplish things. It felt good to succeed. And he liked to be the best he could.

When he discovered he was falling behind in something, he took immediate steps to catch up. Take last year. He'd discovered he was getting out of shape, that both Matt and Caleb could outrun him.

He'd hit the gym, started rowing and biking. He could now beat both of them in a five-mile run. He hadn't thought about why it mattered to him. But ego would definitely explain it.

"Seafood okay with you?" he asked as they made their way toward the parking lot.

"Anything's okay with me. But I can't let you keep paying."

He almost laughed at that. "I've got a lot of paying to make up for."

"With Eli, sure. But not with me. You don't owe me anything."

"Other than nine years of child support?"

"I'm not asking for that." Her tone was genuinely horrified. "I'd never ask for that. None of this has anything to do with money."

"I know it doesn't." How could he not know that?

The fact that he'd found out about Eli at all was a bizarre coincidence. His anger still simmered when he thought about her secrecy. But now wasn't the time to rehash her past decisions. The last thing he wanted to do was fight.

"I won't take your money," she said.

"It's dinner, Sage. I'm buying you dinner. People do that with their friends every day."

"We're not friends."

"Well, I hope we're going to be friends. Things are going to be a whole lot easier if we're friendly."

She didn't seem to have a response for that, and they'd arrived at his car.

"Are you afraid of flying?" he asked as they got inside.

"No," she said. "I mean, it's not something I do. We're hardly in a position to take sun vacations. But I'm not afraid of it." Her tone turned suspicious. "Why? Why are you asking? Are you looking for genetic flaws?"

"Genetic... *No.*"

"I doubt irrational fears are inherited, anyway."

"I'm not looking for genetic flaws. You *have* no genetic flaws." He pulled onto the street.

"I have red hair and freckles."

"The freckles have faded." He'd always thought they were cute. "And your hair's not red, it's auburn. It's a beautiful shade of auburn. Do you know how much women pay to get that color hair? And you're absolutely brilliant. What is your IQ, anyway?"

"I'm not telling you my IQ."

"That high, huh?"

"No, it's not that high. It's not anywhere near..." She blew out what sounded like a tired sigh.

He let it lie as they zipped through the light traffic.

Twelve blocks later he flipped on his signal and pulled up to the Brandywine Hotel.

"Are we eating here?" she asked, glancing around at the brick-lined drive and the lighted gardens.

"Not exactly."

He exited the car and came around to her door.

"We're walking?" she asked as she stepped out.

The valet arrived, and TJ handed him the keys, giving the uniformed man his name.

"Not exactly," TJ answered Sage, gesturing to the revolving glass door.

"I don't understand."

"There's a helipad on the top of the hotel."

"A what?" She looked straight up the outside of the building. "There's a restaurant up there?"

"No." He let her go first through the door. "That's not a euphemism. I mean a helipad, a place where helicopters can land and take off."

"Why?" She looked perplexed.

"You said you weren't afraid to fly."

"You said we were going for dinner."

"We are."

She gave him a look that questioned his intellect. "In a helicopter? Are you showing off?"

"No. I'm being practical." He touched the elevator button.

"This, I have got to hear."

"We're going to the Crab Shack. It's a great little seafood restaurant."

"By *helicopter*?"

"It's faster."

"Faster than what?"

"Than a car."

The door closed behind him. He inserted a key card and pressed the button for the rooftop.

She watched his motions. "Do you have a room here?"

He glanced at the card before putting it back in his

pocket. "No. I made arrangements earlier to access the helipad."

"You planned this?"

"Yes, I planned this. Helicopters don't just swoop in for me on a moment's notice."

She was silent as the floors pinged by.

"Is this place fancy?" she asked.

"You look fine. You look better than fine."

"Is it fancy?"

"Not really. It's pretty down-to-earth."

"Is it on an island? Do we have to cross the strait?"

As the door slid open, TJ turned his head from her and mumbled, "It's in Whiskey Bay."

"What did you say?"

He gave up the subterfuge. "I said it's in Whiskey Bay."

She stopped dead, her eyes going round as she stared at him. "What are you doing, TJ?"

"You might as well see the community."

"Are you kidnapping me?"

"Of course not."

Her gaze slid to the helicopter. "And if I don't want to get onboard?"

"Then you'll miss the ride of your life, a great seafood dinner and a chance to see where I live."

# Four

TJ had been right. The seafood dinner at the Crab Shack was terrific, and the helicopter ride had been the adventure of Sage's life. It took only thirty minutes, and it was smoother than she'd expected. The altitude was low, and her view of the lights on the ground and the stars above had been amazing.

When they'd landed, she'd discovered TJ owned another vehicle. She didn't know why that had surprised her, but it had. This one was a luxurious SUV.

As they drove along the coast highway through Whiskey Bay, he explained that having all-wheel drive came in handy when he wanted to take gravel roads. He liked to mountain bike, but he didn't like taking his sports car off the pavement.

It made perfect sense the way he explained it. If you were a gazillionaire, why wouldn't you have as many vehicles as your heart desired?

"See, it's only about fifteen minutes from my place to the hospital," he said as they turned into the parking lot.

He'd pointed out his driveway, which was close to the Crab Shack.

There was no pay kiosk at this hospital. As far as she could see, parking was free. She had to admit, it was a nice perk for patients and visitors.

"I think you'll be impressed," he said as he chose a spot.

"You're not going to change my mind." She wasn't looking at the Highside Hospital to be impressed. She wanted to be in a position to advocate for St. Bea's. Halfway through dinner, she'd realized she could do that better once she'd taken a look at the competition…and discovered its flaws.

"I'm looking for a conversation, not a debate," he said.

"I don't believe that for a second."

They both climbed out of the SUV.

Both the parking lot and the entrance area were well lit. A few people entered and exited the building, some of them in uniform, some obviously visitors or patients.

The Highside Hospital sign was in stylized red lettering across the front of the building. Inside, the foyer was bright and expansive, with high ceilings and a view of some open hallways above. The colors were bolder than she'd expected. There were comfortable seating areas and a long reception counter with several available nurses, two of whom looked up and greeted them with a welcoming smile.

Before they made it to the reception desk, a slim, thirtysomething woman in a blazer and a straight skirt approached. Her brunette hair was neatly twisted into a braid. Everything about her projected a calm professionalism.

"Mr. Bauer. It's so nice to see you here." Her voice was friendly as she shook TJ's hand. Then she looked expectantly in Sage's direction.

"This is a friend. Sage Costas. Sage, this is Natalie Moreau, the assistant manager of patient care here at Highside."

"It's very nice to meet you." Sage couldn't help but wonder if TJ had called ahead, and she was about to get the full court press.

It wasn't going to help him. She wasn't going to be swayed by his connections to the bigwigs any more than she was by the big lobby.

"I'm sorry to drop in like this," TJ said to Natalie.

Despite his words, Sage still suspected a setup.

"You're welcome anytime," Natalie told him.

"Sage has a nine-year-old son who is ill, and I was hoping we could show her the facilities."

The concern that appeared on Natalie's face seemed genuine. "I'm so sorry to hear that. I can show you around right now and answer any questions you have."

"We don't mean to interrupt your evening," TJ said. "Perhaps one of the nurses might have time to accompany us—"

"Nonsense," Natalie said, her tone going brisk. "You're not interrupting at all. Why don't we start with the lounge and restaurant area?"

She directed her attention to Sage. "There are several visitor lounge areas on the main floor, and two on each patient floor. There are patient lounges too, of course. But we want visitors—especially the parents of young children—to have some space to decompress." She started to walk. "If you'll follow me, I can show you where we converted the cafeteria into two spaces, a full-service restaurant and a grab-and-go coffee bar. Over the past four years, we've put significant emphasis on dining options for both patients and visitors. We're particularly attuned to allergies and sensitivities. Our head chef has started several innovative programs, including using organic and local foods. We're providing better nutrition, a more enjoyable dining experience and improved outcomes all around. It's amazing how a nicely presented, delicious meal option encourages recovering patients to eat. Who could have guessed?" She gave a light laugh.

As they walked, Sage took everything in. It was impossible not to be impressed. The furniture, the construction, the fixtures, everything was good quality and top caliber. Nobody they met seemed rushed or stressed. She knew it was a hospital, but it felt more like a hotel.

They passed through a set of double doors.

"This is a typical patient room." Natalie opened a doorway. "The rooms are private, but the walls are retractable into quads. Occasionally, we have patients who prefer to be in a room with someone else, siblings after a car accident for example. The patient lounge areas provide another place for social interaction. On our pediatrics floors, there are playrooms instead."

"How do kids get to the playroom?" Sage asked.

Eli was bedridden and likely would remain that way for some time to come.

"They can walk, or use a wheelchair, or even have their beds moved for periods of time. Our staff-to-patient ratio is one of the best in the country, so there's plenty of help for patients requiring assistance. The beds are fully automated." Natalie used a remote control to demonstrate. "Each room has a fully capable entertainment and communications station."

Sage took in the wide screen on the wall and the keyboard on a rolling table. "Are you telling me patients can check their email and surf the net?"

"They can. Obviously, many people are too ill to use all the services. But as they recover, we strive to make their stay as homelike as possible."

There were two armchairs with a small table between them in a corner by the window. The colors were warm, green and copper, even the floor was a faux wood grain. There wasn't a speck of beige in sight.

Sage could see why TJ liked the place, particularly when she considered the level of service he must be used to in his life. But she still wasn't changing her mind. Eli was perfectly fine at St. Bea's. He might not have internet access, but he had his mother, and that was far more important.

"Can you talk about your oncology services?" TJ asked Natalie.

"The best, most progressive in the country." She sounded proud. "We attracted top-rated doctors and researchers. Is your son struggling with cancer?" she asked Sage.

"Leukemia," Sage answered.

Natalie touched her arm in sympathy. "Do you have a prognosis?"

"He's just had a bone marrow transplant. At St. Bea's."

"That's encouraging."

"TJ was the donor," Sage felt honor-bound to add.

Natalie smiled. "How fortunate you were to find a match."

"He's doing well so far. It's a good hospital."

"I know some of the staff there. They're very dedicated, with excellent clinical skills."

Sage gave a satisfied glance in TJ's direction.

"I'm interested in transferring him to Highside," he said.

"I'm not," Sage said.

"It's a personal decision." There was a slight rebuke for TJ in Natalie's tone.

"St. Bea's is much closer to my house," Sage said.

Natalie gestured to the hospital room door. "For all our fancy facilities, nothing replaces family."

"Thank you." For some reason, emotion welled up in Sage's throat.

"I'm not suggesting she won't see him," TJ said as they walked, the barest hint of exasperation in his tone.

"Highside is a long way from Seattle," Natalie said.

Sage was now completely convinced Natalie wasn't part of any plot to sway her.

"She can stay in the parents' residence," TJ said.

"I have a job," Sage put in.

Natalie halted. "Mr. Bauer, we love you dearly, and we are beyond grateful for your financial support—"

"This isn't about my money."

"The decision is Sage's alone. It's her son. She knows what's best for her family."

Sage struggled not to look at TJ, but she couldn't help herself.

The set of his jaw betrayed his annoyance, but it didn't look like he was going to blurt out the fact that he was Eli's father.

"Do you have any more questions?" Natalie asked Sage.

"No. Thank you so much for your time."

Natalie took both of Sage's hands. "Good luck with your son. I hope his recovery is fast. We're here if you need us. But there's no wrong choice for you to make."

A wave of guilt passed through Sage. She liked Natalie. She liked her a lot. And she liked everything she'd seen at Highside.

But she couldn't leave Seattle, and she couldn't let TJ pull her and Eli apart. She had to believe Eli would recover equally well at St. Bea's. She had to believe it.

TJ didn't know how he'd failed. But he had. He'd counted on Natalie, or anyone else at Highside Hospital for that matter, to point out the merits of the institution and impress Sage with the level of care Eli could expect. What he hadn't counted on was for Natalie to take Sage's side.

He hadn't wanted to blurt out that he was Eli's father. That wouldn't have been fair to Sage, and he was determined that Eli would be the next person he told. But maybe that was a mistake. Maybe Natalie's attitude would have been different if she'd known that it wasn't just a mother's support at stake here, but a father's support as well.

"Can we go back to Seattle now?" Sage asked as she tucked her phone into her purse.

They were driving down the coast highway toward the Crab Shack. The helicopter was on standby in a parking lot nearby.

"Any news?" he asked, referring to the text message she had just checked.

"He's still asleep."

"That's good." TJ hoped Eli would have a restful night.

"It's getting late." She made a point of looking at her watch.

"I just need to make one stop."

"Are you kidding me?" The exasperation in her tone was clear.

"It's at my house. It's not out of our way."

"Fine," she said tersely.

"Are you angry?"

"I'm frustrated."

"You couldn't make the right decision without all the facts." It hadn't gone his way, but he still believed that. Not that he was giving up this easily.

"I'd already made the right decision."

"You're too smart to make that argument."

"Okay. I saw Highside. It's good. It's terrific. But you already know that. And I never disputed it. My argument was never that Highside wasn't a great facility. It was that *I* wasn't in Whiskey Bay."

"We can change that." They could easily change that.

"I'm not quitting my job. I'm not giving up my apartment."

"It's not much of an apartment. That's blunt. But you know it as well as I do. And you can get another job."

"Really?" She turned her body to glare at him. "I can get another job?" She snapped her fingers. "Just like that, I can get another job?"

He didn't understand her point. "Yes. There are jobs here in Whiskey Bay."

"For people like me."

"For people like anybody. What do you mean, people like you?" He flipped on his signal, taking the road that led to his and the three other properties along this stretch of the bay.

The houses belonged to Matt and Tasha, to Caleb and Jules, and to Caleb's sister-in-law Melissa and her husband, Noah.

"A single mother with no college degree?"

"There are lots of single… What do you mean no college degree?"

Sage was a bona fide genius. She could earn any college degree without breaking a sweat.

"I didn't go to college, TJ."

"What about all those scholarships?" He knew she'd had

a dozen offers, everybody knew that. How could she have turned them all down?

Her tone was flat. "I've been a little busy."

"What about part-time?" Sure, he understood a baby added a complication.

"That didn't work."

"What do you mean it didn't work? What kind of an attitude is that? When it's that important, you make it work."

Her voice rose. "Spoken like a man who hasn't got a clue about taking care of a baby."

"I know there's such a thing as childcare."

"And do you know they don't give scholarships for that? I could get a full ride, sure. But I can't live in the dorm with a baby. So, I'd have to pay rent, buy food, cover day care, study in the evenings instead of reading stories and giving baths."

"And later? When he was in school?"

Surely she could have made something work at some point in the past nine years. She had a brain in a million. It was tragic to let it go to waste.

"Do you have any idea how insulting you're being?" she asked.

He pulled into his driveway and parked out front between the two garages. "Go now," he said.

She closed her eyes, shook her head and gave a long-suffering sigh.

"You're only twenty-seven. Go back to school now. Get a degree."

"Take me home, TJ."

He realized he'd pushed too far. "Come inside."

"No."

"This won't take long. And then we'll walk down to the helicopter."

At first, she didn't move. But then she unbuckled her seat belt and opened the door.

He was sorry if he'd insulted her. But he couldn't believe

she'd given up on herself so easily. There were options. There were always options. There was always an alternate strategy or approach to any situation. You just had to keep looking until you found the right one.

He led the way up the short, concrete staircase and opened his front door. The light was on a motion sensor and came on automatically in the foyer. The living room in front of them was dimly lit by the pot lights above the fireplace to the right side. And the deck and lighted garden beds were visible through the glass wall on the far side of the living room.

Her steps slowed in the doorway and she gazed around in silence.

"It's big for one person," he acknowledged.

"Big?" She took a couple of steps forward. "I was going to go with *huge*."

"Yeah. I barely ever go upstairs."

"There's an upstairs?"

"The stairs are around the corner, across from the study."

"Of course they are," she said a little weakly.

"Are you thirsty?"

"We're not staying."

"Iced tea?" he asked, moving into the living room, taking the right-hand turn that led to the open-concept kitchen.

In front of the kitchen was a dining room and then a family room, where he spent much of his time. It opened onto the biggest part of the deck, where there was an outdoor kitchen and small bathroom.

He gestured to the oversize refrigerator. "I've got cold beer. Or there's always wine."

He glanced behind him, but Sage hadn't followed.

He went back to the foyer. "Come in."

She looked a little frightened. "Exactly how rich are you?"

"I don't know how to answer that question. I guess I'm to the point now where I can do pretty much whatever I want."

She took a couple of hesitant steps into the living room, taking in the furnishings. "Do you have a housekeeping staff?"

"There's someone who comes in to clean. And I have a gardening service. It's a big house," he found himself defending. "But nobody lives in."

She looked to her left, where a short hallway led to his study, his bedroom and the stairs to the second floor.

"Have a look around," he invited. "Maybe a glass of water?"

"Sure," she answered absently, wandering down the hallway.

"The wine cellar is locked, but I can open it up if you're interested."

"Water's fine."

He chuckled. He'd meant if she wanted to have a look. But he'd happily open a bottle of wine if she saw something interesting.

When he returned from the kitchen with two glasses of ice water, she was gone. He guessed she'd taken the stairs, so he followed.

"There's no furniture up here," she said, peering into one of the bedrooms.

"My wife…" He paused to gather himself. "Lauren wanted us to have several children. She expected we'd need the extra room."

"I'm sorry," Sage said. "I didn't mean to bring up painful memories."

"It's fine." He'd told Sage about Lauren while Eli had slept.

Sage gave an apologetic smile. She seemed to sense he'd rather move on, and she obliged him, glancing in each of the five upstairs bedrooms. "You could fit three of my apartments in here."

"It is roomy," he agreed.

Mostly, he ignored this floor. It was a waste of space, but

there was no way he'd sell the house Lauren had designed.
And despite the wasted space, he couldn't imagine having
anyone live with him—except for Eli. TJ would love to have
Eli live here with him.

He knew it was impossible. Though he'd stated a hard
line with Matt and Caleb that night, there was no way he'd
take Eli away from his mother, and no court in the land
would let him do that.

Ironically, there was more than enough room up here for
both Sage and Eli.

His brain took a pause. That would be perfect. It would
be beyond perfect.

He turned to consider her, taking in her profile, his mind
galloping along the idea.

"What exactly is your job?" he asked.

She glanced at him. "What?"

He handed her a glass of water. "What do you do in Seattle?"

"I told you, I plan events for the community center."

"Is it administrative?"

"Mostly."

"That sounds like a transferable skill."

She caught his meaning immediately. "TJ, don't."

"Don't shut the door on this, Sage. You could live here.
You and Eli. There's no reason why not."

From the look on her face, he knew he'd misplayed. He'd
made the suggestion way too soon.

"I mean—"

Without a word, she spun on her heel to march back
down the hall.

He went after her. "I mean that's one possibility. We
should talk about it. Rent would be free. The schools are
fantastic." He trotted behind her down the stairs. "You could
get any job you wanted, maybe part-time. You could go to
college here. I'm a platinum donor, so tuition wouldn't cost
anything. Not that cost matters—"

"Stop!" she shouted, pivoting on him. "Just stop it."

"I'm stopping." He'd gone too far. And he'd gone too fast.

"I'm not moving to Whiskey Bay. Yes, you have a right to visit Eli. And yes, we will work something out. But I'm not walking away from my entire life to suit your needs."

TJ battled the sense of defeat. He didn't want to merely be a visitor in his son's life. He wanted to be there all the time, for all the little things.

He wanted to hear about Eli's day at school, throw a ball with him on summer evenings, tuck him in at night, pour his cereal in the morning and patch his cuts and scrapes. He wanted to do it all in real time, not on two weekends a month and every other Christmas.

He wanted Eli to be with him, day in, day out. But he understood that Sage wanted that too. She deserved that too. To make that happen, there had to be more for her in Whiskey Bay than free rent.

"Thank you," she said. She drew a shaky breath and headed for the front door. "We need to get back to Seattle."

He knew she was right. They weren't going to solve this tonight. He didn't know what he'd expected, but he found himself bitterly disappointed that it hadn't happened.

He followed her, feeling cheated and angry at their circumstance. Parents all over the world lived with their children. It was the normal state of things. He wasn't asking for the moon and the stars.

How were they all more deserving than him? How were they different?

Even as he framed the question, he knew the answer was patently obvious. Those parents were in love. And if they weren't in love, they stayed married anyway.

And then it hit him.

"Wait!" he called out. "Wait just a minute."

Her hand was on the doorknob, and her lips were pressed tightly together. But she waited.

"I'm not being fair," he said.

Her shoulders lowered a little bit, and she looked relieved. "No, you're not."

"I can't ask you to give up your entire life for free rent."

"No, you can't."

"There has to be more to it than that."

She tipped her head to one side, looking puzzled now.

"Marry me," he said.

She didn't react, and he wasn't sure if she'd heard the words.

He continued talking. "Share my life, my whole life."

She started to laugh. Her hand rose to her mouth, and she kept laughing.

He was vaguely insulted. "How is that funny?"

"It's not funny." She removed her hand and schooled her features, swallowing. "It's preposterous."

He'd admit it was unorthodox. "It's logical. We share a son."

"We barely know each other."

"A marriage of convenience, obviously." As he said the words, he pictured her in his bed. The vision startled him. He shook it away and pressed on. "Look at the size of this place. We can stay completely out of each other's way. You and Eli can have the entire upstairs to yourselves."

"Take me home, TJ." She looked sad and tired, really fragile and forlorn.

She also looked beautiful, and he wanted to draw her into his arms and comfort her. He wanted to hold her, and he wanted to kiss her.

"What is wrong with me?" he muttered.

"You're tired. We're both tired."

"Maybe." But he knew there was something more going on.

Exhausted as she was, Sage couldn't sleep. Because, ridiculous as they were, TJ's words kept echoing through her brain.

It was likely the worst marriage proposal in recorded history. But, no matter the complex circumstances, it was also the only one she'd ever received. He'd asked her to marry him. Nobody had ever done that before.

She sat up in bed, gazing at the glow from the street through her thin curtains, hearing the buzz and clunk of the refrigerator and the intermittent drip of the kitchen faucet. A car drove past, its headlights sweeping across the bedroom wall, flashing in the mirror.

TJ was handsome. He was buff and sexy. He was also smart and wealthy. What woman wouldn't want to marry him?

None, that was who.

She tossed off the covers and came to her feet, chilly in the faded tank top and plaid flannel boxer shorts she wore to bed. She headed to the kitchen for a drink of water.

There was no way she could marry TJ and move to Whiskey Bay—even if he did have what was probably the greatest house in the world. It wasn't an idea that was even worth considering. This wasn't 1955. People didn't get married because they had a child.

They made agreements, arrangements. They figured out logical systems that would make it work for everyone. Eli would just...

She retrieved a glass from the cupboard and turned on the faucet.

As she filled the glass, she tried to imagine what Eli would do. Take a bus back and forth between Seattle and Whiskey Bay? Then she pictured the helicopter and gave a fatalistic chuckle. Yeah, Eli's daddy wouldn't let his son ride the bus.

Eli's daddy. It was another phrase to rattle around in her head.

It wasn't that she hadn't known. She'd known all along. What she hadn't known was anything about TJ beyond the little she'd learned in high school. To say the least, he was a formidable man. He was determined. And he was strong. And he was...

She suddenly felt hot instead of cool.

Then a noise startled her. It sounded like glass smashing on the sidewalk, maybe a bottle—possibly soda but probably liquor.

It wasn't the first time it had happened. There would be a mess in the morning for her landlord, Hank, to clean up.

Her phone pinged with an incoming text.

Her first thought was the hospital, and she rushed back to the bedside, picking up the glowing screen.

It was from TJ.

Sorry was all it said.

She sat down, holding it in both hands. Sorry for what? Sorry he'd dragged her to Whiskey Bay? Sorry he'd pressured her to move there? Sorry he'd proposed? Sorry he'd behaved like a lunatic?

She typed back: It's okay. She realized all of those things were okay.

He deserved a little latitude. Okay, more than a little latitude. She'd blindsided him with the knowledge of Eli, and since then he'd stepped up at every turn. He was desperate to forge a relationship with his son. Maybe he was grasping at straws. But at least he wasn't threatening to take her to court.

She sobered at that thought. She'd be completely outgunned if he took her to court. He could out-lawyer her a hundred to one. He could end up with joint custody. Eli could be forced to spend a whole lot of time, likely weekends, summers and holidays, in Whiskey Bay. TJ could play hardball if he chose.

Her phone rang in her hand, startling her.

It was TJ.

She accepted the call and put the phone to her ear. "Hi."

"You're awake."

"I was thirsty." There was no way she was telling him the real reason for her wakefulness.

"Me too," he said.

She found herself smiling. "I'm starting to be able to tell when you're lying."

"You caught me." There was a chuckle in his tone. "I was on a call to Australia."

The gulf between them seemed to widen. "Oh. Well. Yeah, I guess…"

"It sounds stupidly pretentious. That's why I said thirsty instead."

"If you've got business in Australia, you've got business in Australia."

"Forgive me?" he asked.

Before she could answer, another bottle smashed outside. This one was loud, much closer.

"What was that?" TJ asked.

"Glass breaking."

"Are you barefoot?"

"Not me. It was outside."

Concern ratcheted up in his voice. "What's going on? Who's out there?"

"I haven't looked out. It's probably kids. I'm sure they're making a mess."

There was a pause before he spoke. "Does that happen often?"

"Not really. Occasionally. It is Saturday night."

There was a sudden banging on her door.

"What the hell was that?" TJ demanded.

Reflexive fear shot through her and she took a step backward. "There's someone knocking on the door."

"Don't answer it."

"I'm not going to answer it." Did he think she was foolish?

"I'm coming over."

"Don't be silly. The door's locked. They'll go away."

"Are you calling the police?"

"And telling them what?" Sage couldn't imagine the police would respond to someone knocking on her door.

The banging came again, three times, slow and low-pitched like somebody was using the end of their fist.

"Calista?" called a drunken voice. "Honey, let me in."

"They have the wrong house," Sage said to TJ.

"They sure do," he answered.

"They'll give up." She hoped it was soon. She knew the door was locked, but it was still unnerving to have someone trying to get in. Using one hand, she stepped into her jeans and pulled them up. For some reason, she felt more self-confident in her clothes.

"You don't sound convinced, Sage. I'm on my way."

"TJ, no. You're fifteen minutes away."

"Ten."

"Only if you make the lights."

"Who's stopping for lights?"

"They'll be gone before you get here."

The banging came again. Sage hated to admit it, but part of her hoped TJ would ignore her protest and get over here.

"Open the door," the voice shouted.

"Let's order pizza," a second voice said.

For some reason, there being two people out there made her feel less fearful.

She moved a little closer. She considered calling out to tell them they had the wrong place. It was impossible to know if that would make things better or worse. She really didn't want them to know she was inside.

The doorknob rattled, and she backed away, staring at it.

"I'm driving now," TJ said, and she jumped at the sound of his voice.

She'd forgotten she was holding the phone to her ear.

"She changed the lock?" the second voice asked.

"Key's busted," the first voice said on a slur.

"Keys don't break."

"Should I tell them it's the wrong place?" Sage whispered to TJ.

"*No*. Do any of your rooms lock?" TJ asked.

"Just the bathroom."

"Go lock yourself in. Keep talking to me."

She wanted to argue. She didn't want to barricade herself in the bathroom. She didn't want to admit she was in genuine danger.

"I gotta… Where's the tree?" the second voice asked in clear confusion.

"What tree?"

"That big, fat… Whoa, man."

"What?"

"You got the wrong house."

Sage all but sagged in relief.

"I don't… Well, crap on that."

"They're figuring it out," she said to TJ.

"Go into the bathroom anyway."

"Is this even the right street?" the second voice asked.

Sage wanted to shout *no*. It wasn't the right street. They should go find some other street to stagger down.

"We are so wasted," the first man said.

"Two minutes out," TJ told her.

"It sounds like they're leaving."

"Are you in the bathroom?"

"I'm listening to them walk away."

Their footfalls and hollow laughter faded.

Sage realized her legs were trembling, and she backed up, sitting down on her brown armchair. A car engine sounded outside and went silent. She knew it was TJ.

"I'm here," he said into the phone.

"They're gone."

"Can you let me in?"

"Yeah. Sure." She tried to stand up. "Just give me a…" She pushed on the arm of the chair with her free hand and managed to get to her feet to cross the room.

"It's me," he said through the door.

For some reason, that final assurance meant a lot to her. She opened the door.

"Hey," he said, his concerned gaze gentle.

"Hi."

"You okay?"

She nodded, stepping back to let him in.

He pocketed his phone and touched her shoulder. "You sure?"

"Yes. I'm good."

He smiled as he eased her phone from her ear and gingerly removed it from her hand to end the call. Then he wrapped his arms around her, enveloping her in a reassuring hug.

It felt indescribably good, and for a few moments she simply closed her eyes and leaned into his strength.

He smoothed his palm over the back of her hair. She knew she should break away, but she couldn't bring herself to do it.

"You scared me," he whispered. Then he ducked his head to press his cheek against hers.

The contact was electric. Desire raced along her skin, flushing her with heat.

He stilled, and she could hear his breath hiss out.

He was going to kiss her. She could feel it with every fiber of her being. And she was going to let him. She was going to kiss him back.

Her phone rang in his hand, startling them both.

"That's not me," he said unnecessarily. He drew back and held the screen for her to see.

Sage's heart sank. "It's the hospital."

# Five

"It's an infection," Dr. Stannis said.

Eli was asleep, looking pale again. TJ hated the sight of the new yellow-colored bag hanging from his son's IV stand. It was a stark reminder of the setback.

"We caught it early," she continued. "We're treating it with antibiotics. But, as you know, we can't afford to take these things lightly."

"What can I do?" Sage asked the doctor. Her voice was hoarse and her throat worked as she swallowed. She looked almost as pale as Eli.

TJ wanted to suggest Highside again, but the last thing he would do was upset Sage. He looked to the doctor. He could see it in her eyes even before she spoke. She was genuinely worried.

Dr. Stannis touched Sage's arm. "If you can manage the cost, you might want to consider Highside."

"We can manage the cost," TJ immediately answered.

"Would it help?" Sage asked, her voice raspy and paper-dry.

"I'm not ringing alarm bells," Dr. Stannis said. "But an infection at this stage indicates a challenge. Highside has the finest equipment in the country, and their on-site laboratory is state-of-the-art." She paused. "And if things were to get worse—I'm only saying if—our intensive care unit is full."

Sage gave a gasp, and TJ wrapped an arm around her shoulders.

"I'm not expecting that," Dr. Stannis said. "But at Highside, you have more options."

"Can we safely move him?" TJ asked. He'd have an air

ambulance here within the hour if that was the best course of action.

"By ambulance, yes. Moving him won't have an impact on the infection."

"I can order a helicopter," TJ said.

"Wait." Sage looked up at him with near terror in her eyes.

He turned and placed his hands gently on her shoulders, keeping his voice low and even. "One step at a time. Like the doctor said, there are no alarm bells here. This is only a precaution. But it sounds like it's a precaution worth taking."

It took her a second, but then she nodded. "Yes. Let's do it."

TJ retrieved his phone. He didn't feel the slightest bit of satisfaction in this. He'd wanted to move Eli to Whiskey Bay, but he sure didn't want it to be under these circumstances.

He had the air ambulance on speed dial, and his next call was to Highside Hospital to alert them to Eli's arrival. Dr. Stannis contacted the oncology department to transfer Eli's case files.

There was room in the back of the helicopter for Sage to ride with Eli, and TJ sat up front with the pilot. They cruised smoothly over the landscape, following valleys to the coast. There were two nurses and a doctor on the helipad waiting to greet them, and Eli was quickly whisked inside and into a room.

Once he was settled, TJ gave in to temptation and put an arm around Sage's shoulders again, standing at Eli's bedside and gazing down.

"He woke up in the helicopter," she said.

"That seems like a good sign."

"He asked why it was so noisy."

Before TJ could respond, the doctor from the helipad, a lanky, fortysomething, dark-haired man, reentered the room.

"I'm Dr. Westray." He reached out to shake TJ's hand.

TJ shook, cocking his head toward Sage. "This is Sage Costas, Eli's mother."

The doctor turned his attention to her. He had a soothingly gentle manner. "It's good to meet you, Sage. I want to assure you Eli is getting the very best care. I've looked over his chart, and I just got off the phone with Dr. Stannis. We're optimistic we can beat this infection."

"How's he doing?" Sage asked. She reached out to smooth her hand across Eli's forehead.

"His temperature has come down a little bit. It's too soon to conclude that this particular antibiotic will defeat it. But that's a good sign. It's the best sign we can have right now."

Sage gave a shaky sigh.

"Would you like to sit down?" the doctor asked her.

TJ quickly moved a chair, and Sage sat.

"I want to stay," she said.

"You can stay with him as long as you like," Dr. Westray told her. "And we have a residence for parents connected to the hospital, so you can be close by. The nurse will request a room for you there, in case you want to get some sleep, or take a shower."

"Not yet," she said.

"I understand. We'll be monitoring his temperature and his other vitals on an ongoing basis. There's a nursing station across the hall if you have any questions."

Sage took Eli's hand in hers, her eyes shining with unshed tears. "Thank you," she said to the doctor.

"You're very welcome. I'll be on the floor all night, and I'll be in touch again."

TJ shook his hand a final time. "Thank you, Doctor."

"It's good to meet you, Mr. Bauer."

"Please, call me TJ."

Dr. Westray gave a nod. "Let me know if there's anything else."

TJ wished there was something someone could do. But

right now it was all up to Eli. TJ stood by Sage's shoulder for a long while, watching their son sleep.

Eventually, he moved to one of the two armchairs in the corner. It was comfortable, and he was exhausted, and he laid his head back on the cool cushion.

Traffic whizzed by on the coastal highway, and rain tapped lightly on the window beside him. Pings and whirs sounded in the hallway, muted by the closed door.

He shut his eyes, and his mind went back to Sage's suite and the drunken men who'd shown up at her door. She couldn't go back there, not ever. It wasn't safe for her, and it wasn't safe for Eli.

He heard whispery footsteps and opened his eyes. A nurse had entered the room. She spoke softly to Sage as she checked Eli's IV and his blood pressure. When she put the electronic thermometer to his ear, TJ held his breath.

But she smiled at the readout.

"Down a little more," she whispered to Sage.

Sage's shoulders relaxed, and she slumped a bit in the chair.

TJ came to his feet. "It looks good?" he asked the nurse in a low tone.

"Better," she said before leaving the room.

"You'll be more comfortable in an armchair," he said to Sage.

"I'm fine here."

"He's doing better. They recline almost horizontal. You might be able to sleep a little."

She glanced over her shoulder to the two chairs in the corner.

"I'll get you a blanket," he offered.

He recalled from their tour that there were blankets and pillows in the closet.

Sage nodded. "I guess I can stand to be ten feet away."

"That's the spirit."

"He does have a bit more color, doesn't he?" She slowly came to her feet.

TJ wasn't convinced there'd been a change. "He does."

"That's a good sign."

"It is. And his temperature coming down is an even better sign. Are you thirsty? Hungry?"

She thought about it for a minute. "Thirsty."

There was a mini fridge in the room, and TJ checked it while Sage sat down in one of the armchairs. He found water, juices and milk.

"Water or fruit juice?" he asked. "We have orange, cranberry or mixed berry punch."

"Orange would be good."

He cracked a bottle of orange juice and took a bottle of water for himself.

He set the juice on the table beside her, then retrieved a blanket from the closet, shaking it out and draping it over her.

She gave a small smile. "Nobody's tucked me in in a while."

He smiled back. "You need tucking?"

"This is good, just like this." She reached for the orange juice. "I was so encouraged when he drank that milkshake you got for him."

TJ eased down into the other chair. "You should be encouraged now. He's clearly a fighter, and he's almost got this latest thing beat."

"He must get that from you," she said.

TJ's chest tightened with emotion, and he had to blink against a surge of moisture. She saw some of him in Eli. The knowledge was overwhelming. TJ couldn't find the words to answer.

She took a drink. "He has your laugh. And I didn't realize it until I saw you that night in the hospital, but he has your walk. Funny, the little things that genetics do."

"He's amazing. I can't wait to get to know him."

She fell silent at that, and TJ wasn't sure what to say. There were so many things about the future they had to discuss. But she needed to rest. Hopefully, she'd sleep. Everything else would have to wait.

"Looks like you won this round," she said.

"This isn't what I wanted to happen."

"I know. And I agreed because it was the right thing to do for Eli. But we're here now, and he's going to be in this hospital for a while, and I'm going to have to quit my job."

"You don't need a job."

Money problems for her and Eli were off the table completely and forever.

"I do need a job," she said. "I need financial independence and life satisfaction."

He was about to jump in, but she kept talking.

"But my son needs me more. I'm a mom first. I have been since I got pregnant."

"I'm so sorry," TJ said. "I can't tell you how much I've regretted letting myself get talked into that stupid prank. Even before I knew all this, I've wished I could go back and change it."

She was thoughtful for a moment. "I'm not at all sorry it happened. If I had to do it over, I'd take Eli. I'd take him over anything and everything."

"You're amazing too," he said. Then he reached out and took her hand.

It felt small in his, cool, delicate. It also felt right and good. He didn't let go.

Sage awoke to the sound of Eli's voice. He was laughing. It was weak, but he was laughing.

She opened her eyes to see TJ at Eli's bedside. The two were bent over a tablet, and a nurse was standing by. The nurse's presence might have made Sage nervous, but the laugh had to be a good sign.

Eli was in profile, and TJ was in profile. They smiled in

unison, and Sage was dumbstruck by the similarities between them.

"You might want to start slow," the nurse said to Eli.

As she spoke, she put a hand on TJ's shoulder and pointed to something on the tablet screen. She was pretty, and TJ's eyes were bright when he looked at her, and Sage was struck by a wave of jealousy.

As soon as she recognized the emotion, she squelched it.

"Mom," Eli said, noticing she was awake. "They have an interactive menu. I can touch whatever I want, and it'll be delivered."

"Good morning," the nurse said cheerfully to Sage. "We have nothing but good news this morning. Eli's fever is down, and he says he's hungry."

Sage pulled off her blanket and sat the recliner up, pressing the pop-up footstool back into place. "Should he start with liquids?" she asked, coming to her feet.

She smoothed back her hair, finger-combing it. Her jeans and tank top were wrinkled. She felt frumpy compared to the crisply uniformed nurse.

She shouldn't care. And she wouldn't care.

"The menu is customized to each patient's condition," the nurse told her. "And a dietician double-checks each of the orders."

Sage moved toward Eli. "You're looking much better, honey."

"TJ said I was on a helicopter."

She couldn't help a quick glance at TJ.

He looked fresh and handsome as ever.

"You were," she told Eli. "We were worried about you."

"It was weird," he said.

TJ eased out of the way, and Sage sat down on the edge of Eli's bed.

"What was weird?" she asked.

The nurse quietly left the room.

"I remember seeing spotted elephants. And then there

was a pond, but it was chocolate pudding, with marshmallows, and the marshmallows turned into plump little chicks. It wasn't like a dream. It was different."

"That is weird," Sage agreed, knowing it had to have been the fever. She couldn't help putting her hand against his forehead. It was blessedly cool.

"Does this thing have games?" Eli ran his finger across the tablet screen.

"I think you just ordered tomato juice," TJ said.

"Oops," Eli said.

TJ took the tablet. "There's a cancel button."

"Will they let me watch TV?" Eli asked, nodding to the big screen attached to the wall.

"After breakfast," Sage said.

After the words were out, she wondered why she felt like she had to restrict his television time. Who cared if he watched something while he ate breakfast?

"Do they have a sports channel?" Eli asked.

"I bet they do," TJ answered. "Your mom probably wouldn't mind if we found you a game."

"I feel like I should tell you not to overdo it," Sage said. "If you're feeling tired, I want you to nap, okay?"

"I've been napping for weeks," Eli said.

"I know. I'm so glad you're feeling better." She leaned in to kiss the top of his head.

"Do you mind if I take your mom out for breakfast?" TJ asked Eli. "I don't think we can get room service like you do."

"Do you have to go to work?" Eli asked her. "What day is this? Am I missing school?"

She wasn't sure how to begin to answer. "Did TJ tell you we left Seattle?"

Eli looked to TJ with what appeared to be amazement.

"On the helicopter," TJ said. "We're near a town called Whiskey Bay. It's south of Seattle, on the coast."

"We're at the beach?"

"Pretty close to it."

Eli looked at Sage, his brows furrowing together.

"Your teacher says you can catch up," she told him brightly. "And, no, I won't be going to work today. It's too far away."

"Are you going to stay here?" He looked worried.

"I'm staying here just as long as you are."

He seemed to relax at that, and protective instincts welled up inside her. He was still so young.

A different nurse came into the room. She was carrying a tray of milk, orange juice and red Jell-O.

"You must be Eli," she said. "I hear you're feeling hungry."

As he looked at the tray, his enthusiasm seemed to fade. "They didn't bring the ice cream."

"Don't worry," she said. "The ice cream is coming." She set the tray down on the rolling table beside the bed. "Did you see that the menu is in red, yellow and green sections?" She put her hand out, and TJ gave her the tablet.

She touched the screen and put it in front of Eli. "You have to order at least two things from the green section, one thing from the yellow section, and then you can order one thing from the red section."

"Let me guess," Eli said. "I have to eat the green and yellow stuff first?"

"That's a good guess," she said. "That's exactly how it works."

"Okay." Eli drew out the word in exaggerated resignation.

TJ took the remote control from its holder. "We were hoping for a baseball game."

"Sports stations start at three hundred," the nurse said.

He turned on the TV and browsed while Sage watched Eli eat. Three bites into the Jell-O, and he showed no signs of slowing down. She allowed herself a wave of cautious relief. His immune system was still weak, but they'd made it through the immediate danger.

A baseball game playing, TJ spoke to her in an undertone. "You need breakfast too."

She was ready to agree. She also needed a shower and some fresh clothes, which presented a problem. Everything she owned was back in Seattle, and she didn't dare put anything more on her credit card.

"I need to get back to Seattle," she said to TJ. Then she quickly turned to reassure Eli. "I just need to get a few clothes and explain to the people at work. But I'll be back."

"You don't need to leave right away," TJ said with a frown.

She wasn't about to have a debate in front of her son. "You'll be okay for now?" she asked Eli. "Don't wear yourself out. Take a nap after breakfast."

"I'm not a little kid."

"You're not. That's true." She squeezed his hand goodbye, thinking he looked both grown up and so very young at the same time.

Out in the hallway, TJ repeated, "You don't need anything from home right away."

"I need clothes." She hoped he'd be willing to provide transportation. In a pinch, she'd buy a bus ticket. Hopefully, they weren't too expensive.

"You can buy clothes in Whiskey Bay. We do have stores here."

They stepped onto the elevator.

She was embarrassed, annoyed at him for cornering her, and her retort came out more flippant than she'd intended. "I'm afraid I left my platinum card at home."

He looked confused for a moment. Then he shook his head. "Okay, we've got to get this worked out." He took his wallet from his back pocket and flipped it open to extract a credit card. "Take this for now."

She held up her palms and stepped backward. "Oh, no, no, no."

The elevator door opened to a group of four waiting in the lobby.

Even more embarrassed, she slipped out and started for the exit.

TJ quickly caught up. "Take the card, Sage."

"I'm not taking your credit card."

"I owe you nine years of child support back payments. I don't know what kind of a shopping spree you're planning, but I'm betting you can't run through it all in one day."

"You don't owe me anything."

They came to the front door, and he quickly reached to open it for her. "I owe you everything."

As she stepped onto the front sidewalk, she realized she had no idea where she was going. She stopped.

Reality came crashing down. She had no car. She had no money. She had to quit her job. And no matter how hard she'd tried to make the best of it, she didn't want to raise Eli in a basement suite in an area that was heading downhill. He'd be a teenager soon, and the neighborhood influences would get even stronger.

TJ was the answer to all of that. He could solve everything. All she had to give up was her pride.

That was all—such a little thing. She steadied herself. She steeled herself.

For Eli, she'd do it.

"I'll do it," she said out loud.

"You'll take my credit card?"

"I'll do it all." She looked up at him as she took the plunge. "I'll move to Whiskey Bay. I'll live in your house. But I *am* paying rent. I'll get a job of some kind."

He didn't look as happy as she'd expected. In fact, he frowned.

"I've changed my mind," he said.

\* \* \*

Sage's dejected expression told TJ he was botching things all over again.

"I mean," he corrected himself, glancing around for a quiet spot, "we need to talk about our plans."

She opened her mouth.

"Please don't say anything." He gestured to a brick pathway across the drive that he knew led to a garden. "Let's walk instead."

"I don't want to walk," she said, a wobble in her voice. "I don't want to talk. You've changed your mind, and that's fine."

"Please?" he asked.

She hesitated. But then she squared her shoulders, pursed her lips and started for the path.

He gave a silent thank-you as he followed.

"Thing is," he said, formulating his words as they made their way past a carpet of tulips and daffodils, "I'm thinking about what's in Eli's best interest."

Her tone was flat. "Is this your way of telling me you're taking me to court?"

"No. I'm not taking you to court. I mean, I hope we're not going to court." He struggled to get it right. "I have no desire to get lawyers involved."

"I don't have a lawyer."

"I have four." He stopped himself. "I'm sorry. That was supposed to be funny."

He knew he had to get on with it. He was making things worse by the second.

They'd come to a white gazebo overlooking the ocean.

"Can we sit?" he asked, gesturing to the benches inside the octagonal shelter.

She seemed resigned as she took the three stairs up. She perched on the edge of the bench.

"I'm going to start over," he said, sitting next to her, angling himself so he could see her expression. "If you could hear me out, it would be really great."

She stayed silent, giving him hope.

"I want what's best for Eli. I know you do too."

She seemed to struggle to stay silent at that.

"I think Whiskey Bay is best for Eli. I know you can't see the problems with your basement suite. And maybe it's a better neighborhood than I'm giving it credit for. And while it's true I could move to Seattle, I don't want to move. My home is here. Lauren and I designed and built that house, and I'm not ready to give it up. My best friends Caleb and Matt live on either side. I'm not trying to make it a contest. And I really don't want to sound like I'm bragging. I'm not." He took a breath, but she didn't interrupt him.

"I want Eli with me. And I know you want him with you. But I don't want you to be a boarder in my house. I don't want you to feel like a guest. I don't want you to *be* a guest. I want Eli to have a family."

Confusion grew on her face.

"You said there was no one in your life." He swallowed his emotion. "Well, I've already lost the love of my life. I've spent the past year trying, and I know I'm never going to meet anyone who'll hold a candle to Lauren. But I want Eli to have a family. I want him to have his mother and his father both and with him every day, not separate, not shuttling back and forth between us. Maybe one day he feels like tossing a ball around. Maybe he needs some manly advice. Maybe he needs a hug from his mom, a little softness in his world, the security of knowing you're right there, that the person who nurtured him since he was born is right there. Whatever it is he needs, I want him to have it."

The color had gone out of her cheeks. "TJ, we can't—"

"That's the thing. We can. We can try. If it all fell apart, if you met somebody in the future, well, if you had to leave me someday, we'd cross that bridge. But in the meantime, I want to go all in, a ring, a ceremony, a joint checking account." He took her hands in his. "I can't ask you to give up your current life without offering you a new one."

She opened her mouth. Then she closed it again.

He forced himself to wait. He'd said enough.

The seconds dragged before she spoke. "A marriage of convenience."

"Yes."

"A very radical solution to a very ordinary problem."

"There's nothing ordinary about it. And even if there is, it's unique to us. Our circumstances are unique. Why shouldn't our solution be unique?"

She seemed to be searching for counterarguments. "What would we tell people?"

"The truth. We knew each other in high school. We have a son. And we reunited and got married. That's all they need to know."

"Live a lie."

"No. I wouldn't ask you to do that. You can give the details to whoever you want. There are a few people I'd tell. But only a few."

"I can't believe we're having a serious discussion about this."

He slipped his hands from hers and leaned back against the bench. "There are a whole lot of things about the past few weeks that I can't believe."

She leaned back beside him, and they both stayed silent. The breeze rustled the trees, while the waves below splashed against the rocks.

"Before this," she finally said, "before they found you, when I got the bad news, I swore I would do anything, give anything, *endure* anything, if only Eli would get better."

TJ liked where she was going, even if he wasn't crazy about the word *endure*.

"I suppose it wouldn't be the worst thing in the world," she said.

He couldn't help but smile. "That's what a man wants to hear."

To his surprise, she smiled back. She even gave a quick laugh. "I'm not going to start sugarcoating it."

He took her hand in his, raising them both. "Is that a yes? Are we in this together?"

"Raising Eli? Getting him well?"

"Both of those things."

"You are his father."

"I am."

"Yes," she said with a nod. "We're in this together."

# Six

Sage could barely repeat her vows. She swallowed again, but it didn't help. Her voice was paper-dry. She doubted the justice of the peace could even hear her.

They were in a hushed room at the Whiskey Bay courthouse surrounded by mosaic tiles and polished wood. TJ's friends Matt and Tasha had come along as witnesses. The diamond ring felt heavy on Sage's finger. She'd told TJ that an engagement ring was silly, but he'd insisted.

Matt and Tasha knew it was a marriage of convenience, and TJ was open to telling anyone else Sage wanted to tell. But for the public at large, they'd agreed it was best for Eli if their family looked as normal as possible.

She knew it was the right decision. Still, she felt like a fraud wearing a two-carat diamond.

She couldn't help but glance down at it now. The round solitaire gleamed against the gold band. It was as conventional as you could get, for a marriage that was anything but conventional.

She made it through her vows and braved a look at TJ. He was somber, almost sad. But he gave her hands a reassuring squeeze and seemed to muster up a smile.

He had to be thinking about Lauren. Sage knew how much he missed her. She could only imagine their wedding had been worlds away from this simple ceremony.

The justice of the peace asked for the wedding rings, and Matt brought them forward. TJ slipped a ring on her finger. Then she slipped one on his. And it was done.

"You may kiss the bride."

TJ's smile firmed up a little, and he tilted his head, leaning forward. Sage tipped hers, waiting for his lips.

She could do this. She knew what to expect. It wasn't like it was their first kiss. And she'd relived that one a thousand times.

She braced herself for the pleasure she remembered. She was ready.

His lips touched hers, and a deluge of emotion washed through her.

She wasn't ready!

Time must have dulled her memory.

A starburst erupted in her brain. Her skin flushed to glowing. Her toes curled, and the sizzle of passion warmed the roots of her hair.

Her lips parted. The kiss deepened. She leaned into him, and before she could stop it, she'd plastered her body against his and wrapped her arms around his neck.

TJ's hands slid to her hips. He eased her back, breaking away.

She blinked herself back to reality, mortified.

"Congratulations." Tasha's rush of enthusiasm covered the moment and she gave Sage a hug.

Matt clapped TJ on the back and shook his hand. "Congratulations, TJ."

Sage fought to bring her racing pulse under control and to pretend she hadn't just made a colossal fool of herself.

"Caleb set up the private room at Neo," Matt said. "Nothing too much, just us, them and Noah and Melissa."

"The chef at Neo is amazing," Tasha said.

"Wait, what?" Sage looked to TJ.

"We're going to celebrate," Matt said.

"It'll be low-key," Tasha said.

Highly uncomfortable, Sage looked at Tasha. "You know... I mean, you guys know this isn't really..."

"We know this isn't a conventional marriage," Tasha said. "But that doesn't mean you're not part of the family.

I can't wait to meet your son." Concern came into her expression. "How's he doing?"

"Better," Sage said.

It had been more than a week now since they'd moved him to Highside Hospital. Eli was getting stronger by the day.

"He's getting impatient," she finished.

"I don't blame him," Tasha said. "Does he have any interest in mechanics? Boats or cars?"

"He's into baseball," TJ said. "He's a catcher."

"He's going to have to start slow," Sage felt compelled to warn.

The only person who seemed more impatient than Eli was TJ. The two had been bonding over sports. She knew it would be a surprise when they told Eli that TJ was his father. But she hoped it would be a happy one.

She was feeling optimistic on that front, but she didn't want to take anything for granted. They'd agreed to tell him as soon as he was released from the hospital.

"For now," Tasha said, "we're going to celebrate. This is a happy occasion." She gestured for Sage to leave the courtroom with her. "I'll drive."

"Absolutely you will," Matt said with a smile.

"He made the mistake of marrying me," Tasha called happily as they walked. "So now I own half his BMW."

"It's not so bad when she drives the boats," Matt grumbled from behind.

Tasha chuckled. "Have you met Jules?" she asked Sage.

"No. TJ's talked about Caleb and Jules. I know they have twin girls."

"Coming up on five months. They're adorable." Her hand went to her own stomach, touching the denim blue summer dress, and her face lit up with joy. "I'm four months pregnant."

"Congratulations to you," Sage said, happy for Tasha and Matt.

They started down the courthouse steps into the summer sunshine.

"Seeing Matt's reaction to the baby, his excitement," Tasha said, "well, I just want to say, I think you are—"

"A terrible person?" Sage finished, her fragile emotions careening toward a cliff.

She'd been bracing herself for the anger from TJ's friends. She hadn't expected it from Tasha just then. But she understood how they would feel.

"What? No. *No.* That's not what I meant at all." Tasha's hand touched Sage's shoulder. "I think it's great that you're giving TJ and Eli a chance to be together."

Sage's emotions settled partly. "I know it's the best thing for Eli."

Tasha pointed to a gunmetal-gray car halfway down the block. "It is. But you count too. Come with me. Matt can ride with TJ."

Sage glanced back to the two men several feet behind them. They seemed engrossed in conversation. She expected TJ would want the support of his close friends through this.

"I'm getting a lot out of this arrangement," Sage said. She couldn't help thinking about TJ's offer to furnish the upstairs to her liking.

"You mean the money?" Tasha asked. "Money doesn't matter."

"It matters a lot when you don't have it."

Tasha turned to call over her shoulder. "I'm taking Sage. We'll meet you there."

Sage fought the temptation to look back and see TJ's reaction. He wouldn't care. Why would he care? It wasn't like he was anxious to get some time alone with his new bride.

She almost laughed at the thought.

Tasha hit the fob to unlock the car doors, and they climbed in.

Sage straightened her skirt over her bare legs. She hadn't had a lot to choose from when it came to dresses, and it was hardly a formal wedding. TJ had tried to buy her one, but she'd refused.

She'd picked up some of her clothes from home, and she'd gone with the short aqua cocktail dress bought on sale three years ago for the company Christmas party. It had a swath of flat lace across the neckline and the capped sleeves. The waist was fitted, but the skirt was full to midthigh. It was a little loose, but it still looked fine.

"You need enough money for the basics," Tasha said as she started the engine. "But you get to diminishing returns pretty quickly. Matt's got plenty of money—most of it tied up in capital assets, of course—but he has to worry about it all the time. TJ has way too much money. He doesn't seem to know how to spend it, but he doesn't seem to know how to stop making it either."

"He's not going to get my sympathy."

Tasha laughed. "I hear you."

Traffic was light on the coast highway, and the BMW hugged the road as they zipped along above the speed limit. Tasha seemed completely comfortable and in control around the curves.

"TJ says you're a genius," Tasha said.

Sage didn't think getting straight As in high school qualified anyone for that title. "TJ doesn't know me very well."

"He says you skipped college to take care of Eli."

"I did. And I'm glad. And I wouldn't change it."

"I'm sorry." Tasha's voice went soft. "I didn't mean that to sound like a criticism."

Sage regretted her outburst. "Touchy subject. TJ has a strong opinion on it."

"Have you thought about going back?"

"Now I *know* you've been talking to TJ. Is this a setup?" Sage was only half joking.

"It's not a setup. I'm not the type to betray the sisterhood."

It was Sage's turn to apologize. "I'm sorry."

Tasha gave a careless shrug. "No need. You don't know me yet. But when you do get to know me, you'll learn that I'm a huge proponent of women undertaking any career path they want."

Sage knew that Tasha had gone against her wealthy Bostonian parents' wishes to become a marine mechanic.

"I don't know what your passion is, Sage. Maybe you don't know what it is either. But you should find it. Whatever it is, you should go after it. And don't let TJ or anyone else try to tell you what it is."

Sage was liking Tasha. And the woman had inspired her to start thinking.

Once they'd told Eli about TJ. Once she and her son were settled in Whiskey Bay. Once they got into some kind of a routine as a household. What would she do then?

"She seems pretty great," Caleb said to TJ.

They sat at one end of the rectangular table in the Neo seafood restaurant's private dining room. It was Caleb's seventeenth Neo location nationwide, and it had just opened two weeks ago.

TJ's gaze went to Sage, where Tasha was trying to tempt her with something from the dessert cart.

He'd kissed her.

He'd known he was going to kiss her. It was what a guy did at the end of a wedding ceremony. What he hadn't known was that he was going to *kiss* her—full-on, body-wide, every-emotion-and-hormone-engaged *kiss* her. His vision tunneled to her lips, and desire dug deep inside him.

He blinked himself back to reality. "She is great. I never said she wasn't great."

"But she's not Lauren."

"She's never going to be Lauren." As he said the words, TJ was overcome with guilt.

It felt like he'd betrayed Lauren by kissing Sage. Yet he'd somehow betrayed Sage by comparing her to Lauren.

He wasn't going to compare the two women. The situations were completely different.

"I'm still not sure you've thought this through," Caleb said.

"I've thought it completely through." Plus, it was done. TJ wished Caleb could be as supportive as Matt.

"Marriage is big. Marriage is huge."

TJ found his gaze drawn to Sage. He felt the rush of desire again, and he knew he had to find a way to shut it down. "It's not that kind of a marriage."

"There are no kinds."

"There are thousands of kinds. Some people marry for love. Some for money. And some for the sake of the kids."

"Usually that's when someone is pregnant, and—"

"Better late than never," TJ said. To distract himself, he picked up a clean butter knife and spun it in a circle on the white tablecloth. "I thought through the other options. I considered them all. But I want to be fair to Sage. She deserves security. Can you imagine living in someone else's house, at their whim, dependent on their good graces?"

"Are you saying you might kick her out? I don't believe that for a second."

"I'm saying she would have no way of knowing how I'd treat her. This way, the house is half hers. I couldn't kick her out if I wanted to." He kept his gaze firmly on the table. He wasn't going to look at her again and risk that emotional rabbit hole. "And I don't want to. And I never would. But now she'll never have to wonder."

"The house is one thing," Caleb said. "But the prenup better be ironclad beyond that."

TJ didn't answer. He spun the knife again.

Caleb levered forward in his chair. "You did not leave her a loophole."

"I thought you said she seemed great."

"Her seeming great and you being stupid are two totally different things."

"There's no loophole."

Caleb seemed mollified.

But TJ wasn't going to leave the misunderstanding just sitting out there on the table. "There's no prenup."

Caleb blinked. Then he blinked again.

TJ found the stare more unnerving than if Caleb had shouted.

Matt chose the moment to sit down with them. "What's going on?"

He looked from Caleb to TJ and back again, his eyes widening at their expressions.

"What?" he repeated.

Caleb spoke. "Someone drilled a hole in TJ's skull and extracted half of his brain."

"That was colorful," Matt said.

"She's the mother of my child," TJ said to Caleb.

"Who you hadn't seen for nine years. You don't know anything about her. This could be… This could be… It could be *anything*."

"You think it's a setup? You think making me a bone marrow donor could be part of some complex Machiavellian plot to steal my money?"

"Ahh," Matt said. "The prenup. I told you he'd react like this."

"It's not up to him to react like anything," TJ told Matt.

Caleb's voice rose. "How could you be so boneheadedly cavalier? Did you learn nothing from Matt's divorce?"

"How did I get thrown in the middle of this?" Matt asked.

"You're a cautionary tale," Caleb said flatly.

"Sage is not Diana," TJ said. Sage was absolutely nothing like Matt's materialistic ex-wife.

"How do you know that? You barely know her. A prenup is the absolute baseline—"

"Hey!" Jules shouted above them.

TJ suddenly realized how loud their voices had become. He looked up to see Sage and everyone else staring at them.

She was holding an untouched slice of cheesecake on a small china plate, and she looked mortified.

TJ came to his feet.

"Sage…" Caleb began, regret ringing in his tone.

"I'm…" She quickly set the cheesecake down on the table. "Thank you all so much. It's been a big day. And I'm tired." She whisked her small purse from where she'd hung it on the back of a chair. "I'll say good-night."

She started for the door, and TJ went after her.

From the corner of his eye, he saw Caleb get up as well. Then he saw Jules stop him.

TJ didn't call out Sage's name as she made her way through the public restaurant. He kept a distance between them as she went down the curved stairs. He waited until she had gone out through the double doors before stepping up to her side.

"Sage, I'm so sorry."

She shook her head as she walked, chin held high. "You didn't do anything."

"I know it was Caleb. But that was absolutely the wrong place for me to argue with him there, like that, at our wedding."

"I didn't expect drama," she said.

"Neither did I." TJ didn't know what he'd expected. He sure hadn't expected their kiss. "I'm parked under the light." He pointed to his car.

She stopped. There was a note of surprise in her voice. "I guess I'm going home with you."

"That was the plan."

"This seemed a lot easier in theory."

He didn't know how to respond. Did she regret marrying him? He couldn't help but wonder how she'd felt about their kiss. Did she remember their last kiss? Had she been reminded, like him, of why Eli had come into being?

She walked to his car.

They both climbed in and buckled up.

"He's not wrong, you know," she said.

"Who?"

"Caleb. It hadn't occurred to me. But you have all this money. You do need a prenup."

He looked sideways at her. Was that where her head was going? They'd kissed hard enough to rock the world, and she was focused on the prenup?

He jammed into first gear. "You think I want to protect myself against you?"

Abruptly releasing the clutch, he pulled out of the parking lot, heading for the short, steep road that led to his house on the cliffside above. He never imagined himself having this argument.

"It's only logical, TJ. We don't know where this is going, what might happen."

She was right about that. But he was crystal clear on the prenup.

"Eli's my son, Sage. You're his mother, and now you're my wife. You two are my family."

"Only in the most tangential way."

"No. In the most fundamental way possible. Whatever happens, whatever the future brings, whatever money I make or don't make, I do it on behalf of all of us. That's what it means." He pointed back and forth between them. "That's what this means. When I said we were in this together, that's exactly what I meant."

She'd turned sideways in her seat, and now she was gazing at him in silence.

He turned into the driveway and cut the engine before facing her, bracing himself for whatever she threw out on the table.

"I don't understand you," she said, surprising him with her mild tone. "I could take you for, what, half a gazillion dollars?"

"A gazillion's not a real number."

"And you're sitting there making jokes."

"Are you going to take me for half a gazillion dollars?" he asked, knowing the answer.

"I'd never do that."

"I know."

She shook her head, and she gave a crooked smile. She was so beautiful in the moonlight. From a purely objective point of view, she was one of the most uniquely beautiful women in the world. Her green eyes twinkled when she was happy. Her auburn hair shone in any kind of light. And the hint of freckles made what would have been a too classically beautiful face more relatable.

"You don't know," she said. She looked through the windshield at the house in front of them. "Neither of us knows what's going to happen next."

She was right about that.

She reached for the door handle. "This is going to be weird."

Weird was one way to put it. He caught the flash of her wedding band as she moved and felt an unexpected jolt of loyalty and dedication. Weird or not, he now had a family. And he had a new purpose.

Sage felt like a guest in TJ's house. No, more than that, she felt like she was living in the show home in a glossy magazine.

A housekeeper, Verena Hofstead, arrived every morning. She was perfectly friendly and perfectly professional. She dusted surfaces that had no dust and vacuumed carpets that nobody had walked on.

TJ had told Sage there was a cook available whenever they needed one. He ate out a lot and didn't usually make himself complex meals, so he didn't use the cook often. But he'd left the number for Sage just in case.

Sage couldn't imagine calling up a cook to toast her a bagel in the morning or bake her some chicken for dinner. It all seemed surreal.

TJ had given her the keys to the SUV and told her to go into Olympia and buy herself a car. He'd also told her to pick out furniture for the upstairs, suggesting she might want to turn one of the bedrooms into a sitting room. She was trying, but she couldn't wrap her head around so much high-priced shopping.

For now, she was wandering through the enormous kitchen, opening cupboards, trying to familiarize herself with where everything was kept. Verena was down the hall in a main-floor laundry. Sage tried to forget that someone else was washing her underwear.

There was a knock on the front door.

"Hello?" It was a woman's voice.

Sage closed a top cupboard containing rows of glasses.

"Hello?" she called back, cutting through the living room to the front foyer.

TJ left his doors unlocked during the day, and his neighbors seemed to have a habit of dropping by and walking in. It was a strange thing to get used to.

"It's Melissa."

"Oh, hi." Sage had met Jules's sister Melissa three days ago at the Neo dinner.

"Is this a bad time?" Melissa asked.

"It's fine."

Sage had visited Eli this morning, and she'd go back later in the day when TJ got home. For now, she was simply hanging around, trying to find a way to fit into her new life. The only alternative was shopping for the empty upstairs. And she couldn't bring herself to break the ice on that.

Melissa gazed around the high-ceilinged, brightly lit living room. "I love this place."

Sunshine streamed in from the wall of glass that opened onto the deck and overlooked the ocean. Thanks to Verena, the cherrywood furniture gleamed. The leather sofas and armchairs were comfortable and strategically placed.

There was a grouping near the glass wall, another clustered around the fireplace and an intimate setting of two recliners in an alcove.

"I feel like I'm living in a magazine," Sage said.

Melissa laughed. "I hear you. I grew up in a condo in Portland. It was nothing like this."

"Did you go through culture shock when you moved here?" Sage had seen Caleb and Jules's gorgeous home.

"Noah's rebuilt my grandfather's old house. It's nothing like this. You've seen Jules and Caleb's place, and Matt's is impressive too. But TJ wins the prize for grandeur and opulence."

"Lucky me." Sage wasn't feeling lucky. She was feeling disoriented. "Do you want to sit down? A soda or iced tea? Or, really, pretty much anything on the planet."

TJ had three refrigerators, and all were well stocked.

"Love to sit down. And anything to drink would be great."

Melissa chose a big leather armchair near the glass wall while Sage went to the butler's pantry on one side of the living room.

She chose a bottle of ginger ale and filled two glasses with ice from the dispenser. It was like living in a magic house. Everything was always at the ready.

Melissa took two wooden coasters from the holder and positioned them on the small table between the armchairs. When Sage sat, she had a panoramic view of the water. She could see the Crab Shack and Neo off to one side, and the towering cliffs that curved around the edge of the bay and gave the small cluster of houses their privacy.

"Have you heard about the Whiskey Bay Seaside Festival?"

Sage shook her head as she poured.

"We hold it every July in Lookout Park. There's music, food, a homemade boat race, costumes and a scavenger hunt for the kids, and a dance and fireworks to finish up."

"It sounds like fun."

"It is. I'm on the planning committee. So I'm here in an official capacity, for two reasons."

Sage waited.

"I'm looking for a donation, of course. TJ always donates. It's really just a matter of how much."

The question made Sage uncomfortable. Although TJ had given her access to a joint account, she didn't yet feel comfortable spending his money.

"I'd have to check with TJ on that."

"No problem. I'm going to leave this year's sponsorship information. Last year, he sponsored the main tent and the fireworks. But, more importantly, I wanted to invite you to join the planning committee."

Sage was surprised by the invitation.

"It's not too much work, I promise. And it's fun. And it would be a great way for you to meet some of the community members."

Sage appreciated Melissa's efforts to include her. But she couldn't help being nervous. "How would people react to me joining?"

"I expect they'll be happy for the help."

"I meant…" Sage felt like the new kid in school. "What are they all saying about me?"

"They're curious," Melissa admitted, her tone sounding genuinely sympathetic. She lifted her glass and took a sip. "The marriage happened fast, and everyone either knows or has guessed about Eli—since you and TJ knew each other in high school."

Sage couldn't help but worry about her son fitting into the new community. An illegitimate child was hardly a scandal these days, but he would be a curiosity.

"Mostly they're happy for TJ. Everyone in Whiskey Bay loved him and Lauren. They were fantastic contributors to the community and fun to be around."

Sage grew even more nervous. "It sounds like a hard act to follow."

She wondered how deep the stigma of hiding TJ's child from him would go. If TJ was such a beloved community member, people were likely to take his side, likely to look on Sage as the villain for depriving him of his son.

"Oh, no." Melissa looked contrite. "I didn't mean it like that. People are happy for TJ and they want to meet you and Eli. Nobody is aware…"

"That it's not a real marriage," Sage finished the sentence. She knew TJ had taken his close friends into his confidence.

"Nobody knows that it's anything other than a high school sweethearts' reunion. How you and TJ work things out in your family is nobody's business but yours."

"We weren't high school sweethearts."

"TJ told us what happened."

Sage was surprised by that. In fact, she wasn't quite sure she believed it. "What exactly did he say?"

"He admitted to Caleb and Matt that it was a prank."

Sage digested the information for a moment. "I'm surprised he did that."

"It was idiotic, and he felt terrible."

Sage felt an unexpected sense of relief that somebody else knew the truth. "It was hard to wrap my head around it, seeing the man he seems to have become and square that with the entitled jock who slept with a woman as a joke." Sage found herself ending the sentence on a bitter note.

Melissa's brow went up.

The silence stretched to uncomfortable.

"What?" Sage finally asked.

"Is that what you think happened?"

"That *is* what happened."

"Not exactly."

Sage's relief turned to annoyance. "I was there."

"But he was only supposed to kiss you. That was the extent of the prank, to dance with you and kiss you. He never planned…" Melissa paused. "According to Caleb, TJ never intended to sleep with you. And back then he never told anybody he did."

The bottom dropped out of Sage's stomach.

The entire premise of her last ten years shifted.

She struggled for words. "That's… How can it be?"

"Does he know you don't know?" Melissa asked.

Sage shook her head, then she shrugged, then she shook it again. "I don't know."

"You should make sure."

Sage knew Melissa was right. TJ was still in the wrong. He'd still done something terrible. But it wasn't anywhere near as terrible as she'd thought.

Melissa gave a final squeeze and let go of her hand. "Now, the Seaside Festival. Are you interested?"

Sage gave herself a little shake. "Yes. Sure. Thank you for thinking of me."

She was staying in Whiskey Bay. It was time to embrace that reality. She'd been inching toward forgiving TJ anyway, and this solidified it.

# Seven

Back from an evening visit with Eli at the hospital, TJ had convinced Sage to join him and have a glass of wine. He'd chosen a nice vintage from the cellar and was pulling the cork at the butler's counter in the corner of the living room.

She was pacing the room, restless as she often seemed.

He knew she wasn't feeling at home yet, and he wanted to do something to smooth the way. "Why don't you hire a decorator to take a look at the rooms upstairs?"

Maybe once she had her own space, she'd settle in.

"Why didn't you tell me?" she asked, pushing up the sleeves of her hunter-green cardigan sweater. She looked decidedly tense where she stood in the middle of the room.

"Tell you to hire a decorator?" He turned his attention to pouring two glasses of the richly colored Cabernet Sauvignon. "Okay, hire a decorator."

She didn't respond to his joke.

He looked back to see her frowning.

"Why didn't you tell me what happened that night?" she asked.

He lifted the glasses and moved, nodding toward the fireplace. Rain had started outside, and it would be a comfortable place to sit.

"What night?" His brain skimmed from Matt's wedding to the transplant to Eli's move to Highside Hospital.

"Prom," she said.

He stopped.

"The prank," she said.

A wave of disappointment swelled inside him. Their history was the very last thing he felt like revisiting tonight.

It had been a good day. Eli was getting better and better. And all day at his downtown office, TJ had found himself looking forward to coming home to Sage.

He started walking again, setting their glasses down on opposite sides of a small, round table between two armchairs. "You already knew about the prank."

He flipped the switch on the gas fireplace, bringing it to life.

"You know what I thought," she said.

He had a pretty good idea what she'd assumed, judging by their fight the next day.

"You let me keep thinking that," she said.

"You should sit down."

She didn't. "I'm not angry."

He didn't want to tower over her, so he sat anyway. "You sound angry."

"I'm baffled."

"It's ancient history."

"History that's followed us our entire lives. Were you supposed to sleep with me?"

He met her gaze. "No."

"Then what?"

"Meet you, dance with you, kiss you, get your number."

"And never call."

"And never call," he admitted.

"That's horrible."

He closed his eyes, swallowing his regret for the thousandth time. For him, it had been about Sage. But a dozen other girls were involved, even more when you counted the years before and the years after. He wished he'd been strong enough to speak out back then. He wished he'd given more thought to the impact their little game would have on the innocent victims.

"But not as horrible as I thought it was," Sage said, sounding more tired than angry.

He sat forward. "If I could go back…"

She moved closer. "I thought you sleeping with me was part of the prank, that you'd bragged about it to your friends. All these years, I thought the absolute worst of you."

"I tried to tell you. The next day, when I tracked you down."

"I wouldn't listen."

"And then I realized that explaining, excusing my actions, was more for me than it was for you. So I apologized and left it at that."

"And I hated you."

He reached for her left hand, touched the two rings. "You had every right to hate me."

"I might have chosen differently. If I'd known."

He wrapped her hand in his. "Now, this, *this* is why I kept quiet about it after meeting Eli. I don't want you to second-guess yourself. This is on me, Sage."

She shook her head. "I couldn't see past the anger."

He found himself drawing her closer. "You couldn't see past the selfish jerk I behaved like that night."

"I'm so sorry."

"No." He needed to be closer, so he drew her onto his knee. "It's not your fault. It's mine. I pretended it was yours because I felt so damn guilty."

She gazed into his eyes. "You stepped up. As soon as you knew, you stepped up."

She looked regretful and vulnerable. Protective instincts welled up inside him. He couldn't stop himself from touching her face, stroking her cheek, tracing his thumb along her jawline.

Her cheeks flushed and her lips parted. His body shifted to hug her, to draw her against his shoulder, to tell her it was all in the past and they were moving forward to the future. But somehow the motion turned into a kiss.

His lips brushed hers. Then they settled and parted, deepening the kiss as desire, passion and satisfaction flowed through him. His arm went around her waist, hugging her close.

An image of Lauren flashed in his mind, and guilt crashed down on him.

What was he doing?

He drew back, gaping at Sage in shock. "I shouldn't have let that happen."

She breathed deeply. Then she disentangled herself from his hold, rising from his lap.

He wanted to call her back, but he knew he didn't dare.

"We're both emotional," she said without looking at him.

She took the opposite chair and lifted her glass of wine, taking a drink.

He was definitely feeling emotional. Trouble was, he couldn't pinpoint the emotion. What on earth was he feeling?

"I don't need a decorator," she said, her tone growing crisper, more matter-of-fact. "I'll pick some things out. I'm going to Seattle tomorrow."

"You are?"

"I have some issues to clear up, some people to see."

He wanted to ask who and what, but it was her choice to tell him or not.

"And Melissa came by today." Sage kicked off her shoes and curled her feet beneath her on the armchair. It was the first thing she'd done that made her look at home. "She wants me to help with the Seaside Festival. She asked if you'd donate money."

TJ would have to thank Melissa for that. It was thoughtful of her to pull Sage into the community that way.

"Did you agree to help?" he asked, reaching for his wineglass.

"I did. Will you make a donation?"

"*We'll* make a donation."

Sage seemed to need a moment to wrap her head around that. "Can I tell Melissa how much?"

He shrugged. "Donate whatever you want."

Sage stilled. "I'm in no position to make that kind of a decision."

"Sure you are. It's your money too."

"No, it's not."

He set down his glass. "You're going to have to get used to it, Sage."

She didn't argue, but her expression was mulish.

"Tide Rush Investments has a budget for philanthropic donations. It's been mostly dormant for a while because… There are reasons that don't really matter. But it's there. I'll show you how to get into the accounting system. Take a look at what's happened in the past. Get Melissa to tell you what the festival needs. Pick an amount, and call Gerry Carter. He's the chief accountant. He'll process the check."

Sage was still silent, blinking at TJ.

"You'll get the hang of it. I promise. And that platinum card I gave you? Gerry pays that bill too. But you have to take it into a store and buy something before he can pay it. Maybe a bed or a sofa, or a bike for Eli."

"This is hard," she said in a hesitant voice.

"It'll get easier. Break the ice while you're in Seattle. Buy a car or something."

She cracked a smile at that. "Buy a car with your credit card?"

"First of all, it's *your* credit card. And yes, it works on cars too."

She shook her head in resignation. Then she took what seemed like a bracing drink of the wine. "You may regret this."

"I doubt that."

After all she'd been through, all that he'd put her through, there was nothing she could purchase he'd regret. If it made her happy, she deserved it.

After lunch in Seattle with her colleagues from the community center, Sage had stopped to see Dr. Stannis and give her an update on Eli. The doctor was delighted with the news. It seemed she'd been following his case, getting reports from Highside Hospital staff. But she said there was nothing like a firsthand account.

On the way out, Sage stopped at Eli's old room to see Heidi.

"Sage!" The little girl's face lit up as Sage entered the room.

Sage smiled widely in return. "You're looking so good, Heidi." She swiftly crossed the room to give her a gentle hug. "It's so nice to see you. How are you feeling?"

"I'm getting better," Heidi beamed. "It's not a real cast anymore, see?" She pointed to her leg that was encased in a brace.

"You'll be better in no time." Sage smoothed back Heidi's hair, happy to see the color in her face and the animation in her expression.

"I got to see my mom today," Heidi said.

"That's wonderful, honey." Sage assumed that meant Heidi's mother was out of ICU.

That was such a relief. Heidi was such a sweet little girl, and her mother was all she had for family.

"I gave her a picture. I drew it of a tree with apples and oranges and pineapples."

"All on one tree?" Sage asked and settled onto the edge of Heidi's bed.

"It's called artistic expression. I learned that from a book. Nurse Amy read it to me." A cloud came over Heidi's expression.

"What is it?" Sage asked.

"Nobody has time to finish *The Brave Swan*." Heidi named the last novel Sage had been reading to them.

Sage had forgotten all about the book. She felt terrible for leaving the girl hanging.

"Do you still have the book?"

Heidi pointed to the nightstand.

"Good," Sage said, moving to the bedside chair. "Let's read some more of it now."

She read until Heidi fell asleep. As she kissed her on the forehead, she vowed to come back as soon as possible.

It was late afternoon by the time she was on her way home. At the south end of the city, she drove past a car dealership. There were several in the block, their buildings big and bright, rows of shiny new cars parked in formation out front.

She knew she wasn't going to buy one. That would be beyond wild. But she was tempted to look around. She'd never even considered buying a new car before. What would it feel like to sit in the driver's seat of something that had never been used, learn about the features, decide what she liked?

She recognized a brand TJ had recommended and, in a moment of indulgence, she turned into the parking lot. She navigated her way to the showroom, finding several parking spots out front. She didn't even make it out of the SUV before a friendly, well-dressed man approached her.

"Good afternoon, ma'am." He extended his hand.

She shut the SUV door. "Hello."

"I'm Cody Pender. How are you doing today?"

"I'm good." She was a bit surprised at his overly solicitous manner.

Then she remembered she was driving TJ's vehicle. The man obviously thought she could afford a new car. Which, she supposed, she now could.

"Are you in the market for something new?"

"I'm just looking today."

"Just looking is fine. I'm happy to show you around," he said.

"I'd appreciate that. I'm Sage."

"Hello, Sage. Are you considering a trade?" He eyed up the one-year-old SUV that was the same brand as the dealership.

"No, not trading this one in."

"Were you thinking sedan, convertible, minivan, maybe a pickup?"

She smiled. "A car. Definitely not a truck. Beyond that, I really don't know."

"I like a customer with an open mind. It's more fun that way. Let's start with the showroom. That'll give you an idea of what suits you."

Cody led the way through a pair of glass double doors. The showroom was huge, with at least a dozen cars of various sizes and colors.

"Scan the room," he told her. "Don't overthink. What's the first one that catches your eye?"

She strolled down the center aisle, looking from one car to the next. She came to a midsize blue one that looked about right.

"That one?"

"The Medix Sedan. It's a very popular choice. Great for families, good fuel economy, but still with decent acceleration." He opened the driver's door. "Go ahead and hop in."

Sage's phone rang.

"Take your time." He took a few steps away to give her privacy.

The call was from TJ.

"Hi," she answered.

"Hi, back. Are you on your way home?"

She glanced guiltily around. "I'm, uh, still in Seattle."

"Oh." He sounded surprised.

"I stopped at the hospital to see Dr. Stannis, then Heidi. I ended up reading to her for a while."

"Are you still at the hospital?"

"No…" She realized it was silly to hide what she was doing. "I stopped at a car dealership."

"Good for you." He sounded ridiculously pleased.

"I'm just looking."

"Is someone helping you?"

"Yes, they are."

"Let me talk to them."

Her gaze slid to Cody. "Why? What are you going to do?"

"Ask a couple of questions. Or do you want to talk technical?"

"I'm just looking."

"Humor me."

"Fine." She gave an exaggerated sigh.

She caught Cody's eye, and he was quick to return to her side.

"My…" Wow. She'd never said the word before. She cleared her throat. "My husband wants to talk to you."

"Absolutely." Cody took the phone. "Hello? This is Cody Pender."

He listened. Then his brow rose. Then he looked at Sage.

"Absolutely, sir."

Sage got a nervous feeling.

"I would say the LX Two or the Cadmen. We also have the Heckle V series, which is top of the line. It has an excellent safety rating."

"I'm just looking," Sage whispered.

Cody smiled brightly at her.

Whatever TJ was saying seemed to be making Cody happy.

"Yes, sir," Cody repeated. "I can show her each of them." Then he handed the phone back to Sage.

"What did you say to him," she demanded.

"I simply apprised him of your needs."

"What does that mean?"

"That means he's going to show you some very nice automobiles. Have fun. Take some test drives."

"You're up to something."

"Yes." His tone was dry. "It's my secret plot to get you to buy a car. Wait. It's not so secret, since I've *told you all about it*."

"Are you annoyed?"

"No. I'm amused. And I'm serious. Go have fun. If you

like something, call Tasha. She'll ask all the technical questions. I'm texting you her number. Don't disappoint Cody. He seems really excited."

Despite herself, Sage smiled.

Three test drives later, she fell in love with a sleek sedan. It had butter-soft leather seats that hugged her body. It handled like a dream, had terrific pickup from a stop and was smooth and quiet inside. It felt compact to drive, but the back seat was roomy enough for Eli.

She parked it back at the dealership.

"You're grinning," Cody said.

"This is an awfully nice car."

"There's another in the showroom. It has a slightly different set of features." He opened his door. "Let's take a look."

Sage knew she shouldn't be enjoying this quite so much, but she followed him inside.

"This one is midnight metallic blue, one of the feature colors for the model year." Cody opened the driver's door.

She did like the color. It had a subtle sparkle under the lights, and the hue seemed to change as she moved.

"It has upgraded wheels and tires—they're slightly larger, which is good for highway driving—heated seats in the back as well as the front, a radio and communications system upgrade—you'll get superior sound from the speakers—and the feature I like best, the panorama sunroof, which is nice for back-seat passengers."

She couldn't help thinking about Eli. "I'm afraid to ask the price."

"I'm not permitted to tell you the price."

The answer baffled Sage.

"My instructions from your husband were to find you the perfect automobile, have you call someone named Tasha and finalize the details with her. He didn't want your decision to be colored by money."

Sage was speechless. How could she choose a car without comparing prices? Price was fundamental to understanding the value.

"Do you have Tasha's number?" Cody asked.

"Yes."

"You should call her."

Sage wanted to call TJ, but she suspected it wouldn't do her any good.

"I don't usually live like this," she told Cody as she retrieved her phone. "My life is normally, well, pretty normal."

Cody gave a wide grin. "Then you should enjoy this."

"It's not normal."

"It's quite normal. People buy cars all the time."

"Without asking the price?" She doubted that.

"I'll tell Tasha the price."

Sage pressed Tasha's number. "This feels silly."

"It feels romantic and generous to me. Your husband clearly wants you to have the perfect car."

Sage digested the answer, trying to decide how she felt about a romantic gesture from TJ. Then she laughed to herself at the word *gesture*. This was a whole lot more than a gesture.

"Hi, Sage." Tasha's voice was cheerful on the phone. "TJ told me you'd be calling. Did you find something?"

"I did," Sage admitted.

"Tell me about it."

Sage stepped back to look at the car. "It's a beautiful blue, totally smooth on the road. The engine has good pep. It's easy to handle. And the seats are unbelievably comfortable. The salesman, Cody, says the one I'm looking at has larger wheels and tires. It has a panoramic sunroof." She didn't know what else to add.

"It sounds perfect. Let me talk to Cody."

"This is strange," Sage said.

Tasha laughed. "For me, it's fun. And you're going to love the car."

"It's overkill." Sage experienced a moment of serious hesitation. "Maybe I should look at something used."

"That's not going to happen. Give the phone to Cody and stop worrying."

"Okay." Sage told herself to accept the inevitable. She handed the phone to Cody.

He greeted Tasha, then paused. "It's the Heckle V series sedan with the ultra-luxury package." He paused for another moment. "Yes, she does." Then he gave Sage a smile and a thumbs-up and turned to walk away, heading into a windowed office.

She shook her head in bemusement and turned her attention back to the car. It really was amazing. She reached in to touch the steering wheel, imagining herself and Eli touring along the coast highway, the sunroof open, Eli smiling and healthy.

Her eyes unexpectedly teared up. She swallowed and slipped into the driver's seat.

If anything, the seat was even more comfortable than the one in the test car she'd driven. She tipped her head back, seeing the lights suspended from the high ceiling above. The sunroof and windows had a subtle tint, which would be nice in the sun.

"Sage?" Cody interrupted her musings.

She quickly turned. "Hi. Sorry."

"Not at all. You should get used to the feel. Tasha wants to talk to you." He handed back Sage's phone.

"Hi, Tasha."

"You're all set," Tasha said. "I negotiated a great price. They'll put temporary insurance and registration on for you so you can drive it home. All you have to do is give him your credit card."

"What?" Sage was dumbfounded. They expected her to drive it away? "What about TJ's SUV? I can't just leave it here."

"We deliver, ma'am," Cody whispered.

"They'll deliver the SUV tomorrow," Tasha said. "You can't buy a new car and not drive it home."

"To Whiskey Bay?" Sage asked Cody. Surely they didn't realize how far away TJ lived.

"Complimentary delivery anywhere in the state," Cody said. "I'm going to get a technician, and we'll get your features set up." He tapped the top of the roof and walked away.

"Are you excited?" Tasha asked.

"I'm stunned. This isn't how buying a car works." The last time, it had taken her a month to find something decent in her price range.

"It's a great car. You made a good choice. The safety rating is super high, and it holds its resale value. TJ can't wait to see it."

"You talked to him again? Does he know which one I picked?"

"He doesn't care what you picked, Sage. You're the one who'll be driving it. He wants you to be happy."

"It's a difficult adjustment to make."

"I get it," Tasha said. "Don't forget I'm a marine mechanic. Nuts and bolts are my business. And I'm firmly grounded in the real world."

Sage remembered it had been only a few weeks since Tasha married Matt. "Thanks. That helps."

"Drive safely," Tasha said.

"I will." Sage would be excruciatingly careful with what she knew had to be an exorbitantly expensive car.

# Eight

TJ had agreed to give Eli minimal details while he was in the hospital. So, on the day he was finally released, a brilliantly sunny Saturday, the three of them drove to TJ's house, explaining on the way that Sage had been staying with TJ while Eli was in the hospital.

"This place is awesome," Eli said, skipping along the path that led to the front yard instead of going inside.

TJ followed.

"It's practically a ball diamond," Eli said, stopping at the corner of the house to gape at the lawn.

TJ realized how the yard could be a nine-year-old's dream. The basement was grade level on this side of the house, with a patio off the recreational room. In front of the patio and overlooking the ocean was a half-acre lawn rimmed by natural trees and flower gardens.

"We could definitely play catch out here," TJ said.

"Can you get down to the beach?"

"There's a path. It's pretty rocky on the shore, not really good for swimming. But there's a pool beside the patio. And there's an aquatic center about fifteen minutes up the highway. It has water slides."

"Sweet," Eli said, wandering out onto the lawn. He plopped down on the grass and ran his hands through it.

"That's a wonderful sight," Sage said, pausing beside TJ. "I can't believe he's finally home." She seemed to trip on the word *home*.

"We need to tell him the rest," TJ said. He was excited and anxious and impatient all at once.

"I know."

"Now?" TJ looked at her. He could see her hesitation.

"Now," she agreed. "Eli?" She walked forward.

"Have you ever seen such a big yard?" Eli asked her.

She sat down on the grass beside him, and TJ joined them.

"How many people live here?" Eli asked, gesturing to the house.

"Just us," TJ said. "Me and your mom right now, and you, of course."

Eli looked to be in awe. "You live here all by yourself?"

TJ wasn't sure how to answer.

Sage stepped in. She took Eli's hand. "There's something I need to tell you, honey."

Eli's expression turned guarded. "Is it bad? Am I sick again?"

"No. No, no, no." She squeezed his hand. "You are perfectly healthy. Everything is looking good on all the tests. This is about me. And about TJ."

Eli looked to TJ.

"We told you he was your bone marrow donor."

Eli waited.

"Well, the reason he was a match, such a good match, is he's also your father."

TJ held his breath while he waited for Eli's reaction.

It took Eli a minute to speak. "You mean, like, way back before I was born?"

"That's right. TJ is your biological father."

Eli eyed TJ with disdain, looking him up and down. "Where've you been?"

"He didn't know," Sage quickly put in.

"I didn't know," TJ said. "If I'd known, I would've been there for you, for both of you."

Eli set his jaw in a way that looked all too familiar to TJ. "How could you not know? Did you bother to find out?"

"I didn't," TJ admitted. "But I had absolutely no idea you existed."

"That was my fault," Sage said. "I should have told TJ. But I didn't trust him back then. I didn't think he'd be a good father. I honestly thought we'd be better off without him."

Eli's gaze went to the house. "Looks like he could have helped us out."

"That's true," TJ said.

"It's not fair to blame TJ," Sage said.

"It's okay to blame me," TJ said to Eli. "I'd blame me. I do blame me. But I'm so glad I found you. I'm so glad I know you now."

Eli's expression softened a bit. "I guess you did save my life."

"I'm here now for anything you need." TJ meant it with all his heart.

"There's something else," Sage said.

Eli looked at her.

"TJ and I talked about it. And, well, we both want to be close to you, as close to you as possible while you're growing up." She hesitated.

Eli subtly but distinctly angled his body toward his mother.

TJ quickly moved to finish the explanation. "After I found out, while you were recovering, well, we remembered how much we liked each other in high school. We thought it would be best, best for you, best for everyone, if we got married."

Eli blinked at that. He looked to his mom. "You're getting married?"

Sage looked to TJ, clearly uncertain.

"We got married," he said to Eli. He didn't want to leave anything out. "We want to be parents to you together."

Eli's brow furrowed. "Are you moving to Seattle?"

"We thought about that," Sage quickly put in. "But TJ has this amazing big house."

"Here?" Eli asked, glancing sharply around. "We live *here*?"

TJ couldn't tell if Eli was happy or upset.

He felt like he needed to make a sales pitch. "You can decorate your room, pick out your furniture. I've got a wide-screen TV in the basement for gaming."

"What about my friends? And I promised Heidi I'd come back and see her."

"We can go see Heidi," Sage said.

"You can bring your friends here," TJ said. "Or you can visit them in Seattle."

"I know it won't be exactly the same," Sage said. "But I just got a new car, and we can drive up there whenever you're ready."

"I'm ready now."

She smoothed his hair. "Maybe tomorrow."

"*Maybe* tomorrow like you'll tell me *no* tomorrow? Or *maybe* tomorrow like *for sure* tomorrow?"

"For sure tomorrow," TJ said. "As long as you're feeling well enough."

Eli looked skeptically at the house. "Are the games online?"

"Sixteen gigabytes of RAM and an insanity graphics card. I'm set up for four simultaneous players."

"Are you bribing my son?" Sage asked.

"Is it working?" TJ asked Eli.

"Sixteen gig?"

"I looked into going to thirty-two, but the value wasn't there. My buddy Matt's the geek. He tells me what to buy."

The eagerness had returned to Eli's expression. "Can we go inside?"

And just like that, TJ was Eli's father. His heart swelled and his grin went wide. "Yes, we can go inside."


"A nanny?" Sage couldn't believe she was hearing correctly.

Eli was asleep. He'd chosen an oceanside bedroom in the south corner of the upstairs, with a view of the yard out one way and the Whiskey Bay cliffs out the other. The room had a reading alcove with a bay window and its own small bathroom. He was thrilled and couldn't wait to pick out his own, new bed.

"She's not a nanny," TJ responded.

They were in the family room, having loaded the dishwasher after dinner. The views in the room were as spectacular as anywhere in the house, but the color scheme was low-key and earthy, and the furniture was super comfortable. It was becoming Sage's favorite room. She was sitting on the overstuffed corner sofa, while TJ had chosen a leather armchair.

"She's a second housekeeper," he said. "With three of us, the workload is going to increase. I can't ask Verena to do twice the work."

"I'll help. And I'll look after Eli and myself."

"You're going to want to be away sometimes."

Sage wanted to protest. She hadn't left Eli with babysitters in Seattle. Any errands she ran, she took him with her. And she hadn't had a social life. She didn't want to admit that to TJ, but it was the truth. Being a single mother on a budget didn't allow for socializing in the evenings.

"The Seaside Festival, for example," TJ continued. "Not all the meetings for that will be during the day. And I can't always be around in the evenings."

"I can work around Eli's schedule. I've been doing it for years."

"The point is you don't have to anymore. Freedom, Sage. Flexibility. If there's something important you want to do, you just go. And everybody's happy. Kristy starts tomorrow."

Sage didn't feel very happy. "Just like that?" She snapped her fingers for emphasis. "You found a new housekeeper in the blink of an eye?"

TJ looked puzzled. "I have a really good service."

This was too much. "I thought you said we were a partnership, that I had an equal say in decisions?"

"You do."

"But it isn't a partnership if you only consult me at your convenience. You don't get to pick and choose. Is that what you did with Lauren?" Her tone was tart. But as soon as the words were out of her mouth, she regretted them.

His eyes cooled, and his mouth turned into a frown.

"I'm sorry." She quickly backpedaled. "That was out of line. What I meant was…" She couldn't seem to put it into words.

"What you meant was would I behave differently in a real marriage."

She wanted to dispute the statement. But it was true.

He headed for the kitchen and she rose to follow. Opening the fridge, he extracted a beer. "Real or not, our marriage is our marriage, and I'm trying to make it work. You can have veto power over this, as you have with anything to do with Eli. But then I want the same thing. I want veto power over your decisions about our son too."

Sage didn't like the sound of that. It wasn't a very workable solution. They needed to collaborate, not reverse each other at every turn.

He twisted the cap off the bottle.

She hated to capitulate. But she knew it was the right thing to do. She hated it when the right thing was at odds with what she wanted.

"We can give it a try," she said, without a whole lot of enthusiasm.

He gave a short nod.

"This is going to take a while, for us to make this work," she said.

"I know it will." He slid the beer across the counter to her. "Thirsty?"

It wasn't her favorite, but she recognized a peace offering when she saw one.

She took it. "Thanks."

He got another one for himself. "What time are you leaving for Seattle?"

She took a sip. It was a light beer, and it actually tasted pretty good on a warm evening. "I was going to play it by ear. See how Eli was feeling in the morning."

TJ nodded and seemed to consider her answer. He gave his bottle a turn on the countertop. "Mind if I come along?"

She did. She wanted Eli to herself. She wanted things to feel normal again, if only for an afternoon. But they'd just agreed to be partners. And TJ obviously wanted to be with Eli as well. And she was going to have to get used to a new normal.

"Sure," she said.

"Thank you. I appreciate that."

He moved past her, back into the family room, where he flipped a switch on the outside wall. The fieldstone gas fireplace came to life outside.

He turned back to her. "Care to sit outside?"

She nodded. Outside was a good place to clear her head. It was peaceful with the stars, the breeze and the sound of the waves.

He pulled the glass doors all the way open, connecting the family room to the deck, turning it into one giant indoor-outdoor space.

As she followed him out, she realized she was coming to love the smell of the ocean. Maple leaves rattled gently around them, and the heat from the fire swirled out to caress her legs.

She went to the rail, leaning on it, taking in the panorama of the sky, the black water, the white foam of the waves flashing under the lights from the Crab Shack and Matt's marina. Caleb's Neo restaurant was brighter in the distance. It was still open, cars in the parking lot, low lights on the patio.

TJ came up beside her. "It's so good to see him out of the hospital."

Sage relaxed. "He seemed to settle in quickly."

"You were right," TJ said. "Waiting until after he got to know me, until after he was out of the hospital, until he was stronger, that was the right thing to do."

She didn't answer. She'd gone with her instincts, because they were all she had. She was grateful it had worked out.

"I was impatient," TJ continued. "I didn't want to waste a second."

She took in his profile and saw the sadness that still lingered there. She felt a renewed shot of guilt over having kept the secret all these years. "I can understand that."

"I'm trying to hold myself back, but I want to see him run and jump and play."

She took another sip of the beer, liking the taste better and better. "You will. He will. A month from now, you'll be racing to keep up with him."

"I'll like that." TJ turned, bracing his hip on the rail. "I was going to check out the local Little League."

She knew Eli would be anxious to play baseball again. "I don't know if he'll be strong enough this year."

"He can watch. He can meet the other kids."

"I suppose he can."

"So, you're okay with me looking into it?"

Sage realized how far they had to go in getting used to parenting together. "I'm completely okay. He's your son, and you should sign him up for baseball."

TJ grinned. Then he sobered. Then his eyes darkened as his gaze moved to her lips.

The wave of desire was becoming familiar. There was no denying her physical attraction to TJ. Just like there was no denying the danger of that attraction. They were barely comfortable around each other. Anything more than a friendship would severely complicate their situation.

"Sage." He said her name on a sigh.

She put her finger across his lips. "Don't."

He wrapped his own hand around hers, moving it from his lips as he eased forward. "You're an incredible woman."

Her chest went tight. She told herself to back away, but she felt desperate for his kiss.

"I'm incredibly ordinary," she whispered.

"Oh, no, you're not." With his free hand, he smoothed back her hair.

"This is complicated," she warned.

"I know."

He drew her into his arms, cradling her head against his shoulder. He felt so strong, so sure and confident. Years of anxiety she didn't even know she'd been fighting melted away. Eli had a father, and for the first time ever the two of them had security.

"We'll figure it out," TJ said.

She was glad he hadn't kissed her.

She was sad he hadn't kissed her.

Security was one thing, and it was vitally important to a mother. But Sage was also a woman, and TJ was a very, very sexy man.


TJ's house felt full of life. Walking in after a day at his office in Whiskey Bay, he could hear Eli chatting in the basement with a couple of other young boys. By the clacks and clatters, he guessed they were playing air hockey. Music came from upstairs, and he found himself following it.

"It's way too crowded," Sage was saying as he came to the top of the stairs. "I shouldn't have bought the second chair."

"They're so perfect as a set." It was Melissa's voice answering.

"Maybe if we put the sofa against the other wall," Sage said.

"Then you can't fit the coffee table."

TJ came to the open doorway to find the two women standing among a clutter of new furniture. "What's going on?"

"I measured," Sage said to him, her voice defensive.

"It's a tight squeeze," Melissa said.

He looked around, taking in the elements of the apparent chaos. "Please tell me you're not moving furniture yourselves."

"We're just trying something out," Sage said.

"The room's too small." He pointed out the obvious.

"The furniture's too big," she said.

"We can fix it," he said, walking inside to look at things from various angles.

"I don't want to take it all back," she moaned. "Do you know how long it took to pick this stuff out?"

"You should have let me hire a decorator." TJ reminded her of his offer, which still stood.

"I'm not ready to give up," Melissa said, giving an armchair a shove.

"Don't hurt yourself," TJ quickly told her. He could see moving it a few inches wasn't going to help the overall problem. "We should take down this wall."

Sage drew back in surprise, but Melissa smiled.

"And that one," he said, pointing to the wall that separated the bedroom from the hallway. "We can open up the two middle bedrooms and incorporate the hallway. That'll give plenty of room."

There was astonishment in Sage's voice. "Your solution is to *tear down a wall*?"

"I'll call Noah," Melissa said.

"Wait a minute." Sage held up her hand.

"What's the problem?" TJ could picture it already.

"It's a nearly new house."

"We'll still have plenty of rooms left up here. Eli's bedroom at one end, yours at the other, and the main bath and the extra bedroom on the street side."

"A sitting room in the middle will tie it together," Melissa said, putting her phone to her ear. "Noah's great at this."

"You can't just…" Sage's voice trailed off.

"Hey, honey," Melissa chirped into the phone. "Can you come by TJ's this afternoon? He's looking to renovate the second floor."

She paused for a moment.

Then she laughed. "Like you're ever really going to be finished at our house."

"Who's downstairs with Eli?" TJ asked Sage.

She looked puzzled. "You can't make a big decision this fast."

"Why not? I should have thought of it earlier. I want you to be comfortable up here, to have your own space. You want a kitchenette?"

"No, I don't want a kitchenette."

"Noah's coming over," Melissa said, enthusiasm clear in her tone. "He's working on our house today, but that's a perennial project. He can take some time to do this instead."

TJ was glad to hear it. There was nobody he'd rather hire as a carpenter than Noah. "Who are the kids downstairs?" he asked Sage again.

"They're from the Little League team. How is this happening?" She looked helplessly around the room.

Melissa gave her shoulders a squeeze. "This is going to be great."

TJ felt a tiny spurt of jealousy. He wished he was free to touch Sage. He could still remember last week, out on the deck, the incredible feel of her wrapped in his arms. It had been so long since he'd held a woman, so long since Lauren.

He was a healthy, normal man, and he missed lovemaking. But what he truly missed was making love to Lauren, and it wasn't fair to project those feelings onto Sage just because she was here, and just because she was so beautiful.

He gave his head a little shake to clear the wayward thoughts.

Sage's cell phone rang.

"We should really get a decorator," he said. "We'll need to paint and change the carpets and the light fixtures. This is a bigger job than we'd planned."

"No kidding," Sage said as she put the phone to her ear.

TJ couldn't help but grin at her mock indignation.

"Hello?" she said into the phone, pausing. "Yes, it is."

Her expression sobered, and her posture slumped. "Oh, no."

"Eli?" TJ quickly asked.

His son had been back for a checkup and blood tests two days ago.

Sage swiftly shook her head.

"Yes, of course," she said. "I'll be there as soon as I can. Poor thing."

Melissa put a gentle hand on Sage's arm. Once again, TJ was dying to do the same thing, to touch her, to comfort her over whatever she was hearing on the phone.

"Thank you," she said, a quaver in her voice.

"What is it?" he asked as she ended the call.

"It's Heidi. Her mom just died." Sage's tone was filled with disbelief. "They'd taken her out of ICU over a week ago. I thought she was getting better. They even let Heidi see her a couple of times."

"That's terrible," Melissa said. "Were you friends with her mom?"

"I never met her," Sage said. "Heidi was already in the hospital, her mom in ICU after a car accident, when Eli was diagnosed. She's the sweetest little girl. She's asking for me." Sage looked to TJ. "I have to go to Seattle."

"Yes," he said. "Of course. I'll get us a plane."

Sage looked like she was going to protest. But she didn't. She obviously wanted to get there as quickly as she could and recognized that a plane was the way to do that.

"I'll come with you," he said.

"You don't need to."

He kept his tone gentle. "Eli should see her too, and I'll make sure you get there quickly."

"Let him help you," Melissa said.

TJ appreciated Melissa's support.

"I'm sure Heidi would like to see Eli," Sage agreed.

"Coastal West Air Charter," came a pleasant woman's voice on the phone.

"Hi. This is TJ Bauer."

"Hello, Mr. Bauer."

"I need to get from Whiskey Bay to Seattle right away. There'll be three passengers."

"Yes, sir. We have a single-engine Cessna or a twin-engine King Air."

"We'll take the King Air." TJ knew it would be faster.

"What is your ETA to the airport?"

"Thirty minutes." He raised his brow to Sage to confirm. She gave him a nod.

"I'll get the other boys home for you," Melissa offered.

Arrangements made, TJ explained the situation to Eli and made sure he was ready for the trip.

Sage packed her son a sandwich and a drink for the flight. Despite the situation, TJ couldn't help but smile at her maternal instincts. Eli wouldn't realize it for years to come, but he had the most caring mother in the world.

The flight was smooth, and TJ had arranged for a car to pick them up in Seattle. In less than two hours, they were at Heidi's hospital room.

TJ hung back outside the door, letting Sage and Eli go in to comfort the little girl.

He could hear Heidi crying, and he watched Sage take the girl in her arms. Sage spoke to Heidi in soft tones. He couldn't hear the words. But he saw Eli take Heidi's hand and hold it. Eli smoothed her hair and spoke to her.

TJ's heart swelled with pride.

He crossed the hallway to sit down in a chair, content to wait and give the trio space.

"Mr. Bauer?" A nurse said his name.

TJ recognized her, and she was wearing a name tag. He came to his feet. "Hi, Claire. Please, call me TJ."

The nurse's gaze flicked to Heidi's room. "It was nice of Sage to come so quickly."

"I don't think anything would have stopped her. How's Heidi doing?"

"She's upset, of course. And she's frightened."

Sadly, that seemed par for the course.

"And physically?" he asked.

The question brought a small smile to Claire's face. "She's doing really well. She's ready to go home." Claire drew a breath. "We were just waiting for her mom to get stronger."

Sage appeared, and Claire turned her attention, giving Sage a quick hug. "How's Eli?"

"Amazing," Sage said.

"That's good. This is such a tragedy."

"Yes. It is."

"I have some patients," Claire said. "Can we talk later?"

"I'll be here for a while," Sage answered.

Then Claire headed silently down the hall.

Sage's gaze met TJ's, and she crossed the hall to him.

He so desperately wanted to pull her into his arms. He clenched his fists to fight the impulse.

"She's all alone," Sage said.

He nodded. "It's tragic."

"She needs help."

"Whatever she needs," TJ said. "Her medical bills, specialized care."

"Money can't fix this one." There was a shade of exasperation to Sage's tone.

He was puzzled. "Sage?"

Her hand went to her forehead. "Money's good. Money's great. And yes, paying her bills is a help."

"But…?"

Sage looked levelly into his eye. "She needs a family, TJ."

It took him a moment to get her meaning. Then it took him another moment to wrap his head around it. "You're saying…"

"She needs *me*. She's a little girl all alone in the world."

"Grandmother?" TJ asked. "Aunts, uncles?"

"There's nobody."

TJ looked past Sage to Heidi and Eli together on her bed. "You want her to stay with us?"

"I want to adopt her."

TJ had known that was what Sage meant. He looked back into her eyes, seeing compassion, sincerity and determination. "And you called me impulsive for tearing down a wall."

"I need to do this, TJ."

"No," he said, shaking his head. "*We* need to do this."

Her eyes widened, then went glassy with unshed tears. "Thank you."

She surged forward and wrapped her arms around him. "Thank you, TJ."

He hugged her close, telling himself to think about Heidi, to think about Eli, to think about Sage as a caring and capable mother. But that wasn't what he was thinking.

He was thinking about her naked, in his arms and in his bed. He told himself to let go. But his arms wouldn't cooperate. They tightened around her instead.

# Nine

At the kitchen table in Melissa and Noah's house, Sage smiled at a text message from the new housekeeper, Kristy.

"Both kids are asleep," she said to Melissa, Jules and Tasha.

"Wish I could say the same about the twins." Jules looked up from her own phone. "Caleb is sending up an SOS."

"Tell him to call Matt," Tasha said, her hand going to her rounded stomach. "Matt needs the practice."

Sage grinned and typed into her phone.

"How is Heidi settling in?" Melissa asked Sage.

"It'll take some time."

It had been a week since Heidi's mother had passed away. They'd held a small memorial service, where Heidi had clung to Sage. On the recommendation of the head nurse, and with the help of TJ's lawyers, a judge had granted Sage and TJ emergency custody of Heidi. The actual adoption was going to take several months.

For now, Heidi was reeling from the loss and still struggling to heal from her injuries.

"She seems like a strong little girl," Tasha offered.

"She smiled yesterday," Sage said. "She and Eli were painting on the wall, and Eli ended up with red paint on his nose. Heidi thought it was funny."

Sage's heart had warmed at the sight.

"That paint wall is inspired," Jules said.

"It was Lauren's brainchild," Sage said, feeling like she had to give the woman credit.

One entire wall of the big recreation room in TJ's basement was designated as an art area. Once it was covered, the plan was to photograph the artwork, then paint over everything in white and start over. It was a simple concept, but the kids seemed to love it.

"I hear she had a big hand in the festival," Jules said, gazing at the large map of Lookout Park spread out in front of them. "The special lunch made with foods all harvested within a hundred miles and the local art booths were both her ideas."

Sage fought the reflexive feeling of inadequacy she seemed to experience whenever people talked about Lauren. The woman had been beloved by more than just TJ.

"Creativity is not my forte," Sage said.

"What is your forte?" Jules asked.

"She's a fantastic mom, obviously," Melissa said.

"She was a genius in high school," Tasha said.

"That's a huge exaggeration," Sage felt compelled to tell them.

"What subjects did you like?" Jules asked.

Sage thought about it. "Math, I suppose. I did well in physics. I really liked the concrete subjects. You learn the answer, and you've got the marks. The creative subjects frustrated me. How do you get one hundred percent on an essay?"

"I never got a hundred percent on anything," Melissa said.

"That just makes you human," Tasha said.

They all laughed.

"Still, math," Jules said. "I'm not exactly sure how that translates to the festival."

"I can write checks," Sage said.

"That's huge," Melissa said. "Looking at the budget, I'd say that was the best talent of all."

"The budget," Sage said, inspired. "Can I help with the budget?"

"You mean beyond your very generous contribution, actually manage the budget?"

"I'm good with spreadsheets."

"Sold," Tasha quickly said.

Jules's phone chimed and she checked the message. "Apparently, Matt's not going to cut it." She rose to her feet. "I better take off."

"I'll go with you," Tasha said. "Sage, the budget is coming your way first thing tomorrow."

"Thanks," Sage said.

Melissa laughed. "No, thank *you*. It's the least popular job for the whole festival."

"Way to talk her out of it," Tasha said.

"I'm still in," Sage said, feeling happy to be useful.

While Jules and Tasha left, Melissa rolled up the map of the park.

"Glass of wine?" Melissa asked Jules. "I didn't want to offer while Tasha was here, since she can't drink."

"I'd love one." Sage enjoyed Melissa's company.

Eli and Heidi were well looked after, and TJ had said he'd be staying late to teleconference with someone in Australia.

"Noah will be bringing you guys the upstairs plans tomorrow," Melissa said as she opened a cupboard filled with glasses.

Sage followed her into the big, bright, brand-new kitchen. She loved the hunter-green countertops, the sunshine lighting and all the wood accents. There were long banks of cupboards and what seemed like miles of usable countertops.

"I'm sure I'll like it." From what she'd seen of Melissa and Noah's partially renovated house, she very much trusted Noah's tastes.

"It's an amazing thing you're doing," Melissa said as she poured.

"I'm not doing anything. It was TJ's idea, and Noah is the one executing it."

"I meant with Heidi."

Sage mentally switched gears. "It's not altruistic. She's a wonderful little girl."

"Still, TJ said to Noah that you didn't hesitate for a second."

"Neither did he." Sage was still grateful for TJ's quick acceptance of Heidi, and of Eli too, she realized.

He could have made things difficult for her, but he'd come up with a very creative solution. Few men would have opened up their lives that way TJ had done, even for their own son, and certainly not for the woman who'd kept a secret from him all these years.

"What?" Melissa prompted, holding out a glass of white wine.

"Nothing."

"You've got an expression on your face." She gazed closely at Sage. "Are you thinking about TJ?"

"Eli and Heidi."

"You're thinking about a man."

Sage gave a nervous laugh. "Are you a mind reader?"

"I'm an expression reader. But I won't press." Melissa led the way back to the table and set the chilled bottle of wine between them while they sat.

"But I am curious," Melissa said. "Are things going okay with the two of you? There have been some huge changes in both of your lives."

"They're going fine," Sage said. "They're going good." She tried to stop a smile, but it came anyway.

"Okay, now I have to ask," Melissa said, arching forward. "Don't answer if you don't want to, but is there something romantic going on in your marriage?"

"No," Sage quickly answered. She took a bracing sip of the wine.

"Okay." Melissa sat back.

"I've kissed him," Sage admitted.

She wanted to be friends with Melissa, and being completely guarded about her personal life didn't seem like a good way to start a friendship. And they were only kisses.

One of them had been at their wedding. They didn't mean a thing. Well, they didn't mean much.

"Was it a kiss or a *kiss*?" Melissa asked.

"It was a kiss," Sage said. "Okay, it was a good kiss." She slipped her fingers along the stem of the glass. "Some might call it a great kiss."

Melissa raised her glass in a mock toast.

"Am I being stupid? This isn't a romance, far from it," Sage said. "But he's a really hot guy."

"He is handsome," Melissa said. "And he's athletic and intelligent. And he's the father of your child. And you're living with him. I'd say there was something wrong with you if you weren't attracted to him."

"Well, then, there's absolutely nothing wrong with me."

Melissa chuckled. "Would it be so bad? If something were to happen between you two?"

"I don't know," Sage answered honestly. "We went into this with our eyes wide-open. It was for Eli. Neither of us was looking for a relationship, especially not TJ." Her voice went lower. "Especially not TJ."

"Lauren's gone," Melissa said softly.

"But not forgotten."

"You're two healthy adults."

"That doesn't mean we should…" Sage stopped herself, realizing where her mind was going, where it had been going a lot lately.

"It doesn't mean you shouldn't," Melissa countered.

"I'm not going to sleep with—"

"Your husband?"

"He's not…at least not in the conventional sense."

Melissa topped up their glasses. "I'm not saying you should sleep with him. Of *course* I'm not saying you should sleep with him. I'm just saying don't be too quick to write it off. If the idea comes up, I mean. Like I said, you're both healthy adults. And who else are you going to sleep with? I can't see you having an affair."

The words brought Sage up short. "I'm not going to cheat on TJ."

The idea was appalling.

Melissa's brows went up with an unspoken question. If Sage wasn't going to sleep with TJ, but she wasn't going to cheat on TJ, where did that leave her? Eli was nine years old. Heidi was only seven.

Years of celibacy stretched ominously in front of her.

The Seaside Festival was in full swing with hundreds of people, locals and tourists alike, out enjoying what had been a perfect late-August Sunday, with temperatures in the low eighties, breezes light and not a single cloud in the sky. TJ had been gratified to watch Eli participate in the kids' games this afternoon. He and the pitcher on a local Little League team won their age group's egg toss.

Heidi's leg was improving quickly, and her brace had been removed, but it would be a while before she'd be running. She'd loved the art events and spent nearly an hour wandering among the artisans' booths. TJ offered to buy her something, and she'd finally chosen a hand-painted ceramic bowl. It was brightly and cheerfully colored, and he took that as a good sign. She'd also visited the face-painting tent, coming away decorated as a black-and-white kitten. She looked adorable.

The sun had dropped behind the mountains, and the hamburger and hot dog barbecue was winding down. Both Eli and Heidi looked exhausted where they sat on a picnic table bench, Eli beside TJ and Heidi across the table beside Sage.

"I should take them home," Sage said, smoothing Heidi's braided hair and giving her a kiss on the top of the head.

"Kristy will take them." TJ pulled out his phone.

Kristy was enjoying the festival with some of her friends, but she was on call and ready to take the kids home.

"I don't want to bother her," Sage said, rising.

"We're paying to bother her," TJ said, sending the text. "And she likes the job."

Sage obviously decided she couldn't argue with that. Kristy was a college student, and she wanted to earn as much as possible over the summer. She'd made it clear that she liked her job, and she loved the kids. There was no reason in the world for Sage to miss the dance and the fireworks tonight.

"Kristy says we can see the fireworks from the balcony," Eli said.

The first fireworks show was at eight, with a bigger show at midnight to close off the dance.

"Baths first," Sage said.

"What about my kitty face?" Heidi asked.

"It's just for the day, sweetheart," Sage said.

Heidi's expression fell.

TJ's compassion kicked in.

"The paint will smear all over your pillow," Sage said.

"I'll sleep on my back. I won't move. I promise."

Kristy arrived and seemed to take in the scene.

"What's wrong, pumpkin?" she asked Heidi.

Heidi looked up at Kristy, tears forming in her eyes. "I want to be a kitty."

"She doesn't want to wash," TJ told Kristy.

Kristy immediately produced her phone. "I'll take a picture. We'll know what it looks like, and we can put it on again tomorrow."

Heidi's face brightened.

"Or if you want," Kristy said, "we'll paint something else tomorrow instead. That way you won't get bored."

"I want to be a kitty," Heidi said with determination.

"Kitty it is," Kristy said cheerfully. "You can be a gray kitty tomorrow, or an orange kitty."

"Orange," Heidi sang out.

"Nice save," TJ murmured to Kristy.

"Come on, kids." Kristy patted Eli's shoulder, then rounded the table to take Heidi's hand.

"We won't be too late," Sage told her.

"Take your time."

"Can I have watermelon bubbles in my bath?" Heidi asked as they walked away.

Across the table, Sage gave an audible sigh.

TJ turned his attention to her. "Everything okay?"

"Hmm?" She met his gaze.

"You sighed."

"She's talking about bubbles, watermelon bath bubbles. It's such a wonderfully ordinary thing."

"She's come a long way the past few weeks."

"Thank you," Sage said to him.

"You don't have to thank me. You need to stop thanking me. I don't even know what you're thanking me for."

Sage laughed at that, and the sound of it warmed him. "Everything. Nothing. I don't even know. I just know that Eli's getting better and Heidi's settling in."

"I'm as happy about that as you are."

"I know," she said.

The strains from the band came up on the gazebo. They'd installed a temporary wooden floor on the grass and strung hundreds of tiny white lights overhead. Couples were moving toward the dance floor.

TJ couldn't have imagined his life could ever feel this rich. The house was full of sounds and clutter. Sage was fitting in with the community. Eli was making friends on the baseball team. He'd even started doing a little practice with them. And Heidi was a delicate jewel. He couldn't help but imagine how much Lauren would have loved a little girl like Heidi.

But then he reminded himself that if Lauren was here, Heidi wouldn't be here. It would be him and Lauren and possibly Eli, but even Eli would be here only part-time, because TJ would share custody with Sage. His eyes focused on her profile.

He tried to picture himself with Lauren and Eli. But the image wouldn't come. For the first time, he wondered how Lauren would have felt about Eli. Would she have loved him the way TJ did? Could she have brought another woman's son fully into her heart?

Melissa and Noah approached the table.

"Highest attendance ever," Melissa said gleefully to Sage.

"Congratulations!" Sage returned.

"To you too."

Sage waved away the praise. "I didn't do much of anything."

"The drudge work." Melissa looked to TJ. "All that thankless, behind-the-scenes financial stuff, Sage knocked it out of the park. She negotiated prices and found savings. You have her to thank for the awesome sound system."

"It was better this year." TJ had noticed that.

"Clear as a bell," Noah said.

"And her work's not done yet," Melissa said. "The rest of us can stand down after tomorrow, but Sage will have invoices coming in for the next month."

"Not a problem," Sage came back easily. "I may not be good at much, but numbers I can do."

The words surprised TJ. How could Sage sell herself so short?

"Do you want to sit down?" Sage asked Melissa.

Melissa shook her head. "We're going to dance." Then she turned her attention to TJ. "Come on, TJ, get your wife up on the dance floor. She deserves to enjoy herself."

Sage didn't look his way.

They hadn't danced in a long time, and it had the potential to be awkward.

But he was willing to risk it. He wanted to dance with Sage.

He came to his feet and held out his hand. "Let's give it a try."

"That's the spirit," Melissa sang, wrapping her hand around Noah's arm and turning him toward the dance floor. "The night is young."

Sage grinned at Melissa's exuberance. Then she met TJ's eyes, and the grin faded.

He didn't let himself second-guess. He moved around the table to snag her hand, helping her to her feet.

Sage had never danced so much in her life. They laughed through fast songs, swayed through slow songs and stopped intermittently to have a drink and look at the stars. Jules and Caleb left early to get back to the twins, but Melissa and Noah stayed, and even Tasha—while telling them she was more easily tired in her pregnancy—made it through the last song.

There was nothing left but the fireworks, and the crowd made its way to the cliff overlooking the harbor. The fireworks were being set off at the far end of the public wharf.

"This way," TJ said to her, taking her hand again as they moved to the edge of the crowd and around a set of high boulders.

They came out at a small clearing with a sweeping view.

"This is perfect," Sage said.

The noise of the crowd had faded to a murmur, blocked by the wall of rocks.

The first starburst cracked the night, eliciting oohs and aahs. It burst white, then blue, then purple in the sky above.

"Wow," Sage said, watching the flashes and tracing lines.

"Have a seat," TJ offered, gesturing to a rock ledge.

"You knew about this place?" she asked, gratefully taking the load off her feet.

Her shoes weren't particularly fancy, but her feet had been busy all day.

"I've been here a few times before." He sat down beside her on the cool, smooth rock.

The next round of fireworks shot up, three circular

bursts, expanding with multicolors across the sky. Then shining streamers crisscrossed, white and purple.

They sat in silence while golden hues morphed into greens and blues.

She glanced at his profile, seeing the light reflected in his eyes. She could still feel his arms around her, the warmth of him, the strength of him. Out on the dance floor she'd been transported back ten years to another dance, another night in TJ's arms.

He seemed to sense her gaze and turned.

He smiled, and her heart expanded, tightening against the walls of her chest.

Then his smile faded. His eyes darkened, the reflection of the fireworks growing sharper, more distinct.

The bangs and pops grew muffled, the crowd's reaction fading.

TJ leaned toward her, gradually and in excruciating slow motion.

She held her breath. She closed her eyes. Her senses attuned to him.

Then his lips brushed hers and lights brighter than the fireworks flashed behind her eyes. She gasped, and his kiss deepened.

His hands drew her close. Then his arms went full around her, and he tipped his head, arching her backward with the strength of his kiss.

She hugged him tight, parting her lips, kissing him long and hard and deep. Gravity seemed to disappear, and she felt as if she was floating on the salt air, suspended in bliss.

His warm hand touched the small of her back, finding the strip of skin between her top and her slacks. She smoothed her hands up his chest, reveling in his sculpted muscles. She stroked over his shoulders, down to his bare arm, feathering her fingers beneath his T-shirt sleeve.

He broke the kiss, pulling back and staring, a look of astonishment in his eyes. She expected him to back off, but instead he reached for the hem of her top. He peeled it up slowly. She didn't stop him. She had no desire to stop him.

He took it off and dropped it to the side, then he stared for long moments at her purple lacy bra. She reached for his shirt and pulled it off, taking in the breadth of his tanned chest.

Then she stripped off her bra and fell back into his arms, pressing her breasts against him, remembering their long-ago lovemaking, inhaling his musky scent and bringing her lips back to his for another searing kiss.

He reached under her thighs, lifting her, placing her straddled across his lap, her slacks taut against her skin, his jeans rough through the thin fabric. His fingers tunneled into her hair, and his kisses deepened.

Then he cupped her breast. She gasped with the intensity of the sensation, reflexively arching against him. Her thighs tightened around him, and her fingers dug into his bare back.

*This* was what had happened. This was *why* it had happened.

The fireworks going off behind her had nothing on what was happening between them.

"TJ," she whispered. "Please."

He groaned in response.

She reached for the snap of his jeans, releasing it.

But he covered her hand with his, stopping her.

She drew back. What was wrong? What could possibly be wrong?

His eyes were pitch-black. His face was flushed. And his lips were dark red with passion.

"What?" she asked.

He cocked his head sideways to the crowd.

The fireworks banged full volume behind her, and she jumped at the sound. The crowd was behind the boulders, but they weren't very far away.

"Oh," she managed to say, grateful and disappointed at the same time.

"And I'm sorry," he said, handing her clothing back to her. "You didn't sign up for this."

She wasn't a bit sorry. "No, but I—"

"We need to keep it simple." He shifted from beneath her, then he pulled his shirt back on.

She felt suddenly exposed and dressed quickly.

He came to his feet. "We should go home."

She agreed. The fireworks were still continuing, but she really didn't feel like watching anymore.

As they walked, she wanted to ask what keeping it simple meant. From where she was standing, sleeping together would be the simplest thing in the world. They were married after all, and the chemistry between them was still explosive after all these years.

"TJ," she tried as they came to the car.

"Let's leave it," he said, unlocking the doors. "Recriminations aren't going to help anything."

Recriminations were the last thing on her mind. She was thinking about what Melissa had said.

"This isn't anybody's fault."

"It's my fault." He got into the driver's seat.

The drive home was short. All the way there, Sage tried to come up with the right words, the right phrasing, a way to bring up Melissa's idea.

They pulled up to the house, and he shut off the car.

She took the plunge. "We're married," she said, looking straight ahead.

She heard him turn toward her, but she couldn't bring herself to meet his eyes.

"We're both healthy adults. I don't want to have an affair. But I don't want to be celibate." She swallowed. "You were there. You felt it too. I think we should…"

He was dead still and dead quiet.

"I think we should sleep together," she finished in a rush.

The silence was deafening.

"What I mean is—"

"I know what you mean." His tone was flat.

She looked at him then.

It was there—the pain in his eyes, the set of his jaw, the white knuckles where his hands gripped the steering wheel. It was Lauren now, and it would always be Lauren. He might as well be shouting it from the rooftop.

Sage didn't know whether to be hurt or humiliated. But she wasn't sticking around to figure it out. She hopped from the car, went into the house and straight upstairs.

# Ten

When the front door had closed behind Sage last night, TJ sat still for a very long time, his feelings running rampant—a sexual relationship with Sage, sleeping with Sage, making love with Sage. He could picture it so clearly in his mind, and in that moment, he'd desperately wanted to say yes.

But that would have been unfair to both of them, to all of them. He knew he'd done the right thing last night, and he still knew that today.

He'd left early this morning, not even bothering with coffee. He headed straight to his office in the small downtown area of Whiskey Bay. Tide Rush Investments owned the building, but they used only the top two floors. The first floor housed retail space, a jewelry store, a clothing store with local designs and an art gallery. A law firm rented the second floor, while fifteen of TJ's investment managers and their staff took up the rest.

He had other branches, New York, London, Sydney and Singapore. And they were looking at Mumbai. Right now, scanning the proposal for that new branch, he thought what the heck? Why not expand yet again? It seemed there were endless opportunities all around the world. There were days when he wondered if he could stop the money train even if he tried.

Matt appeared at the door of his office, a cup of take-out coffee in each hand. "You're here early."

"I'm looking at Mumbai." TJ didn't feel like explaining his emotional state. Not that he was in an emotional state. He was just confused. No, not confused, disappointed.

He was disappointed that what he wanted wasn't the right thing to do.

Matt crossed the room, holding out one of the cups of coffee.

TJ gratefully accepted it. He'd come in so early that the coffee shop down the street hadn't even opened yet.

Matt sat down in one of two leather guest chairs in front of TJ's desk. It was a pretentious office. Comfortable, but designed to show high net worth investors that Tide Rush Investments was successful, a place where they could park their money with complete confidence.

"What's in Mumbai?" Matt asked.

"Nothing yet. Probably a branch office." TJ looked at the numbers one more time. "Yeah, a branch office." He stroked his signature across the bottom of the page.

"What was that?" Matt asked.

TJ looked up. "What do you mean?"

"How much money did you commit with that stroke of a pen?"

"Fifty million. That'll get things started."

Matt chuckled and shook his head. "I can't even wrap my head around amounts like that."

"Mostly they're just numbers on a page." TJ was feeling particularly disconnected today. "As long as they stay black, it's all good."

"And do they stay black?"

"They always stay black. I sometimes wonder why more people don't do this." TJ peeled the lid from the coffee cup. He hated drinking through those little slits.

"More people can't do this," Matt said. "You're a savant."

It was TJ's turn to laugh. "I wish it was harder, more complicated. Maybe then I'd feel better about earning so much."

"It is harder and more complicated. You just don't see it."

TJ leaned back in his chair and took a satisfying sip.

"I brought you a check," Matt said, dropping an envelope onto TJ's desk.

"I told you there was no rush." Tide Rush Investments had fronted the money for Matt's yacht purchases after a catastrophic fire at his marina.

"It's just the first installment."

"Thanks."

There was a silent pause.

"You have a good time last night?" Matt asked.

"Sure," TJ answered easily, focusing hard on the festival events and not what had happened in his driveway afterward. "You?"

"It was great. Tasha said it was the highest attendance ever."

"Good to hear. The kids had a great time."

Matt smiled. "Heidi is adorable."

TJ returned the smile. "She is that."

It was amazing how quickly he'd grown to love Heidi. Not to mention Eli. TJ's son was smart and reliable, energetic and growing stronger by the day. TJ's pride in him grew by leaps and bounds.

"Did a lot of dancing," Matt ventured.

TJ's radar went up. "Everyone did."

"Not everyone danced with Sage."

"Not everyone is married to Sage." As he said the words, TJ's mind moved involuntarily to her offer.

She was his wife. And she'd offered a physical relationship. And he'd turned her down. He *had* done the right thing, hadn't he?

"How's that going?" Matt asked. "The being married thing."

TJ stared at his friend. "Are you getting at something?"

"I'm curious. I know what you did. I get why you did it. And, honestly, I admire you for it. But I saw how you looked at her last night."

"I didn't look at her last night." As the words came out,

TJ realized how ridiculous he sounded. "You know what I mean."

"You did."

"We were dancing. So yes, I looked at her."

"You're attracted to her."

"You're out of line."

"I'm just saying…"

TJ came to his feet. "What are you just saying?"

Matt stood too. "I guess I'm saying give it a chance. I saw you smile last night. You looked happy, happier than I've seen you…since…"

"I'm not happy." TJ wasn't happy this particular moment.

Matt was suggesting TJ had moved on from Lauren. That was wrong. Sage might be an incredible woman, and Eli and Heidi might be great kids, and TJ was determined to do right by all three of them. But they weren't Lauren's replacement. TJ wasn't moving on to a fairy-tale ending without her. What kind of a man would do that?

Matt held up his hands in surrender. "Okay. But if you ever want to talk."

"There's nothing to talk about."

"Yeah, right." Matt's sarcastic edge obviously came from knowing TJ for years and years.

"She's sexy, okay?" TJ blurted out.

"No kidding."

TJ shot him a glare.

"From an objective point of view," Matt said. "Hey, I'm married. And Tasha's sexier than any woman in the world."

TJ disagreed with that. "She's…" He struggled to put his perception into words. "Her smile, and the way she moves. When she laughs, and you should see her playing with the kids."

A memory of a game of Frisbee came into his mind, Sage leaping in the air and sprinting across the grass, barefoot, laughing, her toned, tanned legs in the bright sunshine.

"It would be strange if you weren't attracted to her," Matt said.

"I can't do anything about it."

"I get that." Matt sat back down. "The two of you have an agreement."

They'd had an agreement. And it was a smart agreement, a marriage of convenience, each living their own lives, sharing responsibility for Eli while staying out of each other's way.

That was, until last night, until Sage tried to change the terms, until TJ realized how very badly he wanted to change the terms as well.

"TJ?" Matt prompted.

"What?"

"You zoned out."

"I'm… It's… Crap."

"What?"

TJ dropped into his chair. "She offered. Last night, she said we should have sex with each other."

Matt's eyes widened.

"And not just last night. It wasn't a heat of the moment kind of thing. She very reasonably and rationally made a case for us sleeping together on an ongoing basis."

Matt remained silent.

Now that TJ was rolling, he found he didn't want to stop. "She said we both needed a sex life. She said she didn't want to have an affair. You have to admire that. I admire that. But she said the only solution was for us to sleep together, with each other."

TJ closed and straightened the Mumbai agreement, tapping the edge sharply against the desk. "Like some kind of friends with benefits arrangement. But we're not friends with benefits. We're married to each other. And for Eli's sake, we have to stay together. If we let it get complicated, somebody's going to get hurt."

"You *turned her down*?" When Matt finally spoke, his tone was incredulous.

TJ didn't think it was an outrageous decision. He thought it was a prudent decision. It was a responsible decision. "What would you have done?"

"If my sexy, beautiful wife suggested we sleep together?"

"You know it's not that simple."

"Simple or not, I would never have insulted her by saying no."

TJ opened his mouth to counter the statement, but nothing came to his mind.

August moved along, and Sage began to think about the upcoming school year. Both Eli and Heidi were now healthy and happy. Heidi still had her sad moments, but the children were making friends and joining in on activities. Eli was playing baseball, while Heidi had decided to join a kids' art club. She loved painting, and the group spent a lot of time with their easels in the park painting landscapes.

While working on the seaside festival, Sage had grown curious about TJ's other charitable causes. He was a stalwart contributor to Highside Hospital, and she wondered if he might also consider supporting St. Bea's. Gerry Carter, the chief accountant, had given her access to part of Tide Rush Investment's accounting system, and she discovered TJ's contributions to philanthropic organizations had fallen off in recent years.

She also came across hundreds of requests that had been submitted through the company website and in letters. She'd sorted through them all, entering them into a spreadsheet that tracked organizations, dates, amounts and causes. Then she added who and what it would benefit, thinking that would be helpful information.

Now she heard the front door close, and she glanced guiltily at the time. It was nearly ten in the evening. TJ often worked late, and she tried to keep to the upstairs while he was at home. They were polite to each other, but their relationship had never really recovered from her suggestion that they sleep together.

It had been an impulsive thing to do, and she regretted it. But she knew she couldn't go any further with her philanthropic ideas without talking to him. She steeled herself and left the office, finding TJ in the kitchen.

He looked up from the refrigerator as she entered, his expression telling her he was surprised to see her.

"Hi, TJ." She moved closer, keeping the breakfast island between them.

"You're up," he said as he selected a soft drink.

"I was using the office computer." She held up a sheaf of papers as evidence.

"Thirsty?" He kept the fridge door open.

She shook her head. Then she thought better of her answer. She wanted this to be a friendly conversation. "Sure. Whatever you're having."

He filled two glasses with ice from the dispenser and split the soda between them.

"I've been looking at the philanthropic accounts," she told him.

A micro expression flicked across his face. If she had to guess, she'd say she'd annoyed him. But she was going to ignore it.

"You've received a lot of requests."

He set one of the glasses in front of her. "There are a lot of good causes."

She slid up onto a stool and put the papers on the island countertop. "I notice you've favored health and educational causes in the past."

"I suppose," he said.

"Other than Highside Hospital and Invo North College, you've mostly donated to national organizations."

His gaze flicked to the papers.

She took the opportunity to turn them to face him. "I've sorted and organized the requests."

He seemed surprised. He flipped over the first few pages. "This was a lot of work."

"There were hundreds of requests. I have some ideas, well, some recommendations on what you might want to consider supporting."

"We," he said. "What we might want to consider supporting."

She met his gaze, feeling a familiar shaft of attraction. It took her a minute to form the word. "We."

"Whatever you want," he said, setting down the report and heading for the family room.

She scrambled to follow. "I don't want to do it that way."

"I don't have time to help. There's a lot going on at the office."

"So I gathered," she said. Her tone came out as a rebuke.

He sat down on the sofa, setting the drink in front of him. "That's how I make my money."

"You don't seem very happy about it."

He glared at her for a moment.

She told herself not to be intimidated. She sat down next to him, this time putting the report on the coffee table. "I was thinking about keeping things local, or maybe statewide. There's a lot of good that can be done by focusing your contributions."

"Our contributions."

Sage sighed. "Whatever they are, they've dropped off in the past few years."

"Do whatever you want."

"I don't *want* to do whatever I want."

"Sage." Her name was a growl.

She looked at him. "What? *What?* I can't figure you out!" Her voice rose. "You don't want to sleep with me. Fine. I won't sleep with you."

The room went deadly silent.

They both breathed deeply.

He broke the silence. "You think I don't want to sleep with you?"

She didn't know how to answer that. She'd offered. He'd said no. Was there any other possible way to take that?

"I'm dying to sleep with you," he said.

She gave her head a little shake, certain she'd heard him wrong.

"You are beautiful," he said, his tone husky. His hand slowly rose, and his fingertips feathered her cheek. "You are so sexy and smart and funny."

"But…"

"I can't look at you without remembering what you offered, remembering my reaction, kicking myself for being such an idiot."

She could barely believe what she was hearing. "TJ?"

"You were right. You are right. That is… I mean… If you still feel…" His head dipped toward her, his lips grazing hers, gently at first and then with clear purpose.

Her surprise had her frozen. But then her body reacted with an avalanche of hormones. She all but fell into him, into his embrace, his name running over and over through her mind.

His forearm was firm on the small of her back, pressing her tighter against him. His spread fingers tunneled into her hair, anchoring her for a deep, passionate kiss.

She tipped her head, and her own arms wrapped around his neck. She could feel his heat, hear the hiss of his breath, smell the spice of his skin. And his kisses tasted like magic.

But she was hot and needy and restless. She reached between them and peeled off her top, revealing her white lacy bra.

He drew back, a look of awe in his expression. Then his tanned hand cupped her breast.

"Oh, Sage," he whispered.

She flipped the clasp of her bra, tossing it aside.

His gaze locked with hers, he threw off his jacket and unbuttoned his shirt.

She was past the point of no return. There was no going back. She stood and stripped off her jeans, dispensing with her panties.

A smile grew on his face. Then he sobered, shucking his own pants. Then naked, he took her back in his arms.

They were skin on skin. Their lips met and their legs entwined. Sage felt herself falling, falling into oblivion. Nothing existed but TJ.

She touched him everywhere, and he returned the favor, her face, her breasts, her thighs. His hands were deft and certain, and her body flushed and sensitized, growing dewy and heated in his wake.

She reveled in the feel of his muscles, his broad shoulders, bulging biceps, the flatness of his stomach, the strength of his thighs.

"Yes," he groaned in her ear. "That is so…"

His entire body tensed, and in a split second she was on her back, sinking into the soft cushions as his weight came down on top of her. She felt like liquid beneath him, and she parted her thighs, wrapping her legs around the heat of his body as they merged together.

As his pace increased, her arms wrapped tighter and tighter around him. Spasms of pleasure began in her toes, pulsating upward. He stroked harder, went deeper. She met him thrust for thrust, sensations intensifying.

He reached beneath her, changing their angle, and a sudden burst of sunshine lit up her brain. Her body catapulted, throbbing hard, contracting right down to her core.

"Yes! TJ, yes, yes."

"Sage," he groaned. "My beautiful, beautiful Sage."

The light in her brain subsided to a glow, first red, then purple, then calming to blue, where she bobbed and floated on joy.

"You were right," he whispered in her ear, his body a soothing weight on top of her. "You were so very right."


"Took you long enough." Matt joined TJ next to the barbecue on the patio in TJ's backyard.

"Long enough for what?"

A round of burgers and brats were sizzling on the grill. Eli and a few of his friends were climbing trees at the edge of the yard. And Sage was standing on the lawn in a white summer dress, chatting with Melissa and holding one of Caleb's twins in her arms.

TJ couldn't pull his gaze from her.

"Don't play dumb. You're staring like she's a bowl of triple caramel swirl."

"Better," TJ said without hesitation.

Matt grinned. "I knew you'd take my advice."

TJ watched Sage sway, gently patting the baby's back. "Right. Because I make all of my life decisions based on your advice."

"You should."

"It had nothing to do with you."

"I'm not saying I came up with the idea. I'm just saying I saw it first."

"Saw what first?" Caleb appeared behind them.

"That TJ was attracted to his wife."

"Who wouldn't be attracted to your wife?" Caleb asked.

Both TJ and Matt shot Caleb a look of incredulity.

"I mean mortal men," Caleb qualified. "I'm obviously not noticing."

"You better not be," TJ said, surprised by his visceral reaction.

After last night, he was feeling very protective of Sage. It was only natural, he told himself. It might not be a normal marriage, but it was a marriage. And now, well, now that they'd made love, he couldn't imagine her being with any other man. Not that he had a right to ask that of her. But she had said herself that she didn't want an affair.

Caleb clapped him on the back, nearly jolting the spatula out of TJ's hand. "Don't look so glum."

TJ suddenly remembered the burgers and quickly moved to flip them over. "I'm not glum."

Matt shot TJ a sly look.

"What was that?" Caleb asked, too quick not to pick up on it.

"Nothing," Matt said.

"That wasn't nothing."

TJ didn't want to play games with one of his closest friends. "My relationship with Sage has shifted."

Caleb looked worried. "What happened?"

"In a good way," TJ said.

Caleb's brow went up. "Seriously?"

"Seriously," Matt said. "And I did notice. And I did suggest it. Unlike you, who's been fixated on I don't know what for the past seven months."

"You try operating on sleep deprivation," Caleb said. "Wait. You're going to be doing precisely that come spring." His tone turned sarcastic. "You're gonna love it."

"I honestly can't wait," Matt said, sounding completely sincere.

Burgers rescued, TJ's attention went back to Sage. She looked so natural holding a baby. She must have looked exactly the same way holding Eli. TJ experienced an acute longing for all that he'd missed.

"I'm happy for you," Caleb said, pulling TJ back to the present.

TJ took in the expressions on both his friends' faces, and he realized where conjecture had taken them.

"It's not like that," he quickly put in, feeling a shot of guilt. "It's…different than that. We're in this thing. We're healthy adults. Neither of us wants to run around with anyone else."

"Does she know that's how it is?" Caleb asked with a frown.

"It was her idea," TJ said.

"You can't see danger signs?" Caleb asked.

"They have limited options," Matt said.

"You're in support of this?" Caleb asked Matt.

"Well, I'm not in support of any of the alternatives. Perpetual sexual frustration? Cheating? An open marriage? Can you imagine TJ standing by while Sage heads out on a date?"

"Stop!" TJ shouted. There was no way in the world Sage was going on a date.

"It may be a bit unorthodox," Matt said.

"It may be playing with fire." Caleb looked to TJ. "One of you is going to fall for the other."

"It won't be me," TJ said.

There wasn't any room in his heart. The knowledge made him sad. He realized he was sad for Sage. Because she sure deserved someone to fall head over heels for her.

"Then it's going to be her," Caleb said. "What are you going to do if she falls for you?"

"It was her idea," TJ repeated with determination.

He told himself she knew what she was proposing. She had to have known what she was proposing. As Matt pointed out, they didn't have a lot of alternatives.

TJ's gaze continued to rest on her holding the baby. He didn't want any of the alternatives. They'd made their choice, and right now he couldn't wait for everyone to leave tonight so they could be alone all over again.

# Eleven

There was a skip in Sage's step as she made her way across the campus of Invo North College. She replayed making love with TJ again over and over in her mind. He was amazing, and she was content to take things moment to moment.

For now, she was enrolling in college. She'd pored over the course listings, coming to the surprising conclusion that she wanted to major in data analytics. Math had always been her strong suit, and anytime her work had involved spreadsheets and data sets, she'd been fascinated with the power of the tools.

After crossing the gorgeous campus, up a wide walkway lined with maple trees, she climbed the stairs to the admissions building. Through the glass doors, it was bustling with activity, lineups and conversations, with signs and monitors providing direction.

She found the enrollment office on a building map and set off down a hallway. The office was large, bright and seemingly well ordered. She joined a lineup being served by at least a dozen officers behind a long counter. Although most of the people in the lineup looked to be in their late teens, she was happy to see a number of twenty and thirty-somethings as well. She hadn't been sure how she'd fit in with the student population.

The lineup moved smoothly, and soon she was standing in front of an older woman in a navy blazer, a pair of reading glasses perched on her nose.

"Do you have your signed eight-twenty-four form?" the woman asked.

Sage quickly flipped through the papers in her hand, finding the right form. "Yes." She handed it over.

The woman scanned the form, then typed something into her computer.

"Did you select your courses online?"

"I was wait-listed for a couple," Sage answered. "But I wasn't planning to take a full course load, so if I don't get into everything this semester, it's fine."

"Hmm." The woman looked worried.

"Is that a problem?" Sage had read through the website. Invo North Pacific definitely offered part-time programs.

"No." She smiled at Sage. "Can you wait just a moment? I'll be right back."

"Why—"

The woman was gone before Sage could finish her sentence. Feeling uneasy, she glanced both ways along the counter. Everyone else seemed productively engaged in the enrollment process. She hoped the length of time she'd been away from high school wasn't going to trip her up. She had checked the mature student box.

Another woman, this one younger, maybe in her forties, slimmer and very professionally groomed, arrived. "Mrs. Bauer?"

The name took Sage by surprise. "It's Costas. Sage Costas."

"I'm sorry. Ms. Costas. Of course. I'm Bernadette Thorburn, college president." She reached across the counter, offering Sage her hand.

Surprised again, Sage shook the woman's hand.

"Do you have a few minutes to talk?" Bernadette asked.

"I suppose." She looked to the admissions officer who was standing to one side. "Are we finished? Is there anything else you need?" Sage had been prepared with an original copy of her high school transcripts and her credit card.

"Bernadette will be able to help you," the officer said.

Sage suddenly understood what was going on. TJ was a

contributor to the college. They must feel his wife shouldn't need to stand in line.

"I'm fine enrolling this way," she hastily told them. She didn't want them to think she expected special privileges.

"There's another matter I'd like to discuss," Bernadette said. She was smiling, and her eyes were friendly. Whatever she wanted to discuss didn't look like it was going to be a problem. She pointed. "I can meet you at the end of the counter."

"Okay." Sage gathered up her paperwork.

She supposed whatever got the job done. Maybe they were going to let her into the wait-listed classes. That would be a bonus. Although she still wouldn't want to take all of them at once. The statistics class would be her first choice.

At the end of the counter, Bernadette held open a half door and showed Sage into an office overlooking the quad. The two sat down at a round table.

"Welcome to Invo North Pacific," Bernadette said.

"Thank you. I'm happy to be here. I'm looking forward to attending."

"I hope your son is doing well."

Sage wasn't sure how to react. "You know about Eli?"

"Whiskey Bay is a small community. The college draws from a much larger area, of course, from all across the country and internationally too. But we like to keep the local culture alive as much as we can. It provides a more unique experience for students. There's a lot to be said for the Pacific Northwest."

"I agree," Sage said. "I grew up in Seattle."

"And I understand you were valedictorian."

"That was almost a decade ago."

"And you've had life experience since."

Sage nodded.

"Community involvement and influence, and I heard you whipped the Seaside Festival into shape. Donations were up. Attendance was up. But expenses were down."

That characterization seemed blown out of proportion. "I didn't contribute much. Just logic and reason where it came to the budget, and I probably had more time than people have had in the past to pore over the books."

"Whatever it was, it worked. I have friends on the organizing committee, and they were impressed."

"Well, then, thank you." Sage wasn't sure what else she could or should say.

"I've been authorized to bring a proposal to you." Bernadette took a beat. "The board has advised me they'd like to nominate you as a trustee."

Sage struggled to understand the statement. "For the Seaside Festival?"

Did it even have a board? Trustees?

"A trustee for Invo North Pacific."

It took Sage a moment to find the words. "For *the college*? I'm not qualified to sit on a college board."

Bernadette gave a light laugh. "If I had a dollar for every time somebody told me that. No, let me rephrase. If I had a dollar for every time a woman told me that. Don't sell yourself short, Sage. They're not looking for a particular skill set. They want community members with life experience who understand the culture of the Pacific Northwest."

"Who can raise money." Sage was beginning to understand. "You want Mrs. Bauer."

Bernadette shook her head. "It's a whole lot more than that. You didn't just hand out a check for the festival. You inspired others to get on board with funding it. Then you managed all that money, spending it prudently. The Seaside Festival is Whiskey Bay's marquee event, and you improved it immensely, and in a very short time."

"Still…"

"Let me add this. Gender balance is an issue for Invo North Pacific, like it is for most college boards. We have less than twenty percent female trustees. I'll be blunt. We need more."

Again, Sage thought she understood. "I'll be a token woman."

Bernadette swiftly shook her head. There was a gleam of determination in her eyes. "There'll be nothing token about it. From what I've heard, you are smart, energetic and determined. I have no doubt you can make a difference. And I can promise you this. It will be a rewarding and enriching experience."

Sage found herself curious about Bernadette. "Is it hard for you? Being a woman at the head of a college?"

"You bet it's hard. But it gets easier over time. And it's important. And I am more than willing to do the work."

"You've sold me," Sage said.

It sounded challenging. It sounded meaningful. It was exactly the kind of contribution Sage wanted to make to her new community.

TJ couldn't stop staring at Sage. The flicker of a hurricane lamp on the deck at Neo reflected off her creamy skin. Her hair was up, wisps brushing over her temples, highlighted by the flash of her dangling diamond earrings that matched the pendant necklace resting against her chest.

He'd given her the jewelry last night at a rollicking at-home birthday celebration with cake and presents and singing. The children had loved it. Sage had been uncertain about accepting the jewelry. He knew she was bothered by the expense. But he wasn't bothered at all—exactly the opposite. She looked stunning in diamonds, and he was thrilled to give them to her.

The waiter had just popped open a bottle of champagne and filled their flutes. The breeze from the ocean was soft, the stars alight, the moon a thin crescent in the distance.

"Happy birthday," TJ said as he raised his glass to hers.

"I don't need two birthdays." But she was smiling as she spoke, and she accepted his toast.

"You deserve two birthdays. You deserve more than that for all the ones I missed."

She touched the necklace. "You don't have to make up for lost time."

He wanted to make up for lost time. He wanted it for Eli and, though he knew it didn't make any sense, he wanted it for Sage too. Her life had been tough while she was alone. There were a thousand ways he could have made it easier.

He wished he could spend every second of the rest of his life with them both. But that was impossible. Reality was already crowding in.

"I have to go to New York," he told her.

Her smile dimmed. "When?"

Guilt and disappointment rushed through him. "Tomorrow. It's just for a couple of days."

"Okay."

"I don't want to go."

"It's fine, TJ." She smiled again.

He still wanted to explain. "There are times when the owner of the company has to show up and sign things in person."

"That sounds important."

"They're closing a very big deal. It's a huge accomplishment for the New York office, and they'll appreciate the attention. Not to mention the client. The client will like the attention as well."

"Can you tell me about it?"

"I could. But the details would be boring. It's a Japanese-American merger of two aerospace companies."

"The space station?"

"Mars."

"You call that boring?"

"They're not actually going to Mars. Not this weekend, anyway. It's all about testing systems and innovations that might someday help with a Mars mission."

"That still doesn't qualify as boring."

"I'm just the money guy."

She touched her necklace again. "That you are."

Inspiration hit him. He leaned forward and took her hand, holding it across the table. "Come to New York with me?"

Her surprise was obvious.

"Come with me," he repeated. "We can stay at the Plaza, dine at Daniel, take in a show."

"What about the kids?"

"That's why we have two housekeepers."

"But overnight?"

"They love Kristy. They'll barely notice we're gone."

"I don't know… It seems…"

He raised her hand to his lips and gave it a gentle kiss. "Come to New York with me. We deserve a weekend to ourselves."

She gazed deep into his eyes, and he felt like time stopped.

He wanted her in New York. He suddenly realized how much he needed her in New York. Making love with her, then sleeping in separate bedrooms wasn't cutting it for him. He wanted to hold her in his arms all night long.

"Please," he whispered.

She hesitated but then gave the barest of nods.

His smile went wide. "If we weren't already drinking champagne, I'd order some."

"This is a strange life I'm leading," she said half to herself.

"Just relax and enjoy the ride." He handed her a leather-bound menu. "Now, tell me about your day?"

She opened the menu on the table. "I registered for college."

"Good for you." He waited. He knew there was more.

"Funny thing," she said, her gaze staying fixed on the menu pages.

"What's that?"

"They asked me something else."

"Oh." He kept his expression neutral.

"They asked me to serve as a trustee."

TJ immediately grinned. "I hope you said yes."

"Bernadette Thorburn was very convincing."

"Bernadette is like that."

"I'm really not sure I have enough experience."

"You're going to be fantastic." He opened his own menu, thrilled to learn she'd agreed to serve on the college board.

It was exactly what she needed to use her talents and get more involved in the community. He wanted her to like it here in Whiskey Bay. No, he wanted her to love it here.

"When are you starting?" he asked.

"Not until October."

The answer confused him. "But they said—" He quickly stopped himself.

She slowly raised her head to stare at him.

He stilled. Then he swallowed.

It took her about three seconds to figure it out. "*You* put them up to it."

He shook his head.

She clearly wasn't about to buy his denial. "You used your money and influence to get me a trustee gig?"

"It wasn't like that."

The tone of her voice rose. "Why would you do that?"

"I merely suggested they might consider you."

"You made a suggestion? Did you threaten to pull your donation?"

"Sage, stop. I only suggested. They could say yes or they could say no. And they knew that. The rest was all you."

She closed her menu. "I don't believe you."

"Have you decided already?"

"What?"

He looked pointedly at her closed menu, hoping against hope to move the conversation along.

"Yes, I have. I've decided to go home and make myself a sandwich."

"You don't want to do that."

She couldn't be that angry. It wasn't possible for her to be that angry over such a little thing.

She reached for her purse.

He touched her arm. "Don't. Stop. Look at me."

She paused, gazing at him with suspicion.

"How do you think these things work?"

"I don't really want to know how they work. And I sure don't want to be involved."

"You wanted to be involved two minutes ago."

"That's when I thought I legitimately had something to offer."

"You *do* have something to offer. You have *a lot* to offer. That's why I put your name forward, and that's why Bernadette agreed to set it up." He took a breath.

She didn't immediately bolt.

He took that as a good sign. "The way these things work is you get a little bit of influence, and then you parlay it into more influence, and so on, and so on. You did a fantastic job with the festival."

"Don't pretend this was my performance at the festival. It was your money, plain and simple."

"Partly. Yes, of course, that was a factor. But so what? That's how everybody gets in. You obviously liked what Bernadette had to say. You obviously think you can make a contribution. So make it. From this second on, I can't help you at all. The door is open, you can walk through it or not."

She glared at him in silent suspicion.

He wanted to say more, but he knew it was smarter to stop talking.

"If that's all true, why weren't you honest to begin with?" she asked. "Why weren't you up-front with me?"

He acknowledged it was a fair question. He hadn't wanted to manipulate her. He'd wanted to make her happy. He'd pictured her conversation with Bernadette over and over in his mind, and he quite simply got a kick out of thinking about her joy.

"I wanted it to make you happy," he said.

She heaved a sigh. "It did. But then it made me mad. And now I'm not happy anymore."

"I'm sorry. I didn't think it through."

"You mean you didn't think you'd get caught."

"I normally don't."

*"You do this all the time?"*

"No, no." He could feel himself losing ground. "Not at home. In business. Just a little bit. Sometimes the direct approach isn't the best approach. Sometimes it's better to plant a seed and then stand back and let it germinate."

"I'm not a seed."

"I know."

"I don't want to germinate."

"I understand."

"I don't want you germinating me ever—" It was obvious she struggled but then failed to stop a smile. "That didn't sound right."

"It sounded sexy." He dared to take her hand. "I won't try to manipulate you again. I promise. But as for the germinating part…"

"It's not the manipulation." She paused. "I mean, it is the manipulation. But it's more the money. You don't need to use your money to make me happy."

"I'm not." He wasn't.

She gave a sad smile. She obviously wasn't convinced. He'd have to work on that.


"You're going on an airplane?" Heidi asked in a wary voice.

Both kids were on the sofa in the family room, still in their pajamas after breakfast. Sage and TJ were in the armchairs across from them.

"Kristy will be here the whole time," Sage said, her guilt surging.

"We'll have a great time," Kristy chimed in from where she was loading the dishwasher.

"I've never *been* on an airplane," Heidi said.

"I was on a helicopter once," Eli said. "I don't remember it though." He looked to TJ. "Will you go to the Mets game?"

Sage and TJ exchanged a look. She hadn't seen this one coming.

"Are you telling me there's a Mets game tonight?" TJ asked Eli.

Eli moved up to the edge of the sofa. "It's their first home game this month."

"I like baseball," Heidi said, her expression growing hopeful.

TJ closed his eyes and his chin dropped to his chest.

"I've never seen a live major league game," Eli added.

"He's your son," Sage said to TJ, struggling not to laugh. "Dropping seeds and letting them germinate."

"Do they have ballpark franks?" Heidi asked. "Do they bring them to your seat?"

TJ raised his head. "Are you two saying you want to go to New York?"

"Yes!" both children sang out in unison.

TJ raised his hands in defeat. "Kristy?"

"Yes, boss?" Kristy moved from the kitchen into the family room.

"Would you be able to come to New York overnight?"

"You bet I can."

"Yippee!" Eli sprang to his feet on the sofa.

Heidi followed a little more slowly.

Sage felt her heart swell with joy. Seeing the kids this excited was so wonderfully ordinary.

She leaned closer to TJ. "Thank you."

He retrieved his phone from his shirt pocket. "I told you,

you never have to thank me for taking care of my son." His gaze went to Heidi. "Or my daughter."

"Upstairs," Kristy said brightly to the kids, urging them down from the sofa. "We need to pack your things."

"Our flight is in an hour," TJ told her. Then he pressed a speed dial button on his phone. "I'm still getting you alone," he said to Sage.

She grinned, feeling lighthearted, happy and excited. She wanted to be alone with TJ too.

"Hi, Danica," he said to his assistant. "We're going to need a second suite at the Plaza. There'll be five passengers on the jet. And can you get us some Mets tickets. We'll need five." He paused. Then he frowned. "True. You better cancel that reservation. It sounds like we're having hot dogs at the stadium."

Sage chuckled.

"Thanks, Danica." He ended the call. "This isn't funny," he said to Sage.

"It's a little bit funny."

"Do you know how hard it is to get reservations at Daniel?"

"Poor baby." She rose and cradled his face in her hands.

"Kiss it better?" he asked hopefully.

She leaned slowly down. He closed his eyes and raised his chin.

At the last moment, she planted a kiss on his forehead instead.

"Oh, no, you don't," he said.

Before she could react, she was in his lap, pressed against his chest, his arm firmly around her shoulders.

"That's not going to cut it," he told her.

"You must be really upset," she teased.

"Devastated," he answered, and then he was kissing her mouth.

She kissed him back, her lips melding with his, softening and parting. Her arms went around his neck, and she held him tight, her emotions in a free fall. He was such an amazing man. He was a wonderful father. Their lives might be exceptionally complicated, but right now, right this minute, for today and tonight and tomorrow, she would let them be simple.

She and TJ and their children were taking a short vacation, just like families did all over the country. Well, most families likely piled in the minivan and drove down the highway to a seaside motel. But a private jet and the Plaza were almost the same thing…almost.

"What is it?" TJ drew back and took in her expression.

It was hard for her to put into words. Instead, she made a joke. "Like I said before, this is a strange life I'm leading."

"It's a perfectly normal life."

"I feel like an impostor." There. That was closer.

It took him a second to answer. "The last thing you are is an impostor. You're my wife. You're the mother of my son."

His words warmed her, and she let herself lean into his strength.

He smoothed his palm over the back of her hair. "Like *I* said before, relax and enjoy the ride."

"I will. I am." It was the only thing that made sense. And it was what she wanted, anyway.

She touched his face, smoothing her fingertips along the curve of his cheek and the jut of his jaw. Then she kissed him again.

The children's voices echoed down the stairs, and she knew they had only moments alone, but she kissed him deep and long, falling into the moment and into the fantasy she intended to perpetuate for the next two days.

# Twelve

By the time the game had ended, both kids had been asleep on their feet. Kristy had taken them into the suite across the hall, promising them bubble baths in the oversize tub and a story once they were tucked in. TJ was finally alone with Sage.

Theirs was a two-bedroom suite, but he had no intention of using the second bedroom.

"I have room service coming," he told her as she kicked off her runners.

"Hot dogs and malted milk balls weren't enough for you?"

"They weren't exactly what I had in mind when I planned this."

She was smiling as she made her way into the living room. "But it was fun."

"It was fun," he agreed, peeling the heavy foil from the top of the bottle of Cabernet Sauvignon that was waiting for them on the bar.

The game, in fact the whole day, had been more fun than he'd expected. They'd gone to the zoo, where Heidi had fallen in love with the cats. TJ had bought her a stuffed snow leopard, while Eli had chosen a rubber snake. Both Heidi and Sage had shuddered when Eli draped the python around his neck. TJ was gaining a whole new appreciation for the differences between boys and girls.

"Thirsty?" he asked Sage, sliding two red wine goblets out of the overhanging rack.

"Is that a thirst-quenching red?" she asked, coming up behind him.

"It will complement the charcuterie board that's on its way up. I'm chilling champagne to go with the chocolate strawberries."

"Are you planning to get drunk?"

"We don't have to drink it all." He started to pour.

She glanced around the room. "Does this seem normal to you?"

"Does what seem normal?"

"This room. The wine. The strawberries."

"I haven't had this vintage before." He glanced at the label. "But Caleb highly recommended it."

"You consulted with Caleb on the wine?"

"Before we left Whiskey Bay. I didn't call him between innings or anything." TJ offered her one of the glasses.

"Because that would be odd?" She accepted the glass.

"I called him last night, after you agreed to come along."

"Before Eli and Heidi decided to crash."

"The night is still young." TJ raised his glass and waited for Sage to take a sip.

Strangely, although he was more than glad to be alone with her now, he didn't begrudge having the kids and Kristy along for the day. It had been fun. It had been great. As a package, the day had been perfect.

"Do you like it?" he asked Sage.

"It's delicious."

TJ took a taste. It was everything Caleb had promised.

There was a knock at the door.

The waiter entered with a rolling cart and took a few minutes to set up the table that was positioned in a turret of windows overlooking the park.

TJ saw the waiter to the door and gave him a tip. When he turned back, Sage was biting into a chocolate-dipped strawberry.

"Those are supposed to go with the champagne," he said, making his way toward her.

She grinned unrepentantly. "I'm a maverick."

"The tastes will clash." He wanted her to have the best possible culinary experience.

A gleam in her eyes, she took another swallow of her wine. "It all tastes good to me."

"Bohemian."

"Snob."

She was clearly teasing, but the accusation hit its mark anyway.

"You think so?" he asked, suddenly worried he'd overdone the evening.

"Oh, I do think so, Mr. Phone-a-Wine-Consultant."

"It wasn't the most expensive bottle in the cellar."

She took another sip, then wrinkled her nose. "Cutting corners, are we?"

He waltzed forward and swung an arm around her waist. "I can't win with you, can I?"

"Oh, I wouldn't say that." She went soft and supple against him, and a sensual glow came up deep in her jade-colored eyes.

"I take it back."

"Oh, you will." She moved to disentangle herself.

"What? What are you doing?"

She took a step away from him.

"Where are you going?" he asked.

"To change."

"Please don't change." Even as he made the joke, he realized he didn't want her to change. He didn't want to change a single thing about her.

"I took your advice," she said.

He moved toward her, but she backed off some more.

"Clearly, I'm giving you very bad advice."

"I'm going to change my clothes, TJ. I took your credit card."

"*Your* credit card."

"And bought a little outfit."

He stilled. His mouth went dry. "Define *little*."

She gave him a saucy grin. "I think you'll like it."

"Then what are you waiting for?"

"You don't want to finish the snacks?"

"The snacks will wait." He couldn't. He couldn't wait to see what kind of an outfit she'd bought.

"I wouldn't want to compromise your culinary experience."

"You can compromise anything you want."

She laughed at that. Then she turned for the bedroom, sauntering through the door and closing it behind her.

TJ took a deep breath, telling himself to stay cool.

He moved to an armchair and sat down, taking a swallow of the wine.

Whatever she looked like when she walked back through the door, he absolutely was not going to rush things. He'd take his time, just like he'd planned. He'd make it romantic, just like he'd planned. They had all night to—

She appeared in the doorway, and he nearly dropped his glass.

She was draped in purple satin—a short spaghetti-strapped nightie with flat lace panels along the neck and hem. Her shoulders were smooth and slender, hair copper under the soft lights. Her thighs were shapely, her calves sleek, and her feet were bare. Her auburn hair billowed around her face, bouncing to her collarbone and framing her slim neck.

He abandoned his wine, rolling to his feet, stripping off his polo shirt as he crossed the floor.

"What do you think?" she asked a bit breathlessly.

"Huh?" He had to shake himself out of a daze.

"Do you like it?" She spread her arms and did a pirouette.

By the time she'd turned, he had her in his arms. "I love it."

"You've barely seen it."

"I'll see it more later." He kissed her, bending her backward, going deep, drinking in the taste of her.

She held on to his shoulders, and he wrapped an arm around her, stabilizing her, using his free hand to roam the satin of her breathtaking outfit, smoothing his palm over her stomach, her breasts, her rear. Every inch of her felt fantastic.

Her breathing rate increased, her chest rising and falling. She kissed him with fervor, thrusting her tongue to parry with his. Her lips were so sweet. Her thighs were sleek and firm. And her breasts were soft beneath his hand, her nipples peaking against his touch.

She arched her back, and a soft moan came from her lips.

Desire flashed through him, and he scooped her into his arms, carrying her back into the bedroom, laying her on the four-poster bed, atop the crisp sheets, the moonlight filtering through sheer curtains to dance on the sheen of her skin.

He shucked his pants to lie down beside her, peeling the spaghetti strap from her shoulder, kissing his way to her breast, drawing her nipple into his mouth.

Her hands buried themselves in his short hair. She moaned again, gently flexing beneath him.

The silk bunched up at her waist. He drew back to stare at the sensual picture she made against the stark sheets, arms above her head, one knee bent.

"You are beautiful," he whispered, brushing the back of his hand from her elbow to the side of her breast, then farther down to the nip of her waist and the curve of her hip. Her eyes were buffed jade, her hair a dark halo.

His touch followed her hip bone to her navel and below, dipping farther and farther.

She closed her eyes, and her thighs twitched open.

He dipped into her heat, his pulse pounding, his breathing labored.

When he couldn't stand it anymore, he stripped off his boxers and covered her with his body.

She wrapped herself around him, kissing his mouth, her fingers kneading the muscles of his back. When her heat and softness engulfed him, he groaned her name, balling his fists, searching for strength.

He was determined to take it slow. She deserved romance. She deserved to be cherished. She deserved to be the only woman in his world. Just for tonight, he told himself. Just for tonight, he'd banish everything from his mind, everything but Sage.

He drew his head back, just far enough to focus on her. Her eyes were closed. Her lips were deep red. Her cheeks were flushed.

She moved with him, their rhythm easy, their bodies in sync. Pleasure ebbed through him, pulsing, growing, taking over his body and his mind. His pace increased, and her hold tightened. Before he knew it, he was out of control, moving faster, reaching higher, holding, holding, holding back every second that he could until a world of color, heat and light exploded behind his eyes and his muscles convulsed with release.

"Sage!" Her name was wrenched from his lips, then it thundered over and over inside his brain.

It was midmorning, and the house was completely quiet. Sage stood in the opening between the living room and the family room and drank in the stillness.

Eli and Heidi were at their first full day of school. Whiskey Bay Elementary was a fifteen-minute bus ride away, and they'd been thrilled to hop on the school bus at the end of the driveway. TJ had gone to the office, and Kristy was back at college. Verena wasn't due for at least an hour.

Sage tried to remember how long it had been since she'd been completely alone.

There was course reading waiting for her in the office, and two reports from the college board. Plus, there were always the philanthropic requests for Tide Rush Investments. Although she had that part down to a system, it was always satisfying to find a new project that fit their criteria.

But for now, just for a few minutes, she wanted to savor the peace.

Maybe some tea—since she'd learned how to use the cappuccino machine, a latte was her beverage of choice in the morning. But today didn't feel like a latte day. It felt like herbal tea, maybe something with lemon.

The family room wasn't messy, but it was comfortably disheveled. She liked that.

On the way past the table, she closed Heidi's coloring book and put the stray pencils into the case. Eli's rubber snake was coiled up on one of the chairs. It had stopped startling Sage a few days ago. TJ's plaid shirt was draped over the back of a chair.

She reached out and touched the shirt. He'd been wearing it yesterday playing catch in the backyard with Eli. He'd stripped down to his T-shirt before dinner, because the sun was hitting the deck, and it was hot in front of the barbecue.

They'd grilled burgers and eaten ice cream. Yesterday had come close to being perfect.

Sage lifted the shirt and pressed the soft fabric to her face. She inhaled the subtle scent of TJ, emotions rushing through her. TJ himself was close to perfect.

Maybe he was perfect.

He was perfect for her.

"Hello?" Melissa's voice called out from the front foyer.

Sage lowered the shirt from her face to call back. "I'm in the family room."

She was getting used to the casual drop-in culture of the four oceanfront houses. She couldn't quite bring herself to walk into anyone else's house yet. But she was getting there.

"Kids get off all right?" Melissa asked.

"They couldn't wait to leave."

"That's the spirit."

"We'll see if the novelty lasts." It was a lot to hope that they'd love school every morning all year long.

"I didn't mind school," Melissa said, her glance going to the shirt in Sage's hand.

"Laundry," Sage said, hooking the shirt over the back of one chair, wondering why she felt flustered. "I was about to make tea."

"Love some."

Sage headed for the kitchen, and Melissa followed.

"When do your classes start?" Melissa asked.

"Thursday. I decided to just stick with the two. I don't want to shortchange the philanthropic work for Tide Rush. There are a lot of requests coming in."

"Free money is popular. Who could have guessed?"

Sage gave an eye roll to Melissa's sarcasm as she began filling the kettle.

Melissa laughed. "I say that as the person who asked you first."

"That's true. You did. Do you need a contribution for next year?"

"Not yet. I'll hit you up in the spring."

"I'll be here." As she spoke, Sage realized her future looked bright.

Her future with TJ felt good. Maybe it felt too good. She found herself glancing at his shirt again. Before Melissa interrupted, Sage had been cuddling his shirt, smiling and musing on his perfection.

That couldn't be good.

"Sage?" Melissa asked.

"Hmm?"

"The kettle's overflowing."

Sage glanced down. "Oops." She quickly shut off the tap.

"Is something wrong?"

"No. Nothing's wrong."

Melissa moved up beside her at the sink, concern in her tone. "Is it TJ? Are there…problems?"

Melissa knew about their unorthodox sex life. It had been her idea in the first place.

"It's good," Sage assured her. "Really good."

Melissa's gaze sharpened. "Too good."

Sage opened her mouth to lie but then changed her mind. "He's… Yeah. Maybe too good is the right way to describe it. He's so incredible. He's great with the kids. Eli adores him. He's patient and gentle with Heidi. She's gaining confidence by the day."

"And with you?"

Sage paused. "He's off the charts. In every way you can imagine. I… We…"

Melissa's arm went around Sage's shoulders. "You're in love with him."

Sage closed her eyes, anxiety and relief washing through her in equal measures. "I can't believe I let it happen."

"Do you know how he feels?"

"He seems happy. He's attentive. He's relaxed. Our conversations are fun and funny. He trusts me with his money. Our sex life is terrific."

"Are you going to tell him?"

Sage immediately shook her head. She backed away from Melissa, holding up her palms. "No. Oh, no, no. That wasn't part of the deal."

"The deal can change."

"Not this deal. We're co-parenting."

"And you're living together. And you're sleeping together. And you're sharing a bank account. That sounds a whole lot like marriage to me."

"The marriage part isn't the problem." Sage stepped back and removed the kettle from the sink, drying it off with a towel before setting it on the stove.

"I've seen the way he looks at you," Melissa said.

"That's lust." Sage knew TJ desired her.

"I bet it's something more."

"You can't read his mind." Sage set the burner to high.

"I can see love in his eyes."

Sage swallowed. She wanted to hope, but she didn't dare. "It's not going to end that way."

"You have no idea how it's going to end."

"Lauren," she said simply.

"People get over their losses. They move on."

"Do you think?" Sage turned to look Melissa in the eyes. She wanted to hope. She very desperately wanted to hope that TJ could love her. "Do you actually think it's possible?"

"I do think it's possible. I think it's likely."

"I don't know…"

"Just consider telling him," Melissa said while the kettle began to boil.

Sage nodded.

She did think about telling him. It circled through her mind through their tea and conversation. What would happen if she told TJ she loved him? She pictured him looking confused. Then she pictured him looking horrified. Then she pictured him looking delighted. She let her fantasy TJ say he loved her back.

He smiled. He hugged her close. He kissed her and told her he loved her more than anything else in the world.

The image was so compelling, that by the time Melissa left, Sage was ready to take the risk.

She held his shirt in her arms, hugging it to her chest, inhaling the scent again. Then she laughed at herself. She wasn't going to spend the rest of the day mooning around the house like a lovesick calf.

Gripping the shirt, she marched down the hall to TJ's bedroom. The door was open, as it generally was, but she found herself hesitating in the doorway.

She'd never gone into TJ's room. They didn't sleep together. Sage stayed upstairs with the children, and TJ slept in his own bed.

At first, she'd respected his privacy, and then it had become habit. There was little reason for her to come down to this end of the hall.

Now she took a step inside.

His bed was perfectly made, even though Verena wasn't here yet—interesting. The curtains were closed over two windows on either side of the bed. The en suite door was open, and she could see a laundry hamper inside. She looked down at the shirt, laughing at herself for wanting to preserve his smell.

On the way past, she pulled the curtains open. Then she dropped the shirt in the hamper.

When she turned in the bathroom, her gaze caught on a small crystal bottle that sat on the counter. It looked like perfume.

Her heart stilled and her breathing stopped. Next to the bottle was a container of scented soap, and a glass jar of makeup pads, pink bath salts and three copper-colored candles. It was as if Lauren had just stepped out and was coming back any minute.

Sage backed out of the bathroom. As she went to leave the bedroom, she caught a glimpse of TJ's dresser. The top was covered in photos of Lauren, everything from a formal wedding shot to a picnic in the park where they were laughing and embracing on a blanket. And in the center of it all was a set of glass jewelry boxes.

Foreboding drew her forward. There were three boxes in the set, and the biggest one had Lauren's name etched on the top. The smallest held rings—a diamond engagement ring, a woman's band and a man's band beside it. Everything inside Sage turned to ice.

"What are you doing?" It was TJ's voice.

Sage whirled. She had no idea what to say. Maybe she should feel guilty. But instead she felt angry and betrayed. And intensely sad.

"Do you still have her clothes?" she asked.

TJ's jaw went lax.

"This is practically a shrine. Have you kept everything that was hers?"

"That—" his tone was rock-hard "—is none of your business."

"I'm your *wife*."

He seemed to stumble for a split second. "It's not the same thing."

Her brain reeled from the hurt and disappointment. "You mean I'm not a *real* wife."

"I was honest with you from the start."

Her heart split in two. "In other words, I'm right."

He'd acted like he cared for her. Everything he said and did made her feel like she mattered, like she was more than just Eli's mother.

"Right about what?" he asked, looking confused.

"Not right. Wrong." She made for the door.

He didn't step aside. "Wrong about what?"

She swept her arm across the room. "About this. About you. About us. I thought I could do this, TJ."

"We *are* doing this."

"No." It was crystal clear to her. "*You're* doing this. I'm doing something else altogether."

"You're not making sense."

She squeaked past him. "I have to go."

"Go where? Why? What?"

She didn't answer but kept walking.

"I never pretended I was over her," he called out.

He was right. He hadn't pretended he was over Lauren. His progress was all in Sage's mind.

"Tell me you're exaggerating," Matt said.

"Tell me you're not that stupid," Caleb said.

Afternoon sun rays bounced off the smooth water beyond the marina's rooftop patio.

"I was completely up-front with her," TJ defended. "She's known all along this was about Eli."

"You're *sleeping* with her," Matt said on a high-pitched note.

"It was *her* idea."

"People can get emotional about that sort of thing," Caleb said.

"Are you saying I should stop sleeping with her?"

TJ didn't want to do that. He truly didn't want to give that up. It was one of the few things that kept him sane. Those moments in Sage's arms, was whole, complete. He wasn't lonely anymore.

"I'm saying you should stop lying to her," Matt said.

"I'm not lying to her." Had TJ's friends not been listening? "I've been excruciatingly honest. From minute one, I've held up my end of the deal."

"You mean the money," Matt said.

"Sure, I mean the money. Not that I can get her to spend much of it. Well, except on other people. I got her to buy a car and a few clothes. Melissa had to twist her arm to get her to buy furniture."

"It's only money," Caleb said.

"That's what *I* keep telling her."

"I mean, she doesn't only need money."

"She definitely needed money."

"You're more than generous with your money," Matt said.

TJ would have liked to take credit for that. He needed some points in this conversation. But money was easy. It was easy to make, and it was easy to give up.

Caleb leaned forward in his chair. "Eli needed more than your money. All the money in the world wouldn't have saved him without you. And Sage needs more than just your money."

"Sage isn't sick."

Caleb winced. "She needs your love."

A pain shot through TJ's head. It was as if his friends had never even met him. "I love Lauren."

"Lauren is gone," Matt said.

"Just because she's gone doesn't mean I've stopped loving her."

"Maybe not," Caleb conceded. "But it also doesn't mean you can't love Sage."

"I don't love Sage." TJ stopped himself. That sounded harsh. "I mean, I'm not in love with Sage. I love her. In a way. I guess." He suddenly felt disloyal to Lauren. "I'll never love anyone the way I loved Lauren."

Matt's tone went low, sympathetic, understanding. "Nobody is suggesting you forget Lauren. But Sage is here. She's real, and she's in your life. You can go forward, or you can go backward. But you can't do both."

"Do you want to lose Sage?" Caleb asked.

"No." TJ's answer was instantaneous.

"Do you want to hurt her?"

"No." TJ didn't want to hurt Sage.

He'd been trying his utmost not to hurt her since they'd reconnected. He owed her. What was more, he liked and respected her. He was attracted to her. He loved her.

He suddenly pictured the hurt in her eyes as she stared at his wedding picture, his wedding rings, his world with Lauren. He felt a brick hit him in the side of the head.

He'd let Lauren hurt Sage.

How could he have done that?

Lauren was forever his past. But Sage… Sage… Sage was here, and she was his future. She was warm and loving and…

He raised his chin to look at his friends, regret washing through him. "Oh, no."

"He's got it," Caleb said.

"I think he's got it," Matt echoed.

"I'm in love with Sage," TJ said. "I have to apologize."

"Not with words," Caleb said.

"Not with money," Matt said.

TJ understood. He rose. "I have to show her that there's room in my life for her."

"He's not as stupid as he looks," Matt said with a chuckle.

"Thank goodness for that," Caleb deadpanned.

TJ gave them a crooked smile, grateful as always for their blunt honesty—no matter how painful it sometimes felt.

He left the marina, striding up the pathway to his house. Sage was still gone, but he'd expected that. He was even glad. He had some work to do before they talked.

It was a good bet that she'd be back when the kids got home from school, which gave him a couple of hours. He pulled some packing boxes out of the basement and took them to his room.

He started with the easy stuff, Lauren's soap and perfume, and the clothes that were in the dresser drawers. As the items piled up, his chest grew lighter. There were hundreds of happy memories in her possessions. But that was all they were now, happy memories.

By the time he removed the last picture from the dresser, the daylight was fading through the windows. He checked his watch. Sage hadn't come home, and neither had the children.

A block of fear settled into his stomach. Where were they? Had she taken them? What if he was already too late?

# Thirteen

Sage had been halfway to Seattle, her phone switched off and the kids buckled into the back seat when she'd realized she couldn't do it. She couldn't run off without a word to TJ. It was a cowardly thing to do, and it was just plain wrong to yank the kids out of school.

Sure, she was hurt. She was humiliated. But TJ was the one sticking to the terms of their agreement. She was the one who'd decided she wanted more. He was right when he said he'd been honest with her all along. He had.

She'd turned around at a rest stop and headed back home.

When she'd arrived, both kids were asleep. TJ had rushed out the front door. When he saw the sleeping children, he'd pressed his lips tight in silence and lifted Eli into his arms.

Sage carted Heidi up to her room. The little girl had barely stirred while Sage slipped her into a nightgown and tucked her into bed.

Then Sage had steeled herself to make an apology. The best thing for everyone was to get back to an even keel. For Eli's and Heidi's sakes, she'd bury her feelings for TJ.

She'd have to stop sleeping with him. She couldn't do friends with benefits, certainly not with TJ. It would be heartbreaking to hold him in her arms and know his love was still with Lauren. She couldn't bring herself to do that.

But she could do everything else. And she would.

She made her way downstairs. It took a few minutes to find him sitting on the deck outside the family room. Her stomach fluttered, and her heart pounded in trepidation, but she forced herself forward.

"Hi," she said in a tentative voice, coming out on the deck.

He looked up quickly, as if she'd startled him.

He seemed to take in her appearance.

"I'm sorry," she said, perching on the edge of the chair next to his, gripping the armrests to steady herself. "I shouldn't have left like that."

"I tried to call," he said.

"My phone was off."

He gave a nod.

She pressed forward. "You were right. I overreacted. I mean, I reacted. I mean, I shouldn't have been surprised—"

"I didn't think you were coming back." His expression was grim.

"Like I said, I overreacted. I just needed some time, a few miles I guess, to get my head on straight." She sat up. "We had a deal, TJ. I'm prepared to honor it."

He gave a ghost of a self-deprecating smile. "To be my wife?"

"Yes. And Eli and Heidi's mother. It's better if we're together, no matter…" She cleared her throat. "It's better that we stay together."

Unexpectedly, he reached out and took her hand, stroking his thumb across her knuckles.

She wanted to snatch it away. It was just too painful to have him touch her.

"I can't—" Her voice cracked. And then all she could manage was a whisper. "I don't think we should keep sleeping together."

His thumb stilled.

"That was a mistake." She forced herself to rush on. "I know it was my idea, but it was a mistake to think it wouldn't get too complicated."

She fell to silence, and the waves below echoed in the night.

"I thought your logic was impeccable," he said.

She had too, at the time. But that was before she let her

heart get in the way. She'd risked her heart, and she'd lost her heart. She was numb now, but she knew she had some very painful days ahead while she tried to get over her feelings for TJ.

"Can I show you something?" he asked.

The question took her by surprise. "Uh, sure. What is it?"

He came to his feet, centering his hold on her hand. "This way."

"Are we leaving? Is Kristy here?"

"Kristy's not here. And we're not leaving." He led her across the family room and the living room to the hallway and started down.

She stopped dead. "TJ, no. I can't."

There was no way she could go back into his bedroom.

"It'll be okay. I promise."

She shook her head, trying to pull her hand from his. "It won't be okay."

He turned to face her. "Sage." He brushed her cheek. "Trust me. I'm not going to hurt you again."

"You didn't—"

He cocked his head with an expression of disbelief.

"It was my fault, not yours," she said.

"No. It was my fault. Let me make it up to you."

Sage swallowed against the lump in her throat. Embarrassingly, tears tingled behind her eyes. "I can't go in there."

"She's gone, Sage."

His words didn't make any sense. Sage needed to flee. She needed to get away from all this.

"Lauren is gone," he said. "She's gone from my room, and she's gone from my heart." He gave a tiny smile. "From most of my heart. I'll always love what she and I had, but it's in the past. Come and see."

Emotion swelled in Sage's chest, making everything ache. How was she ever going to stop loving him?

He took her hands, backing up, drawing her down the hall with him. "You are my present, Sage."

The light was on, and she saw the cleared room, blinking to take in the enormity of it. "TJ, you didn't have to..."

"And you are my future. If you'll have me. I love you, Sage."

Her gaze darted to his. She couldn't believe she'd heard right. "You what?"

He smiled. "I love you so much. If we weren't already married, I'd be proposing right now. I never, ever, not in a million years thought I could feel this way. Stay with me." He pointed to the bedroom. "Stay here with me, every night, all the time. Let's make it real. Let's have some babies. Let's fill this house with love and laughter." He paused. "That is, if you want to. I mean, if you..."

"Love you?" she asked, feeling the brightest of joy take over her world. "I love you, TJ. I didn't mean to, but I fell very, very hard in love with you."

He wrapped his arms around her, lifting her from the floor. "I should have known."

"That I loved you?"

"That I loved you. When I saw you holding Caleb's daughter, you looked perfect. I wanted our own baby, another baby."

"More babies," she mused.

"Would you be okay with that?"

"Mommy?" came a little voice behind her.

Sage turned to see Heidi. It was the first time Heidi had called her that.

"Yes, sweetheart?" Sage let go of TJ and dropped to one knee.

"I had a bad dream."

"I'm so sorry, sweetie."

TJ crouched to join them. "Would you like Daddy to come upstairs and read you a story?"

Heidi nodded.

"Okay, pumpkin." TJ lifted Heidi into his arms.

Then he took Sage's hand.

She leaned her cheek against his shoulder as they walked. "You're the best daddy in the entire world."

Heidi's arms tightened around his neck. "Best daddy," she murmured.

"I love you both," TJ said. "I love you all."

* * * * *

# THE BABY CLAIM

## CATHERINE MANN

To Dad and Betty,
and the joy of a second happily-ever-after.

# One

"Do you live to infuriate me, or is it a pleasant pastime for when you're not wining and dining the single females of Alaska?"

Glenna Mikkelson-Powers splayed her hands on her day planner to avoid launching herself from behind her mahogany desk to confront Broderick Steele.

Being so close to the man had never been a wise idea.

The sensual draw was too strong for any woman to resist for long and stay sane. His long wool duster over his suit was pure Hugo Boss. But the cowboy hat and leather boots had a hint of wear that only increased his appeal. His dark hair, which attested to his quarter Inuit heritage, showed the first signs of premature gray. His charisma and strength were as vast as the Alaska tundra he and she both called home.

In a state this large, there should have been enough space for both of them. Theoretically, they should never have to cross paths. But their feuding families' constant battle over dominance of the oil industry kept Glenna and Broderick in each other's social circles.

Too often for her peace of mind.

Even so, he'd never shown up at her office before.

She pressed her hands harder against her day planner and fixed him with her best icy stare. "I have an assistant. Zeke—the grandfatherly looking gentleman—can announce you. Or you can knock. At least attempt some semblance of a normal greeting."

Not that anything about Broderick was in any way calm or normal.

"First of all—" he tossed his snow-dusted hat on her desk "—I do not live to infuriate anyone. Your assistant wasn't out there."

Glenna glanced through the open door and found his statement to be true. She repressed her inclination to roll her eyes anyway. Surely Broderick could have waited for Zeke to return instead of barging in here.

"Second..." He peeled off his leather gloves one at a time, revealing callused hands. A man of brawn, he also happened to have an extraordinary chief finance officer aptitude that had served his family's business well. "...I am far too busy to have the sort of sex life you've attributed to me."

That dried up any words she might have spoken, and made her stomach flip more than it should have.

"Third, Glenna, I have no idea why you're acting like the injured party when I'm the one who had a bombshell dropped on my desk today." He leaned closer, the musky scent of his cologne teasing her senses like breathing in smoky warmth on a cold day. "Although once we sort this out, let's come back to the obsession you have with my sex life."

Light caught the mischief in his eyes, bringing out whiskey tones in the dark depths. His full lips pulled upward in a haughty smile.

"You're being highly unprofessional." She narrowed her own eyes, angry at her reaction to him as she drank in his familiar arrogance.

Their gazes held and the air crackled. She remembered the feeling all too well from their Romeo-and-Juliet fling in college.

Doomed from the start.

And yet…those memories had never faded.

One weekend long ago. A passionate couple of days in her attic apartment. Fireplace blazing. Snow piling on the skylight.

Steam filling the shared shower stall.

Still, those two days were nothing compared to the love she'd felt for her late husband during her six-year marriage. The deep emotional connection, the respect they'd felt for one another. The work they'd invested in overcoming hardships.

And the grief they'd shared over their inability to conceive a child.

Her job was everything to her now. Glenna refused to put it at risk, especially for Broderick.

He was her rival. He wanted his family's business to dominate the oil industry and she simply could not allow that. She was the CFO of Mikkelson Oil, and she'd make sure *her* family's business came out on top.

His mesmerizing eyes and broody disposition would not distract her.

She eased back in her chair. "This is the last time I will ask you. What are you doing in my office?"

"Like you don't know." He dropped a large envelope on top of her day planner. "What would you call this?"

"Mail," she said, giving herself time to figure out his game.

So much had been upended in the company since her father had died of a heart attack two years ago. So much loss. First her father, then her husband. She'd been left reeling. But if she allowed grief to consume her, Mikkelson Oil would lose out…to Broderick.

"Do you care to elaborate?" she asked.

He shrugged, his starched white shirt rustling against his broad shoulders.

"Printouts, technically, with some kind of bogus report on a stock share buyout. It makes no damn sense, but my people have traced it back to your office."

She reached into a drawer, pulled out a manila envelope and placed it next to his file.

"Really?" She tapped the envelope. "Because I could ask you about a similar buyout. In reverse."

His forehead furrowed before he dropped into one of the two leather club chairs in front of her desk. "Our companies are exchanging shares? That doesn't make sense."

She jabbed a manicured finger in his direction. "Your father is up to something and I don't appreciate this pushback since my dad died. It's sexist to assume we're weaker without a man at the helm."

Her shoulders went back defensively as she sat taller and straighter. She would not allow Broderick Steele or his father to intimidate her.

"You talk about sex a lot." He tipped his arrogant head to the side and glanced at the yellow sofa tucked behind him. One damn look loaded with suggestion.

"Shut up and listen to me." She barely resisted the urge to stamp her foot.

"I am. It's fun to watch your cheeks go pink." He clapped a hand to his chest. "And by the way, my mother always told me it's rude to tell people to shut up." A sardonic smile played along his lips.

"Rude? Talking about sex in a business meeting is rude." She scooped up a brass paperweight in the shape of a bear that had belonged to her father. Shifting it from hand to hand was an oddly comforting ritual. Or perhaps not so odd. When she was a small girl, her father had told her the statue gave people power, attributing his success to the brass bear. After the last two years of loss, Glenna needed every ounce of luck and power she could get. "I'm not in line to join the Alaskan female dating population ready to fawn over you."

"I didn't ask you to, and there's no need to threaten me with your version of brass knuckles. You're safe with me." Humor left his face and his expression became all business. "But since you're as bemused by this data as I am, come with me to speak to your mother."

"Of course. Let's do that. We'll have this sorted out in no time."

The sooner the better.

She wanted Broderick Steele out of her office and not a simple touch away.

Broderick was pushing his luck with Glenna, but this woman got to him in a way no one else ever had.

When they were in college, he'd told himself it was the warring-families, forbidden-fruit thing that had drawn them to each other. Except, he still craved her.

Usually he kept those feelings in check by staying as far away from this particular blonde bombshell as possible.

But today he'd received disturbing paperwork about stocks changing hands.

"Are you ready to speak to your mother about this now?

We need to know who on your board, or on mine, is messing with our companies."

She looked up, her blue eyes as crystal clear as the Alaska sky after a storm. "Yes, absolutely, the sooner the better. She's here today. I met with her earlier this morning." Glenna nodded, rose and stepped to the front of her desk.

Holy hell. He damn near swallowed his tongue.

Her pencil skirt hugged her curves and set his imagination on fire. The suit jacket plunged, and even though a white blouse covered almost all her skin, that *V*... He forced his eyes away out of respect.

And to preserve his sanity.

"After you," he said.

He worked to keep himself in check, to stay steady even though proximity to her sent him reeling. He followed her past a sitting area in her office with that yellow sofa and two chairs clustered around a fireplace.

She glanced over her shoulder, blond hair swishing in a golden curtain. "Mother's office is two floors up. We'll settle this. Not to worry."

Without another word, she charged through the door, boot heels muted against the plush carpet. The wall of windows along one side of the corridor provided an awe-inspiring view of the mountains. It might be spring everywhere else in America. But here in Alaska, snow still capped the peaks.

Sunshine streamed through the windows and over Glenna. To keep his eyes off her swaying hips and the killer leather boots, he checked out the art on the other wall. Yet again he was struck by the differences between the Mikkelson corporate offices and his family's building on the other side of Anchorage's business district. The Steele headquarters had a more modern look, sleek and tall in a way that reminded him of his home state, like an ice sculpture filled with coal and grit and gold.

The Mikkelson offices harkened back to old-school Alaska, with a rugged elegance denoted by pelt rugs and wooden furniture heavy enough to remind people nothing fragile lasted in this land. To make it here, you had to be born of sturdy stock.

The file crinkled in his grip as they walked, reminding him why he was here. What did his father know? Broderick hadn't been able to find him this morning, and he'd tried hard. Damn hard.

Lately, his dad had been distracted and inaccessible. Unusually so, and at the worst possible time. Bids were going up for the major pipeline from Alaska to the Dakotas. This wasn't just about money or energy independence. It was also about keeping projects ecologically friendly, making sure the land they loved and called home was protected.

They were a family of engineers and ecologists, working like hell to present a balanced plan.

Broderick knew his reputation for being a cold bastard, but he didn't see the point in getting emotionally invested in anything—or anyone—outside of work.

Something had gone haywire in him when his sister died. He understood it intellectually, but that didn't make it easier to get past. Maybe if he hadn't lost his mother at the same time, she might have helped him find his way out of the maze where he sabotaged relationship after relationship. Now his dating life consisted of women who had no interest in anything more than being casual.

Glenna often stated—emphatically—that she was all about her job. He understood. He was married to his work, too.

That's why this ridiculous rumor of a merger had to be squelched.

"You don't act like most number crunchers."

He cocked his head to one side. "Practical, you mean?"

"I guess. You're just so…outrageous. Illogical. Unpredictable." She picked up her pace.

"And you are very much a buttoned-up numbers gal." Heat fired inside him as he thought of a time he'd *un*buttoned her, very thoroughly.

She seemed to read his mind. "Keep your eyes forward, cowboy."

"Do you think I brought a hidden camera to steal secret formulas from your office?"

He met her eyes full on and found those blue depths too alluring. Something about them made words slip out before he could stop them. "I would very much like to know your secret desires."

Her breathing deepened, her chest rising and falling quickly. She licked her lips. "I prefer we keep things all business. Do you think you can respect my wishes for at least the next half hour? If not, we'll be doing this meeting via videoconference."

He nodded, backing up a step, knowing he was playing with fire. Still, she was right about him being unpredictable. Despite the complications, he found himself plotting to press for more from her. Later, of course. Timing was everything.

"Of course I'll respect your wishes."

"I wish I could trust that," she said softly, before walking to the elevator and pushing the button.

Her words stung. Did she think so little of him? He joined her at the elevator, watching her, musing.

She felt for a hairpin, tucking it inside a sweep of hair that pushed the golden length over one shoulder. Her pale pink nail polish was barely perceptible. Classy. Understated. Like her. "I can't help but be concerned about you getting an insider's peek at our business and financials."

The elevator dinged, the doors slid open and she stepped inside.

He joined her in the circular enclosure, which provided a panoramic view of the harbor with a few boats still floating between chunks of ice. "Maybe you should worry about your files. There are all sorts of cloning devices for computers and—"

"I'll have the security guards strip-search you on the way out."

Just as he'd decided her word choice was accidental, she glanced back over her shoulder, blue eyes glimmering with mischief.

Heat spread and he moved to her side, ducking his head toward hers. "Will you personally supervise the search? Lucky for me I wore my favorite comic-character boxer shorts."

She arched one delicate blond eyebrow. She'd always had a way of putting a person in his place quietly, succinctly. "You flatter yourself."

"I dream, oh lady, I dream."

She tipped her head, her eyebrows pulling together. "I have to ask. Do you treat all business professionals this way?"

"Only the business professionals I've already had an affair with. Actually, strike that." He held up a hand. "Only you. Everyone else at work, it's all business."

"A poor choice during one weekend in college is not the same as an affair." Her hands on her hips accentuated her curves in that killer power suit.

He ached to peel it off her.

Broderick clapped a hand to his chest. "You wound me.

That weekend is my benchmark for all other relationships. Every woman falls short after you."

Had he really said that out loud? It had almost felt like he'd meant it.

He was saved from pondering that uncomfortable thought when the elevator bell dinged. They'd reached their destination.

Glenna surprised him by pressing the button to keep the doors closed. "Your board of directors may buy your bull, but I'm not fooled by your smooth talk."

She was right. Whatever he was doing with her, it had no place in the office.

But they were in the elevator. Alone.

He was not one to let an opportunity pass by.

He stepped closer, inhaling the scent of her. Almonds… Unexpected. Sensual. "What if I'm serious?"

Her eyes widened before she touched his elbow. "Then I am so very sorry you were hurt." Her throat moved with a swallow. Then her elegant nose scrunched and she pointed a slim finger at him. "But I'm not buying that line about all women falling short. Now stop playing me and let's speak to my mother."

Glenna let the elevator open, then charged ahead of him around a corner to an empty receptionist's desk. "I'm not sure where Sage is—"

Glenna's young cousin Sage Hammond rounded the corner just then, smoothing her simple turtleneck sweater dress as she took her place at her chair. "I've been away from my desk. I was meeting with your assistant in the tech department. I'm sorry to have left things unattended. Your mother was busy with a call when I left." She tapped the phone console, strands of her whispy blond hair falling across her shoulders. "But the light's off now so she must be finished, if you wish to go inside."

Broderick nodded. "Thank you, Miss Hammond."

Glenna muttered, "Eyes off my cousin," as she reached for the door handle of the next office.

Jealous? Interesting. "I don't pluck wings off butterflies."

Glenna's sky-blue eyes shifted with something he couldn't name, just briefly, then she turned away and walked into her mother's office.

The interior held more of that Mikkelson charm. Antiques and splashes of light green filled the room, as if to bring life inside. Two walls of windows let sunlight stream into the corner office, and more rays poured through a skylight. Outside, the streets teemed with people, cars and even an ambling moose.

But the office itself was empty.

"Mom? I'm here with Broderick Steele. There's been a misunderstanding, a rumor we need to clear up." Glenna looked around. "I know she's here. There's her leather portfolio bag and her coat, even her cashmere scarf. She must be getting coffee."

Or in the powder room? Glenna's gaze flicked to the private bathroom.

Muffled sounds came from within, like a shower maybe, soft and indistinctive. Steam seeped from under the door as if the water had been running a long time. A moan filtered through. From an enjoyable shower? Or was that a sound of pain? He wasn't sure.

Broderick backed into the sitting area, away from the line of sight of the bathroom. "I'll step out so you can check on her. If you need any help, just say the word."

"Thanks, I appreciate that. Mom?" Concern laced Glenna's voice. "Mom, are you okay?"

There was no answer.

Glenna looked at Broderick. "I hate to just burst in, but if she's ill… If it's an emergency…"

"Your call. Do you want me to leave?" Maybe health issues might explain the strange business behavior.

"How about you stay back, but nearby in case I need to send you for Sage." Glenna tapped lightly on the door. "Mother, it's me. Are you all right?"

He studied the top of his boots, keeping his eyes averted.

"Mother, I'm worried. I don't want to embarrass you, but I need to know you're okay. I'm coming in."

When the doorknob rattled, Broderick glanced up and saw Glenna shaking her head. His concern ratcheted a notch higher.

"It's locked." She knocked harder on the door. "Mom, you're scaring me. Open up. Please." She reached into her pocket. "I'm going to use my master key to come in." She opened the door—and squeaked.

She clapped a hand over her mouth, launching Broderick into motion. He rushed forward and rested a palm on her back, ready to help with whatever crisis might be unfolding.

Glenna pressed a steadying hand on the bathroom door frame. "Mom?"

Broderick stopped short. Blinked. Blinked again. And holy crap, he still couldn't believe his eyes.

Glenna might have been surprised, but Broderick was stunned numb. He even braced his booted feet because his world had done a somersault.

Jeannie Mikkelson stood wrapped in a towel in the steam-filled, white-tiled bathroom, and she wasn't alone.

An all-too-familiar figure edged in front of her—pushing Glenna's mother safely behind his broad chest.

Confused, Broderick couldn't stop himself from asking the obvious. "Dad?"

# Two

Pacing in her mother's reception area, Glenna struggled to push through the fog of…confusion? Shock? She didn't know how to wrap her brain around what she'd seen, much less put a label on it.

Her mother was having an affair with their corporate enemy.

Okay, so, technically, Glenna had done the same in college, but she and Broderick hadn't held positions in the family businesses then. Even now they weren't the owners and acting CEOs of both companies. They weren't the parents who had perpetuated the feud with dinner table discussions of suspicions and rumors.

Back in college, Glenna had felt so guilty, like such a turncoat because of her attraction to Broderick. She'd felt that way just fifteen minutes ago in her office.

Now, she glanced across the waiting area at…the son of her mother's lover, boyfriend, whatever.

This was so surreal.

And Broderick was still infuriatingly hot. But things were more complicated than they'd been before, which had been mighty damn complicated.

He rested one lean hip against a wingback chair, his booted foot tapping restlessly. Her cousin looked back and forth between them. Sage obviously sensed something was wrong, but she kept her lips pressed closed. She wouldn't ask.

And she wouldn't gossip. Very likely that had been a quality high on Jeannie Mikkelson's list when she'd chosen her assistant.

Did Sage already know about the affair? And perhaps about whatever was going on with their stocks? If some hint of the relationship between the two oil moguls had leaked, that could explain the odd fluctuations in stock holdings as investors grew unsure, some selling off their interests while others scooped up more, based on their own hypotheses.

So many questions.

Starting with…how long did it take to throw on some clothes? Glenna winced at the thought.

The door to her mother's office finally swung open, the Alaskan yellow cedar panel revealing her mom, with Jack Steele standing tall right behind her, a gleam in his green eyes. Protective. Territorial. An unrelenting look Glenna had seen before in his business dealings. But this was different. So different.

She shifted her gaze to her mom.

Her mother's damp hair was pulled back in a clip, but otherwise there was no sign of what had happened. Jeannie Mikkelson was as poised and strong as ever. She'd run the corporation alongside her husband for years, and then taken the helm alone after his first major heart attack debilitated him.

She'd kept the business running at full speed through his entire health crisis and even held it together after that final fatal heart attack. The whole family had been rocked. But Jeannie? Glenna had seen her cry only once.

Her mother excelled at keeping her emotions under wraps.

So it was no surprise she remained unreadable now. This wasn't about her mother having a relationship with someone other than Glenna's father.

It was about her mom having a relationship with *this* man.

Jack Steele looked like an older version of his eldest son, with dark hair more liberally streaked with gray. He'd kept in shape, but age had thickened him. He was a character, similar to all three of his sons. He was executive and cowboy. And Alaskan.

One of the many headlines from his magazine profiles scrolled through her mind. *The CEO Wore Mukluks.*

Jeannie nodded toward her assistant. "Sage, could you hold all my calls and redirect any visitors?"

"Of course, Aunt Jeannie." Sage already had her notebook tablet in hand and was tapping with delicate efficiency.

"This may take a while."

"I'll reschedule your eleven o'clock and send Chuck to take him out to lunch."

Chuck, aka Charles Mikkelson III, was Jeannie's son, Glenna's brother and second in command of the company. Heir apparent to take over when Jeannie retired.

If she ever retired. Jeannie was still vibrant and going strong, only in her sixties.

"That's the perfect plan. Thank you, dear." Jeannie

waved Glenna and Broderick into the office and Jack closed the door behind them, clicking the lock to ensure there would be no interruptions.

Glenna swayed and Broderick palmed her waist. She couldn't help but be grateful for the momentary steadying, even as his hand seared her.

Jack raised one eyebrow before saying, "Let's all have a seat."

Glenna self-consciously stepped away from Broderick, the tingle of his touch lingering.

The Steele patriarch pulled one of the green club chairs closer to the other, then touched Jeannie's arm lightly as she took her seat. He eyed the sofa, making it clear that Broderick and Glenna were to park themselves on it like two kids waiting to be put in their place.

Broderick still wasn't speaking, although he settled beside her on the apple-green sofa. Glenna couldn't get a read on him, but then her brain was jumbled again just by the simple brush of his knee against hers.

What the hell was it with the Steele men?

Her mother and Jack were now holding hands like teenagers. It was sweet—sort of—but still such a jarring sight. "Mom, I know this is your personal business and I don't want to pry, but you have to understand how confusing this is, given our families' histories."

"I realize this is more than a little awkward, Glenna, and we'd hoped to talk to everyone as a family soon."

Broderick tapped the file against his leg. "Talk to us about…which part? The relationship between the two of you, or is there something else you want to share? Something, say, business related."

Jack's thumb caressed Jeannie's wrist. "We want you both to know that this has come as a surprise to us, as well.

Nothing happened while either of us was still married. We were very happy in our marriages."

Her mom leaned forward, reaching out to Glenna. "I loved your father, you know that. I still do."

Jack cleared his throat. "Son, you understand how… difficult… How…your mother's death…"

Looking over with a sympathetic smile, Jeannie squeezed his hand before continuing, "Jack and I have spent a lot of time together these past months dealing with different EPA issues and concerns with the economy."

"But our companies are in competition," Glenna pointed out, still not understanding the situation.

"Our companies were eating each other alive. We would have been at risk from a takeover by Johnson Oil United. Their CEO, Ward Benally, has been making acquisitions and filings on their behalf that are concerning. We decided, out of a love for what we've built and for our home state, that we needed to talk."

Talk? Glenna couldn't help but note, "Clearly you've been doing more than talking."

After the words fell out, she winced at her own lack of diplomacy.

Her mother, however, laughed with a light snort. "Clearly. We were as surprised as you are." She tipped her head to the side. "Well, maybe not literally as surprised as the two of you were when you opened that bathroom door."

Jeannie's mouth twitched at the corners, then laughter rolled out of her. Jack's deep chuckles joined hers and they exchanged an unmistakably intimate look as they sagged back into the chairs, hands still linked.

For some reason, that moment made Glenna far more uncomfortable than seeing them in towels earlier. This was about more than sex. This truly was a relationship, a connection, something she didn't have in her life anymore, now that her husband was dead.

She might not have been married as long as her mother, but Glenna understood the pain of widowhood. And her deepest regret beyond losing him? She didn't even have a child of theirs to love.

Glenna pinched two fingers to the bridge of her nose, pressing against the corners of her eyes, where tears welled. So much loss. So much change. Too much for her to process.

Broderick inched forward and slapped the file down on the coffee table. "If we're all done with laughing, let me get this straight. The data and rumors that point to a merger of our two companies are not rumors. You're genuinely planning to dismantle both corporations, and you expect us all to join forces without input or discussion."

"No," Jack stated.

"Of course we don't," Jeannie echoed. "We're all adults and we have always intended to treat you as such. Things just happened so quickly between us we haven't had a chance to bring you up to speed."

"But," Jack interrupted, "we intend to. And soon. Very soon, son."

Broderick frowned. "Please say you don't intend to put us all in a room together, Dad."

"Not for the initial discussion," his father answered. "We are smarter than that."

Good thing. Being this close to Broderick, even for such a short time, was interfering with Glenna's ability to focus. And it seemed she would need to keep her wits about her now, more than she'd realized even a half hour ago. "Mom, what exactly do you have in mind?"

"We want to arrange family meetings separately first," she explained, her blue eyes worried but resolute. "We'll need to allow everyone time to process what we have to say."

"But then…" Jack held up a finger in a lecturing style that made Glenna wince. He wasn't her father. And he wasn't her boss. Yet. "We fully expect everyone to accept our decisions."

Broderick gave a hefty exhalation as he sat back for the first time. "Dad, I think you're expecting a lot awfully fast." He turned to Glenna. "I don't know about your family, but my brothers and sisters? They're going to blow a gasket."

Glenna was completely in sync with Broderick on that point at least. Because expecting her siblings to end a decades-long family feud after a simple conversation, expecting them to accept what appeared to be a blending of the businesses, too?

Blow a gasket?

Understatement of the year.

Broderick had eaten in restaurants around the globe, with food cooked by the finest chefs, and he'd enjoyed every meal.

But none of them outstripped the cuisine here at Kit's Kodiak Café in the little town outside Anchorage. The diner, a rustic barn type structure, was perched along the bay's edge. The paned windows presented a clear view of a dock stretching out into the harbor, an occasional whale's back cresting through floating chunks of ice. Inside, long planked tables accommodated large, noisy groups—like his family.

Menus crackled in front of the others, but he knew what he wanted, so his menu stayed folded. He flipped his coffee mug upright to signify java would be welcome. The waitress took their orders with quick efficiency and no pandering, another reason they all enjoyed coming here. Their family was well known in this café, but they appreciated not receiving special treatment.

He and his siblings had been coming to Kit's since they were children. Their father brought them most Saturday mornings and sometimes before school so their mother could sleep in. He would bundle them up. Half the time, their gloves didn't match, but they always had on a hat and boots as they piled into the family Suburban.

Broderick hadn't realized then how his billionaire father was trying to keep them grounded in grass roots values by taking them to "regular Joe" sorts of places, the kind that played country music and oldies over the radio. The air smelled of home cooking and a wood fire. Back then, he'd thought the stuffed bear was cool, the music loud enough and the food almost as good as his mom's.

And he still did.

As kids, the Steele pack had ordered off the Three Polar Bears menu. He'd taught his younger siblings to read their first words from that menu, even though they always ordered the same thing: reindeer sausage, eggs and massive stacks of pancakes served with wild berry syrup.

These days, he opted for the salmon eggs Benedict.

Their dad always said their mom had the hardest job of all, dealing with the Steele hellions, and the least he could do was give her a surprise break. He'd rolled out that speech at the start of every breakfast, and reminded them to listen to their mom and their teachers. If there were no bad reports, then they could all go fishing with him. Looking back, Broderick realized his father had done that so they wouldn't rat each other out and would solve squabbles among themselves.

It had worked.

He and his siblings had a tight bond. A good thing, sure, but both a blessing and a curse when they'd lost one of their siblings in that plane crash along with their mom...

Even when the table was full, it felt like there was an empty place without their sister Breanna there. Sometimes they even accidentally asked for six seats.

Today, though, their uncle sat with the five remaining Steele children, pulling up an additional chair as he joined them.

Uncle Conrad, their father's brother, hadn't been a part of building the Steele oil business. He was fifteen years younger than Jack, and had been brought into the company after finishing grad school with an engineering degree. He'd been a part of the North Dakota expansion. The Steeles had started in Alaska and moved toward the Dakotas, and the Mikkelsons had grown in the reverse direction, each trying to push out the other.

Uncle Conrad reached for the coffee carafe as he scooted his chair closer to the table. "Where's my brother? He's been in hiding since those rumors started flying yesterday morning. Damn rude of him to wait so long to meet with us. Marshall, Broderick? Somebody?"

"I only just got here. I was out with the seaplane, surveying," Marshall pointed out. The family rancher, he oversaw their lands, as well as doing frequent flyovers of the pipelines.

Conrad cupped his coffee mug in his hands. "You'd think he would have returned calls from his own brother."

The youngest Steele sibling, Aiden, reached for the pitcher of syrup. "You would think so. It sucks being discounted because you're the last in line." He smiled, but it didn't reach his eyes. A thick lock of hair fell over his forehead. "Right, Uncle Rad?"

"Don't call me that, you brat. You're as bad as your brother here." Conrad gestured to Broderick. "You both carry that sardonic act a little far. We're your family. Tell us, Broderick, is it true that you and Glenna Mikkelson-Powers found your dad with…"

Conrad shuddered and took a bracing swig of coffee, then refilled his mug, emptying the carafe. He held up the silver jug and smiled at the waitress as she swept it from his hand on her way to another customer.

"I couldn't begin to say what you're all envisioning. And it was even tougher to see…" Broderick leaned toward his youngest sister.

"Tough to comprehend," Delaney responded, spooning wild berries onto her oatmeal.

Naomi, the wild child, older than Delaney and the boldest, most outspoken sibling of the pack, leaned her arms on the table. "Was he really going at it with Jeannie Mikkelson?"

"In the shower?"

"In her office?"

The questions from both brothers tumbled on top of each other.

Broderick forked up a bite of salmon and eggs. "Sounds like you don't need me to tell you anything."

Naomi slathered preserves on her toast. "What the hell is up with Dad?"

Conrad lifted his coffee mug. "Oh, I think we all know what's up."

Delaney snapped her napkin at him before draping it in her lap again. "Don't be crude."

"He's older, as am I—" Conrad waggled his eyebrows "—but not dead."

"Eww." Delaney pushed her oatmeal away, her dark

eyes widening and her nose scrunching. "Too much information."

A cluster of tourists walked by the table, cruise ship name tags on lanyards around their necks. The Steeles went silent until they passed.

Naomi tapped a pack of sweetener against her finger before opening it into her coffee. "Do you think that's all it is? An affair with a Mikkelson, the forbidden fruit?" She slanted a glance at Broderick. "I mean, you had that—"

Broderick leveled narrowed eyes at his sister and mentally cursed himself for a drunken admission in a quest for advice.

"Okay, okay." She opened another packet of sugar into her coffee. "Damn, everyone's testy around here."

"Well…" Delaney admitted softly, "I did get Dad on the phone, and while he wouldn't give me details, he admitted they're in love."

A series of hissed breaths and heavy exhalations sounded, along with silverware clanking.

"Broderick," their uncle interjected, "what do you think? You actually saw them together."

"I would say Dad's serious about her," he answered without hesitation.

"You don't think this has been going on for a long time? A very long time?" Naomi's dark brown eyebrows, already plucked to high arches, went even higher.

"Could be, but they say their feelings caught them by surprise. I choose to believe them."

"How serious do you think this is? Like…marriage? What's going to happen to the business?" Marshall forked a hand through his loose brown curls, his face full of questions.

Delaney stirred the berries through her oatmeal before spooning up a bite. "Were you able to get details about their plans? Do they want to make changes to the company's safety standards?"

Broderick shook his head. "We didn't get that deep into the discussion. Dad said he wanted to speak to all of us at the same time Jeannie Mikkelson speaks to her children, but separately."

Aiden pulled three more pancakes from the platter in the center of the table. "I'm still stuck on the fact our families hated each other for years."

"Maybe just the fathers?" Delaney asked quietly.

Broderick shook his head. He knew differently, first-hand. He and Glenna both did. "Jeannie Mikkelson was as much a part of that business as her husband. She's different from Mom."

At the mention of their mother, his siblings went silent in a new way, leaving a heavier atmosphere around the table. None of them had really come to peace with losing her or their sister Breanna in such a violent and unexpected way. A plane crash into a mountain... There hadn't been much left in the wreckage after the flames. Their father had been allowed to view the bodies, but he'd kept his children away.

Broderick could see the memories ripple across each face at the table.

Naomi finished chewing her toast and took a swallow of her coffee. "Maybe this group meeting with Dad will be a golden opportunity to get him to see that...hell, this is a mess for the business. The board will go haywire over this. The stockholders will react violently to the uncertainty."

Broderick scrubbed his hand along his jaw. "You're going to tell them to break up for the sake of profit? That's not going to float, not with our dad."

His youngest brother's eyes went wide with a hint of

fear, giving Broderick only a moment's notice before a familiar voice rumbled over his shoulder. "What's not going to float with me?"

*His father.*

Jack Steele had arrived.

# Three

Broderick carefully set aside his coffee mug as he crafted an answer for his father that wouldn't send the old man— and the table full of edgy people—spinning.

His family had a way of letting their tempers fly. Especially since the peacemakers had died…his mother, his sister. These days, Delaney often tried to rein in family squabbles, but she was only one soft voice against a tide of pushy personalities.

Just as he was about to opt for a Hail Mary distraction instead of a logical plea, he was saved from answering when Conrad stood and pulled up another chair.

"Have a seat, Jack. You're the man of the hour. We've all been on pins and needles, waiting to hear from you about your, uh, *news*." Conrad clapped his brother on the back.

"Thank you for meeting me here on such short notice." Jack waved to the waitress as he took his seat. "The usual order for me, please," he called, requesting sourdough waffles, as he had for decades. The only difference lately? These days he topped the waffles with fruit rather than syrup.

They'd gathered at this table more times than Broderick could count, until it had become a de facto family dinner table. One his father loomed large over when sitting at the head.

Being Jack's oldest son hadn't been easy. Broderick's father's boot prints in the snow were large to fill and he cast a long shadow in the business world.

But damn it all, Broderick wouldn't stand idly by and watch the Steele business be placed at risk. He knew Glenna felt the same about her family's legacy.

Strange to be on the same side with her.

Broderick watched his father with analytical eyes. He wasn't going to weigh in recklessly. He needed to wait for the right opportunity and choose his words wisely. The stakes were too high for misplaced speech. The fate of his company—and his place within the family business—depended on rationality, not impulse.

Conrad took his seat again. "Thank you for putting your clothes on for us. Poor Broderick here still looks like he needs a bracing drink."

Jack scowled, his lips so tight his mustache all but hid them. "You can zip your mouth, brother."

Conrad smiled unabashedly. "Do we really want to talk about zippers right now?"

Leaning back in his chair, Jack crossed his arms over his chest. "My sense of humor on this has run out. You're being disrespectful to Jeannie and I won't stand for that."

"Fair enough," Conrad conceded. "You have to understand we're all more than a little stunned by what's transpired."

To hell with waiting. Broderick saw the opening to take

control of this conversation, not only for his family's sake but also for Glenna's. "We grew up believing our families to be enemies. I can't count how many times I've heard you curse both of them—Jeannie and Charles Mikkelson."

"Things change," Jack said simply, pouring a mug of coffee. The statement was casual, as normal as the black coffee he had drunk every day for as long as Broderick could remember. "I don't have to explain myself to any of you, but I will say that Jeannie and I love each other. Very much. We intend to be married—"

"Married?" Aiden interrupted, his voice cracking on the word.

Everyone else stared in stunned silence, then looked at Broderick as if he'd kept a secret from them. Shaking his head, he pressed his fingers to his temples against the headache forming. He'd had no sleep, instead wondering how serious his father's relationship with Jeannie really was, if it might wane with time. A litany of questions had kept him awake. Not to mention being tormented by visions of Glenna in that tight skirt every time he closed his eyes. Seeing her again had brought back memories, vivid ones.

"Yes," Jack confirmed, in a no-nonsense tone, the kind he'd used on his children when they were younger, "married. Sooner rather than later, especially now that our secret is out. Jeannie and I discussed it at length last night, which was why we didn't answer any of your phone calls."

Broderick focused on a crucial word in his father's answer. "Sooner?"

"Yes, now that you know, why wait for the perfect time to break the news? Jeannie and I *had* planned to tell our children in a more…prepared, controlled manner this weekend. But yesterday afternoon's events forced our hand. Jeannie is speaking with her children now." He glanced at Broderick. "As I'm sure you already know from talking to Glenna."

The mere mention of the Mikkelson CFO drew a few raised eyebrows at the table. His siblings looked at him with sidelong glances, understanding that their father had tipped the balance of power in the conversation. Shifting slightly in his chair, Broderick pushed the image of Glenna and her sunset-blond hair out of his mind. Far away.

Broderick had no intention of letting his father distract them from the topic at hand. After all, the old man had taught that diversionary tactic to each of his kids.

Leaning forward with elbows pressed on the wood table, Broderick levied his own power. "Let's stay on target, Dad. You're here to fill us in on your engagement plans to a woman we thought you didn't like. Do I have that right?"

"More than engagement plans. As I said, we are getting married." His tone was as stern and certain as an Alaskan winter.

"A long engagement?" Broderick said it hopefully.

The extra time would give their relationship a chance to cool. Perhaps even allow Jack to see the madness of this whole situation. To really evaluate what this meant for their companies.

Jack's eyes warmed, wistful and sentimental. Something Broderick hadn't seen in his father's expression since before the plane crash.

"*Short* engagement."

"How short?" Naomi asked. She was more of a daddy's girl than she liked to let on.

Jack waited until the waitress set his waffles in front of him and walked away before he continued. "Jeannie and I are getting married on my birthday. Surefire way I'll never forget my anniversary." A smile cracked his wind-weath-

ered face and a slight chuckle escaped his mustached lips.
Jack had clearly amused himself.

The hair stood up on the back of Broderick's neck. A
guttural, visceral reaction to the realization of what his
father was saying. "Your birthday is—"

"In two weeks." Jack's chin dipped with a quick affirmation.

"Oh God," Naomi whispered, but every member of the
Steele clan felt the words echo deep in the pit of their
stomachs.

Broderick sagged back in his chair. He sure as hell
hadn't seen that coming. Anger simmered deep in his gut.
He'd let go of Glenna after one of the most memorable
weekends of his life because of family loyalty. Even now,
when he should be concentrating, he could almost taste her
full lips… And yet he had pushed their attraction aside.
He'd given everything for the Steele mantra of *Family
Above All Else.*

Where was family loyalty now?

The anger kept his mouth closed tight. He didn't trust
himself to speak and not say something he would later
regret. His siblings had no such problems. Their shocked
words tumbled on top of each other in a jumble that made
it tough to gauge who said what.

Broderick pried his thoughts away from Glenna and
back to the future of the Steele oil empire. "And the business leaks about stock sales? Does someone else already
know about your relationship? If you've been meeting in
the office, then others may already be talking. Dad, you
have to know the implications to the fiscal health of both
companies."

"Yes, about that…" Jack sawed into his waffles and
speared a bite. "We want to work with you all on a presentation to the board for our plans to blend the companies."

Blend?

*Blend* the companies?

Normal businesses could blend. But this would be like combining flint and matchsticks. This was fire, an explosion—the end result possibly destroying everything they'd built.

The confirmation of Broderick's worst fear since he'd learned of those damned stock purchases stoked the flames of his anger to a full blaze. In a simple sentence, a single revelation, his father was risking what Broderick had devoted his entire adult life to preserving and growing.

"Blending the companies? As in blending everything? You can't just expect that we'll—I'll—accept that."

Jack leaned in nose to nose with his oldest son, a gesture of dominance. "That is exactly what I expect. I'm still the majority shareholder in Steele Industries, and Jeannie is majority shareholder in her company, as well. The board may have concerns. You and Glenna may have concerns. But Jeannie and I have thought this through. It's time for the feud to end. We *are* merging the companies. She and I are prepared do whatever is necessary to make that happen. You can join forces to make us a more powerful entity, or you can cash in your portion and I'll buy it at fair market value. Your choice."

"Think about what you're saying, brother," Conrad hissed in alarm, placing a hand on Jack's arm. "Are you prepared to cut out your children? Your flesh and blood?"

Broderick was wondering the same thing. If his father expected him to surrender their company without a fight, then his old man was going to be very surprised.

Jack chewed thoughtfully. "I did not say anything about cutting anyone out. I said if anyone wants to walk away from the business, they can. Family will always be welcome in my home."

Marshall spoke up. "And what about our jobs? Our family land, our heritage?"

"You're getting ahead of yourself, talking about things we haven't gotten to yet," Jack explained, looking too much at peace, considering he'd overturned their whole world. "Restructuring will create opportunities, too."

*Restructuring?* The word casually rolled off his tongue in the manner of someone mentioning that Alaska was cold this time of year.

The word knocked around inside Broderick's head for all of five seconds before gelling into an image that would create utter chaos for the Steeles and the Mikkelsons, both personally and professionally.

"Dad, I've given this same talk to employees on their way out the door."

His father smiled with a hard-nosed determination they'd all seen before. "Then that gives you an edge that will put you in the running to be CFO of the whole operation."

Just when Broderick thought his world couldn't be any more upended, he learned otherwise. Because his father had left no room for misunderstanding.

It was Broderick or Glenna for CFO. One of them would be ousting the other.

"I hope you don't mind that I brought my puppy."

Kneeling, Glenna nuzzled her face into the fluffy husky puppy sitting pretty in front of her. Her heart filled with tenderness for her pup, such a source of comfort and joy after her husband's death.

Feeling the weight of eyes on her, she glanced up to find Broderick studying her intently from the other side of his office. Electricity danced in the air between them.

"I don't mind a bit," he answered. "What's the little guy's name?"

"Kota. As in Dakota." She unhooked the leash and stood, monitoring Kota as he sniffed around the room. The dog sniffed the leather boots curiously. The husky pup stood at attention next to the sleek black chair, glacier-blue eyes trained on Broderick.

Clearing his throat, he walked around his desk to a minibar, pulled out a sparkling water that had been bottled locally from the Kalal glacier. The fizz and bubbles jumped around the glasses as he poured.

For a microsecond, she caught his gaze and it sent tingles down her spine, flooding her awareness. Images drifted into her mind that she knew she had to temper. This was business.

"Thank you for understanding. Kota was at doggy day care while I was at work, and even though I know he's cared for, I still want him to know me." She ruffled Kota's black-and-white head.

"He's a great pup, well behaved. You're clearly doing a good job. I don't mind at all," Broderick answered. They'd been number crunching for an hour, so far all business, leaving personal matters undiscussed.

Never in her wildest dreams would Glenna have guessed that in the span of thirty-six hours Broderick would storm back into her life again and she would then be working with him.

But that had been her mother's firm request after dropping her bombshell about the companies merging. She wanted a joint report.

"How did your meeting with your siblings and your mom go?" His whiskey-warm tones tingled through Glenna's veins like a hot toddy on a snowy day.

Glenna focused on her puppy, who was staring up at

her with ice-blue eyes, trusting and pure. "Well, that's a complex question. I'm not sure we got a true read on things, since the conversation was on speakerphone. My younger brother's plane had trouble making it in from North Dakota. Everyone on the line stayed quietly civil during the news."

"That's good, though, isn't it?" Broderick said, leaning toward her.

She raised her eyebrows in answer and shrugged. "I'm cautious in saying for sure, because I fear an explosion could happen later."

In person.

And that storm would be unforgiving, filled with emotion and lengthy, loud conversations that would send the dogs and cats at the ranch house fleeing under tables and chairs.

Ice clinked and drew her attention to Broderick, who was preparing their water glasses with slices of lime. Then he dumped the candy out of a crystal dish and filled the empty bowl with the rest of the water.

The thoughtfulness, the precious gesture for her pet, melted her heart faster than sun baking a snowman. "My oldest brother, Charles, sounded calm, most likely thanks to his wife. I could tell, though, his teeth were grinding on the other end of the phone. Trystan, well, he's gruff but quiet, so who knows."

"And your baby sister?" He placed the glasses and bowl on a tray before returning to the table in the corner, not a full-out conference table, rather more of a cozy meeting area. Not nearly large enough for her liking right now.

"Alayna's a peacemaker. So unless I'm looking into her eyes, I don't know for sure." She reached for the glass, her hand brushing his. Crackles of awareness sparked along her every nerve. She took a quick swallow of water to cover her nervousness. "Thank you for this."

"I've ordered food to be brought up. If you're starving now the minibar has some granola bars—"

"This is fine. Thanks. I'll wait."

"I ordered extra. We have a long night ahead of us."

Her gaze shot to his, searching for a double entendre, but his eyes were serious tonight. None of the teasing from that first day in her office was visible.

It had been a sobering three days since then. "I'm not sure how we're supposed to do this."

She jabbed a pencil into her loose topknot. "How do we work together while protecting the interest of both companies?"

"One company, if we can take what our parents said at face value." He knelt to offer Kota the crystal bowl of water.

"I don't understand how they expect the employees to get over decades of secrecy agreements and distrust. I'm not sure how we're all supposed to get over it."

"I don't think we have a choice in the matter." The tenor of his voice struck something in her.

Only the sound of Kota lapping water and icy rain beating against the windows cut through the silence.

She drummed her fingers along the edge of her laptop, still not sure how much to share in spite of what her mother had said. But Jeannie and Jack wanted a board of directors' packet to reassure investors, and that would require Glenna and Broderick working together. "How did the meeting go with your father and your family?"

"Stunned surprise."

She lowered the laptop screen, sliding back in her leather seat. "Not a surplus of congratulations, huh?"

"We're all still in shock."

"Less than an hour after the call, my sister-in-law and baby sister started sending out texts about organizing an impromptu shower or bachelorette party or something like that for the females in both families. Made me feel bad for not jumping on board with the congrats and felicitations."

"You have to remember that they weren't blinded by the—"

"Right. Don't remind me. I feel bad about my reaction. My mother's an adult. She's entitled to her own life. It's just tough to turn on a dime and see this relationship positively, after a lifetime of our parents bad-mouthing the business practices of the other family."

He flipped a pencil over and over, tapping it on the tabletop rhythmically. She watched it linger between his fingers, mesmerized by the small, controlled gesture. Only the challenge in his voice broke her trance. "The business practices? What exactly do you object to in the way we do business?"

"I'm not trying to pick a fight." Her voice rose, and her puppy sat up, whining. "We're going to have to sort this out."

"No. We just have to come up with a cohesive plan for the financials that we can present to the board. Ways to combine assets while preserving jobs."

She snapped her fingers for Kota to come to her. "And staying on track for a pipeline."

He dovetailed on her thoughts. "Building it faster and safer, to pipe more and be competitive. It's a matter of self-preservation. Our parents haven't given us any choice."

"Right, of course." She stroked her puppy's back, the fluffy texture of his freshly washed coat soothing.

And she could definitely use all the comfort she could get right now, being closeted in this room with Broderick. Her senses were on overload from the fresh cedar scent of his aftershave, teasing and tempting her every breath. Her body wanted him...but her mind rebelled.

She still grieved for her dead husband. She'd loved him during their marriage. She'd loved him through every conflict as they'd worked so damn hard on their relationship. Yet on an earthy level, her body ached for closeness with a man. With Broderick.

Inhaling, she shivered at the delicious tingle of his scent even as she resented the tightening of her nipples. "Do you ever want more than...this? The job, the office?"

"No," he answered without hesitation. "Does that mean you do want more? What would that be?"

Was it just her wayward imagination or had his voice lowered to an intimate level on that last question? His eyes locked on hers with a heat that seared right through her.

Her heart slugged faster in her chest even as she fought for composure. A professional distance.

"Oh, you're not getting rid of me that easily. My job's not up for grabs." She pulled the pen from her hair and pointed it his way. "And neither am I."

She needed to remind herself as much as she needed to tell him.

*Hands off Broderick Steele*, she reminded herself.

"Why not? The wall's been torn down." He gave her a truly quizzical look, as if he was genuinely considering the idea and not just flirting.

Something about his tone made her wary. And very, very hot.

She breathed deep, too aware of her body's every response to this man.

"No, no, stop right there. From the minute you walked in my office door three days ago, you've been filling what you say with sexual overtones." She had to halt this line of discussion before she started questioning if maybe he had a point. "Now more than ever, sex between us would complicate things."

"How so?" That sly grin formed dimples in his cheeks.

"You're smarter than that." She looked down, shaking her head while pretending to scrutinize his boots. "We don't need to add more tension to an already strained situation. We're not college students who've had a bit too much to drink at a party."

"You're right. We're not rebellious kids. We're adults who know exactly what's going on. Our parents are getting married. We'll likely have to share Christmas dinner year after year. That's a fact." He leaned closer to her, across the table. His musky scent mingled with the playful growl in his voice. "But there's always the mistletoe."

At the mention of such a cozy scene, the fire in her belly cooled. The image he painted was too...personal. "This isn't funny. You're sexy as hell, and clearly, I'm attracted to you. But I've lost enough. I'm not going to risk losing my job and my family, too."

"I like hearing that the attraction is mutual." He twined his fingers with hers on top of her puppy.

"Again, I will say, you're a smart man. You had to know." Her fingers curled for an instant before she pulled away.

"I didn't, not for sure. You made a hasty run for the door all those years ago after what I thought was an incredible weekend."

"It was...memorable," she said, then rushed to add, "in a good way. But we can both see now how difficult that would have been. Think how impossible it feels to have your dad marry my mom. How tough would it have been back then after that impulsive weekend to combat our families' feuds?"

"And after that you got married." A flatness entered his voice.

"Yes, I did." She tipped her chin defiantly, then tried to lighten the mood. "And you have to admit your reputation as a ladies' man is well earned. Those tabloid articles can't be all rumor."

"The gossips are going to be busy enough right now with my father and your mother. I don't think they'll have time left over for the two of us." He skimmed his knuckles along her cheek in a flash of sensation before returning to his computer. "Think about it."

There was no missing the invitation in his eyes. The attraction echoed inside her. And as lonely as she'd been, her body ached for the simple touch of a man. This man.

But no.

With Broderick, it would be more than a touch.

And it would never be simple.

# Four

Jack Steele had known it would be tough getting his off-spring and Jeannie's adult children on board with merging their two warring companies. But hell's bells, he hadn't expected such a massive wall of bullheaded resistance.

His redwood mansion in the distance now, he settled deeper into the saddle, hoping the quarter horse's rhythmic gait crunching through snow would settle his frustration. Riding had saved him from losing his cool more than once. In fact, riding had saved his sanity after his wife and daughter died in that plane crash. The open sky was his sanctuary, day or night.

Right now, the sun glistened off the snowcapped trees and mountains. Glistened off Jeannie's hair as she rode beside him. He'd dreamed of taking her horseback riding once they could be seen in public together. Another reason he should be happy, but the world was topsy-turvy.

Jack gripped the reins loosely in his hands. He'd saddled

up the Paint—Willow—for Jeannie. She was a natural. Just as he'd known she would be. The sunshine brought out the lighter shades in her golden hair, which was slipping free from the hood of her parka. She perched confidently in the saddle, the gentle curves of her slim body calling to him. The cinched waist of her parka. Her long legs that made him think of how much he would enjoy tugging off her boots, her jeans and silk leggings.

He would never forget that moment six months ago when they'd found themselves alone at a business conference in Juneau. He'd looked at her. She'd looked at him.

And the world had changed.

He'd felt it. Seen it echoed in her eyes. He'd asked her to have a drink with him. She'd said yes…and here they were. Together. Committed.

Clearing his throat with a breath of icy air, he returned his attention to the present. To the ride. His first with Jeannie. He could envision many more such outings in their future.

Once they settled the controversy between their children.

Damn it all. He scrubbed his gloved hand under the lamb's wool collar of his coat. He and Jeannie were adults, for God's sake. Their spouses had died years ago. He wasn't ready to crawl in the grave, not by a longshot.

Maybe if he'd found someone else, someone without the surname Mikkelson… But life had always thrown him curve balls, and apparently, his love life wasn't any different. Knowing how precious happiness was made him all the more determined to enjoy what he'd found.

He glanced at Jeannie as she swayed alongside him, so regally beautiful she threatened to steal his breath all over again. "Thank you for coming today, to my home."

She smiled back at him. "Our home, soon."

"That it will be." He still couldn't believe she'd agreed to leave her own home for his. "We could build a place of our own, if you wish, or if you think it would make things easier for your children."

She scanned the stretch of land from his sprawling mansion to the seaplane bobbing on the lake. "This place is lovely. I promise I'll be slow in putting my own stamp on things so as not to upset the Steele applecart."

"It's your home, too," he said firmly. "Your choices are mine."

Her exhalations puffed a cloud of white into the afternoon air. "If only it could be that simple. Are you sure you're prepared for this fight? For what it could cost us?"

"Nothing in life has come easily for me or mine. My children are made of tougher stuff. Once they get past the surprise—"

"Shock," Jeannie corrected.

"Well, that's one way of putting it." He couldn't hold back his chuckle at the memory of Broderick's and Glenna's faces when they'd opened that bathroom door. "They certainly didn't learn in the gradual way we'd planned."

Jeannie laughed along with him, the sound of their voices floating together on the wind. Damn, he was getting downright poetic these days.

Love did that to a man.

He reached for the reins to Jeannie's horse and guided both animals to a stop. He reached out to stroke back Jeannie's hair and tuck it into her hood, then cupped her neck. "What we've found together is a gift."

Her blue eyes glistened with tears and she touched his wrist, squeezing. "One I didn't expect to have again."

"And one I'm not giving up," he said without hesitation.

"Even if it threatens your business?"

"Even if it threatens yours?"

"Ours," she answered with a smile. "Like the houses."

"Exactly." He slid his hand down to grip her waist, then lifted her from the horse and onto his lap.

"We are a team now." She looped her arms around his neck, leaning against him. "This is real."

"Yes, my dear, it is very real." As real as his growing need to have her right now. But this was more than an affair. He loved her. "Our families need to get on board with our engagement. No more separate explanations, separate family meetings. They have to learn how to be together if the business merger stands a chance at working."

"You're right." She kissed him once, twice, enticing as hell. "And the sooner the better. For them as well as for us, because I love you, Jack Steele."

"I know you do. I love you, too, lady." He hugged her closer, securing both sets of reins in his fist. "And you know what else?"

"Do tell?"

"I want you. Right now."

And lucky for them, the plane hangar was very, very close.

Glenna clutched the edge of her chair. She was in the glassed-in sunroom at the Steele family lodge for their first big co-family gathering. It was so surreal.

Not that it was a completely blended family get-together. The women sat on different sides of the room, based on family affiliation. Glenna and Alayna stayed closer to their mother, along with their sister-in-law, Shana. Whereas the two Steele hostesses, Naomi and Delaney, stood like bookends near the wet bar, so alike in appearance even if opposite in temperament, Naomi being a partying wild spirit, Delaney an intensely serious green-issues crusader.

The men were outside, horseback riding on a sunny day

that melted snow into a glistening display. It could have been a gathering at Glenna's mother's home—her parents' home—except more than double the people were present.

Through the window she could see her two brothers riding expertly alongside the five Steele men. But Broderick drew her eyes most today, his Stetson a hint higher than the others since he was so tall. His collar was flipped up, with the lamb's wool against his ears. His hand held the reins loosely, confidently.

Broderick's bay quarter horse, Abacus, demanded nearly as much attention as his rider. They were a matched set. Dark, muscular—commanding. Even the way the bay tossed his mane said something of his wild, albeit tempered, nature. The two moved like one, almost as if Broderick's soul had been fused to the bay. Every response, every turn seemed to happen from instinct.

Was there anything this man couldn't handle?

Glenna's hand dropped to Kota, stroking the puppy's fur for comfort. Each touch of his coat soothed her ragged nerves.

She'd thought about Broderick's proposition again and again throughout the night. But they weren't two strangers meeting for the first time, with no entanglements. He had to understand they couldn't just resume where they'd left off long ago.

But if she *were* meeting him for the first time?

Her gaze wandered back to the sight of him tall and strong on horseback. Her stomach lurched with awareness—and apprehension.

Yes, even if she were meeting him for the first time right now, she would still run. Because truth be told, this attraction was more than she could risk. Her emotions had to be off-limits. Losing her husband had already decimated her heart.

Glenna drew her attention back to the rustic luxury of the sunroom, a room that was the direct opposite of the Steeles' sleek office space. Fat leather chairs and sofas filled the expansive, light-filled room. Rafters soared upward, dotted with skylights, as well as lantern-style lights for the long winter nights. One stone wall held a fireplace crackling with flames. Elk antlers hung above the mantel. The wet bar was laden with snacks and drinks.

The room was packed with wary women, gathered at the edict of Jeannie and Jack.

Glenna's sister-in-law, Shana shot to her feet. "We're going to play a party game. I reached out to Naomi and we've come up with some icebreakers to help us all—" she gestured weakly "—get over the *newness* of this."

Well now, wasn't that diplomatic? Kudos to Shana.

Jeannie waved from a log-style rocking chair. "Please, not one of those wedding shower games where we all end up wearing silly hats covered with bows."

Glenna's baby sister winced. "Or please say we don't have to tell lies and truths and guess. I never win those because people can always tell when I'm lying."

Edgy, Naomi stood, wearing brown leather leggings with a thick Sherpa vest. "We're going to play the dating game."

Alayna frowned, peering around the room at each woman. "But she's already engaged, and she's already married, and I suspect that she—"

"No," Naomi stated, "this is a different sort of dating game. I've been consulting with a company that helps people write their bios for online dating sites—"

Her sister chuckled. "You've done *what*?"

"You heard me, Delaney. Guys in particular have a tough time expressing themselves with words, so they ask for help. It's like marketing or editing. I have some samples and we're going to figure out who's for real and who's a poser."

Shana gathered her thick caramel-colored mane and tossed it over her shoulders. "Like the kind of guy who hangs out in a bar and claims to be an astronaut."

"Great example." Naomi walked to a corner table with the laptop computer connected to three wide screen televisions. "The names have been changed to protect the guys. Now are we ready to play the game?"

A dating game? Glenna would rather do the polar bear plunge, jumping naked into icy water. But she said, "Let's get started." So they would be done all the sooner and she could go home, away from this awkward gathering and the tempting view of Broderick as his horse galloped along the fence line.

Shana clapped her hands. "Good. Here are the rules. One point for every warning sign, five points if you can catch an outright lie."

Delaney's expression said she was clearly not sold yet. Glenna wasn't, either; her eyes kept returning to the window, to the wild scenery and the precision with which Broderick moved with his horse.

"I was thinking for each correct guess, pick your poison for someone or yourself—a champagne Jell-O shot or a chocolate truffle?" Shana suggested.

Forcing herself back into the present moment, Glenna decided to be helpful. "Where are the truffles and alcohol?"

Naomi and Shana each swept a silver cover off a platter just as the wide screen televisions hummed to life. Each TV went to split screen, with multiple profiles.

"Oh, oh!" Her cousin Sage's hand shot into the air. "Well, this is easy enough. I see five guys with creepster in their profile name. Like 'Legman.' Four guys reference their penis length."

"Eww." Alayna shook her head. "And there are two with 'hard' in their name." Both she and Sage rushed to the minibar and popped an assortment of champagne Jell-O shots and truffles into their mouths. They savored them with closed eyes, *yums* and *mmms*.

Glenna crossed her arms tightly over her chest. "Do guys really think we go for that level of slime?" She pointed to another screen. "The guys on the left side appear real."

Yes, for the moment, she would play this game and drink a little champagne, then she'd be on her way.

Her eyes went to Broderick again. She wasn't in any condition to be in the same room with him once the men came back inside. She'd spent so much time with him this week, she couldn't handle being in this house with him surrounded by family. It was too close to the cozy mistletoe image he'd painted for her back in his office.

Naomi nodded. "Well done, future stepsister. Help yourself to the treats."

Stepsister? Glenna made a beeline for the champagne shots. Another mark on the why-anything-with-Broderick would be infinitely complicated. The sweet, slippery shot with a kick sent a delicious tingle along her senses. Yes. Just what she needed. This would be her treat of choice for the duration of the game.

Especially if she expected to get through an evening with Broderick and keep her sanity.

"I'm sure there are good ones out there, too. Honest ones." Glenna considered another shot, just for the hell of it.

"We could do a percentage chart of how many there are, and I'm guessing it will all average out. The point here is to be wise, ladies. Be wise."

Naomi snorted. "Or stay single."

Shana laughed. "Cynic."

"Realist." Naomi waved to the minibar. "Please help yourself to the food before the men return."

"What?" Alayna stood, swaying a little, clearly a drinking lightweight. "That's it?"

"Would you have preferred a male stripper?" Naomi's laugh was hoarse and deep. Genuine. Glenna liked her honesty.

"Let it be known for the record," Naomi continued, winking with playful mischief that almost hid the tension in her face, a tension echoed in all of them at this forced gathering. "I would have voted for a stripper, a cowboy. Or at the very least a lingerie shower, but your sister-in-law shot down those ideas."

Shana shrugged. "I wasn't sure Jeannie would approve. Now, let's enjoy this amazing food. The Steeles' chef is truly exceptional I have to say. Jeannie? A Jell-O shot?"

Jeannie shook her head, her shoulder-length hair brushing her shoulders in a blond-gray echo of her children's coloring.

Alayna stumbled over and gripped her mother's arm. "You're not pregnant, are you, Mom? Do we need to have a talk with you before the wedding?"

Glenna's thoughts winged back to the night before her own wedding. Her mom and sisters had gathered around her as they ate ice cream and watched chick flicks. Nostalgia and regret rolled over her.

Jeannie patted Alayna's hand, dismissive and amused. The matriarch winked. "I think I've got that covered."

"Clearly." Glenna's mind skipped over the images of that fateful walk in and moved right to memories of a similar shower moment with Broderick back in college. God, she needed to speed this party along, snag her coat and leave. "Perhaps you could give us some notes—"

The burgeoning camaraderie was cut short by a swelling of voices outside. Louder and louder, even shouting. Glenna shot to her feet, searching through the windows. The men were sliding from their horses beside a Range Rover. A young woman stood beside the car, holding a baby swaddled in a pink parka.

Curiosity brought Glenna to the edge of her seat, her eyes drawn to that precious bundle. Murmurs filled the sunroom, but Glenna only half heard. Her gaze was still trained beyond the windows. Before she could question the wisdom of her action, she stood and reached for her white wool coat and cashmere scarf.

Two guards raced from the fence line, closing in on the group of men dismounting.

Inside, the other women at the party gathered up their coats, too, without a break in their buzz of chatter, but Glenna led the pack, being the closest to the exit. She tugged on her coat and pulled open the door. A blast of crisp air washed over her.

Voices carried on the breeze.

"Ma'am." Conrad held up two hands. "I've never touched you."

What the hell? Glenna's eyes shifted back to the baby, her heart aching as it always did when she saw a child, given the loss of so many pregnancies. She'd never even made it to the second trimester. Never felt life move inside her.

The stranger jostled the baby on her hip and fished an envelope from her jacket pocket. "I'm not little Fleur's mother. I work for Mr. Steele—the senior Mr. Steele. Someone—I don't know how—left the baby in the barn and I found her while I was refilling the food and water troughs for your return. Security is still trying to figure out how the baby was brought in. But there was a note on top of her…"

Jack took the envelope from her hand, glanced at the outside. Blinking fast, he looked sharply at Broderick, then Glenna, giving only a moment's heart-stopping warning before he announced, "It's addressed to Broderick...and Glenna."

# Five

Glenna's stomach clenched as Jack read the outside of the envelope...addressed to her and Broderick?

Gasps rippled through the family crowded around her, sending puffs into the cold air. She glanced at Broderick, but found no answers on his handsome face. He looked as puzzled as she felt. He rubbed his temple, just under the brim of his Stetson.

Glenna pulled her gaze away from his strong, beard-stubbled jaw. What did this child have to do with her? With both of them? Even as she thought the question, she couldn't help but reach for the little bundle in a pink parka and a blanket. The sweet weight settling into her arms was a precious, squirming joy. Her heart swelled. She stroked a knuckle along the cherub's cheek. Wide blue eyes blinked up at her, the tiny mouth sucking on a pacifier.

She felt Broderick step up behind her, his boots crunching through the snow. She glanced back to see him look over her shoulder at the baby, then over at Jack, who was still staring at the letter.

Glenna hugged the child closer, the pink blanket trailing from her arms. "What does the note say?"

The paper crackled as Jack handed it back to the secretary who handled it carefully, as if preserving evidence, and then withdrew a sheet of paper. A swirly scrawl filled the pristine white surface. "Um, sir…" The woman from the barn passed the paper to Jack Steele. "You may want to read this. I'm not comfortable with, um, well…"

A hint of snow started whispering from the sky as Jack took the paper and then pulled a second typed document from the envelope, scanning both while tipping them for Jeannie to see. "The note says she isn't sure who the baby's father is," he reported. "She sent a birth certificate for a three-month-old baby named Fleur Wilson. It lists the mother's name as Deborah Wilson…"

Jack looked over his glasses at his oldest son and Broderick's eyebrows shot up. Tellingly so. Glenna swallowed hard. The name was unfamiliar to her, though.

Jack glanced down, swiped a few snowflakes from his glasses and continued. "She goes on to write there's no use in looking for her. She's already in Canada and will contact us when she's ready. But for now, she wants her child to be with family." He cleared his throat. "Her message says she isn't sure if the father is Broderick or…"

Jeannie rested a hand on his shoulder, took the papers and walked over to her daughter, worry was stamped across the older woman's face. "Glenna, the note says the father could also be Gage. I'm sorry to even have to say that out loud."

Glenna bit back a gasp. Her dead husband could be the father of this child?

Even with the gentle voice of her mother delivering the

words, Glenna felt the blow of each syllable in her gut. She gasped in a gulp of the crisp air, swaying and forcing to herself to hold on to the baby more securely. She felt the weight of so many eyes on her, this strange mix of family and long-time enemies as she processed news that threatened to bring her to her knees.

Silence reigned, as if the group held their collective breath. Behind her, she heard the snort and stamp of one of the horses.

In some distant part of her consciousness, she realized that Broderick had placed a steadying hand on her waist. Surely he had to be staggering at this revelation, too. She looked into the baby's face, searching the features for a magic clue to the parentage. She eased back the baby's hood and knit cap to find light brown hair. No real clue there. She shielded the tiny face with her hand to keep the snowflakes from landing.

It seemed the more she stared at the infant, the more this little girl became her own person. With each passing second, her face became more distinctly different from Gage's or Broderick's.

Glenna shook her head while swaying to rock the baby. The swishing movement calmed her as much as it did the little babe. With a slow exhalation, she said, "It's okay." The words steadied her. "Don't tiptoe around or worry about what needs to be said. The most important thing is that we focus on this child and making sure she's safe and healthy."

Broderick nodded tightly. "We should contact the police. She could be a kidnapped child."

"Oh, God," Glenna gasped, and studied the baby's face again. Such innocence, unaware of the chaos in her world. Thank God. "I never considered that possibility. We should check with the authorities."

Broderick's brother Marshall—the middle Steele son—took the papers from Jeannie. "I'll meet with our security team here and we'll contact the police. We can find out if there are missing child alerts, and let them know the baby is here."

"Thank you, son," Jack said.

Glenna's mind began to clear. "We should go inside where it's warm and dry. We also need to make sure she has fresh formula." She found comfort in taking control as she charged toward the towering redwood mansion. "I'm assuming the note doesn't say when she ate last. She could be hungry any moment now, and she's been through enough change without having to be uncomfortable for even an instant."

Broderick scooped up a pink checkered diaper bag and walked beside her. "Apparently, she came with this." He unzipped the sack. "It looks like there are some of her things inside."

What was he thinking right now? This could be his child. Had that registered with him? Glenna couldn't envision him as a single father.

Truly, she couldn't envision much of anything at the moment. "I'm not sure I trust anything dropped off by a stranger who dumped her baby with people the poor little tyke has never met. At least we can use the formula brand to go shopping." She climbed the wooden steps to the back deck of the Steele mansion, all too aware of Broderick's bracing hand on her back. A steadying and unsettling assurance all at once. "Bottom line, this baby is an innocent and she needs our help."

Her thoughts winged fast to the reality of sharing this baby with Broderick, even for a short time. She couldn't help but feel the strength of his touch, and yes, a tingle of awareness where each of his fingers settled on her back. He would make a powerful partner for a woman.

And she couldn't deny that seeing him in this new light was flipping her world upside down.

Broderick paced around the lodge's great room.

Even in this expansive space, he felt caged in, waiting for Glenna to join him with the baby…

The baby.

Potentially *his* baby.

Fleur.

He didn't know what he thought about the possibility of being a father. Of what this would mean for his attraction to Glenna or the fact that he wanted to pursue her even in the middle of family drama.

He couldn't help but think about the possessiveness he'd felt earlier when he'd placed his arm around Glenna. Seeing the way she cradled the child—possibly *his* child—had burned through him with a fierceness that rattled him even now.

Each successive lap on the thick rug brought more questions, more unease.

Every stable aspect of his life had been yanked from him in a very short time.

Boots thudding off the carpet, Broderick made his way to the stone fireplace. Flames danced along the logs, casting orange-tinged shadows in the room lit only by a small table lamp.

A stranger walking in would mistake the space as soothing and luxurious. But right now, tension hummed so palpably through Broderick that he was sure it filled the space around him.

And he wasn't sure how to fix the world again.

He paused in front of the fireplace, kneeling to stoke

the flames to a crackling blaze. One of the logs settled with a shower of sparks.

Hungry for normalcy, he surveyed the room. The fireplace wall was dominated by massive moose antlers—a family heirloom that had belonged to his great-grandfather when Steele Industries was just getting started. Back when Alaska was a wilderness to be conquered. Tall ceilings normally provided an airy balance to the thick leather sofas that filled the room, but did nothing to alleviate the pressure and confusion jackhammering in Broderick's mind.

Pacing again, he wandered with determined footfalls to the other side of the room, to a painting of an Alaskan forest. He was no art aficionado, but he appreciated the vivid colors and strong brushstrokes that seemed to capture so perfectly the nuance of light in early springtime.

Some of the family had gone with Glenna's sister-in-law to the store to get supplies for the baby. Other members were in the kitchen putting together food for the adults, as the evening threatened to stretch beyond the hours allotted for the party. His father and his father's *fiancée*, a word Broderick still had to get used to associating with Jeannie, had given Glenna and Broderick the chance to speak privately. Here, in this room, where he was waiting and pacing.

Raking his hand through his hair, he let out a sigh at the exact moment he heard the door click open.

Spinning around, he saw Glenna, baby in tow.

Damn.

Glenna was always stunning. For as long as he had known her, her slender frame and bright eyes had drawn him in. As did her intelligence and generosity. All the layers that made her Glenna were undeniably attractive.

But seeing her with the baby sent his heart pounding. This was a softer side of Glenna he'd never glimpsed up

close before. A tender, nurturing side that made him…
damn. He didn't know. He'd never been with a woman
who looked like that.

In his gut, he felt a stirring. He wanted to protect his
potential child.

And Glenna.

Her smooth voice interrupted his staring. "Fleur's
calmer now, and I imagine once she eats she'll sleep for
the night."

Sitting in a plush padded rocking chair, she settled herself with the baby. A heavy sigh slid from Glenna's lips as
she gave him a weary but valiant smile.

Broderick crossed to the sofa adjacent to her, his leg
brushing hers. Even with the barrier of his jeans and her
wool slacks, he could still remember the feel of her skin. A
hint of her almond scent teased his senses and threatened
to distract him, making him want to lean closer and inhale.

And now wasn't that distracting as hell?

He gathered his thoughts and sat. "I think we're all
in agreement that you and I need to talk." He glanced at
his boots, the leather still damp from his ride earlier. The
world had gone haywire in less time than it took water to
evaporate. "As awkward as this is, we need to know what
we're facing, depending on whose child this is."

The weight of those words hit Broderick as he fully
realized how awful this had to be for Glenna. He'd been
so wrapped up in his own shock, he hadn't thought about
how hurtful this had to be for her. "God, Glenna. I'm sorry.
This has to be painful for you. I assume since you haven't
shut this paternity question down altogether, there's a possibility the baby is Gage's?"

Her brow furrowing, she shook her head, a whisper
of blond hair escaping her loose topknot and grazing her
cheek. "I don't know for sure. We were having a…rough

patch. It's not…impossible that she could be his. But I have no knowledge of her and he certainly never mentioned any pregnancy."

Her eyes looked past him, drifting to the painting of the Alaskan forest. A moment of weariness flashed over her face, but he watched her quickly gather her composure, a skill developed in boardroom meetings. Her attention returned to the baby. Smiling again, she rocked the tiny girl gently.

"I'm sorry about the problems you and your husband had." And he was. If this was indeed Gage's child…

"Me, too. But you can tuck away your pity for me and save it for Fleur." Glenna looked up from the baby. "And you? You didn't shout 'hell no, not my kid.'"

"It's possible." He had to admit it. "I met Deborah Wilson when she came up here to do a series of articles on the likelihood of us pursuing a pipeline. She and I went out. It wasn't serious. But there is a possibility. Not probable, since I was only with her once and we, um, used protection. But then nothing's one hundred percent except abstinence."

"Then she could be yours." Glenna bobbed her head up and down, her loose topknot glimmering in the warm light.

He gave her a sidelong glance, weighing his words, but knowing he needed to share what was on his mind. "We went out a few times, but I ended it when she broke down in tears telling me she was involved with a married man."

There were some lines he did not cross. He might not want marriage for himself, but he still believed firmly in the sanctity of the union. Even when dating, he stayed monogamous for the duration of that relationship.

Glenna inhaled sharply. "You believe that married man was my husband."

"I didn't say that." He reached across to touch her elbow,

to comfort her. "I'm only saying this baby is here, and there's a chance she's family."

Family to one of them. That alone was enough.

His touch lingered, and he found himself unable to pull away.

"And we have to watch over her until we know..." Glenna rocked gently. "If Fleur is my husband's child and Deborah Wilson has given up her rights, then I could be a potential guardian, legally. Right? Because if he had lived, this would be my stepchild." The pronouncement was filled with logic, acceptance and generosity. Everything that made her so damn attractive to him. But he knew they needed to slow this down.

"That's a complicated issue, Glenna, with a lot of ifs—"

"But possible." Her interjection betrayed her determination. Looking back at the baby, she leaned forward to kiss the tiny pink forehead and smooth the whispery hair.

And just like that, the tender gesture made him feel as if he had walked in on a private moment. As if he was seeing a side of Glenna no one but him had ever witnessed—one she perhaps would not want him to see.

He cleared his throat. "The word of the night. *Possible.* She could be my child and I will operate from that perspective starting now. I won't have her ever thinking I wasn't her champion." He and Glenna would figure this out. But if this was his child, he would be there for his daughter.

"I'm not sure I trust you to mix formula."

A smile twitched his lips. He raised his brows high. "I can do fractions."

"Can you burp a baby and change diapers?"

He shrugged. "I can find a sitter."

"Or we can work together." Her eyes were glassy in the muted light, but still fierce. The question of paternity meant neither of them would relinquish the child.

The idea settled in him, the rightness of the solution. Working with her to care for Fleur would only further his goal of pursuing Glenna. Yet even as he thought of the advantages, he forced himself to keep things light so as not to scare her off.

"Are you propositioning me?" he teased.

Snorting on a laugh, she shifted in the rocking chair, lightly patting the baby's bottom. "With baby puke on my shoulder?" She winked, her mouth smiling but her eyes still holding a hint of hurt, fear. "Sure."

"Damn, you're making me remember why I liked you."

"I'm sure I can make you forget just as quickly."

He knelt beside her, avoiding her challenge and truly studying the baby for the first time. How was it he didn't know somehow if this was his child?

Regardless, he felt protective toward the innocent life. "She will have the full weight of my protection."

Glenna's face knotted briefly in surprise. But as soon as their eyes met, a cord tightened between them. He felt it in his stomach, knew that he had to have her, convince her. Even amid all these complications...

There was something tangible between them.

His cell phone chimed, a loud ding that knocked his gaze away.

Broderick bit back a hiss of frustration and pulled out his phone. "That's my dad. They've got formula for the baby, a nurse practitioner...and an attorney, my sister Naomi, who's speaking with the police."

As the early Alaska dark settled, Glenna realized she and Broderick had unexpectedly joined forces.

They had both positioned chairs by the new portable crib. Fleur snoozed with a full stomach, oblivious to the massive changes going on around her.

The house was stocked with baby gear and food. The nurse had checked the baby over and she appeared healthy. The police had determined there were no missing child alerts that matched Fleur. The birth certificate had been registered, and an APB on Deborah Wilson's car had turned up that she had indeed crossed into Canada. Beyond that, she'd disappeared.

Which left Glenna and Broderick as this baby's only possible family.

Broderick's sister Naomi was a fierce lawyer. Sure, she had a brilliant legal mind, but she was also a bit ruthless and certainly didn't sugarcoat a thing.

Naomi's eyes narrowed as she spoke to them. "Let me talk to a friend of mine in child services. There are so many children in the system… Given that you're willing to admit possible paternity, we'll try for a temporary guardianship until the matter can be settled with DNA tests. If you're amenable. Glenna, the lab can use something of your husband's, like an old hairbrush, or perhaps his mother once saved his baby teeth…"

Glenna's already overloaded mind balked at Naomi taking over in such a complete fashion. Suspicion inched up Glenna's spine. Her mom might trust the Steele family, but that didn't mean Glenna was on board with letting a former business rival make choices for her life. Naomi was a well-known shark and her loyalty would be to her own family. "Temporary guardianship? For which one of us?"

"Just what it sounds like. While you two were talking, I chatted with Dad and Jeannie. And since none of us could envision either of you two backing down, we thought it would be best for the two of you to take care of the baby together until we sort this out—paternity and legalities."

Broderick bristled. "That leaves the baby and all of us

open to more gossip at a time when there's already enough going on."

Glenna turned to stare him down, her softer feelings toward him starting to evaporate. So much for unity. "You're really worrying about the company right now? This has nothing to do with business."

Broderick held up a hand. "The way I see it, the less negative gossip about our families the better for Fleur if this goes to some kind of custody battle."

Warning bells sounded in Glenna's mind. She knew the Steele family was a force to be reckoned with. But they could stuff their take-charge attitude. This baby could well be tied to her. It could be a tie to her husband—a reminder that their marriage had been troubled, yes, but also an answer to her prayers for a child she could love as her own. She wasn't giving up even a few days with the baby. "I'm not leaving. I won't be pushed out of Fleur's life—"

Broderick touched her elbow again in that comforting way that also launched butterflies in her stomach. "What if we care for her together, somewhere outside of the Steele or Mikkelson backyards, so the baby isn't a distraction from the merger?"

Naomi nodded curtly. "I have to agree with my pigheaded brother on this. Speaking as a part of this family-company-merger mess, I think getting away is best for the two of you, as well. You'll have the quiet you'll need to sort out the financial side of blending our businesses, to figure out what to present to the board. It benefits all of us if the two of you mend personal fences."

All eyes focused on them with a new intensity.

Glenna raised her eyebrows. "Personal fences? You can't possibly expect us to fix the family feud."

"Don't play coy with us. I'm not talking about the Steele-Mikkelson battle. Neither one of you is fooling me."

This must be that famous courtroom face that Naomi wore to win her most difficult cases. "I went to the same college and was only a couple of years behind you. I heard. I know."

Broderick straightened his spine. "Naomi. Stand down. This most certainly isn't the time or place and it definitely isn't any of your business."

She flicked her long brown hair over her shoulder, not in the least intimidated. "I'm not a gossip. But I am smart and I see the wisdom of getting the hell out of Dodge. The wisest thing for you two to do now? Make the most of the window of time I can get you with a temporary custody order while DNA tests are run and a search is made for the child's mother. Use that time to figure out how to get along and settle our companies' business. Take your own advice, Broderick, and lie low."

The words sank in. Hard. And Glenna couldn't ignore the wisdom of Naomi's plan.

Which meant she would be stuck playing house, alone with this baby she already loved…and Broderick.

# Six

Cold light reflected on the pristine shore of the Steele family compound an hour outside of Anchorage. The rays bounced up at Broderick in an unforgiving manner. Reaching for his sunglasses tucked into his shirt pocket, he breathed in the crisp air, enjoying the frigid burst against his lungs.

For his whole life, he'd been taught the importance of family. As he surveyed the distant snowcapped peaks from his spot on the runway behind the family compound, his desire to protect this place—and what might be his infant daughter—filled him.

With a bag slung over his back, he made his way to the seaplane bobbing alongside the dock. Two pontoons kept it afloat. Last year, they'd invested in the modified amphibious aircraft version that could take off and land on either water or runways. That choice made sense for flexibility, and was a benefit now, with Glenna and the baby, if an emergency arose.

The blue of the water intensified next to the piercing white of the plane, looking more like a painting than reality. The rustic mansion on the hill seemed to demand that he act now to save his family's legacy. He gave a cursory glance to a smaller, pale yellow aircraft peeking out of the hangar. He preferred that twin engine plane, but the floatplane was more practical for where he and Glenna were headed.

Together. With a baby.

They would be staying at a Steele family cabin along a secluded bay on Prince William Sound in the Gulf of Alaska. The two-bedroom A-frame with a sizable loft had served as a welcome retreat anytime one of his family members needed to recharge.

He flipped up the collar on his coat, the wind pulling so hard today he'd opted for a cap rather than his Stetson. Hopefully the crosswinds would ease up soon so he could fly the aircraft out on schedule.

He and Glenna would be alone together, plotting the financial future of their families' combined companies and caring for a tiny baby. And yes, the thought of taking care of that infant made him nervous. He didn't know a damn thing about babies. Still, he knew he needed to learn, especially if this child turned out to be his.

A possibility that still stole his breath.

Hoisting an oversize suitcase onto the seaplane, he felt his muscles strain. They had packed formula and baby supplies, all collected within two hours of the baby's arrival. These next few days would be challenging.

From the corner of his eye, Broderick saw his father help Glenna into the plane, then hand her the baby carrier. Not that he'd ever been a gambler, but this scene was not one he'd ever thought he'd witness.

A whip of Alaskan wind tore across the dock, ruffling

the pale pink blanket draped over the carrier. Next, his father hoisted Kota's crate up into the plane. Kota's intense blue eyes regarded every movement with curiosity. Broderick's brother Marshall checked the instruments, making sure the plane would get to the cabin safely.

Broderick clapped his father on the shoulder as Marshall left the craft, stepping onto the dock beside them. "Thank you for your help finishing up here. And pass along my thanks for all the shopping and packing up of supplies."

Marshall passed along a travel mug of coffee. "No worries, brother. The plane's fueled and everything checks out. I even took her up for a spin this morning."

"I appreciate that."

Jack shifted his weight, straightening his puffed insulated jacket. "I called the service. The cabin has been aired out and stocked with food. The heat's been turned on."

"Thanks, Dad."

A full smile pushed up his father's mustache. "Anything the three of you need, just let me know. We'll send it up."

"I need you to let me know if you and Jeannie change your minds. You're sending me off to review our company's financials with our biggest business rival. And to be fair, Jeannie Mikkelson is asking Glenna to do the same. Be one hundred percent certain this is what you want."

"Son, we have to stay united and strong. Otherwise, our competition will gain traction during this time of transition. We're all family now. I'm certain this is what I want." Jack hauled Broderick in for a back-thumping hug before stepping away. "Now get to work."

"Yes, sir." He'd been given his marching orders in clear terms. And to be frank, he was looking forward to this time with Glenna. Maybe he could figure out this tenacious attraction between them. Maybe they could put their feelings to rest, find peace. The baby only made the stakes higher. They needed to find common ground so they could move forward as a blended Steele and Mikkelson company—and family.

Broderick stepped onto the plane, his eyes immediately finding Glenna. Somehow, she managed to look radiant strapped in the backseat, attentively bent over Fleur, cooing reassurances. The smells of cold air, pine and salt drifted into the cabin on a gust of wind. This might be a turbulent ride.

Kota let out a quiet whine beside Glenna from the secured crate, tail wagging in hopes of some attention.

She looked natural, sitting between a baby and a puppy, her hair pulled back into a loose bun. She seemed to notice Broderick's gaze, because her blue eyes met his. He gave her a curt nod and smile, then continued to the front of the plane to check the equipment himself in spite of his brother's assurances. Safety was too important.

While strapping himself into the pilot's seat, he glanced at Glenna and Fleur again, enjoying the sight of them from his mirror. He had to focus. He settled his headset into a good fit and felt the rush of preflight squarely in his stomach, right up until he accelerated the plane. The drumroll before being airborne had always thrilled him. He longed for the feeling when the craft lifted from ground or sea and found life in the air.

As he saw the panorama unfold before him, his breath caught. Untamed wilderness flooded his vision.

He felt connected to the wild land in his home state— an heir to tenacity and resilience. Off to the left, he saw a herd of caribou galloping in the spring sunshine.

Broderick called over his shoulder, "We're level now if you would like to move forward and talk." He studied her in the rearview mirror. "Looks like the munchkin is sleeping hard. You can watch her in the mirror up here."

Glenna worried her bottom lip, then reached for her seat belt. "Sure, we could get started on work."

Or they could talk.

Yes, they were here for Fleur and for their families, but he also needed to use every moment of this time together to figure out his attraction to Glenna. If the opportunity presented itself, he wanted back in her bed. Because his desire for her messed with his thinking at a time when he needed clear focus.

The plane hit a pocket of air, bobbling for an instant, then settling. He latched on to Fleur as a topic that could open an honest dialogue with Glenna about how they would move forward. "Looks like Fleur is sleeping well. She's a cute little munchkin, for sure."

Glenna didn't immediately respond, but when she did her words hit him with an emotional punch. "She could be *your* munchkin. Have you thought about being a father? And please don't make a joke. I'm asking a serious question."

He thought it over while the plane slid through the clouds, the white puffs dragging along the windscreen. He needed to offer up honest answers if he wanted her honesty in return.

"I'm known as the commitment-phobic sort, so I guess the answer naturally follows that I never expected to be a father." He shrugged, eyes darting to the equipment on the dash. Everything was as it should be. "I'm careful," he added, hoping the comment reminded her just how attentive he could be.

She inched down the zipper on her parka, the sound hinting at the intimacies he wanted to share with her.

"Broderick? Do you like children?" Her question corralled his heated thoughts.

"I'm not sure I'll be a good father, but yes, I like children. I thought—hoped—I would be an uncle several times over by now." Like him, his siblings were focused on their careers and less focused on child rearing.

"I just wondered, because you've made a concerted effort not to hold her, even though I could swear I see the hint of a natural."

He thought about her words and the squeeze to his heart each time he saw the kid. "Oldest brother syndrome, I guess. I helped out with my siblings. But I honestly don't have much experience with babies beyond the occasional employee bringing in a new son or daughter to show off around the office."

"I hear Steele Oil has a top-notch on-site child care facility. I would assume you've seen it."

He nodded in her direction, keeping his eyes on the horizon. "Yes, I tour every part of the building."

"Hmm. So, the magazine photo shoot of you on the floor in the child care facility playing with toddlers wasn't a publicity stunt."

He could hear the playful smirk in her voice.

"You set me up with that lead in about the on-site day care."

"I did. Although I am curious. Was it a ploy to win women?" she asked with a challenge in her voice.

"I was there visiting a friend's child. I didn't know the photos had even been taken until they showed up in the article."

"That's nice to know."

"Don't let those photos fool you, though. I'm still not the go-to guy on anything more than the fractions for mixing formula. I'm hoping you know more than I do about what we're supposed to do with her." They'd been dropped into caretaking with no warning. If Fleur was his, he would read all the books, figure it out.

"I have taken care of friends' babies," she said. "I have the nurse practitioner on speed dial, and we can look up answers on our phones. I expect you to give one hundred percent."

"Totally on board with that. Willing to learn what I don't know." He'd always been willing to solve tough problems. He just needed the chance to get acclimated.

"Which brings me back to my original question. What happens if she's your daughter?"

"Then I will be a father and I will work to be the best father I can be."

And he meant it.

Although with each moment that passed, he saw Glenna growing more attached to the baby. He couldn't help but worry about what it would mean for her to have no claim to the child.

His hopes of conversation making things easier between them had only reminded him of all the reasons this wasn't a simple getaway meant to end with them in bed.

Broderick was certainly full of surprises. Or perhaps, more accurately, she was seeing a version of him that she'd forgotten about.

His commitment to the potential of being Fleur's father reminded her of a twentysomething Broderick.

Memories floated in her mind's eye as she watched him check some equipment, his lips forming a satisfied curl as he read the numbers.

In college, it had been Broderick's confidence that attracted her. They'd been assigned a group project—a task she normally dreaded. But he'd proved to be just as dedicated to the presentation as she was. He'd pulled all-nighters with her and they'd been excellent study partners, pushing each other to be better, smarter.

His gaze had always been electric and his body delicious.

It was still delicious. When he'd hefted the suitcase and supplies into the seaplane, he'd proved his muscles were just as tight and enticing as they had been over a decade ago. In that moment, the careful way she'd forced herself to think of Broderick as a cutthroat businessman faltered.

Chewing the inside of her cheek, she realized how much more there was to him and how damn difficult it'd be to spend all this time alone with him.

He was a *man*. In every sense of the word.

She tore her eyes off him now, searching for some distraction. She looked up into the mirror, half hoping Fleur would be waking and need her. But the infant slept on.

The plane dipped, hitting harder pockets of air as they made their way to the mountains.

Glenna devoured the sight of springtime in Alaska, particularly from the sky. A field of impossible emerald green and pockets of lakes served as contrast to the snowy mountains. When Glenna was a child, she'd thought of the land as a magical space. When she'd gaze out at the backdrop of green land and white mountains, it'd always seemed as if two seasons existed simultaneously.

She reached out to touch the cool glass at her side. The engine rumbled, reverberating slightly. "It's been so long since I flew in one of these."

"Perhaps because your family spent more time operating out of the Dakotas. I'm sure there are equally awesome sights you could show me there that I've missed."

"Sure, sure," she said, enticed by the idea of showing this man her stomping grounds. She folded her legs under her, sitting in the lotus position. "One good thing will come from this family merger. We'll bring new experiences to the table."

"I imagine there can be some other positives."

Did he have a hidden meaning in those words? His face appeared honest, calm, focused on flying. Lord, but he was handsome. The sun streamed through the window, playing across the strong line of his jaw, his broad shoulders in that plaid shirt, those jeans fitting him like denim was made just to hug that fine butt.

Her eyes roamed back up to the hard angles of his face. He always had that five o'clock shadow, even when he wore a crisp suit.

The man freaking oozed testosterone.

And her body sensed every pheromone.

She pulled on her black cashmere sweater, hoping the ritual tug on the sleeves would calm her. Ground her.

Staying in that cabin with him was going to be…difficult. To say the least.

She pulled her attention back to work and the more manageable reason for their retreat to the mountains. "Figuring out the corporate logistics of blending both employee rosters will be challenging," she reminded him, simultaneously reminding herself that Broderick Steele should be off-limits to her wandering feminine imagination. "There's no way everyone can keep their jobs at the current level. Demotions are inevitable. Everything can't be a co-job. Someone has to be the boss. CEO… CFO…" She ticked the list off on her fingers.

There. That should put some distance between them.

"We'll work it out," he answered vaguely, his hands clenching briefly on the steering yoke.

Strong hands. She remembered how they felt on her last night, his palm steadying her, burning through the fabric of her shirt.

"This peace between us can't last." She looked away from him, fingers tapping on her denim-clad thigh.

And no, she wasn't thinking about Broderick's touch on

her thigh. It must be the cashmere sweater that was over-heating her to this degree.

"Why not? Isn't there anything else in the company you would enjoy overseeing?" His question was a welcome distraction.

Did he really think she would give up her job without a blink? "Why should I be the one to find a new place in the business? What about you? Isn't there something else you would 'enjoy overseeing'?"

"In the end, it may not be up to either of us. Let's not make this getaway more difficult by arguing."

She studied him. No question, he had on his poker face today. She'd seen it often enough across the boardroom or on an occasional television show as he made a comment on behalf of his business. He was charming, sure, but gave little away.

Glenna played with the zipper on the folded parka in her lap, finding the interior of the small plane still too warm. "You're not going to attempt to push me out or seduce me into stepping aside?"

"Is that what you think I'm trying to accomplish here? Seducing you for Machiavellian gains?" His voice was dry as he adjusted their course.

"Aren't you?" There. She'd said it. Put it out there. Her heart picked up speed as she wondered what he would say.

And wondered even more what she *wanted* him to say.

His eyebrows shot up. "Well, in the past couple of days I've realized you're more plainspoken than I remembered. I'll answer as plainly as I can. I'm attracted to you and that has nothing to do with business. I always have been. Is that so difficult for you to believe? You're the one who walked out on our relationship. Not me."

*Relationship.* The word hit her hard. In fact, she never

would have anticipated he'd characterize their time together that way. "It was a weekend."

He didn't back down. "It was a friendship that led to a weekend."

"A friendship? Are you sure? We barely knew each other. We thought we were Romeo and Juliet, rebelling against our parents."

"You were using me to get back at your parents?"

She stared hard out the window as they descended toward a lakeside cabin. Where they would be together. The flight had passed all too quickly.

Kota whined from the back, and Glenna's eyes flicked to baby Fleur. Still sleeping.

Broderick's question still hung in the air.

Looking intently at the cabin, noting the large fenced-in area and kidney-shaped hot tub, she spoke. "Isn't that what it was about for you?"

"Not at the time. No."

His words stole the air from her lungs and her stomach lurched as if the plane had just taken a significant plunge. "Then I'm sorry."

"But knowing that wouldn't have changed your leaving."

Would it have? She wasn't sure. It had been so long ago. And in the intervening years, she had met and loved her husband. His betrayal had shredded her heart. His death had nearly finished the job.

And now all the changes to their lives that had come so quickly? She couldn't afford the emotional stakes of another relationship.

"Our parents may have found a way to be a couple, but I can't envision that sort of strange, statistical improbability happening again in our family."

"Then it sounds like we have a challenge in front of us.

Take care of the baby, who loves to sleep. Work on financials, which we can't start until tomorrow, when the latest reports come in. And work on becoming friends again, because, lady, we're stuck with each other."

After securing the plane, Broderick fixed his eyes on the mountainside cabin where Glenna and Fleur waited. That A-frame building held a lot of memories of family retreats for him.

The place had been one of his father's earlier acquisitions, when the stresses of work had started to take a toll on family time. Jack Steele had always told them family came first or the rest would fall apart. They'd been tight-knit, no question, and that had made it all the tougher after his mother's and sister's deaths.

He pulled gear out of the plane, one bag at a time, remembering so many other trips. Each kid had been responsible for packing his or her own duffel bag, and if they forgot a crucial piece of snow gear, that meant limited activities for that person. Jack made them learn their lessons the old-school way.

But they sure didn't forget a second time. Or in other cases, they learned to share and work together. Corporate team building, even back then.

Broderick's cell phone rang and he fished deep in his parka pocket. Reception up this way used to be tricky until his dad added a booster tower. Money sure did have its perks.

Broderick read the screen, but didn't recognize the number. Still, given the unknown situation with Fleur and the merger mess, he figured he'd better take the call.

"Yes, Broderick Steele speaking. And this is?" He hitched a carry-on bag and a large duffel with a portable crib over his shoulder, tucked the phone under his chin and then grabbed two more suitcases. Damn, babies came with a lot of stuff.

"Steele, this is Trystan Mikkelson," a gruff voice barked.

Glenna's brother, the one who worked their family ranch. The voice sounded familiar now that he'd identified himself. What did the guy want? "Is there a problem?"

"I'm checking on my sister."

Oh-kay. Broderick started his hike up the dock toward the cabin. "We arrived at the retreat on schedule. We're unpacking now and setting things up for the baby. Any news?"

"Nothing to report."

He frowned at the oddness of this call coming out of the blue from a man he barely knew. "Then please pass along the message to the rest of the family that we're fine. I'll send out periodic texts and emails with our progress on the business front. We would appreciate you sharing any news you receive."

There. That should appease his father that he was trying to make nice with the enemy—aka, his future stepsiblings.

"Can do," Trystan answered, his tone clipped. "And Steele? One last thing."

Broderick started up the steps, his eyes locked on Glenna. She stood at the floor-to-towering-ceiling window wall. "What would that be?"

"Hurt my sister and I will kick your ass clear to Canada."

The phone line disconnected.

Broderick dropped a suitcase and caught the cell as it slipped from under his chin. He studied the screen and saw the connection was fine, plenty of signal. Trystan had hung up on him. Plain and simple.

But the message had been clear enough, and oddly, for once, Broderick found himself commiserating with a Mikkelson. As a man. As a brother. Because if anyone hurt one of his sisters, Broderick would hunt the bastard down and pummel him personally.

His gaze trekked right back to the window and the woman who tugged at him in a way no other ever had.

With all that was going on in their families, he would have to tread very, very carefully.

# Seven

Needing to collect her thoughts, Glenna sat on her bed, while Kota patiently settled at the door, head cocked to the side.

All her clothes had been neatly unpacked, hung in the closet or tucked away in drawers. Throughout dinner, she'd been the one to take care of baby Fleur. Not that she minded, but it concerned her. If the child was not Gage's... If the child was indeed Broderick's, then his avoidance was worrisome.

Perhaps he needed more time. Or perhaps she'd found the one area in his life where he didn't have a skill set and bravado.

She walked out of her room and into the main living area, the scent of pine furniture and floors cleaned with lemony oil filling the air. Broderick sat on the couch, eyeing Fleur in the baby swing. He seemed wistful, eyes warm, but he made no move toward the child.

Kota made laps around the baby swing, tail wagging.

Protective. Eventually the dog curled on the dark brown throw rug in front of the hearth. They looked like a still life from a family vacation promotion.

Glenna scooped up Fleur, looked intently at her little face, again hoping a distinct feature would manifest and hint at her father.

Instead, she met Fleur's fluttering eyes, felt a connection to the infant and her innocence. Baby cradled in her arms, Glenna walked to the bedroom and put her down for the night. After turning on the monitor, she returned to the living area, fully taking in Broderick for the first time since supper.

Dressed comfortably as he was in navy jogging pants and a long-sleeved gray T-shirt, his muscles were on display. His dark hair slightly askew, he looked up at her.

The baby monitor hummed in her hand, giving her a sense of peace.

He jabbed a thumb in the direction of the French doors leading out to the deck. "I'm going to the hot tub. And that isn't a come-on line."

Hot tub?

Her body tingled with awareness at the suggestion. She tossed her hair over her shoulder with a nonchalant air she was far from feeling. "Glad to know you're not hitting on me, because if that's the best game you've got, you need help."

A masculine, throaty laugh rolled free. "I'll save my good game for later." He winked. "For tonight, after the stress of our parents' engagement and a surprise baby bundle, I could use some relief. I'm hoping to catch the northern lights. I never grow tired of seeing them stream across the sky and we're almost out of season. If you wish to join me, there are always extra swimsuits of all sizes in the changing rooms."

She studied him, wondering, assessing, and realized… "That's a dare, isn't it? To test your non-come-on line?"

"I'm simply stating where I'm going and inviting you to join me." He winked again. "If you dare."

How much did she trust him? Hell, how much did she trust herself?

But then ignoring him sure hadn't worked out all that well for her, given how much he occupied her dreams at night. "Fair enough. I'll bring the nursery monitor and join you once I choose the most boring swimsuit in the collection."

"I can't wait." His chuckle rumbled over his shoulder and hung in the air long after he stepped outside.

Once in the changing room, she thumbed through the neat stacks, her fingers lingering on an array of swimsuits stockpiled in the drawer until… There. She found it. The perfect boring suit in her exact size: a solid navy blue one-piece. Nothing would set the "hands off" tone quite like that. But a rush of impulse made her reach back into the drawer to a skimpy black string bikini.

She slid out of her clothes and into the bikini, then stared at her reflection in the mirror. Feeling confident and ready. Removing the hair tie from her wrist, she piled her strawberry-blond hair on top of her head—ready.

Before she lost her nerve, she shrugged into a luxurious spa robe and yanked fluffy boots onto her feet. She wasn't exactly a showstopper right now, but she couldn't deny she looked forward to knocking Broderick's socks off once her robe hit the deck.

Kota followed at her heels as she made her way to Fleur's room for a final check on her way out. The young pup wagged his fluffy tail in anticipation.

Kota bounded to the crib, his icy blue eyes curious and interested. While the dog meant well, he was too young to be left alone with Fleur. Glenna could too easily envision Kota jumping into the crib to curl around the baby. A well-intended action, but not one she could risk. Satisfied that Fleur was peacefully sleeping, she checked the monitor's setting once again before picking up her receiver, then guided Kota into the laundry room.

"Come along, boy. With me. With me," she commanded. She'd set up his crate, with a doggy bed so it felt like and smelled of home. Beside it, his bowl of water and a bowl of kibble waited. She'd even left some treats.

He pranced right to his bed and curled up with a sleepy sigh.

She smoothed the black-and-white fur along his side. "I love you, sweet boy. I do." She'd made sure to take him on extra long walks so he wouldn't get jealous of the attention she had to give Fleur. "You're a good pup. I'll see you soon. Night-night."

Standing, she turned on an iPod she'd rigged in the room to play soft, soothing music, the same she played for him at home. Then she dimmed the light and secured the gate in front of the door.

Turning on her heel, Glenna strode through the rustic cabin, her fluffy boots making muffled sounds on the stone floor in the kitchen. She made her way to the glass door that led to the picturesque deck extending out around the isolated cabin.

A watercolor sunset of reds and oranges melted over the snowcapped mountaintop, while to the east the evening's first stars appeared in the sky. She glanced about, taking in the serenity of the water, the slow bobbing of the parked seaplane. She followed the sound of churning water, walking past a latticework partition to the hot tub, which provided an uninterrupted view of the mountains.

And an equally chiseled Broderick.

The cold air urged her to move, but so did his whiskey-eyed stare. After stepping onto the heated stairs, she kicked off her fluffy boots, deciding somehow she could resist him better if she quickly slid into the warm, welcoming depths.

Although right now she was having trouble remembering why she needed to resist him at all.

Swallowing hard, she discarded her robe and draped it over the railing. Her breasts tightened at the chill.

Or perhaps at the sight of the Broderick's bare, broad shoulders and his muscular arms stretched out along the edge of the hot tub as he leaned back. His smoldering gaze met hers. Then stroked over her from her nose to her toes.

He lifted one dark eyebrow. "If that's the most boring swimsuit in the collection, then heaven help me if you'd picked something else."

His words eased the stress knotting inside her and she stepped into the welcoming waters.

She sat next to him, careful not to get too close, not yet, not trusting herself. Leaning back, she rested her head on the edge, eyes fluttering shut at the caress of the jets easing her tensed muscles. "I'm sure there must be something in the code of ethics about a business meeting like this."

"Who says it has to be about business? We've crunched numbers, taken care of the baby…" His voice rumbled gently in the night air, soothing and intoxicating. "And we've helped our families. I say it's fine for us to decompress. I would have brought wine, but I want us both to be completely aware and in control of our senses."

She opened her eyes to find him staring at her, a hungry smile on his face. Her throat dried up as an answering hunger churned inside her.

One she tamped down with both fists clenched in the water. "Would you care to clarify that?"

"I want us sober for the baby, and in case I need to fly the plane, of course. What did you think I meant?" he asked, with such overplayed innocence, she splashed him.

He splashed her right back, and then they both eased deeper into the swirling water, their legs brushing ever so briefly.

Emotional distance. She needed to keep finding some.

"Do you really think my mother and your father are going to get married?"

"What do you think?"

She shrugged, playing her fingers along the top of the water, popping bubbles. "My mother has dated a couple of times since my father died, but no one serious. For her to say she's marrying Jack is huge. I don't know your father well, only from business meetings and what I've heard."

"What do you think of him?" The timbre of Broderick's voice issued a bit of a challenge.

"He's fearless in the boardroom. His devotion to his family has always been without question."

"He loved my mother, deeply." Broderick held up a hand. "Sure, I know there are kids who wear rose-colored glasses where their parents are concerned. But he grieved so hard when we lost her and my sister. I don't believe the company would have survived if Uncle Conrad hadn't stepped in for a year."

"Somehow I never knew your uncle did that. He always seemed to have his own side projects going, independent of your father."

Broderick swirled the water and she felt the small current against her tummy. "The family kept it on the down low to protect the stability of stocks. Uncle Conrad was masterful at reassuring the board. He comes across as such a jokester, but don't underestimate him. He's a smart man who doesn't care about recognition."

Stars twinkled in crystal brightness across the inky sky.

"Lack of ego in a man." She laughed softly. "What a novelty."

"Ouch." Broderick flicked water at her. "Surely you didn't mean that for humble me."

"Of course not." She crinkled her nose at him, feeling her body drawn toward his. Just like she had been over a decade ago. The laughter between them felt natural, familiar.

And so very enticing.

His hand lifted from the water to point to the beginning of the northern lights. Preternatural greens and purples filled the sky, dancing with no regard for anything besides the present moment.

Somehow, she and Broderick were closer than just a moment ago. She felt his body next to hers, aware and awake. Present.

Her eyes found his. Her own heart felt foreign in her chest, beating hard under his gaze. She wasn't sure who moved first, or if they perhaps moved at the same time.

Because without question, they were now a breath away from a kiss—a kiss of passion and longing and a promise of so much more.

And she didn't have the least inclination to stop.

So much for all his good intentions.

When she looked at him like that, he couldn't keep his distance. When her shoulder brushed against him, she released the desire he'd tamped down for a decade.

Her mouth parted, ever so slightly, anticipation pulsing in the small gesture. Broderick was filled with the urge to wrap his arm around her. Pull her onto his lap. To let her legs straddle him, for her to open to him, accept him as he plunged deep inside her body as he once had. As he wanted to do again.

This woman had always had the power to bring him to his knees with desire. And yes, the thought of being on his knees in front of her, with her legs parted, ready for him to tease her to completion—

He exhaled long and slow, willing his heartbeat to slow from a gallop to something vaguely close to normal.

The last time he'd surrendered to that temptation, she'd walked away, married another man and ignored him for a decade. Did he have the will to stop if he let himself have a taste of her?

Broderick stroked Glenna's cheek and plucked at a damp lock of hair clinging to moist skin. The silky softness of her sent a bolt of heat through him far hotter than the bubbling tub. Her pale blue eyes glistened with the reflection of the stars and hints of the northern lights.

Her creamy shoulders peeked above the rolling waters. The thin black ties reminded him she still wore a bikini top, and with one tug he could free those ties, baring her beautiful breasts for his eyes alone. He recalled in vivid detail what she looked like wearing nothing.

Yet there were more mature curves to her now and he ached to explore every inch with his hands and his mouth. To make love to her under the stars with the northern lights streaming through the sky.

He wanted that.

But if he didn't want another decade of regrets, he needed to bide his time. Take things slow.

For tonight, he needed to relearn the feel and taste of her lips.

Angling forward, he waited a hairbreadth away, giving her the chance to protest. Praying she wouldn't.

Then she slid closer. All the encouragement he needed to taste her, and for an instant he let himself do that. He brushed his mouth along her cheek, where his fingers had stroked only an instant before. Her skin was creamy soft. Her light gasp enticing as she swayed closer, her knees brushing his underwater.

Her breasts pressed against his chest with a sweet pressure that had him throbbing, longing to sweep aside her swimsuit and his and be inside her. The ache was intense, but the will to win her over for more than an impulsive hookup was stronger.

His mouth skimmed around to capture hers and her arms slid around his neck in a smooth affirmation that she wanted him as much as he wanted her. Heat and desire and the fragrant blend of Glenna mixed with the Alaska air threatened to send him over the edge of reason. Of control.

And in that moment, he realized just how very much he longed to be in her bed again. And again.

That second *again* being the operative word. If he moved too fast now, this could well be his only time with her. And once would definitely not be enough. He'd learned that long ago from a weekend that had tormented him for over a decade. He needed to be smarter this time.

With more than a little regret, he eased away, stroking his hands along her shoulders. "Glenna, continuing is not a smart idea."

"So you keep saying." Her breath caressed his face. Her own voice was ragged as she looked at him through her lashes. "You know how much I want you."

"Is that a proposition?" He stared deep into her eyes, a moment too long—just in time to feel more awareness pass between them.

"I'll let you know." She leaned in so close her lips feathered against his ear.

"Glenna, as much as I would like to continue this, it's too soon for both of us." He allowed himself one final stroke of her shoulders and a kiss on the tip of her damp nose. "Good night."

Easing away from her was no easy task, but he knew the time wasn't right. Not yet. With an extra dose of that regret charging through him, Broderick hefted himself from the water. And hell, yes, he welcomed that bracing cold wind whipping across the bay.

Jeannie Mikkelson didn't doubt her course. She'd been a businesswoman and a mother long enough to know her mind.

But she still found herself reeling from the impact of her feelings for Jack. A man she'd known for decades, only to suddenly find herself falling head over heels, passionately in love with him. How strange to fall for someone at first sight even when you already knew him. But that's what it had felt like. Seeing him with fresh eyes that day at the conference.

Now, stretched out on a leather sofa with him in his bedroom suite, the fireplace crackling, she was a part of his life, just as he was a part of hers. Not just dating or sex. Their daily routines were blending now that their romance was out in the open.

She looked at the remains of the simple dinner they'd shared, the tray on the coffee table. She knew well not to take the simple pleasures of life for granted.

If only others could understand that. "How can our children have so much in common and still be ready to knife each other in the nearest dark alley?"

His dry chuckle rumbled against her. "Might have something to do with the Hatfields and McCoys upbringing we gave them."

"You and Mary bad-mouthed the Mikkelsons?" She glanced at him, tracing his bristly mustache. Gracious, he was handsome, in a tall, dark and weathered way that launched flurries in her stomach. "I'm astounded."

Laughing, he nipped her finger. "Not Mary, but I may well have shouted my frustration at the Mikkelsons over dinner."

"Why does that not surprise me?" She settled against his side, his arms warm and solid around her. "I guess we're reaping what we've sown."

"There's truth in that, I believe, but I also feel they're adults living their lives and we should be able to live ours."

Jeannie admired Jack's steadfast spirit, but wondered if they were being too rigid in their approach. "I don't mind being accommodating and reaching out."

"They're not babies to be coddled anymore. And this is about the business, as well. They can get on board or not."

There was no mistaking the steel resolve in his voice. He was aptly named.

"Jack, we can compromise with them."

"Bargain from a position of weakness?"

She turned to face him, resting her palms on his broad, flannel-covered chest. "We're talking about our family. That's much more important than the business."

"Once the kids realize that, they'll be fine." He clasped her hands and kissed the top of each. "But until then, someone's always going to feel they got out maneuvered by a new stepsibling. And we can't negotiate that. They need to figure it out on their own."

She could see his point. If only she could be sure he was right. "I just wish I knew your children better so I could gauge the dynamics."

He shifted his mouth to kiss her ring finger. "We need to go shopping for an engagement ring."

"I just want a band."

His mustache tickled her skin as he smiled. "Your feelings are heard, and I want to buy you an engagement ring."

Lord, he was stubborn. So was she. "Can you donate the money to charity instead?"

"I can do both."

Shaking her head, she eased her hands free and cupped his face. "You're a tough negotiator, Jack Steele."

"You keep me on my toes and I like that." He rested his forehead against hers, then angled his face to kiss her lips.

She welcomed him, thoroughly, opening and tasting.

Yet even as she lost herself in the moment, she couldn't stop her mind from spinning. She loved him, deeply. She would live the rest of her days with him. But she would never have children with him. All of that took some adjusting in her mind, given she'd expected to spend her life with Charles, the father of her kids. Things had upended for her when he'd died, and there were days she'd been certain her heart had broken so fully her body would follow. But somehow, she'd pieced herself back together.

For her children.

She'd held on for them. And now she couldn't deny a feeling of resentment that they were holding back. She'd always supported them in their decisions. Could they really cut themselves out of her life over this? Could she live with that?

Could Jack?

He'd truly lost a child, in the worst way imaginable. He had to be aching inside over this new rift. If it came down to calling off the wedding to keep their kids, even if *she* could commit, could she ask him to give up that much for her?

# Eight

What. The. Hell.

Even fifteen minutes after Broderick left, Glenna was still stunned to her curling toes from his kiss—and his abrupt departure. She slumped against the side of the hot tub, the water bubbling just under her chin.

Broderick had literally walked away. After luring her out here under the stars. Kissing her as sweetly as if he was savoring the world's finest wine. Touching her as if she were delicate china to be adored. He'd then left her feeling more than a little crazy. Breathless and edgy, she could barely tell what side was up right now.

Leaning her head back, she stared up at the shimmering streaks of the aurora borealis. Early spring wasn't the optimum time to watch, but the lights were still magnificent. Romantic. She wasn't sure what game he was playing, or if it was even a game. He was attracted to her. He had high stakes here, too. Could he be as confused as she felt?

Asking seemed to be a dangerous proposition right now, though. Not until she was prepared for whatever his answer might be.

A wail interrupted her thoughts, sending her limbs into motion. Little Fleur's cry set off a maternal drive in her heart, and she barely registered the cold whip of Alaskan night air across her exposed skin as she leaped out of the tub and reached for the baby monitor. More discontented cries sounded from the machine.

Fumbling for her robe, she pulled it on as she made her way across the patio, dripping water as she went. She left her fluffy boots behind, determined to be there for the baby who might be her only physical link to her deceased husband.

Glenna yanked the door open, water pooling at her feet in the momentary pause. Entering the cabin, she heard another voice emerge as a rustle from the baby's room. A male voice.

Broderick.

On her tiptoes, she listened, trying to distinguish the words.

His tone, gentle and soft, made it hard to determine exactly what he was saying. Glenna touched a hand to her throat, held her breath.

Silence.

Little Fleur's crying eased.

Glenna scooped up a towel off one of the chairs at the rustic wood table. Patting herself dry, she strained to hear him, noting the warm shadows the yellow lamps cast in the cottage. A homey glow. There was no other way to describe this space.

"Shh, shh. It's okay, little one." His normally deep rasp carried a softer cadence.

Her head cocked to the side as she let him take care of

the child. If Fleur was his baby, then this moment mattered for their bond. She didn't want to intrude on that.

Instead, she wandered around the cabin, reaching up to touch the moose antlers above the hearth. All the charm of old Alaska seemed distilled in this space. Glenna dropped her hand to the wood-burning stove. The metal was cool to her touch. An absence of fire. Refreshing, because her own conflicted desire felt like a roaring inferno.

"Ahh. There we go."

Broderick's voice sliced into her thoughts.

She kept moving around the room, her bare toes trading cool stone tile for a warm fur throw rug that sprawled in front of the couch.

Gazing about her, she took in the small details of the place. An old barn-style wooden sliding door separated the two rooms. As she drew closer, her breathing quieter now, she fully appreciated the softer side of Broderick.

Hand braced outside the door, she listened in on his one-sided conversation. Apparently, he'd picked up the baby, and she heard him say, "Yes, ma'am, we'll get you in a dry diaper and take a little walk around to look out the window…"

Her chest went tight as she envisioned him holding Fleur, carrying her to the window to gaze at the stars.

Glancing over her shoulder, Glenna noticed a family photograph hanging on the far wall, beneath massive elk antlers. The whole Steele clan… Crossing the room, she scrutinized it, aware of how different Broderick's family looked now. Aware of how strange it must be to go through life without his mother, without his younger sister who'd tragically passed away…

Fleur cooed, a gentle sound interrupting Glenna's melancholy thoughts.

A smile pushed at her lips and her heart beat a bit too

fast. Glenna felt herself slip into dangerous territory, practically tap-dancing on thin ice.

Broderick's interaction with the child warmed her core.

Dangerous territory indeed.

A few hours had passed since he'd settled Fleur back to sleep. His potential daughter. The thought still sent him reeling.

He opened the door to the fridge, cool air dancing on his cheeks. Pulling at his soft navy T-shirt, he scanned the shelves for enticing treats for a late night work session. He had made progress with Glenna. He was playing a long game here. More than a one-night stand, and that required patience and persuasion.

Bold had always been his signature move, even as far back as that weekend in college. Broderick didn't back down from challenges. And he needed her in his bed.

He would keep his cool, take his time and appeal to her more logical side. There was only one way to resolve this issue with the baby and with the business.

He needed to persuade her to make this about more than sex. They needed a serious relationship.

Then, problem solved with the business and the baby. They would be aligned on everything. He had no plans of marrying or falling in love, and she'd made it clear her dead husband was the love of her life. The notion of dating her, of taking it to the next level, should have surprised him, but it didn't. It settled in place like a well-formed plan for a profitable merger.

Reaching into the stainless steel refrigerator, he pulled out an assortment of cheeses—brie, feta and mascarpone. He stacked the wedges on the counter, then rummaged for the raspberries, blueberries, strawberries and smoked salmon.

He looked over his shoulder to where Glenna sat in the overstuffed chair, computer screen washing her face in a blue light. Her damp hair was gathered back in a lazy top-knot that called to his fingers to pull it free.

After their hot tub dip, she'd pulled on silky sleep pants and a matching top. Sure, it covered her, but the outfit reminded him they were here for the night. The sea foam color brought out different hues in her blue eyes, like waters churned by a storm.

He understood the feeling well. But soon enough, they would have relief from this frustration—long-term relief—if he simply presented his plan in the right manner.

Arranging the bounty next to a sliced baguette on a cutting board, he felt resolved. Broderick would play his hand carefully. Walking away from her in the hot tub had been damn hard, but it had given him time to think. Time to come up with a better plan.

After bringing over the platter, he snaked two wine-glasses between his fingers and grabbed a bottle of chilled prosecco.

He arranged the spread on the rustic dinner table, poured the sparkling wine and popped some strawber-ries into the stemmed glasses. Setting one to his right, he opened his laptop, ready to get down to business.

Looking up from her perch on the armchair, Glenna glanced at the food. She picked up her computer and brief-case, then headed for the chair next to his. The light scent of her cologne and shampoo wafted by him as she took her seat, so intoxicating his mouth watered.

After scooping smoked salmon onto a piece of bread, she studied him, her gaze so intense Broderick felt she could peer into his mind. There were a few moments of silence between them, interrupted only by the soft classical cello piece pouring through the nursery monitor, music for baby Fleur.

Kota groaned, extracting himself from his spot underneath the table to nuzzle Glenna's hand. Out of the corner of his eye, he watched her ruffle the pup's ears. Kota let out a large yawn, teeth flashing bright even in the muted light.

Broderick took a sip of his wine, peering over his computer screen. "We should talk about what happened out there."

A flush brightened her cheeks. "Let's not."

He squinted, taking in her forward-leaning posture. He wasn't buying for a moment that this attraction between them had simply been extinguished. She circled the rim of her wineglass with an idle finger, staring back at him.

In a throaty voice, he pressed on. "I want it to happen again, and more, and from your response it's clear I'm not alone in feeling the attraction."

He watched as she popped a raspberry into her mouth, the slight red stain of the juice accentuating her full lips with a sweetness he wanted to savor. Reminding him of the earlier kiss that still seared his brain and left him feeling more than a little uncomfortable.

She wasn't easily swayed. She shrugged her shoulders. "It's biology. And abstinence—" She winced. "I didn't mean to say that part about being abstinent. That's personal. Private. None of your business. Please don't speak right now."

The scarlet in her cheeks deepened.

After spreading goat cheese on a piece of baguette, he eased back in his chair and gave her his best, wickedest smile, teasing her just a little. Although the fact she hadn't been with anyone since her husband's death reminded Broderick of how much she'd cared for the other man.

He moved his neck from side to side to work out a sudden kink.

The knowledge also reminded him that he was on the right track with his plan for something more serious with her. She preferred sex within a relationship.

"Really, don't say a word." She buried her face in her hands, then fluffed her hair and returned to her wineglass. Glenna's next swig seemed full of determination.

Silently, he held up his hands.

She threw a pillow from the neighboring chair at him. "You know I'm attracted to you, but you made it clear in the hot tub that nothing is going to happen," she said boldly. "I don't know what your angle is, but I'm not into game playing. You've only served to remind me why it's unwise to act on those feelings, especially with all that's going on." She made a gesture that seemed to suggest she was talking about all the general chaos of their lives.

For him, that chaos wasn't insurmountable. If she wanted to opt for a no-holds-barred discussion, he could handle that. In fact, he welcomed the challenge of sparring with her.

"I walked away earlier because I wasn't sure you're ready. Am I right?"

Her eyes narrowed and she scratched under her topknot in a gesture he was beginning to realize was her nervous twitch. A poker "tell" that she was rattled.

"Maybe. But you could have said all of this out there instead of just strutting away like the lord of the manor."

"I could have, but you tempt me, lady. In spite of my very best intentions, you tempt me."

"I guess that's a compliment." Her throat moved in a long swallow. "Things are difficult and complicated here. I'll admit that. It would help if you weren't so smart. So charming. So damn hot."

The way she spit out the words, they didn't sound much like compliments. Still, he grinned.

Broderick grabbed another handful of berries. "I'm glad you feel that way. Those should be good things, because you're one helluva sexy lady. I'm pacing myself. You're worth the wait." He finished his white wine and popped a berry in his mouth.

She pursed her lips, shaking her head. "That still doesn't answer the question of how we're going to work together and be in the same family."

He scooted his chair closer. "What if we work together, at the office, and take Fleur with us?"

"What do you mean?" Her brow furrowed. Glenna downed her last bit of wine, then licked her lips. Driving him mad.

He needed this to work.

"You don't want to get married again. You've said as much. I'm devoted to my job, but I want a steady relationship."

"Just not the commitment?"

He nodded. "I don't want my heart stomped by someone too upset by the hours I pull, and I sure as hell don't want to go through what my father went through when Mom died. So let's give this a try hanging out together. Seeing where the attraction takes us."

Broderick tucked a loose strand of hair behind her ear. Let his other hand graze her knee ever so slightly.

"You're serious? You're not just hitting on me for a one-time deal?" Glenna leaned into him, her voice soft.

"I'm very serious. Look at this as the most important business decision of our lives. We'll be together, connected. Then whoever turns out to be Fleur's new parent, we can help the other."

Her blue eyes searched his. "You really mean this."

"Can you think of a good reason why not? Let's decide now."

"Whoa. You're asking us to make this kind of decision right now, this fast." She held up her hands, shaking her head until that topknot slid to the side, threatening to fall altogether. "That's crazy."

"Maybe. Maybe not." He slid a berry between her lips. "Think on it."

Her throat moved in a long, slow swallow. Yes. He was making significant progress.

He eased back. "Now let's get to work on the last set of financial quarterlies."

Kota had limitless energy, or so it seemed to Glenna. For the past hour, she'd played fetch until her arm grew weary. Kota dashed into the snow, a sleek black line of ambition. Then he'd bound back to Glenna, practically prancing with the ball wedged between his teeth.

And maybe she'd been trying to work off the nervous energy from the chaos Broderick had brought to her life with his proposition.

She pitched the tennis ball again. Harder.

The midmorning sun hung heavy in a cloudless sky, and the cabin's isolation provided her with time to think. Much needed time to think, as it turned out.

Sure, she felt a visceral attraction to Broderick. But his proposition about starting a serious relationship and co-raising Fleur?

*That* she still had to work out. Her feelings ran rampant, and over breakfast, she'd snapped at him. Not on purpose, but she'd known she'd been prickly.

Too much had changed in a week. Nothing about her life felt normal or manageable. The only things that had become increasingly clear were her affection for Fleur—

and her desire for Broderick. She knew she had to consider his offer.

She called Kota back to her, and they made their way from the fenced-in backyard to the deck and hot tub. Broderick opened the door, a concerned look on his face.

The echoes of hurt on his face slammed into her. "I'm sorry for being irritable earlier. Truce?"

"Absolutely." His smile rested easy on his tanned face. Those whiskey eyes warmed.

"Would you like to come with me while I walk Kota? I think Fleur could use some sunshine, too." She gestured to the small nature path she'd spotted just outside the fence.

He gave a backward glance into the cabin, where Fleur sat in a baby carrier. "Won't she get sick from the cold?"

"Seriously? Were you Steele children pampered wimps?" Glenna laughed, welcoming a moment's levity.

"Don't let my dad hear you say that. He believed in making us work hard. No silver-spoon, trust-fund kids in his family." Broderick took a step back so she could make her way into the cabin. Even so, her body rubbed against his, sending electric awareness into her limbs.

Glenna ignored it, responding instead with a tidbit about her own life. "Mom and Dad were the same way. We even had price limits on eating out. I remember someone commenting on it at a restaurant. Mom said, 'Yes, Charles and I have a healthy portfolio. Our children, however, have yet to earn their fortune.'" Glenna did her best to impersonate Jeannie's dramatic hand waving.

Broderick let out a chuckle, nodding as if thinking of some distant memory. "Sounds like Dad... And if we're not careful, they're going to fire all of us and start with a fresh staff."

A deep, rich laugh emerged from her. Shook her back to life. "Okay, now let's get you ready for that walk."

"What do you mean?" He pointed to his coat, as if that was all there were to their excursion. "I have my winter gear."

Raising a brow, she gestured to the carrying pack in the living room. "You'll need to keep Fleur close to your chest so she'll be warm and secure."

"What about a baby sled instead?" he asked quickly.

He was obviously nervous, but Glenna recalled how he'd handled Fleur last night when no one was looking. A natural. Though he clearly needed encouragement.

"This is a difficult time, with her being away from her mother. The baby needs as much human contact as we can give her."

"I could walk the dog." His counteroffer was smooth, but didn't completely mask his unease.

"Are you afraid of babies?"

"No. I'm afraid of that contraption." He walked to the swaddle pack, picked it up. He examined it gingerly, as if it might move of its own volition.

"Think of it as a hiking pack on your front."

She quickly assembled Fleur in the pack on Broderick's chest, showing him how it worked and barely resisting the temptation to take a little extra time touching him. Things were…complicated. This walk would do them good. If Fleur was his, he had to learn.

Glenna playfully squeezed his arm. "And now we're ready to walk."

She let him lead. After all, these were Steele family grounds. He'd grown up here, knew the trails. Kota walked in step with them, and Glenna drank in the untouched scenery. Not another building in sight. Perfection—she'd found it.

They hiked toward the mountain, boots crunching in the unmarked snow. Silence descended between them, the comfortable familiar kind. Fleur made giggling noises, soft and lovely. Broderick seemed to calm down the farther they went.

Feeling empowered and brave out in nature, Glenna asked, "Do you think our families would have been friends if they'd all worked for the same business or if we'd lived in the same neighborhood?"

"Hmm… That's an interesting thought. The Steeles and Mikkelsons going to block parties together."

Her lips felt slightly chapped by the persistent wind. "Silly question. I'm just feeling whimsical, I guess."

"It's not silly at all. I imagine we would have built forts and had snowball wars."

She chewed her lip before adding, "Boys against the girls, naturally."

"I bet you girls would have won. Especially with my sister Breanna on your side."

"That's the first time I've heard you mention her." The loss must have been monumental. She felt for him. She understood loss well.

"That seems wrong somehow, that I don't talk about her more. She should be remembered." His voice sounded honest and raw. She knew sharing this must be hard for him, but he'd said he wanted to be friends. He wanted more. Could she be there for him?

"Do you want to tell me something about her?" When her grandmother was alive, she'd often talked about people in her life who had already passed on. She'd tell stories of their lives, and in doing so, had preserved a part of them. That was a small gift Glenna could offer Broderick.

"She was full of spirit and one helluva leader in the making."

Glenna snorted. "Naomi is spirited."

He laughed and rolled his eyes. "Naomi is a rebel. Breanna was more focused, always charging forward, so I figured I better keep up. She made me stronger."

"Losing someone you love is so hard. There's no set way for how to deal with it. We're all different. Losing your mother at the same time is just horrible." All losses hurt. To death, to divorce, to time.

And therein lay the core of why this offer to start something serious with him gave her such pause. She needed to make him understand that committing to a relationship, even without being in love, wasn't something to be taken lightly, no matter how much it streamlined their practical concerns.

"We were all changed because of it." Broderick stopped walking for a moment to stare at her. "I'm so very sorry about your husband's death. This has to be hell for you, waiting for the paternity results."

She swallowed, pushing her feelings to the pit of her stomach. "I'm sure it's difficult for you, as well, not knowing if Fleur is yours."

"It's different for me. I understand that." He squeezed Glenna's hand.

"Are you trying to ask me if I really think she could be his?" She found it impossible to keep a neutral tone.

"There's no need for me to ask. The test will speak for itself." His evasive answer did nothing to soothe her.

"But you want to know if I believe my husband would cheat on me." That was the question he wasn't asking.

"It's not my place to ask. But I do care if he hurt you or betrayed your trust." Broderick looked at her.

She inhaled deeply, smelling the pine, letting the crisp air steady her. In a small voice, she answered him. Gave him a secret few people knew. "He had an affair three years ago. We worked through the problem with a counselor. It wasn't easy, but we put our marriage back together."

"Damn, I am so sorry." He turned to face her, concern etched in the lines on his brow and at the corners of his mouth.

"He's dead." She could barely choke out the words. "I'm sorry most of all about that."

"Of course," he said gently.

"I told him if he cheated again, that would be a deal breaker. But I can't help thinking that if he *had* cheated again, he wouldn't have risked telling me because he knew I would walk."

"And?" Broderick's head tilted.

"What do you mean? Isn't that enough?"

He stared intensely at her. "There's more on your face."

"If Fleur is his child…it means he betrayed me again. And yet I don't know how I can let go of her. She's the last piece of him. I know that sounds all tangled up—that I would have left him for being unfaithful, but thinking of her being his child makes me ache. We had trouble conceiving. I have endometriosis and lost an ovary during an ectopic pregnancy." She drew a deep breath. Then another. All the pain of the last few years rushed through her.

Broderick reached to stroke her hair.

She leaned into his touch for an instant before pulling away. "I don't want sympathy. I just want answers." She cleared her throat. "What are your plans if the test shows you're her biological father?"

He looked down at Fleur, whose eyes had shut. Her breath was deep as she slept. He smiled at the baby. "I'll be her father. She's already suffered enough rejection from her mother."

"One way or another, she will be staying with our new extended family."

"Appears so. You're good with her."

Glenna smiled as she moved closer to look at Fleur. "I love children. I've always wanted to be a mother."

"You can still be a mother, no matter the outcome of the DNA test."

There he went. Pushing that offer at her again. The one she had no idea what to do with. "I realize that, but I don't want to discuss it. Thank you for caring."

He touched her face. This time, she lingered, staring into those eyes. Lifting her head, she closed her own, and her lips found his…

Instantly, she was entranced by the warmth of his tongue, a brilliant contrast to the cold of the air. His hands found her hair, pulling her closer, becoming more urgent…

The world tilted. Literally.

Kota pounced on them, flattening Glenna to the ground. As she stood, dusting off her jacket, she couldn't help but think how the pup had saved her from herself.

# Nine

Losing himself in memories of past winter meals at the cabin, Broderick flipped open the lid of the slow cooker. He checked the status of his family's recipe for caribou stew. A roll of steam billowed out with the scent of thyme. He waved some of the fog toward his face, breathing in the smell of the hearty meal promising a flavor he found only in Alaska. Comfort food, really.

His personal favorite, and he looked forward to sharing it with Glenna after she finished putting the baby to bed. At the moment, she was oblivious to his nostalgia, sitting on a quilt on the living room floor with Fleur and some activity toy.

His parents would sleep in the master bedroom. The girls slept in the small spare room—a room Fleur would use now—and the boys would sprawl out in the loft. Family time was full of snowmobiling, fishing and hikes, until they came back to the cabin exhausted and famished, leaving a trail of soggy snowsuits, caps, gloves and boots behind them.

This recipe came down from his grandmother. Every time he made the stew, he envisioned his grandma and mother dicing the tomatoes and onions. They didn't need to measure the broth and spices. Everything was done by eye, and even when his family had become richer than Midas, with a crew to help in the home, his grandmother had insisted the recipe wasn't falling into any stranger's hands. And that even if a staff chef attempted to recreate the recipe, no one could cook the stew as well as she could. Broderick agreed.

The caribou stew recipe was a part of their family DNA.

Taking a wooden spoon off the ceramic spoon rest, he stirred the chunky soup, which had been simmering all afternoon, checking the color and consistency. He felt as if someone was staring at him and looked up to find Kota sitting pretty. Those icy blue eyes left no mistake. The puppy was working his charm for a treat.

"Kota, buddy, I'm not sure I'm supposed to feed you table scraps," Broderick said. "Glenna would probably kick my butt."

"Yes," she called out, "I will kick your butt if you mess with my pup's good manner."

The pup tilted his head and let out a whimper.

"Yeah, yeah, puppy," Broderick continued, half amused at her speedy response. "I know it's not fair. But I'll tell you what. I do have a soup bone tucked away in the fridge and if your mama says it's okay, you can have that all to yourself. Right, Glenna?"

"After I check to make sure the bone won't splinter or make him sick," she called back, tapping a jingling toy, enticing Fleur to reach for it.

Kota kept waiting expectantly, making Broderick feel

like the meanest human alive. He checked that Glenna wasn't looking, and then pulled out a chunk of cooked meat and rinsed it.

Kneeling, he whispered to the puppy, "Our secret. You can have it if you work for it, okay? Your mama says the key to a balanced, well-trained dog is the motto 'Nothing in Life Is Free.' So here's the deal. You do one of your tricks and I'll give you this piece of meat. Fair enough? Now shake, Kota, shake," he commanded.

Kota lifted his paw on cue and Broderick felt as if he'd clinched a million-dollar deal. He shook the paw, then passed the nibblet to the dog on an open palm. The puppy took the treat with a gentle lick.

"Good boy, Kota." Broderick gave the husky a scratch behind the ears before standing, washing his hands and returning to his meal prep.

He scooped up a taste, assessing the balance of game and spices to make sure none overpowered the other. His taste buds all but moaned in pleasure. Sure, it could use a little tweaking, but the stew was almost perfect. Almost. He looked forward to sharing the meal with Glenna tonight as he stepped up his plans to persuade her they could be good together—

His cell phone chime cut through his thoughts.

Leaving the spoon half submerged in the contents of the slow cooker, he fished his phone out of his pocket as Kota trotted into the living area and sprawled out in front of the fireplace a good inch away from the baby's quilt, as Glenna had already taught the puppy. Glenna promptly pulled two all-natural doggy treats from her pocket to reward him.

Nothing in life was free.

Chuckling and impressed, Broderick looked back at his chiming phone. A picture of his brother Marshall popped up on the screen. Sliding his finger to answer, Broderick scanned the spice rack, looking for black pepper, to kick up the flavor a notch.

He held the phone to his ear, instinctively lowering the volume. A silly gesture, really. Glenna could hear his side of the conversation from her spot a few feet away.

Regardless, he stole a glance at her, taking in the tight-fitting dark-wash jeans and blousy aqua top that suggested the beauty of her curves. She wasn't paying attention to him, though. Instead, she'd scooped up Fleur and was cradling the baby in her arms with a smile.

"Hey, Marshall. Good to hear from you. Any news on tracking down the baby's mother? Or the father?"

That last question had his gut in knots, because he didn't have a clue which way he wanted this to shake down.

"No answer yet on either front, I'm sorry to say," Marshall said, the sound of a horse's whinny floating through the phone line. "She disappeared into Canada and not a peep since then."

Broderick ground more black pepper into the slow cooker, then stirred the stew as he watched Glenna coo to Fleur some nonsensical words that made him grin.

"Damn, who dumps their baby and just disappears? Doesn't check on the child? Nothing?" He turned around, eyes skating to baby Fleur.

Her round face beamed with happiness and light. All things good and innocent. Fleur grinned up at Glenna, whose face was obscured by strawberry-blond tendrils. A stranger peering in through the window at this moment would easily believe Glenna was the mother. Her attentiveness and empathy manifested in every movement.

Damn. This woman pierced him. Humbled him.

"I don't have the answer for that," Marshall said, always matter-of-fact.

"I realize Deborah didn't have any family to support

her when she had the baby. But if Fleur is mine, why didn't Deborah reach out to me before?" Broderick felt sick at the idea that she would think he wouldn't have assisted her. Things might not have worked out between them, but there'd be no way in hell he'd let his child suffer because of that. Family over all else. And if Fleur was his, he intended to ensure that.

"Maybe she was worried about the family money and losing her child," Marshall offered.

"I wouldn't deprive a child of its mother. I would just want rights—" Defensiveness and anger weighed down his heart.

Marshall interrupted, "I know, brother, I know." A long sigh filled the earpiece. "But it's obvious she's not thinking clearly. And then perhaps she became overwhelmed? I'm just guessing."

Exhaling hard, wanting to accept that explanation, needing some reason for this, Broderick willed his frustration down a notch. He set aside the pepper mill and sampled the stew again. Hmm…almost but not quite. And as he tasted it once more, he couldn't help but wonder if he was substituting a fixation on food for his hunger for Glenna, trying to ignore the other appetite that threatened to burn him.

Patience. The key for winning the battle with Glenna *and* with conquering this recipe. He hoped if he kept at it, he'd match his mom's skill one day. Was it a small way of recapturing a bit of the people he'd lost? Maybe.

The stew still missed something. He stared blankly at the spice rack, phone pressed hard into his ear. "I guess we'll never know until she tells us. Hopefully sooner rather than later."

"No kidding." Marshall gave a low whistle. "Naomi is working hard to research all legal aspects so we're prepared, whatever we face."

"Glad to know, for Fleur's sake. Naomi's a fierce advocate." Thankfully. He had a feeling they needed Naomi's ambition and ferocity.

Glenna had laid the baby on a blanket decorated with blue and pink polar bears. She patiently changed Fleur's diaper, making silly sounds as she went. Even from this distance he could see how comfortable the child was. The baby had two mighty advocates on her side with Glenna and Naomi. And he couldn't deny the protectiveness for the kid building in him. "I've wondered more than once why Dad doesn't put Naomi in charge of the company. She's a fighter."

He could practically see his brother shake his head, scratching under the brim of his Stetson. "You're telling me. Naomi actually asked Dad about a prenup for his marriage to Jeannie."

"Holy crap," Broderick said, then whistled softly. "Did he explode?" Naomi had never been shy by a longshot. Their father said she'd come out of the womb arguing, already a lawyer in the making. She always spoke her mind, even in difficult or touchy situations. His sister had a way of seeing the world through Lady Justice's eyes—objectively and full of reason.

"Not really, surprisingly. He said he understood those prenups were to protect the husband and the wife so their interfering children knew where things stood. And so we won't have to feel conflicted, he and Jeannie are using independent counsel to set up the will." On the other end of the phone, Broderick could hear more whinnying of horses. Perhaps Marshall was getting ready for a ride to clear his mind. Broderick could only imagine how chaotic it must be at the family property right now.

"Okay, then. So we have no idea what's going on?" His eyes slid back to Glenna. She'd put the baby in pajamas.

Scooping Fleur up, she cradled the child to her chest, completely unaware of Broderick's gaze.

Or the fact that he was remembering the perfection of her curves in that bikini she'd worn for their dip in the hot tub.

"Correct. He said it was none of our business. They are adults. And that we all have our own fortunes, so we don't need anything from them."

Broderick laughed, respecting the old man more than ever even when, sure, it would have been a lot easier to be in the loop. "Fair enough. Looking at the financials I've seen so far, the two companies are fairly evenly matched. I'm actually surprised. We've both been so damn busy trying to convince the other we had the edge, we didn't realize we were running neck and neck."

Even while he talked to his brother, Broderick's thoughts were on Glenna and how soon he could get her back into the hot tub. Or better yet, stretch her out on that bearskin rug and make love to her by firelight.

"We don't have to worry that Jeannie and her kids might try to take advantage of Dad for his money."

"And they don't have to worry we're trying to take advantage of their mom, since we're all standing soundly on our own fiscal feet."

Marshall's tone was indifferent. Broderick knew something was weighing on his brother's mind. "That's worth a bit of peace, at least."

Broderick leaned back against the counter and watched Glenna rock the baby. Fleur burped, then giggled. "Remember Mom's friend, Christy Shackleford, who married Dad's doctor? Her two sons were hell-bent from day one that their mama wasn't getting enough of the old man's estate even though he'd made provisions for the rest of her life backward and forward."

"Yeah, I do," Marshall said drily. "They guilted their mama into sneaking them money under the table while the old man was alive, and then when he died, they took the rest."

Turning back to the stew, Broderick tasted it again. There. That was right. He closed the lid. "He'd left a rock-solid will, but those boys beat the hell out of things in the legal system. Whittled the estate down to next to nothing just getting them to back off, and the poor woman barely had anything left."

"Things can get touchy when two families come together so late in life," Marshall said pointedly. "And I don't have the past you and Glenna do. You're stuck up there together with the baby and that whole paternity issue hanging over your head. Watch out for yourself. Okay?"

Broderick bristled as he chose two deep pottery bowls from the cabinet. "Greed is a hungry beast. No matter how much you feed it, it still dies of starvation."

"Are you saying we should count our blessings?"

"That's one way to look at it." He pulled out a loaf of crusty sourdough bread and set it on the wooden carving board. With a ceramic knife, he sliced thick pieces. The perfect accompaniment to the stew.

Marshall paused before continuing, "What's your take on Glenna?"

"She's worried her job will go away," Broderick said without hesitation, settling on the most benign answer he could find, because he was not talking about the kiss or his hopes of renewing their relationship.

"Valid concern about the job, really."

It was premature to discuss who the CFO would be. He was still hoping she would choose a different job and remove the controversy altogether. "She wants her mother to be happy." There was plenty of drama to go around. "And she's attached to the child already. She's afraid of the kid getting lost in the system and she is not going to want to let that child go."

A pause stretched over the phone line before Marshall continued, "Even if the baby was the product of her husband cheating?"

"I believe so." And what did that mean for him? Broderick wanted Glenna, but was he prepared to use, really use, the baby to get her? He was a tough businessman, but the harshness of using a child for leverage gave him pause.

"If she already is so attached to this kid, what's going to happen if the baby turns out to be yours?"

Damn good question. He hoped she'd say yes to his proposition and make that question void. But no matter what occurred, their time together was only going to get more complicated once the answers about the baby came through.

Leaning back against the counter again, he watched Glenna stand, then her slender silhouette disappeared as she went into Fleur's room to put the baby down for the night.

Complicated didn't even begin to describe this scenario.

If he wanted to win Glenna back in his bed—and he did—he would have to step up his game.

Jack dived into his indoor pool, the warm waters enveloping him. He had never been much for team sports, other than watching his kids play. His life was already complicated enough, at home and at work. He enjoyed recreation that afforded him time alone or one-on-one moments with those important to him. Outdoors when possible, but he kept indoor options available for himself and wearing out his kids. Like with this pool and an indoor gym.

He gravitated toward activities like fishing, hunting, swimming and sledding. He'd tried teasing Glenna that he could turn Kota into a sled dog.

She hadn't laughed.

Stroking easily, he kicked toward the other end of the pool, where Jeannie lounged on the steps. The rippling water did little to mute the appeal of her body in a sleek black swimsuit. He got plenty of time alone with her these days as their kids kept their distance, communicating via email about progress on baby Fleur and the merger of the companies.

The child was about the only issue where they agreed.

His and Jeannie's efforts to smooth over the blended family transition weren't going as planned. And he could sense her frustration growing. More and more each day. If she asked him one more time if they should delay the wedding, he was going to blow a gasket.

A final kick underwater propelled him the rest of the way to Jeannie's side. He broke the surface next to her and turned to sit on the stone steps. The hot tub bubbled a waterfall into the main pool.

She skimmed her elegant arms along the surface, trailing her hands. Her ring finger was still bare, but they'd met with a jeweler to have one custom made. "Maybe we should delay the wedding."

Damn it.

He ground his teeth and held his temper in check, wishing some of the snowflakes on the glass ceiling could rain down on his heated feelings. "Jeannie, if we back down now, our stubborn children will just keep pushing. We taught them their negotiation skills. We shouldn't be surprised they're using them against us."

"What if this push and tug isn't a game?" She tucked a damp blond strand into her hair band, gathering her locks on top of her head. "What if they really mean it? What if one or more of them cuts off from the family?"

"You're borrowing trouble. They're blood. They're not going anywhere." He refused to accept otherwise. This was the time in their lives where he and Jeannie should be handing over the reins and enjoying at least a partial retirement. He wanted her to enjoy these recreational moments and relax.

Except life kept getting tenser. He pressed his leg against hers.

"Jack, are you certain?" Her forehead furrowed and she inched away from him. Again. "Because I'm not."

"Yes, I'm sure of that." He reached for her hand, only to have her avoid his touch. "But I'm starting to wonder if there's something more going on here. Do *you* want to delay the wedding because *you* are having doubts?"

"Honestly?" She inhaled deeply, her hands clenching into fists. "I'm worried about you. You lost a child already. I don't want to be the cause of you losing another."

Her words chilled him as surely as if the ceiling had opened up to dump the snow on top of them.

"That's not the same, Jeannie, and not playing fair."

Her jaw thrust forward, stubbornness stamped all over her features. "You wanted to know what I'm thinking and there it is. I don't know if I can live with myself if I cause you to lose another child in any fashion."

"I call bull." He pointed, stabbing the water with his finger and letting flow the words he'd been bottling, the thoughts he'd been denying. "I think you're looking for an excuse to back out because things are getting tough and you're afraid of losing your kids. You're flinching at the clinch of the negotiation."

"This isn't a negotiation, Jack," she said, her voice rising with frustration. She shot to her feet, water dripping from her body as she stalked out of the pool. "This is our lives. Our children. Our hearts."

He followed her, fear filling his gut. He took her hand just as she reached for a fluffy towel. "You are my heart."

"It's not that simple." She turned to face him, their hands clasped between them.

"For me, it is just that simple."

She shook her head, backing away. "You're deluding yourself. Life is never as simple as 'love solves all.'"

Her words sank in, but more than the words, he saw her face. Felt her letting go, his whole world slipping out of his grasp. "You're breaking things off."

"I just… I need…" She gathered a towel to her chest and backed toward the changing room. "I'm going home, and no, I don't know when I'll be back. Jack, please honor that. We need space right now."

As he stood with water pooling around his feet, he could do nothing more than let her go. For now. His heart was broken, but he would not let that defeat him. He refused to believe he wouldn't have the chance to place an engagement ring—and wedding band—on her finger.

He would do whatever it took—when the time was right—to convince that stubborn woman they were meant to spend the rest of their lives together.

Glenna had just settled Fleur down for the night. The day in the snow had been exhausting—and rewarding.

Quietly, she slid shut the barn-like door to the baby's room and made her way back to the living area where—

Her stomach flipped and her heart squeezed. She blinked, barely able to believe her eyes. But sure enough, a lovely, thoughtful gesture was laid out for her. A small dinner table had been pulled in front of the crackling fire. A romantic gesture—the kind born of simplicity and earnestness. This man could afford to hire legions of caterers. Writing a check was easy for someone like him—or her. She knew the effort that had gone into what he'd done for her.

Two bowls of stew with steam rising framed a plate of thickly sliced bread. The Steele family's personal beer label on a large longneck bottle glinted in the firelight. Two beer mugs were filled with the pale foaming brew.

A real home-cooked dinner. It'd been ages since she eaten something that wasn't ordered in or prepared by professional staff. Even when home, she avoided the kitchen. Cooking for one had been difficult, a glaring reminder that rendered her husband's death all the more palpable.

This gesture touched her heart on so many levels.

A candle flickered on the table, adding to the spicy aroma of the caribou stew. They both could buy whatever they wanted, which made the personal touch and effort mean more to her.

He draped a hand towel over his arm and smiled with that wicked glint in his brown eyes. "Dinner is served."

His attention was completely on her. A heady sensation. She felt the warmth of his gaze touch her skin, send her reeling. He looked so sexy, standing with the chair pulled out for her, his dark hair slightly messy.

"Thank you, Broderick. This is truly thoughtful of you." She took her seat, enjoyed the brush of his fingertips as he guided the chair forward.

"I realize you've been doing the bulk of baby care. It's only fair I pull my weight where I can. I'm definitely a better cook than I am a diaper changer," he joked, his laughter rumbling up to the vaulted ceiling.

The beauty of the fire was nothing compared with the magnetism of this man as she sat across from him. Needing to break the spell, she looked out the window, drank in the fading sun splashing the little valley in orange and red, recalling an artist's palette.

The scenery, too, failed to distract her, being just as romantic as this dinner. She might as well surrender to the moment.

She picked up her spoon, scooped up a bit of stew. Silence lingered between them as she tasted the first bite. The flavor rolled along her taste buds. Bliss. She'd had caribou stew before but nothing like this. She couldn't hold back a sigh of delight.

"Oh my, this is… I don't even have words to do it justice. Such rich flavor. I could go on, but I'm too hungry." She spooned up another taste as he laughed.

His smile of appreciation sent a thrill tingling through her. Everything about this moment had her senses on high alert, like a conduit in a lightning storm.

Across from her, the fire whispered its approval, flames leaping like dancers in a perfectly coordinated ballet. A structured, beautiful dance. Much like the one she had to perform now, to keep this surprisingly thoughtful, yet devilish man from making her life more complicated.

They ate quietly, the food so delicious she realized how truly famished she was. Her finger brushed his when they both reached for a piece of bread. Glenna's cheeks flooded with heat, but she hoped the firelight disguised the betrayal of her feelings.

Zeroing in on the sight of the mountain and elk emblem on the Steele logo, she realized she felt strangely comfortable here. Glenna felt the weight of his gaze on her, and looked up.

He tipped his head to the side, his eyes narrowing quizzically. "What happened to you?"

Such a loaded question.

"Care to be more specific?" She took a slow sip of her beer, enjoying the hoppy flavor.

"You used to be so...open." He set aside his half-eaten piece of bread and leaned forward.

"You mean back when I was naive? Before I married a man who cheated on me?" The darkness in her tone came as a defense to the pain she'd experienced.

Broderick shook his head, eyes shifting to hers. "No, I don't mean that. Not at all. In college, you were funny and you smiled. God, you smiled in a way that slayed me."

"I haven't lost my sense of humor. I smile, and I help others. Maybe you're the one who's changed," she volleyed back. And damn it all, she'd lost her husband barely a year ago.

She'd only just started to venture into the dating world and she hadn't slept with anyone. She couldn't deny, though, that she craved companionship. She'd missed these sorts of meals and conversations with a man, sharing daily life. And she didn't know how to reconcile that with her fear of investing in another relationship.

"Oh, there's no question that I've changed," he admitted. "But we're talking about you. I know you're funny and I see your smile, but it's so dark."

Playing with her spoon, stirring it through the stew, she shrugged to keep her eyes from lingering on his bold jaw. Yet dropping her gaze only brought into view his strong hand holding the mug of beer.

She cleared her throat. "It's called seeing the world." Of course she wasn't doe-eyed anymore. Reality had forced her to adapt her fairy-tale dreams.

"Not everyone lets the world make them into a cynic. I know you've been hurt, but—"

"But nothing. I don't think you're one to offer advice on getting over loss." Her head tilted toward the baby's room. Pushing out her chair, she stood, attentive and determined. "I think I heard Fleur again."

Thankfully.

He would have thought she was lying about the baby needing her. And perhaps that had been her original intent in shooting up from the table to get away from his attempt at a more serious conversation.

But now the baby's screams were piercing, so much so even Kota was running in circles, agitated and fretting.

They'd both dashed to Glenna's room, where the portable crib had been set up. Broderick's heart hammered at the distress—hell, ear-popping misery—in Fleur's cries. He scooped her from the crib, pulled her close, but the cries didn't stop.

Working as a team, wordlessly he and Glenna channeled through the obvious. They changed her diaper. Tried to feed her, but Fleur rejected the bottle and it wasn't really feeding time, anyway. They burped her again and again in case it was gas. They took her temperature. Played music. Kept quiet. Gave her a bath.

And now nothing worked except pacing the floor.

He held the baby to his shoulder and patted her back like he'd seen the child care workers do at the on-site center. But damn it all, it wasn't working. "I think I'm doing something wrong." His forehead creased, anxiety flooding back into him.

"You're doing fine." Glenna shook her head, offering an encouraging smile.

"Maybe I'm patting too hard." What if he was hurting her? He would never be able to live with himself if that was the case.

"You're probably not patting hard enough. She's not a butterfly."

Her lashes sure felt like butterflies against his cheek. Damp butterflies as big fat tears rolled down her face. God, she was breaking his heart and driving him batty at all once.

Glenna walked out of the room, motioning him to follow. "I'm no baby expert, not by a long shot, so let's see if we can figure this out. You keep holding her and I'll run an internet search. Somewhere on some forum there is an answer for this." She opened the laptop and began typing.

How had his parents survived this? Before the internet? Especially with so many kids, even a set of twins?

The thought of Breanna blindsided him.

He swallowed hard and yanked his thoughts back to the present. To this baby. This moment. And how he could get this kid calmed down and go outside to deal with the memory of losing his younger sister, Naomi's twin. "Have you found anything out on that internet search of yours? Because if you've run out of ideas, I'll look around for a while."

Glenna waved a hand at him dismissively as she scanned, a harried expression spreading across her face. Somehow…somehow this worried, harried look suited her. Glenna's dedication to this child, even in this moment of uncertainty, made her all the more alluring. She glanced up at him, exhaustion mixing with fire. "I'm still looking…"

"Look harder. Maybe we can take her on a plane ride in lieu of a car ride." He knew his parents had used the car to put Breanna asleep. They joked that even as an infant, she'd needed to travel, to move. He shoved the painful thought back down, needing to focus on the present. On Fleur. On being there for his possible daughter.

"I'm not comfortable with an impromptu plane ride in the middle of the night with no flight plan."

Damn. That made sense. His unease grew as Fleur's crying continued, becoming even more urgent. For the first time in his life, Broderick felt the tug of failure, felt he wasn't enough for the task at hand. "Fair enough. Maybe you could walk her and I'll look on the internet."

"What else do you expect to find? We've covered all the steps in Baby Care 101."

"I have friends I can ask." There were a few people at the office dancing in his mind's eye. Surely one of them would know what to do.

"Are you planning to tell them what's going on in your life? Because I'm not sure that's wise."

"I can be subtle," he protested, heat flooding his cheeks.

She burst out laughing, launching a fresh wail from the baby.

Broderick winced, not sure when he could recall feeling this helpless. "Shh, shh, shh, Fleur. I'm here. I would sing, but my voice would hurt your ears."

Glenna leaned back in her chair, her eyes softening. "You really are doing everything right. Just keep walking and let her know you're there. When you're tired, I'll have a turn. We'll keep walking until she falls asleep. Maybe it doesn't sound like much of a plan, but from everything I've read, it's a timeless one."

"Timeless plan it is. I guess there is nothing left to do." He paced around the room, slowly and gently rocking Fleur.

"If someone had told me a year ago I'd be in a cabin with you and a baby, I would have called them a lunatic. And yet here we are." She folded her arms across her chest, her expression surprisingly light and inviting.

"Yes, this was never a scenario that entered my mind, either." He walked toward the window, drawn to the blanket of stars.

"Funny how things work."

He chuckled wryly. "Truth."

Silence hung between them for a moment.

Actual silence. The baby had stopped crying.

In a softer voice, one barely above a whisper, he asked, "What do we do now?"

She pointed at the crib. "All the blogs say you should lay the baby down while she's drowsy. Let's do that. I'll be right there with you for moral support."

On creeping toes, they made their way into the small nook area with the crib. Broderick laid the baby down carefully.

The only sounds were the quiet ones of a snoozing baby. His eyes met Glenna's. And though shadows cloaked her face, she seemed calm. A small smile rested on her lips.

He realized right then why he'd jumped at the idea of making their relationship more serious.

This wasn't a casual weekend rekindling for him.

# Ten

The next morning, Glenna woke to streaks of sunlight coming in through the windows. The days were lengthening, but Alaska nights were still long, even in the spring. She stretched and wriggled her toes to work away the remnants of sleep.

And then the night came flooding back.

How she and Broderick had decided to stay in the room with Fleur. How they'd fallen asleep while waiting to make sure she was really okay. They'd had the small parenting victory of figuring it out together.

She found herself drawn to the word *together*.

Sleep had come so quickly in that domestic scene. She opened her eyes fast and found—

The bed was empty. The pillow held the indention of his head and the Egyptian cotton sheets were tangled. The fat comforter dragged off his side of the bed. She touched the space and found the fine thread count sheets to be cool. He'd been up for a while.

Her gaze skirted over to the portable crib. It was empty, as well, the whale-and-fish mobile swaying lightly. The house was silent, with not even a bark from Kota.

Curiosity, along with a hint of panic, wafted through her.

She swung her legs off the bed, the furry rug warm on her bare feet. She tiptoed along the floor until she found her fleece-lined slippers and shoved her chilly feet inside. Threading her fingers through her tangled mass of hair, she padded to the bedroom door...

And oh my, the sight took her breath away.

Broderick stood by the soaring window overlooking the water, Fleur in the crook of his arm as he fed her the last of a bottle. Kota snoozed on the sofa with an unrepentant air. The whole tableau had such a natural look, the epitome of so many dreams she'd had for her life back when she was married to Gage.

Except right now, she was having trouble remembering her dead husband's face. All she saw was Broderick's tender expression as he talked to the swaddled infant.

"Shh, little one. Let's not wake up Glenna. She's been taking such very good care of you. She needs her rest." He set aside the bottle and eased the baby to his shoulder, and a rag draped over his shirt. He patted her back a little awkwardly still, but was becoming better and better with practice. A tiny foot in a pink bootie slipped free from the blanket and Broderick ensured the little leg was well covered.

His attempt touched Glenna deeply. She leaned against the door frame, tilted her head to the side as Broderick continued, "You know, one day I'll help you with homework. We'll discuss $y=mx+b$ and other mathematical equations that will blow away the rest of the class. And I'm sure you will be the smartest kid in the room. Hey, probably even the whole school—"

Then he stopped short, as if feeling Glenna's gaze. He turned on his bare heels, a sheepish grin on his face. "She seems to like math."

Glenna laughed softly and padded closer, her heart warmer than her toes curling inside the fleece slippers. "So much so, you put her right to sleep."

He ducked his head to peer at Fleur's face. "Well, what do you know? She's out like a light." He softened his voice. "It's mind boggling how much babies sleep. Seems like she just woke up."

Glenna extended her arms, wanting a turn, hungry to feel that tiny weight curled against her. "Thank you for taking her so I could sleep in this morning."

"We're a team here. For the new family order."

Broderick placed Fleur in her arms, his hands brushing hers in the process. Little sparks of electricity danced in her stomach, awareness building.

Her gaze flashed up to his. Any question about whether or not he felt the same way was answered in that heated look. Her heartbeat quickened; her breath caught.

How long could she pretend that attraction didn't affect her? From the look in his eyes, pretense was drawing to a close.

Glenna gingerly walked to the crib and set Fleur down, caught in a dream of what this life might be. After smiling down at the baby, she kissed the top of Fleur's head. The moment her lips touched skin, she realized those test results would be back soon. The business merger would begin. And this idyllic time away would end.

Sooner rather than later.

She didn't know if she wanted to accept Broderick's offer of a serious relationship. But she knew she wanted him. And she didn't have much time left here with him. This was her chance. She intended to take it. Well, as soon as she brushed her teeth. And wasn't that a silly thought?

She sprinted into the bathroom, afraid if she took too long the baby would wake up again. Was this what being a parent felt like?

As quickly as the thought tickled at her mind and tempted her bruised heart, she pushed it aside, before it could distract her. Hurt her.

She stepped out of the bathroom in winter silk pajamas, checked on the baby again and made her way back into the living room. Broderick stood facing the window, his shoulders as broad and strong as ever. Before she could second-guess herself, she walked across the thick woolen rug and slid her arms around his waist. Wrapping herself around him.

Only for a moment did the muscles along his back ripple with tension, with awareness. Then he placed his hand over hers.

"Glenna, you have to know if we do this, it won't be a one-time deal."

His words unnerved her even as the reverberation of the sound of his voice rumbled over her skin where she lay her cheek against him.

Still, she also knew those words were very likely true. "I hear what you're saying."

She wanted him, and yes, more than once. Her body ached for a deep and sensual meeting and mating with this man. He felt so good against her, his muscled body, his callused fingers that were still so gentle.

"Good. I'm glad we have that cleared up." He turned and faced her, brushing her hair back with his hands as she linked her arms around his neck.

She trembled against him, her whole body attuned to his and the way they seemed to fit together so naturally.

Her breasts tightened against the fabric of her silk winter sleepwear, the tips aching for his touch, for his mouth. It didn't help that his fingers teased a path down the back of her neck and along her half bared shoulder, making her skin tingle in anticipation.

Her head fell back to give him better access…and she caught sight of his cell phone and computer resting on an end table, bringing reminders of work too easily to mind. Damn it, she wanted to will them away. "I do have to wonder, though, Broderick. How are we going to work together if we start sleeping together? Everything is complicated enough—"

He pressed a finger to her mouth, his voice a soft brush of sound along her ear. "Let's talk after. We're in agreement now, aren't we?"

To hell with computers and phones and business. This was their pocket of time together.

She all but swayed on her feet from longing as she nipped the tip of his finger. "Yes, we are."

Arching up, she pressed her mouth to his, and oh my, he tasted familiar and new and exciting all at once. His tongue stroked over hers in a way that made her weak with longing. Hungry for more. She opened to him, pressing herself into him. The past blended with the present as she remembered that weekend so long ago and kisses they'd shared more recently. She'd always been attracted to him. Somehow, she knew that wouldn't change with time. She knew that wasn't the same as love, but damn, the feeling was strong.

Powerful.

Her hands took on a frenzied life and hunger of their own as she tore at his T-shirt, bunching the cotton in her fists and pulling it up over his head. And as she felt the air brush her stomach, she realized he'd done the same with her sleep shirt, until they both stood flesh to flesh. Only their pants and her sports bra separated them.

He was all muscles and calluses and hints of bristly masculine hair under her questing hands, his strength formidable as she took in the breadth of his shoulders. He felt so good she could just melt all over him. Into him. She dropped kisses onto his shoulder and down his powerful chest.

She played her fingers along the warm planes of his shoulder blades, down his spine as he backed her toward the fireplace. Their shoes fell away; his jeans and her sleep pants peeled down and off without either of them pulling away from the kiss. When she stumbled slightly the hard strength of his arms banded around her. Lowering her. Laying her to rest on the bearskin rug. The fur tickled her tingling skin, almost as tempting as Broderick's lips kissing up the inside of one leg and down the other.

Moving upward again, he tugged at her waistband of her panties with his teeth, teasing without pulling them off, then nuzzled her stomach, stroking until it seemed his touch and mouth were everywhere. When she thought she would combust from the fire inside her, he stretched over her and kissed her. Oh my, how she'd missed being kissed, and kissed well.

"More, now," she whispered, nipping his bottom lip. "We can go slower the next time."

"Next time," he growled softly. "I like the sound of that."

Cool air brushed over her tightening nipples an instant before his mouth closed over one taught peak. His tongue flicked and circled until she writhed with pleasure. He teased the other with the stroke of his nimble fingers, and she ached to feel him, too, and explore, relearn the texture of him. Her hand glided down to cradle the rigid length of him, to stroke.

To remember.

His breath hissed from between his teeth, an encouraging moan stoking her desire until it was hotter than the flames in the fireplace. "My jeans. Pass me my jeans, so I can protect you."

She didn't question him for a second, just used her other hand to reach off to the side and pat until she found his pants, the denim still warm from his body. She fished in the pocket until she found his wallet, the condom. More than one. But for now, one would do.

He kicked free of his boxers at the same time he twisted the string along the hip of her bikini panties. Her lacy underwear had long been a favorite indulgence to wear under all the layers of clothes she needed to stay warm. Although right now, staying warm was the last concern on her mind.

Between the fire and this fiery man, her body was a delicious lava pool of need. She tore open the condom packet and sheathed him, held him. His eyes met and held hers as she guided him...

Inside.

A moan of pleasure rolled up her throat and free. She arched against him, the sweet pressure of him filling her, that first deep thrust almost sending her over the edge. She could have chalked it up to abstinence, but she knew better. Their connection was chemistry on overload. There was no need analyzing. And quite frankly, the last thing she wanted to do now was think. She only wanted to feel and absorb every sensation.

The bristle along his legs was a sweet abrasion as she brought her own legs up to wrap around his waist. The taste of the perspiration as she kissed his jaw was like ambrosia. The slick glide of their bodies against each other ramped up her pleasure with every roll of her hips. Each gasp of pleasure took in the scent of him mixed with the earthy air of the fireplace.

Timeless aromas and feelings imprinted themselves in her mind as they made love in their cabin, sequestered away from the world.

The pressure and pleasure built inside her in time with his speeding heartbeat until she flew apart in his arms. The force of her orgasm sent her head pressing back into the bear rug. She held Broderick tighter, closer, taking every ripple of pleasure from the moment. And more. His shudder of completion sent a fresh wave through her, stronger than before.

So much. Almost too much. Making her wonder how she would ever be able to walk away from him a second time.

Not in a million years did Broderick imagine one day he would be sitting in sweats at his cabin retreat, sharing computer files back and forth with Glenna—who was currently rocking the hell out of her sleep pants and one of his T-shirts.

They had been crunching numbers for the past hour, preparing a plan for their parents to present to the board. Glenna sat with her knee tucked to her chest as she looked at the screen.

How in the world was he supposed to concentrate with this woman in the room?

After their frenzied lovemaking, he'd taken his time. They'd moved to his bed, where he'd touched and tasted every sweet inch of her luscious body. They'd showered together, the steam of the water and their passion mingling to fog the oversize stall. A shared snack had rejuvenated them enough that he would never again be able to stand in that kitchen without thinking about lifting her onto the counter. Finally, they'd both fallen into an exhausted slumber, waking long enough only to feed the baby and go back to sleep.

Being with her shook him. Rattled him right down to the core. More than he'd expected. He had to figure this out. How to be with her in the middle of their crazy family drama.

He took a sip of coffee, counting on the caffeine to provide focus and answers. Breathing in the spiced smell of the hazelnut coffee—Glenna's favorite—he tried to focus on the low hum of the baby monitor. Still, remaining focused was hard.

He picked up an apple pastry from the plate and bit off a large bite, chewing thoughtfully.

"This financial merger is going to send us all through the ringer." Glenna's husky voice caressed him, spurring him to find the best fit for her in this new age of their merged companies.

He nodded, glancing at the various career positions on the screen. Glenna was organized and dynamic. Perhaps more of a public relations job would suit her?

"Also, about our parents... I'm still processing that." Glenna rubbed her temples before scooping up a puffed pastry. She tore an edge off, popped it in her mouth.

"I sure as hell never saw that coming between the two of them," Broderick agreed, wondering about the implications of his father and Glenna's mother as a joined force in the business world.

"They kept their secret well. Maybe we can keep what we're doing a secret, too?" Glenna teased, looking at him sidelong.

A rumbling laugh rolled up his throat. "We didn't manage that before when our families never saw each other. I doubt we'll be able to pull it off now that we'll be working together." He dimmed the light on his screen, then swiveled to really look at her. "Not to mention sitting at the holiday dinner table together. At least our discovering them in the shower kept them from eloping. I would have been sad to miss out on the wedding."

"It's still…strange. Thinking of the two of them together."

He sipped his coffee, the java warming him. "Unexpected, that's for sure. But maybe it's a sign we should take a fresh look at what happened between us in the past. We've spent so many years avoiding each other. Hearing horror stories about the other family's sharkish dealings."

"I wonder how long they've felt this way?" Glenna's voice trailed off and she seemed miles away from him as she turned to stare out the window.

"Is that your way of ignoring my question?"

She snapped back into focus, eyes narrowing as she tugged a hair band off her wrist and gathered her tousled locks on top of her head. It seemed that pulling that mane back helped her create distance. "It's my way of staying on topic. Your question is another subject for another time. Back to our parents. How long do you think this has been going on?"

Broderick couldn't help but ask, "You think our parents cheated with each other?"

"No—at least I don't think so. Even considering it makes me…unsettled. But I wonder if they had feelings for each other. It's upsetting to think back on my childhood and wonder if it was a lie." She tore off another piece of the pastry and chewed thoughtfully.

He could tell the idea upset her, perhaps because of her own experiences.

"Do you think you're feeling this way because of your husband? Afraid to trust people could really love each other and be honest? I would apologize for asking such a personal question, but our lives are already tangled up—and they will be forever." He needed to know what was going on with her. Wanted to understand.

"It's okay. You're not saying anything I haven't already wondered, too. Life is just so…" She bit her lip and waved her hand in the air.

"Complicated," he offered, giving her fingers a reassuring squeeze. At the touch, he saw her eyes widen. Dropping her hand, he smiled at her encouragingly.

She grabbed her coffee mug, holding tight to the handle. "Definitely. I take it you don't think there were any feelings between them until recently."

"I think if there were, they didn't act on them. I know none of this changes who my mother was or how much she loved her kids." He could feel emotions pull at him—the pain of losing his mother and sister so palpable.

"That's beautiful."

"The stew was one of her recipes. She only taught me and Breanna how to make it. She said just the oldest children—son and daughter—got to have the recipe."

His throat tightened and his eyes grew heavy with feeling. The conversation wasn't supposed to go here. Broderick ran a hand through his hair, trying to regain his composure.

Fraying nerves made all the colors in the room too bright.

Glancing at his drained mug, he got up from his seat and headed to the coffeepot. He focused on the darkness of the drink, the way the aroma filled the air.

Broderick needed his defenses back up if he was going to make it through the remaining days with Glenna. But damn the next few days. He needed to figure out his next few words.

Reality pushed hard on him.

* * *

Glenna couldn't help but make the most of the chance to study Broderick as he walked across the cabin's living space to refill his coffee. With his back to her, he reached for the carafe, his shoulders heaving with a heavy sigh.

In that moment, she realized that she'd pushed on a wound in his personal life that hadn't healed, still caused so much pain. Part of her considered giving him space, but a larger part of her accepted that she needed to know more. With his proposition looming between them and the DNA test due any moment, she had decisions to make.

Despite telling him no, she couldn't help but consider his offer of starting something long-term with him, to join forces for Fleur and the company—and for that explosive attraction between them. What he said made sense. But still she balked, craving a sign.

Wanting to understand him better.

Needing to tend to this wound he'd been dealt.

She understood what it was like to be emotionally raw. And really understood the value of sharing the painful memories, of giving them breath and life. So difficult, but she would push a little bit more, a little more gently.

Glenna set aside her laptop and shoved back her chair to join him at the counter. She rested a tentative hand on his solid biceps. "I'm sorry if I pushed too much with the personal questions."

"No need to apologize. We've crossed a line here today and there's no going back to the way things were."

Oh Lord. The line. She'd known that at the time, but it didn't really sink in until this moment. In this space between syllables where she and Broderick were undefined.

Kota trotted up behind her, his white-and-black snout finding her fingertips. Scratching between his ears, Glenna waited for whatever Broderick would say next. For wherever this conversation was going.

In spite of having just downed an apple pastry, Broderick pulled out the leftover stew from the fridge without looking at her. He grabbed a bowl from the cabinet and a ladle from a drawer. Eyes flicking toward her, he pointed at the food. An offer.

She shook her head, anchored herself by stroking the fluffy fur on Kota's head. Broderick shrugged, still not speaking as he poured a few scoops into the bowl.

Maybe she should stop waiting for him to share and instead offer up something of her past. For the first time, it dawned on her how closed off she'd been, expecting everything to come from him. Afraid of being vulnerable.

Glenna poured another cup of coffee, added sweetener along with half and half. Absently stirring it, she realized what she had to do, what she needed to share, how to connect with him in hopes of coming to her decision. "We rigged a zip line through the backyard over a frozen pond."

He paused midbite. "You did…what?"

"A zip line. We were young engineers and ecologically minded kids. We figured out the aerodynamics." She held the mug with two hands, blew on it to cool it. Then took a sip and nodded at him.

His face relaxed, seemed less contorted than before. "I imagine that was quite a ride."

"We were kids. Our math was good." She set the mug down, laughing softly. "Our sewing? Not so good. The sling gave way."

"Ouch. Broken bones?" he asked, pulling the stew from the microwave.

"A fracture and a dunking." She shuddered at the memory.

"Through the ice?"

She nodded. "It was scary. So scary."

"You're the one who went through?"

"Worse. My cousin Sage did. But I knew it had to be my fault." She'd been the mastermind—the one who'd suggested the zip line. Sage had volunteered to go first, trying to prove she was brave. It had been a rite of passage, one that went terribly awry.

"How did you and your brothers haul her out?"

There had been no option except action. Even now, Glenna could feel her brothers' grip as she'd gone in after Sage. Her arms reaching and thrashing in the cold water for any trace of her cousin.

"We held on to each other and went in as a human chain until she was safe."

"You could have all died."

"She would have done the same for us. We were close. You understand. You have siblings."

"We were more…competitive. But yes, I like to think we would have gone to any extreme to save each other. Actually, I know we would have." He looked down at his stew.

Glenna ran a light, encouraging hand down his back. "What about you and your sister Breanna?"

"Ah, so now we get to the heart of what you're pushing for. You want the emotional grist."

She chose her words carefully. "Your sister is clearly important to you and yet you and your family don't mention her very often."

"It was—is—painful to think about her," he admitted hoarsely, staring down into his bowl of stew. "Most people don't know, but we didn't get a clean goodbye. Long after that crash, we were tormented by calls from sick bastards who wanted to milk us for money with everything from offers to speak to her in the afterlife to people who said they'd seen her. None of those leads turned out, of course. My father had each one investigated, no matter how crazy."

"But I thought she died in the crash…"

"She did. Her body was—" he choked up "—badly burned. But there were a couple of teeth in the ashes. Her teeth. All evidence pointed to her dying that day and no ransom note ever came. We waited, even hoped for a long while, because at least that hell was better than death."

"I am so very sorry. I had no idea your family went through that. That had to be difficult for all of you, not having the official closure of saying goodbye to your sister and mother."

"Mom's body was thrown from the plane before the fire really took hold. She was already…gone. It was hell, but at least we knew."

Forget distance and boundaries. Glenna closed the space between them, slid her arms around his waist and rested her head against his chest. "Oh, Broderick, I am so sorry."

He set aside his stew and held her closer. "My father was always nervous about someone kidnapping us because of his fortune. After the crash, I thought he would lose his mind. He assigned a bodyguard to each of us twenty-four-seven. I can assure you, that gets awkward at school." He chuckled.

She didn't. Because her heart was breaking for him. She touched his face, stroking his cheek. He captured her arm to stop her, and slowly, deliberately, kissed the inside of her wrist.

"Glenna, the last thing I want is your pity. The very last thing."

His mouth sealed over hers with unmistakable possession.

# Eleven

After the passionate night they'd shared, Broderick couldn't imagine they would have the energy to make love again. But already he felt desire building inside him with each stroke of his tongue against hers. His erection throbbed between them. No question, he was ready, eager, wanted to be inside her again.

Morning sunlight streamed through the skylights over them in the kitchen, helping guide him, giving him an even better view of temptation.

Glenna's arms glided up, her hands behind his neck, fingers feathering lightly. He knew the feel of her touch against his skin, the tips of her fingers teasing along his hairline. Yes, he remembered. And she was everything from all those years ago—and more.

His hands traced her sides, then cradled the sweet curve of her bottom. He lifted her, bringing her flush against him until her feet dangled off the floor. Her personality was so strong and magnificent he sometimes forgot she was so much shorter than him, slighter in frame. She was an oxymoron of delicate power.

Her legs locked around his waist. He carried her to the kitchen table, kissing her every step of the way.

Carefully, he eased her back on the tabletop. A sexy smile spread across her face in invitation. Her hair fanned across the wood. She looked like a goddess—gorgeous, sexy, strong.

And his for the taking.

His hands stroked her shoulders, her breasts, the smooth flat planes of her stomach, until he swept her silk pajama pants down. Her sigh of anticipation drew a growl of appreciation from him.

Dropping to his knees between her legs, he caressed her, nuzzled, found her with his tongue. Her hands gripped him in encouragement. Each time they were together, he learned more about her body, her wants and her desires. He burned to glean more insights; pleasuring her damn well pleasured him.

With each touch and tease along the tight bundle of nerves, he called on the ways he knew to bring her to completion in an intense rush. Her breath came faster and faster until…

Yes.

Her back arched in pleasure as she bit back cry after cry. Her legs clamped harder at his shoulders, her fingers digging in. He guided her as each aftershock rippled through her, until she relaxed with a sated sigh.

He inched up her body and cradled her face in his hands. "Let's be together. Really together."

"You don't have to say that to get me in bed." Her eyes were heavy lidded, her cheeks still flushed from her release.

"I noticed. Now say you're ready to get serious with

me." He cradled a breast in his hand, his thumb stroking over the tightening peak.

She clasped his wrist. "Don't use sex as leverage."

"Be with me." He rested his forehead against hers, his voice hoarse with emotion.

"I heard you the first time." Easing out from under him, she righted her clothes again. He could feel her body tense as she moved away.

"I'm going to keep asking." He couldn't back down from his proposition. Not now. Not after the last few nights together. Not after all their shared history and twined futures.

"Even if it turns out Fleur isn't your baby, you want me in your life long-term?" Her tone was dark, as sharp as a knife leveled at his heart.

Broderick crossed his arms, staring hard at her. "You think I want to be with you for free babysitting services? I can pay someone for that."

Child care wasn't his concern. He had enough money to make sure Fleur had the best care possible, around the clock.

Glenna's eyes turned melancholy—with a hint of steel. "I think you're looking for a mother for her, and I'm the one who comes with the least complications."

She raked back her hair, a shudder falling from her lips down to her toes. Broderick couldn't help but note how ragged she sounded.

He laughed darkly. "If you actually believe you come without complications then you are not thinking clearly."

Nothing about their situation was simple. A decades-long family feud, engaged parents…a passion that had danced between them since they were teenagers. Now precious baby Fleur.

"There's no need to be sarcastic." She paced away from him. Creating distance. Old habits. Just like a decade ago.

She doubted him? Well, he could dissuade her of that notion. This time, he'd make sure she didn't walk away.

He followed her and rested his hands on her shoulders. "I'm serious."

"Then I will rephrase." Her face was sad, her hair a tousled mess. "You know I'm the person least likely to complicate your life by falling in love with you."

Ouch. "That's harsh. And also a weird compliment, if you think every woman is at risk of succumbing to my charms."

He ran a light finger down her arm. For a moment she leaned toward him. Almost an answer to his call.

Her face softened. "I don't mean to insinuate that your feelings don't matter. You're offering something serious. That's a big deal. But I know you're not in love with me."

*Love.* A word that only brought pain.

She had to know that. He'd thought his plan would appeal to her. God knows, the idea of a lifelong passionate friendship enticed him. A way to be connected to someone without the emotional risk, without laying bare his heart and having his scars flayed open.

Had he been wrong in his approach with Glenna? If so, it wouldn't be the first time he'd royally screwed things up when it came to this woman—or to relationships overall. "Is that what you want me to say?"

"No!" She almost shouted the word, then glanced toward the baby's room. "No," she said more softly. "I just want you to stop pressuring me. Give me time to think. I hear what you're saying and how it makes sense. But everything is happening so fast. I need time to sort through the implications. I need time. Please."

Spinning away before he could answer, she raced back

to the baby's room, the room where Glenna slept, too. Without him.

Strange how he'd been on board with an analytical decision when it came to himself, but hearing that same need for logic come out of Glenna's mouth was hard to accept.

Eyes averted, she closed the door behind her, making it clear he was not welcome.

Glenna gave up trying to sleep by five in the morning.

She'd been tossing and turning restlessly all night. The silence in the cabin was deafening. Her fault. She'd kept to her room after her argument with Broderick, stepping out only to get supplies for Fleur. However, the time alone gave her too much room to think. And feel guilty for the way she'd rejected him out of hand.

With heavy, burning eyes, Glenna glanced at the baby. Fleur still slept, her little breaths providing a steady rhythm to the early morning.

Dragging heavy limbs from bed, Glenna wondered again what to think of all this. She made her way to the crib, drinking in the peaceful scene.

She had enough financial means to make it as a single mother if Fleur became her responsibility. But if Fleur was Broderick's... Sadness slid into her throat, forming a lump at the thought of losing daily contact with the child.

In such a short amount of time, she'd become bonded to the baby. She enjoyed Fleur. And sharing the baby's smiles and sweetness with Broderick.

Thinking back to Broderick's proposition had her stomach moving like an out-of-control Ferris wheel. Perhaps... perhaps they did make a pretty good team.

Was his suggestion of attempting a real relationship just ill timed?

On tiptoes, she walked out of the room with a rumbling

stomach. In the still dark hours of the morning, she made her way toward the fridge.

The stress of the last few nights translated into a sweet tooth. Time for leftover tiramisu and a glass of milk.

She could hear it calling her name.

Lifting the container from the fridge, she caught movement out of the side of her eye. For a terrifying moment, Glenna convinced herself there was an intruder.

As her vision adjusted, she recognized the form. Broderick sprawled out on the sofa.

Relief washed through her.

"Oh my God, you scared me. I thought you'd gone to bed." Her free hand covering her mouth, she willed her heartbeat to return to normal.

He sat up, stretching, a blanket around his waist. "I fell asleep here."

The sexy timbre of his morning voice stirred something inside her, reminding her of things he'd whispered in her ear last night. The sweet litany of lover's words that made her feel beautiful. Desirable.

"I'm sorry to have woken you." Sheepishly looking at her plate of dessert, she raised it to him.

"Is the baby okay? I can feed her." All remnants of sleep left his face.

"She's sleeping well. I'm the one who was hungry." She held up a spoon. "Tiramisu for breakfast. Want some?"

"I'm good for now." He stoked the embers in the fireplace back into a blaze. "Thanks."

Broderick tossed two thinner logs into the grate. The dance of the flames reflected on his bare chest, turning the rippled muscles to burnished bronze.

Glenna sat on a bar stool, the leather cover creaking as she settled. She traced the wood grain along the breakfast bar, circling the food in front of her. "I owe you an apology for the way I behaved last night. And a thank-you for all you've done to help since we got here."

"No apologies or thanks necessary." His gaze fixed hard on the fire.

She tipped her head to the side. "Ah, come on. Your mother's stew recipe was epic."

Rising, he grinned. Half a grin, anyway. "Glad you enjoyed it."

"I liked hearing things about your family, too. Those stories make it easier for me to envision how the business is going to work after the merger. How we can all make it work." She hoped, anyway, because there wasn't a choice. The company merger was going to happen.

And a merger—a personal partnership—with Broderick?

She was still considering it.

"My dad had this annual tradition for the family. We all spent a winter weekend camping out in glass igloos. Sure, they were temperature controlled, but still it was the ultimate blending of sleeping outdoors under a clear sky with all the luxury of a hotel."

"That sounds amazing."

"It was. Dad did it for Mom, in recognition of her heritage, ours, too. You remember my mother was a quarter Inuit?" He shifted over on the sofa, making room for her.

His gesture inviting Glenna to sit with him touched her. Abandoning her breakfast, she slid from the stool and plopped down next to him. She tucked her feet by her side and positioned herself to face him. Even now, electricity hummed between them, adding fire to their conversation.

"That was incredibly thoughtful and romantic of him."

"I remember my parents being very in love. To be clear, she didn't grow up in an igloo." He chuckled. "She was the daughter of teachers, and was a teacher herself. She valued our education. My siblings and I joked we were homeschooled *and* went to public school." Pivoting on the couch, he faced her, the flickers of the fire enlivening his dark features.

"I remember when she died. The community was rocked by her death and your sister's. We all saw your father's grief." Glenna's lips formed a tight smile, and her heart was heavy with an acknowledgment of his suffering.

"You were at the funeral?" Silence fell for a moment, and even in the muted light, Glenna noted the lump is his throat. He swallowed hard, shaking his head. "I don't remember that day."

Her fingertips found his muscled arm. "We were there. My whole family."

"Thank you. I know your parents were considered a great romance, as well." He opened his hand and she slid her palm into his. Warmth and serenity seemed to emanate from him.

"I guess we both imagined our parents would stay single forever."

"The way you plan to stay single."

She avoided his searching gaze by looking toward the fire. "Work and family fill my life."

"Yet you are prepared to parent Fleur." He angled forward, examining their hands. He brought her knuckles to his lips, planted a soft kiss on them. Butterflies tickled her spine. He pressed on after a pause. "You have to realize that no matter whose child Fleur turns out to be, she's another symbol that our families need to unite."

"I want to raise her, regardless. You have to know that." She squeezed his hand before dropping it, coiling back into herself.

An exasperated sigh pushed out of his mouth with a

hissing sound. "Then let me help you. You can be her mother no matter the outcome. We can parent her together."

He sounded so urgent. Yes, Glenna's past had made it difficult to trust, making it nearly impossible to believe his motives were pure. "Are you actually using that innocent baby to get me to give up my job with the company so you have a clear shot at CFO for the combined corporation?"

"No," he said, almost too emphatically. "Of course not. I'm just tossing options out there for us to discuss."

Ah, right. Options.

Which meant changes for her.

She shot up, headed back to the counter and the abandoned tiramisu. She shoveled a bite into her mouth, a poor substitute for all the things she hungered for in life right now. "Why don't you spell out these 'options' a little more clearly."

"You can consult, be the epitome of the working mom, have it all."

Ah, there it was. The catch. Disappointment filled her, over a hope she'd only just begun to embrace. "Why is this job so important to you?"

"Why is it important to you?" He matched her fiery tone with his own.

"It's my family's business. My legacy." Her work identity and her role in the family were integral to her self-concept, providing a rock to build on after her husband's cheating and then, later, his death. "There's your answer. Why should it be any different for a man than a woman?"

"How long have you been working for the company?"

"Are you going to dare say that because I'm a woman and was trying to start a family I care less somehow? Because if you go down that path…" Pacing restlessly, Glenna became mercury rising, fury mounting as her voice rose an octave.

He held up a hand, his eyes brokering for peace. "That's not what I meant."

"Are you sure? Because I'm not. If you find out you're Fleur's father, will you cut down your hours to work part-time?" She read his face, then her brows rose in bittersweet victory. "I thought not."

He began to speak, but stopped, his gaze pushing past her, above her. Growing...softer as he focused on the skylight. Following his glance, she found herself settled by the bit of northern lights visible. Blues, purples and pinks streaking across the sky in a shimmering nimbus. For a moment, the fight left the room. Or at least went on pause.

She nibbled her bottom lip. "I never get tired of seeing this."

"Me, either. My sister says this is why it's so important we're careful about the pipeline." Alaska's unearthly beauty never grew old for him.

"She's right. Our state, this place, is a treasure to protect. The Dakotas, too." Glenna couldn't keep the regret from her voice as she asked, "How can we have so much in common and be so far apart at the same time?"

"We don't have to be far apart." He said it quietly, without fuss or his usual hustling pressure. Genuine. Earnest.

Maybe he was right. Perhaps her own stubbornness wasn't that different from his. Without compromise they would never run the company or parent well. With so much at stake, she needed to take a step toward trust.

Her heart sped up ten beats faster than normal.

*Leap.*

It wasn't her normal policy, but it felt right. Leaning back on the countertop, she felt the words in her heart before they came out of her mouth. "Okay," she answered before she could second-guess herself. "Let's be a real couple."

Broderick's face twisted in surprise. He blinked. Once. Twice. As if blinking replied to her words. She saw his disbelief fade, traded for happiness. And yes, she saw victory in his expression, too.

"Really? Wait, don't answer that. I don't want you changing your mind."

In a moment, he had closed the distance between them. Strong arms found her waist, lifted her up. They spun, her head back in a wicked laugh, hair fanning around her.

Broderick brought her back down. Kissed her deeply, his hand cradling the back of her neck.

Anticipation pulsated between them.

A sharp ping burst into the air.

Then another.

Broderick's ring tone.

He set her down, grabbed the phone off the counter. Moments that felt like hours passed as Glenna watched him take the call.

"Yes. Okay. I understand. We'll be there." An abrupt conversation. Everything about his features changed as he hung up.

"There's news. Good news and, um, I-don't-know news."

"What the hell does that mean?" she asked in frustration.

"Good news? The authorities have found Deborah and she's continuing to assert she wants to sign over her legal rights to the family of Fleur's father."

Relief and trepidation warred in Glenna's stomach. "And the other news?"

"The DNA test is back. Except the lab won't reveal the results to anyone except Fleur's family. They're asking us both to come in, but they won't say which of us they wish to speak to."

Just like that, Glenna knew this moment would change

everything. They wouldn't have the opportunity to start a relationship on even footing, where neither of them knew who had parental rights to Fleur.

The scales were going to shift.

The next several hours blurred. She barely registered the too-bright light of the waiting room or how uncomfortable her green chair was.

They'd packed up everything and made it back to Anchorage in record time, with little conversation beyond the practical words needed to move things forward. For the past half hour, they'd been outside the doctor's office. Waiting.

Her stomach somersaulted, revolting against her.

Broderick paced with baby Fleur. Had it really only been a few days ago that holding her had seemed to scare him to bits? Now he looked as though they'd been together since birth. Fleur rested comfortably in his arms. While that should have reassured some part of Glenna, her heart hurt.

They'd both told their respective families they didn't need support here today. This was a matter they could handle alone. But Glenna's sister-in-law, Shana, saw through that line and made sure to be in the doctor's waiting room, anyway.

Glancing down the hallway, Glenna watched the doctor talk on his phone. Torture. The information was so close to being revealed. So close to changing their lives.

Putting her hands in her lap, Glenna took a deep breath, trying to focus on that simple action.

Shana stroked Glenna's back, reassuring as ever.

In these moments, the world seemed so clear. Hindsight being twenty-twenty and all. Why didn't she delay the results? Why didn't she ask for that?

She wasn't ready to know the truth. Not really. A lump pushed into her throat.

Except she knew why they had come straightaway. She and Broderick had both rushed here. Once those results were in, they'd needed to get back to Anchorage as quickly as possible, for Fleur's sake. They couldn't risk even the slightest delay that could cause a hiccup in custody. Even with Deborah Wilson's signed statement surrendering rights to the baby, so much could go haywire. Fleur had to be the number one priority.

Which meant Glenna should have accepted his offer to start something real between them sooner. Any relationship—if it was still going to happen—would come second to fighting for custody of Fleur.

It had been a long, quiet flight home.

Images of what could have been her future sucker punched Glenna.

Shana's low, honeyed voice cut into her thoughts. "Are you sure you're ready for this?"

Blinking, Glenna sat up straight. "Of course. I have to be."

It was a lie and the words tasted like ashes in her mouth.

"For the baby or for the business?" Shana scrunched her nose, looking at Glenna sidelong.

"Both, of course. They're tied together because it's all about the future of our family."

"I hear you." Shana shook her head, cutting to the quick of the matter. "But that's still not my question. Are *you* going to be okay if you have to let the baby go?" She never pulled punches with Glenna. Always said what was needed, even if her words were difficult to confront.

"I have to be."

"Even if Broderick is the baby's father?"

Another question Glenna couldn't answer. She wasn't

even sure if her answer mattered or not. But however this turned out…it would be difficult. Painful as hell, actually. Because, oh God, she wanted this baby to be hers. And even as she thought that, fast on the heels of that possibility was the reminder that becoming Fleur's mother meant she would have to face what a sham her marriage had been. Face the fact that Gage had broken his promises after the tremendous effort it had taken to repair their marriage after his first infidelity.

Or had it been his first?

Glenna swallowed down bile.

"Thank you for your concern. But I can't worry about what I can't control." If the baby was Broderick's, then would she always wonder if he'd asked her to play house with him just so she could be a surrogate caregiver? An easy two-for-one option that would take care of his child and streamline matters at work?

As much as she wanted to pour out her fears to Shana, she couldn't bring herself to say the words out loud for fear she would fall apart.

"You keep talking about the practical concerns, but there's so much more going on here than that. I can see it in your eyes." Shana rested a hand on Glenna's arm and squeezed lightly. "Honey, I can't help but worry you're going to get hurt."

Glenna felt transparent. So she pushed back, injecting ink into the situation.

"My heart is closed up tight." Her fist clenched involuntarily.

"Ah, honey, take care of yourself." Her sister-in-law slid an arm around Glenna's shoulders and hugged her close for a moment. "You know I love you as much as any sister. No in-law part to it."

For a moment, all Glenna could do was nod before speaking. "I know, and I feel the same."

"Good, very good." Shana hugged her tight and said with a catch in her voice, "Call me if you need me."

"In a heartbeat." Glenna hugged back before easing away. She hesitated, something keeping her from ending the conversation, after all. "And you? How are things? Are you all right?"

"Fine. Just tired… And no," Shana said with a sad smile. "I'm not pregnant. Definitely not."

"I'm sorry." She knew they'd been trying for so long and understood the heartache of infertility all too well. There were no words to make it easier. There was no "right" thing to say.

"Thank you for not telling me 'It will happen.' I'm really tired of that." A forced smile pressed her lips tight—

A receptionist in a bright pink dress walked out, clipboard in hand. Pushing a piece of mahogany hair behind her ear, the woman cleared her throat.

The name she was about to call would be Fleur's parent.

The moment seemed to last forever, tension building like a terrible storm. Glenna's breath caught in her throat as she waited.

"Glenna Mikkelson-Powers, the doctor will see you now."

Her stomach lurched with the reality that Fleur was her baby. Her dead husband's child.

Her hand trembled as she pressed it to her lips, as if somehow that could hold back the reality. "Gage," she said in a tortured whisper. "Gage is Fleur's father."

So many thoughts jumbled on top of each other—especially the realization that Gage had cheated again in spite of his vow. He'd betrayed her. Once more.

Eyes flicking to Broderick, she took in his features

and the pain there, as well. A wave seemed to knock into him, pushing against him with force. Heartache twisted his normally handsome features, made him clench his jaw.

He'd been hoping Fleur was his.

In that instant, Glenna realized how much he cared about the baby, enough to offer a relationship to a woman he didn't love. Even though he was hurting, she realized that now his need to have Glenna as the baby's mother was gone.

Her chance to have something real with Broderick had ended.

Because even if he still wanted to take that leap for himself or family unity, her dead husband was Fleur's father.

And Glenna's already fragile ability to trust had just taken a fatal hit.

# Twelve

Jeannie sagged back against the hospital vending machine, cradling a cup of coffee. Needing the caffeine, the warmth. And knowing it wouldn't come close to heating the chill inside her while she waited for Glenna to finish her meeting with the doctors. Broderick had left, his face stormy.

How would this family ever heal now? She hadn't even told them about her breakup with Jack. So much had been going on with the baby. Plus, she and Jack needed to talk practically about the merger plans that had already started...

Such a tangle.

Her heart ached for all of them. Her daughter's husband had cheated. God, that was such a betrayal, and there was no recourse to fix things since he was dead. This situation would have been so much easier if Broderick had been the father.

But he wasn't. And they had to deal with that.

The child was a part of their family.

Her family.

But Jack's?

Broderick said he still loved the child, but she and Jack had split and life was such a mess. She'd thought her heart couldn't hurt this much again.

She was wrong.

Heavy footfalls pulled her from her thoughts, familiar steps, steady and sure. Jack's. Her eyes closed as she drew in the scent of him and waited for him to speak.

"Jeannie, we need to talk."

Biting her bottom lip, she glanced down the hall toward the doctor's office. "Glenna—"

Jack held out her coat. "Her siblings are waiting. I told them to call you the minute she's done. Let's walk, outside. Please. I may be a businessman, but my thoughts work better out in the open. In my Alaska."

As much as she wanted to challenge him for taking over, she also saw the heartbreak in his eyes. She dropped her coffee into the trash and slid her arms into her parka. "How did you know I was feeling restless and in need of a walk?"

"It was a guess," he said, as he led her toward the small courtyard, with a path and benches cleared of snow. "We share so much in common with how we embrace this home of ours. Am I wrong?"

"Of course you're not," she answered as the doors closed behind them. A brisk wind churned flurries and she shivered.

"You don't have to make that sound like a bad thing." He looped an arm around her and pulled her to his side, warming her through and through. "I happen to think it's very good. I like who you are—a boardroom goddess and an earthy woman all at once."

"Things haven't changed for the better with the news

today. If anything, they've gotten more complicated." She'd missed talking to him, working problems through. She valued his feedback, as she knew he valued hers.

Had she been wrong to break things off between them? Even now, it seemed impossible to pull away from the warmth of his touch. The comfort of his embrace. How had she walked away from him the first time?

"I suspect that will be the case more times than we can count. Yes, things are complicated for us. But there's only one way around those problems."

She glanced up at him, his wind-ruddied face so handsome her teeth hurt. "What way would that be?"

He stopped and clasped her shoulders. "Together."

Her heart swelled to hear those words and she knew she had to pull back before she caved.

"Jack—"

"Jeannie, hold on. Listen, please. I'm not dismissing your concerns. God knows, the thought of having one of my kids walk away forever scares the hell out of me." His exhalation was full of emotion, swirling between them in a white cloud. "I know they're as stubborn as their old man. But I also know they're the amazing people they are, in great part, because Mary and I didn't compromise our principles. I suspect the same was true with how you brought up your brood."

She nodded, unable to deny it. And also unable to deny how much sense he was making. Could she trust him to put her fears to rest?

"Then you know, my dear, if you love me even half as much as I love you, we have to stay the course." He brushed a snowflake from her nose, then stroked her cheek, his gloves scratchy, but his touch gentle. "I love you. I want to spend the rest of my life with you and I believe you feel the same. You love me so much you were willing to give me up because in some convoluted way you thought that would make me happier."

She blinked back tears. "I can't bear the thought of causing you hurt."

"Jeannie, love. Being with you makes me happy." His words rang with certainty. "The thought of my life without you by my side is unbearable."

"And you are sure?" She had to ask again. Or maybe she just wanted to hear it, the truth that made her heart sing and gave her such joy and hope.

"Absolutely."

"Okay then." She blinked back the tears, nodding, peace rushing through her for the first time since she'd walked away from that pool. "We're getting married."

"On schedule." His tone left no room for misunderstanding.

"Yes." She laughed at her stubborn man, but then she was stubborn, too, just subtler about it. Luckily, they wanted the same thing. "On schedule. As soon as possible, I want to be your wife, wearing your ring and sharing our lives."

He sealed their promise with a kiss, one that mingled all the textures of their feelings for each other. Friendship. Passion. Constancy. And before she finished her thought, he eased his mouth away.

He rested his forehead against hers. "Our children will come around and we will help them through the tough times life brings. Like now. We just need to be here to listen, support them, help if the opening arises. Jeannie, they *will* come around," he repeated.

"I think so, too."

And in that beautiful truth, she realized that even though they hadn't borne children together, they would celebrate and enjoy grandchildren together. In fact, they'd already welcomed their first. A precious, innocent life that had helped bring them all together.

Their beautiful future stretched out before her, a future full of family and love.

Fleur wasn't his daughter.

Glenna was walking away again.

Considering flying back to the cabin to lick his wounds, Broderick leaned on the dock railing at the Steele family compound, his coat zipped up tight and his Stetson holding firm in spite of the wind whipping off the water. Chunky bits of ice floated in the private bay, leaving spiky shards in their wake, much like the emotions inside him.

Once the doctor had called Glenna, making it clear she was the one with legal rights to Fleur, Broderick hadn't been able to stand around idle with his world crashing down on him. He'd pushed back the roaring denial and passed the baby over to Shana.

Then he'd made a hasty as hell retreat out of there.

He should be relieved to resume his old life before things had gone haywire. Before his reunion with Glenna. Before a certain infant had wriggled her way into his heart. But he wasn't relieved. Somewhere along the way, he'd grown to enjoy—deeply—that pattern at the cabin.

What he'd found with Glenna and Fleur had become about more than settling family drama. He wanted Glenna and Fleur in his life. Because damn it all, he couldn't deny the truth. They were firmly lodged in his heart.

And he didn't have a clue what to do next. Because he'd heard the pain and betrayal in Glenna's voice when she'd said, "Gage is Fleur's father."

He'd seen just as clearly in her eyes that she was crushed over this new infidelity from her now deceased husband, even though she loved the baby. There was no way Glenna would have faith in a man after the way that bastard had abused her trust.

So Broderick had left, giving her the space she would need to process her grief, with the support of her sister-in-law.

He gripped the dock railing until splinters pushed through his gloves. Normally, a dose of the outside world was a remedy for him. But as the cold wind pushed against his face, he felt an answering coldness rise deep within his chest.

A sharp inhalation burst through his lungs. Breath had become hard. He'd hated the look of utter betrayal on Glenna's normally composed face. He couldn't protect her from the truth any more than he could make Fleur his biological daughter.

He tried to stabilize his world. Another gust of wind pushed on his chest, threatening to take his Stetson on a journey toward the bobbing seaplane in the nearby bay. Hands flying fast to his head, he pushed the hat back down. Took another breath and then let it go toward the tall, sturdy mountains in the distance.

Everything had changed in the span of one sentence. His shoulders sagged under the weight of it all. He felt a hand touch his shoulder. He knew without turning.

Glenna.

Somehow, she'd already come to him, only a couple hours after he'd left the doctor's office. Her hand slid away and she stepped beside him, leaning on the railing. Her purple parka was zipped up tight, the hood on her head. Hints of hair blew from the side.

His throat raw from the wind and emotion, he asked, "Where's Fleur?"

She gestured toward the mansion on the hilltop. "Your family is watching her, and Kota, too."

"Good, that's good." He nodded tightly. "Why are you here?"

"I wanted to check on you. You left so quickly we didn't have a chance to speak."

"What more is there to say? You can't tell me you aren't in full retreat mode. So why are you here?"

Was it his imagination or did she flinch, her eyes dimming.

"It's…difficult. I'm reeling. But that doesn't mean I don't care about you."

*Care?* A wimpy damn word. Of course, he hadn't offered her much better. "I'm relieved to know her father isn't a stranger. That's good news for Fleur's security."

Glenna rested a gloved hand over his. "Broderick, I'm sorry you're hurting over Fleur not being yours."

"How do you know I'm not relieved?" he asked with a tight bravado he was far from feeling.

"Because…" She angled sideways, her cheeks and the tip of her nose pink from the cold air. "I could see it in your face, then and now. You're attached to her."

The baby wasn't the only one who'd become important to him. Seeing Glenna now, remembering what they'd shared, hurt like hell. Because he knew it was over.

"Who wouldn't?" he admitted, thinking back to the way the baby giggled. To all the innocence and trust in her alert eyes. "You're an incredibly capable woman. I believe you have this covered. You can handle parenthood without me." Though his words were dull and hollow, he attempted to smile at her encouragingly.

One of her eyebrows shot to the sky. Then he saw her features school themselves into boardroom neutrality.

Her chin trembled, before it tipped with strength. "I'm overwhelmed at the reality of being her mother. I can't deny that. And I have to admit that I'm tempted to ask for all the help I can get."

She was actually still considering coparenting with him? "But you don't trust me. Your husband hurt you. He betrayed you again. It doesn't matter what I feel. If you can't trust me, then there's no way a relationship between us will work."

Her forehead furrowed. "Don't put this all on me. You're the one who had the practical, no-emotions proposition. And now that I've accepted, you're ready to run. Or fly away. I can see it." She gestured to the plane.

"You're suddenly a mind reader?" Well, she was in a way, but realizing she read him so well only made him even more frustrated.

"Broderick, I don't know what you want from me." Her voice sounded weary, defeated.

As much as he wanted to take her up on the offer of seeing what they could be to each other, to help in a future with Fleur, he realized now that if he couldn't have it all with Glenna, it wouldn't be enough. He didn't want just an affair or a partnership for the baby, or for her to move in with him. He wanted her love.

But she loved a man who'd betrayed her, who'd damaged her heart quite possibly beyond repair. Broderick knew what it was like to live with the pain of loss and how it could damn near cripple a person's emotions.

They'd both suffered enough.

"Glenna, we're just torturing each other, dragging things out. This conversation is leading nowhere good."

The world pushed too hard on Broderick today. Fulfilling Glenna's prophecy, he practically ran to the plane. Slamming the door behind him, he took to the skies. Didn't care where he was headed.

So long as it wasn't here.

* * *

Glenna's thinly constructed scaffolding of emotional coping mechanisms began to give way as she watched the seaplane fade from view.

Broderick had left her.

Left her.

The realization tore at her already frayed nerves, slowed her heartbeat. How could he leave her without a real explanation?

Already, today had been too much. Her world had tilted when the receptionist called her name. The truth of her late husband's infidelities had crashed into her.

Somehow, she'd foolishly held out a sliver of hope that when she walked out on the dock to talk to Broderick, things would be okay. She'd make peace with him, at least for the moment. Doing that had been hard as hell on the heels of realizing Gage's betrayal, but she'd tried. And Broderick had literally run away from her. God, it hurt.

Too much.

Her heart ached, and she felt the melancholy in her bones.

"Come fishing with me," a rusty masculine voice demanded.

Jack Steele?

She turned to find that, sure enough, Broderick's father stood a few steps away. She hadn't even heard him walk across the planks of the dock.

His request more than stunned her. She spun on her heel. Jack stood in a heavy flannel shirt with two fishing poles. She blinked, taking him in, fighting back the tears that threatened to spill over. "Excuse me, sir? You want me to do what?"

"Girls can go fishing, too. My daughter learned early and I expect you to bait your own hook." He extended a sleek blue fishing rod in her direction.

"I'm not arguing. I'm just surprised that this is how you would choose to, um, bond." She chewed the inside of her lip and cast a nervous glance toward where the seaplane had been only a few minutes ago.

"That goes to show you don't know me or my family. I hope we can change that, for your sake and for my son's." He thrust the fishing pole at her along with a tackle box. "Let's walk farther down the shore, where my son hasn't scared away all the good fish with his takeoff. Give a little here, okay? Let's get to know each other."

Their boots clinked in time as they walked side by side on the dock. The midday sun sparkled along the cresting ripples of the water.

She laughed drily, attempting to go with the flow in this bizarre outing. "With all due respect, sir, it's not like we have a choice. You're marrying my mother, so we're going to see each other."

They made their way off the main dock, turning a corner. Their boots crunched on stray snow as they made their way out onto a fishing platform.

Glenna grabbed the bait bucket, then stuck her hand in the chilled water, searching for the right fish. Satisfied with the one she came up with, she backhooked and cast her rod. They both heard the sound of the reel releasing the line far out into the bay.

Jack whistled softly. "Color me surprised. You're really good at that."

"My father taught me. In the early days of the business, all the extra cash went back into the company. We fished and hunted to save money on groceries. We ate well. Didn't Mom tell you?" Glenna spun the reel, comforted by the clicking sound.

"Hmm, not in so many words," he said. "Looks like

we'll all be eating well. You'll be stocking the freezer."
He cast his own line.

"This is better fresh. These days when I fish, we split
it up among the staff."

Scanning the horizon, he said, "That's thoughtful."

"Our family is so large now, I may need to stay out
here longer." Her breath caught for an instant over the
word *family* connected to the Steeles and Mikkelsons. Her
gaze drifted off to the empty horizon where Broderick
had flown away. "Our family. I'm still getting used to the
sound of that."

"Both of our families have been through a lot of pain,
a lot of loss." Jack's dark eyes searched her face.

Glenna swallowed a lump in her throat. All she could
do was nod.

His rod bent, went taut, then slack. Something had nibbled and gotten away. "I just have one more question."

"What would that be?" Glenna asked, reeling her line
in. She sent it back out, and it landed with a resounding
plop. Minor in comparison to the splash of a whale tail in
the distance.

Broderick was out there somewhere on the horizon,
hurting, aching from another loss. She couldn't help but
worry about him and what he was feeling.

And she couldn't deny she still wanted him. She wanted
to comfort him. Wasn't that why she'd come out on the
dock in the first place, instead of rushing back to her own
family home?

Heaven help her, she didn't want to let Broderick go.

Jack angled his head her way, mustache curving with
his smile. "Why do you keep calling me sir?"

His question surprised her. "I'm, uh, just trying to keep
from calling you Mr. Steele or, um, boss man?"

"At least you're not calling me that hard-nosed something or other, or worse." He pulled his line back in. Then gave another cast.

They laughed. The family feud seemed so distant, for this moment at least. "I'm just not sure what to call you."

"I prefer Jack, but that's up to you." His rod bowed deeply, and he fought with the line for a moment. Soon, he'd reeled in a fat, wriggling trout. "But we'll all have time, because there's no dodging each other. We are family. And family is everything."

Broderick was her family.

That fact truly dawned on her, causing her to reevaluate the last few hours. He was family in the most important way. He'd never turned his back on her. She'd been the one pushing him away, even as far back as college. In spite of the pain of his losses, he'd still been willing to risk it all to commit to her.

He was a man of honor. A man of deep feelings. She knew that in her heart. Her mind had just been too stubborn to listen.

But not any longer. She turned to Jack. "Is there anyone here with a pilot's license who can fly me to Broderick?"

The cabin had been colonized with so much meaning over the last week.

Sure, he had memories of the cabin from childhood. However, the memories that attacked him now were of Glenna and baby Fleur.

He sat on the deck, trying to shove the past week out of his mind. But the hot tub undid any and all progress he'd made.

He looked skyward at the sound of an airplane engine, realizing what approached wasn't a seaplane, but a twin propeller plane with wheels.

The plane touched down beautifully on the lawn, settling in a surprisingly small area. Which meant it could be piloted only by his brother Marshall. He was one hell of an aviator, though these days Delaney was giving him a run for his money.

Marshall hopped out of the plane, with no hat, his curly hair in serious need of a cut as the wind tore at him. Family support. That had been something Broderick could always count on. He drew in a breath, ready to shout. Then he saw strawberry-blond hair and a slender frame. His breath caught as Glenna darted down the steps of the plane, clutching a simple overnight bag.

A feeling like hope kicked around in his gut. No. More than that.

A rush of love so strong it threatened to take him down faster than an Arctic wave.

Marshall stopped at the bottom of the deck and cupped his hands around his mouth to shout, "Brother, are you good with me leaving?"

Looking down the steps at Glenna, Broderick saw the hope glimmering in her blue eyes. He should never have walked away from her. Should have stayed and worked things out back on the Steele family dock. But maybe he was getting a second chance. A way to put the past behind them.

He shifted his attention back to his brother and nodded. "We're good, Marshall. Thank you."

Broderick walked down the steps as Glenna walked up. He reached for her overnight bag and resisted the urge to touch her. To haul her into his arms and hold her until they both froze to the spot.

They needed to talk. He wouldn't rush her. She was here, for him. Right now, that was everything.

Walking toward the cabin steps, he asked, "Where's Fleur? And Kota?"

"We have a family full of very qualified babysitters and puppy sitters who lined up to help."

"Fair enough." They walked into the house. A fire crackled in the hearth, casting an orange glow into the room. She shimmied out of her thick coat. Damn. Glenna was elegant even in dark wash jeans and a tan cashmere sweater. It didn't matter what she wore. She always took his breath away. He couldn't imagine ever seeing her and not wanting her.

Gesturing to the leather sofa, he asked the question searing his brain. "What are you doing here?"

She eyed him warily, half reaching for him, then pulling her hand back. "I came for you. For us. If you still want to talk." She sat on the sofa, cross-legged. "Really talk. You ran off before we even had a chance to let the news about Fleur settle in." She looked at her hands. "Before I had a chance to process what Gage had done."

God, that had to have hurt her. Broderick took her hand in his. "I'm sorry. Genuinely sorry. I know you loved him."

Her eyes met his, no tears. Just full of regret. "I'm finally learning to accept the marriage for what it was. Flawed, and likely destined to fail." Her mouth half tipped in a bittersweet smile. "You may have noticed, I don't deal well with failure."

Dealing with failure? That's something he understood well. Yet, he'd never shared the greatest failure of his life, and it wasn't a story that would come out easily.

However, Glenna had made the effort to chase him. It had gotten his attention. It had given him another chance at this relationship they seemed to be starting, and he needed to deserve it. He offered up a piece of his soul—an aspect of himself that he guarded carefully.

In a quiet voice, he began, "I'd like to share a story with

you that will help you understand me better, a story passed down through my family."

Glenna stroked his hand softly, then curled her fingers around his. "I would like to hear it."

Hard as it was to say, he found he wanted to tell her. Very much. "My mom used to arrange sleigh rides for us."

"That's a beautiful memory." She stroked her thumb along the inside of his wrist.

He looked around the room, taking in the decor. He felt as if he saw the past, his former life, and the life that didn't have a chance to happen because of the plane crash. "She loved this place, her home state. We vacationed in the Dakotas when Dad had business, but this was home. For her. For us."

"She's the one you got the stew recipe from?"

"Her, and she got it from my grandmother. Yes. My mother wanted to teach us about how her Inuit grandparents lived as much as possible. We hunted, moose mostly, and fished, to fill freezers for orphanages and local food pantries. We still do."

"I've gotten a sampling of your father's fishing skills."

What? Interesting, and worth talking about later. Right now, he needed to stay on task. "Caribou, too, obviously. We even hunted some seals."

Surprise washed over her face. "You caught a seal?"

"With some serious help from my great-grandpa. I was more of a lightweight participant. It was a memorable day, to say the least. But I learned lessons from them that stay with me now."

"Such as?" she pressed.

He adjusted his body on the couch, facing her, hoping she would grasp the importance of what he was trying to explain. "In the pure Inuit culture, there was no social structure or class, no ownership. The earth and its resources belonged to all of us. It was shared property for living and hunting."

"Everyone was equal?"

"To a degree. There were people with a higher status based on things like seamstress skills. Being a shaman. Others. But you had to pull your weight." He chuckled. "Now that's a credo my father wrapped his brain around."

A small smile played at the corners of her lips. For the first time since she'd arrived at the cabin today, she seemed calmer. More assured. "I can see more and more how our parents are going to mesh well."

"My grandparents made sure we heard the legends directly from them, not from a book. Like the legend of the Qalupalik. She was green and slimy and lived in the water. She hummed and would draw bad children to the waves. If you wandered away from your parents, she would slip you in a pouch on her back and take you to her watery home to live with her other kids. You would never see your family again."

The story had terrified him and his siblings when they were younger. A small memory wafted through his mind as he recalled how Delaney had cried the first time she'd heard it.

"Sounds like a certain fish movie that's quite popular."

He spread his hands. "Hey, when a life lesson works, it works." Which brought him to his point, what he needed her to know. "We also had our own werewolf legend about the Adlet. They were said to have the lower body of a wolf and the upper body of a human—"

"Like centaurs," Glenna said, leaning forward. Her attention fully on him.

Good. This was progress.

"I guess so. And apparently, they still roam. My

brothers and I tried to hunt one once. We had to turn back because Naomi tagged along and Aiden followed her... Are you just being polite? You have to have heard all of this."

"I haven't heard it this way. Not from you." She narrowed her eyes as if trying to discern his intent. "What are you trying to tell me?"

The thoughts sliced at his insides like more shards of ice. "Naomi and Brea were twins. They were supposed to have that special bond. People worried more about her after we lost Brea, and I understand that. But she and I were close, too." A pained smile tugged at his mouth. "She was even given the name I was supposed to have if I'd been a girl. She was my baby sister. I was supposed to protect her."

He swallowed hard before continuing, "Since my sister Brea died, I've felt like half a person—like the legend of Adlet. I didn't think I had anything of substance to offer another person, not until these past days with you and Fleur."

Glenna's blue eyes melted, tears glimmering. She squeezed his hand. "For a confident businessman, you vastly underestimate yourself."

Hope kicked up another level, along with awareness from the feel of her hand in his. "I think you just complimented me."

"I did. You are an incredible man on so many levels." She took his other hand, as well, pinning him with an intense gaze. "Why would you want to settle for a loveless relationship? I accepted a half measure in my marriage for years and I can tell you, it eats at your very soul."

He ached for her and the pain she'd been through. She deserved better.

He wanted to give her better. "I wasn't settling, not by

a longshot. You are everything I could ever want in my life. I realize now I was more concerned about being what you need in *your* life."

Her eyes filled with more of those tears and she moved forward as he leaned toward her. Their mouths met, not in a kiss of unbridled passion, but one of relief, connection.

And love.

He felt the emotion without hearing the word. The connection went beyond the electrical current that set their senses on fire. This feeling was more like northern lights of the soul.

Her hands rested against his chest, sending his heart slugging against his ribs. "Broderick," she whispered against his lips, "we haven't made our report to the board. What about our jobs?"

"I'll step aside," he said without hesitation. And he meant it.

To win over Glenna, there was no sacrifice too great. And with her at his side, he knew he could achieve success beyond any preconceived plans he'd set for his life. She opened his horizons.

Enriched his life.

Her eyebrows shot up in shock. "You'll do that? You can't possibly mean to give up your job, your stake in the Steele business."

"No job is more important than you." He meant those words more than any he'd ever spoken. "There is more to life than work. There is family."

"But…your job *is* your family."

"No. Not anymore," he said simply.

"You really mean this." Amazement entered her blue eyes as she scanned his face.

"Whatever I need to do to prove to you I want to be the man you deserve."

She flattened a hand to his chest. "You don't have to do this for me."

He smiled unrepentantly. "It's not like I'm lacking financially. I work because I want to, not because I need to. I can consult. Spend more time with you. With Fleur."

She blinked fast, nibbling her lower lip, then blurted out, "What if we both consult?"

"Run that by me again? I'm not sure I heard right. You've been so adamant about your family legacy. I don't expect some kind of quid pro quo on the job-quitting front. We'll both be making sacrifices along the way. I get that. And I also get that our relationship, our marriage, will be worth it."

"Broderick…" She squeezed his hand hard. "*Family*. Isn't that what we're talking about? You and I building a family together? Marriage, even. This is *our* legacy, one we build together. We can consult for the company and create our own schedules."

He stroked her face, feeling a joy he was beginning to realize could be his for life. "I like the sound of what you're saying, but I want to make sure you really understand you don't have to give up your career for me."

"Oh, Broderick, don't you see? I'm not giving up anything. I'm healing broken relationships and facing new challenges instead of just protecting myself from possible hurts. I'm embracing a life with you. And if our parents say no to this plan of ours—" she inhaled deeply "—then *we*, you and I—a family—become oh, say, accountants maybe, and live off our portfolios and hunt and catch fish while we play with Kota and bring up Fleur. Our daughter."

The beauty of her offer and the magnitude of her sacrifice filled him, making him feel whole for the first time in a very long while. "I am totally in love with your plan, and I'm totally in love with you, Glenna."

Her arms slid around his neck and she wriggled closer, leaning into him. The softness of her body against his fit with perfection, giving off a hint of the scent of almonds. "Well, isn't that a magnificent coincidence? Because I am wildly, passionately in love with you, too, Broderick Steele."

And if he had any remaining doubts—which he didn't— he intended to prove just how strong their love was. He hauled her closer and gently rolled her to the bearskin rug where he would prove it all night long, for a lifetime.

# Epilogue

*Two weeks later*

Glenna knew she wasn't the only mother ever to spend time simply gazing at her baby, so she refused to feel guilty about her lazy afternoon in the sprawling Steele family home, watching Fleur sleep in her swing. Nearby, Naomi worked on her tablet, her dark head bent over the screen as she tapped and scrolled. The quiet hum of the swing motor and the soft taps were the only sounds in the sunroom, and Glenna's life felt absolutely perfect as she watched the baby's head cuddle deeper into the side of the pink cushioning.

Glenna's whole world had changed since the "bache-lorette" party for Jeannie in this room, the day Fleur had come into their lives. Now, she felt at home with the Steele family, her heart expanding to take in all of Broderick's relations. Turning from Fleur's swing, Glenna peered out one tall window where a slight snow fell outside. Below, Broderick sat easily on his horse, returning from a ride with his family.

Her heart flipped in her chest. Broderick was such a strong man of honor. The love of her life. She still could hardly believe how much joy filled her world these days.

A breathy baby sigh drew her attention back to the room. Fleur's eyes were fluttering awake as she cooed happily, but Naomi's brow was deeply furrowed as she stared at her tablet.

Glenna leaned toward Naomi. "Are you alright?"

Broderick's sister looked up, her face smoothing. "Yes, just preoccupied." She set aside her tablet, and reached into the baby swing to scoop up Fleur. "Come here to Aunt Naomi."

"You're a natural with her."

Naomi shook a fuzzy bear rattle in front of the infant's face. "I love babies."

Glenna hesitated to mention children further. She understood too well how sensitive fertility issues could be. Broderick had told her about Naomi's cancer battle as a teen, and how Naomi's eggs had been frozen for a possible in vitro fertilization procedure later. What a traumatic thing for a teen to have to think about. "Well, Fleur definitely adores Aunt Naomi."

Naomi leaned her forehead to the baby's, then gave Fleur the gentlest nose to nose kiss. "I know people see me as a work hard, party hard type, but family is important to me. Much of my workaholic nature comes from wanting to pull my weight."

"You're invaluable to the company." Glenna had never seen anything to give her the impression that Naomi was a wild child, but she'd heard the rumors. Sometimes, she knew, those labels could be unfairly earned.

Naomi's dogged determination made her an indomitable attorney. They were lucky to have her on their side. Still, there was a flicker of insecurity on the woman's face that surprised Glenna.

"I'll feel better once I've figured out a way to land Royce Miller's research for our company."

Royce Miller? That was a lofty goal. The recluse's oil industry inventions that melded efficiency with environmental safety were legendary—and much sought after by their competitors. "It would be a coup to land him—or even get a peek at his research. Of course, gaining access to even speak with him would be a good start."

Behind them, the exterior door opened a moment before footsteps sounded on the tile. Fleur heard it too, her little face straining to turn toward the noise before Naomi shuffled sideways.

A moment later, Broderick stood in the doorway in his jacket and Stetson, a dusting of snow on his shoulders. His eyes locked on Glenna right away, an electric look passing between them before he swept off his Stetson. Her skin heated, anticipation curling her toes at just the sight of the man she loved. How was it possible he made her so breathless with just a simple look?

Naomi cleared her throat, standing with the baby in her arms. "Glenna, how about I take the little one and feed her a bottle. It'll be good practice for…uh…one day. I imagine you two new parents could use some time alone."

"Are you sure you don't mind?" Glenna asked without taking her eyes off Broderick's.

Laughing softly, Naomi angled past. "I don't mind at all." She elbowed her brother on the way out. "Have fun."

Glenna walked to Broderick and slipped her arms around his neck, breathing in his scent. "Did you have a good ride?"

"I sure did." He skimmed a kiss along her mouth. "Although it would have been better with you along."

His touch gave her butterflies.

"For a gruff businessman, you sure have turned into a romantic."

"You bring out the best in me." He swept his hand along her hair. "And I mean that."

"Thank you. I do believe we were meant for each other."

His smile made her senses tingle. He backed away, his fingers trailing down her arm. "I think it's time we made this very official."

She angled her head. "What do you mean?"

He dropped to one knee and pulled a ring box from his jacket pocket. "Glenna, I was going to take you out for a romantic meal, tonight—and I still want to do that. But when I looked into your eyes just now, I couldn't wait any longer."

Emotion swelled. Her hopes and happiness were all tied up in this man and their future together.

She pressed her hand to her heart, savoring every detail of the moment to keep it in her memory so she could relive it again and again. "The feeling is mutual."

She wanted every day to be like this one, spent with Fleur and Broderick, surrounded by family.

A smile creased his sun-ruddied face. "Glenna, my love, my lover, my life, will you do me the great honor of becoming my wife?"

Her heart squeezed around the words. She dropped to her knees in front of him, clasping her hands around his holding the ring box. "Of course I will. I'm yours and I'm so glad you're mine. Forever."

He opened the ring box to reveal…a stunning canary yellow, square cut diamond. He slid it on her finger and she realized her fingers were trembling just a little. The ring was a perfect fit. Just like their love.

"Oh my," she whispered, extending her hand and capturing the sunlight in the facets. Rainbows floated around the room from the bright, beautiful stone. "It's gorgeous. How did you know it was the perfect choice?"

He kissed her nose. "I had some help from your mother and your sister. So, I take that to mean you like it?"

She liked what it symbolized more than anything. But the ring was breathtaking.

"I do," she said, thinking how someday she would say those two words to him again. She couldn't wait to speak their vows for all the world to hear. "And I have an idea. Let's skip dinner out and celebrate in our suite."

His eyes went a shade darker as he sent her a heated look that smoldered over her skin.

Clasping her hand, he stood, guiding her with him. "I think that's a brilliant idea, from my brilliant future wife."

\* \* \* \* \*

# LET'S TALK
*Romance*

For exclusive extracts, competitions
and special offers, find us online:

**f** facebook.com/millsandboon

**⊙** @millsandboonuk

**🐦** @millsandboon

Or get in touch on 0844 844 1351*

For all the latest titles coming soon, visit
millsandboon.co.uk/nextmonth